MOTHS AND MOONLIGHT

MOTHS AND MOONLIGHT

A FLEUR HARKYN MYSTERY

KRISTA FAZENDIN

to Wade—
Who gave me wings

Death is not the opposite of life, but part of it.

— HAUKI MURAKAMI

PROLOGUE

My last thought was of sunlight—not panic, not loved ones, but of warmth. I slumped against the back of a wooden bench. Damp hair plastered to my brow, my skin swollen and gray. It might have been the stench that gave me away. Not even an orchid's heady fragrance could mask the putrid odor of death.

My lungs, their fragile lace unable to withstand the poison's onslaught, tightened. I wheezed, sucking in air and releasing it in the same breath as I struggled to remain whole. I lolled, heavy and limp, my body paralyzed. My stunted gasps echoed in my ears, loud and intrusive, until nothing else mattered.

Some poor janitor found me. He shrieked. I don't think I'll ever forget the sound. I hovered over us, watching as he regained his confidence and pressed two fingers to my neck. He stumbled back, shaking, and pulled his phone from the pocket of his green jumpsuit.

Next came the bevy of coroners and inspectors. They poked, prodded, and photographed me, recorded my death on their tablets. Speculated, searching for answers, and found none.

I watched with a morbid fascination reserved for voyeurism, not realizing I was watching myself. That this was real, not some horrible nightmare. I lifted my arms to steady myself against the shelving behind me but couldn't grasp it. My energy fizzled and sparked as it passed through the metal. I inhaled, but instead of the deep swell of air in my chest, light filled the room, unseen but by me. Instead of a heartbeat, luminescence flickered softly like a light bulb at the end of its life. I laughed bitterly, relieved I could still hear the echo of my voice in my ears.

The coroner and a medic lifted my body onto a gurney. My light flickered faster. Colored rays fluttered around me like cards in a bike's spokes.

NO! I screamed. *Don't go. I'm not finished yet!*

But they left. The gurney's wheels creaked as they rolled my body through the double doors, vanishing into a labyrinth of glass corridors. One by one, the police and medics ambled out of sight until I was alone in the gloom with only the flicker of my light for company.

They left police tape in their wake, banning the door with a bright yellow sash. I looked at the tiled floor, expecting to see some kind of outline or an impression of what was once my life—but there was nothing, no trace of me.

My light beamed, spotlighting the absence of my body. Purpose surged within me. There was something I was meant to do, something I needed. The urgency colored my aura red, then drained, disappearing into obscurity.

I was dead. Killed, I was sure of it. But why? And by who? I closed my eyes, probing every inch of my memory.

A shudder raced through my phantom limbs, wracking my light. Why couldn't I remember my name? I thought of something simple, something everyone had—a favorite food.

My mind drew an image of hot mead and barley in a tankard, but I couldn't taste it. I pulled at the tangle of images swirling around me, images of a stone building, church-like with a wide spiral staircase, and books, massive amounts of books—a man sat in a wing back chair beside a fire, he was young, his face unlined by the weariness of time. His close-cropped gray hair curled over his forehead. A small girl raced up to him, her cheeks flushed, the same gray curls tumbled down her back. The air smelled of musk and strawberries. The man smiled down at the young girl.

"What do you have for me, Fleurie girl?" he asked, his cheeks dimpling.

I pulled back, reeling. I would have stumbled if I were still made of flesh and bone.

This was not my memory.

CHAPTER
ONE

FLEUR

The dead had no concept of boundaries, much to Fleur's increasing irritation.

A chill trickled down her back, icy fingers poked and prodded the sleeve of her jacket, but she kept her gaze on the lamppost across the street. She didn't budge, didn't look. It didn't matter how many whispers or moans the spirit beside her uttered. Fleur would not acknowledge it. She shifted from one foot to the other, stuffing her hands into the pockets of her leather jacket, and tried to think of anything but the scene the spirit was making.

Just because she could see and speak to them didn't mean she had to. She finished with that five years ago. This was her life. And it was about time she invested in a little self-care.

And that meant no more Atua.

The Atua flickered, its light fading slightly, but that didn't deter it from raising its ghostly silhouette into Fleur's line of view.

Fleur cursed and turned, fisting her hand around the small set of tarot cards in her pocket. The spirits were getting bolder, and it was damn annoying. Sure, once she would have engaged the Atua, asked questions, sought to right whatever wrong they left before their death. But that was before ... Fleur frowned. She didn't want to think about that.

The light changed, and Fleur stepped onto the crosswalk, tucking her chin into her fleece scarf. The November wind grew brisk, pulling the few gray curls escaping from her beanie across her eyes. She pushed them back and hurried across the intersection at 15th Avenue toward the university library.

The tall arched, cathedral-like windows of the Suzzallo Library rose up to meet her as she cut across the square at the heart of the University of Washington's main campus. Fleur kept her gaze forward, ignoring the few greetings tossed her way as she climbed the shallow steps to the library's entrance.

As always, Atua littered the square, their light casting shadows beneath the overcast sky. Shadows only Fleur could see. A school as old as UW had its share of spirits, and Fleur was well practiced at ignoring them. Pushing open the glass door and sidestepping the Atua loitering near the curved staircase, Fleur headed to the circulation desk. Lindy sat glaring at his computer. Apparently, a lunch break was too frivolous for her coworker.

"You're late." Lindy didn't look up from the stack of books beside his computer.

"Am I?" Fleur checked the time on her phone as she set her messenger bag on her desk and began taking off her jacket. "Thirty-minute lunch, and I'm back after twenty-nine. Seems on time to me."

Lindy grumbled, "Don't be a smart-ass. Those books won't catalog themselves."

Fleur bit back a reply. Provoking him wouldn't help, no matter how much she wanted it to. Despite his plans, Lindy was not her superior, a fact Fleur was eternally grateful for. She'd rather have Dolly Swinkle's toxic positivity any day. "Is Dolly back?"

"Am I the only one to take our job seriously? No. She hasn't returned."

Fleur sniffed, settled into her swivel chair, and turned on her computer. Lindy was in a fine mood. She glanced over at the older librarian. Curiosity bloomed on her tongue, but she bit it back. Lindy's troubles were his own, as he never failed to remind her.

He looked up, catching her gaze, and frowned. His thinning dark brown hair tufted above his ears, outlining the slight indent of his typical tweed flat cap. "Did you want something, Harkyn?"

Fleur shook her head and looked back at her computer. She used to ask questions, offer customary greetings, and trite small talk, but after almost a decade of being told to mind her own business, Fleur was tired of trying. She didn't care if Lindy wanted to keep to himself, but he didn't have to be rude about it.

Truth was, Fleur preferred Lindy's ask-no-questions approach. It allowed her to keep her secrets without having to bend the truth.

Not that anyone would believe her anyway.

It was one thing to be able to see ghosts. It was another to be from a completely different realm where such things were common —at least in her family.

Lindy's wrinkly little head would probably explode if Fleur ever told him that Earth was just one of ten realms—that magick was common and expansive and that this realm was the most dangerous of the ten, simply because of its magickless existence.

Yeah, that would definitely make his head explode.

This world—Mundad, or Earth. Fleur wrinkled her nose at the informal name, used to be infused with magick, second only to the core realm, Evirdahl—her home. It was a land of storms and moon-light. But that was before the Great Betrayal—before the invasions that led to the creation of a sheath to protect the realms from each other and that sheath's destruction. Like the imperialist rulers of this world, the realm chieftains sought resources and people to conquer, growing their power like a weed. Mundad's power dimmed long before the realms' current troubles, leaving it blind to the truth.

Not that she gave it much thought anymore.

She was kicked out. The damn Legacy Council sent her and her father through the Henge Veil days after her mother's death, and why? Because she had a vision of the Queen's demise. Didn't they know her visions were subject to interpretation? No, the council thought they could hide from Fate. As if the Goddess Hemsut would let them. The Goddess of Fate held the threads, despite how hard they tried to manipulate them.

The past was past, and Fleur had a life in this world ... and a giant stack of books to get through.

She came from a family of archivists. Her oldest ancestors were the bards and historians of Evirdahl—the first and oldest realm, and like them, Fleur understood the calling of quill to parchment, but for her, it wasn't to record, like her uncles. Instead, she watched over them—the scratch of ink bound in limitless volumes.

However far from her realm, the call was still there. In her blood.

Fleur hated how much she loved it.

Her degree in library science could have opened doors to archival pursuits or digitizing catalogs, or even a museum curatorship, but to Fleur, there was nothing better than policing patrons behind the circulation desk.

Someone coughed. The gasp echoed and bounced the more the poor student tried to hold it. Fleur opened the drawer to the left of her, fished out a bag of cough drops, and slid from her chair. The heels of her combat boots tapped quietly against the polished oak floor.

"Here." She held out the bag, startling the student from his reverie. He looked up, smiling sheepishly as he reached for a wrapped drop.

"Thanks," he whispered, slipping the lozenge into his mouth.

Fleur nodded once and lifted her finger to her mouth, making her way back to the desk and Lindy's disapproving frown.

～

A SPIRIT HOVERED beside her car. Fleur gritted her teeth as she pulled her keys from her bag and unlocked the ancient Subaru. Tossing her bag onto the cracked red leather passenger seat, she climbed inside. Fleur knew her 1971 Subaru 360 was impractical—that was one of its main attributes. Its white paint was faded, its chrome rusted, and it barely made it over forty miles per hour on a good day. It was a mess, like her—there was only one person in all the realms that Fleur bonded with as much as she did this car.

She didn't understand why Theda picked her. Fleur knew she was a handful, but Theda embraced it—all of it. Meeting her at the library fundraiser was the kick in the pants Fleur needed to be the person she wanted to be. Not the failed medium, not the orphaned woman exiled from her home with only a nosy stepmother to nag her.

When Fleur told her she was born in a world of magick and creation, the core of the universe, there were plenty of questions, and Fleur answered them as truthfully as she could, expecting Theda to run screaming from the room at any minute.

But she didn't.

When she told her about her talents as a medium and seer, about the magick that ran through her ancestry—Theda smiled and snuggled closer.

Tonight was Theda's night to cook, which meant another quiche. Fleur smiled and started the car. She was sick of quiche, but Theda was determined to remember her mother's recipe, no matter how many variations. Theda was searching for a remnant of her mother, before the drugs, the men, the overdose—for a piece of the woman she had only a glimmer of, and Fleur would eat as many quiches as it took to give her that.

The drive home should have been quick. Fleur frowned as another SUV pulled out in front of her, splashing water from a massive puddle onto her windshield. "Hey!" she exclaimed, giving the dark blue SUV a thumbs-down gesture. "Gods," she muttered, deftly maneuvering into the right lane.

Seattle traffic was at its worst after three o'clock when the frenzy of tech workers were finally unchained from their desks, each one of them in a rush to … well, wherever the masses flanked to on Friday nights. Fleur wasn't much for the bar scene, or the music scene … or any scene, really.

Too many spirits. Sometimes it was just an excuse, but most of the time, it was true.

The Subie slid into the lone parking space in front of their apartment, and Fleur exhaled, turning off the car. It sputtered once before falling silent. Plumes of white exhaust faded in the surrounding damp air.

The off-key melody of a half-forgotten Nina Simone song feathered through the air as Fleur opened the door to their apartment. She sighed, dropping her bag and jacket onto the chair by the front door, and moved toward the kitchen. Theda couldn't sing. Her voice, although beautiful, couldn't carry a tune, no matter how hard she tried. Fleur's heart swelled as she watched Theda sway to the rhythm of the whisk in her hands.

Like her, Theda's mother died early in her life. Unlike her, Theda found a surrogate in her mother's sister, Alma. What would it be like to know someone had her back, no matter what? She envied the understanding they shared. Theda would do anything for Alma. Maybe it wasn't the relationship she envied, but the certainty.

Fleur slipped her arms around Theda's waist, pressing a kiss to her cheek.

"Oh! You're cold." Theda set the bowl of whisked eggs on the counter and turned in her arms.

"It's freezing out." Fleur nuzzled her. "But you're warm." She looked up, meeting the warmth in Theda's brown eyes. "Hi."

"Hi, yourself." She glanced at the clock on the microwave. "You're early."

Fleur released her and nodded to the bowl. "It's quiche night."

"You hate quiche. Don't pretend."

"Yeah, but you like it." Fleur shrugged. "Besides, I couldn't handle another hour of Lindy."

"That bad, huh?"

"Like, I want to care, but he just makes it so hard. Anyway, how was your day?"

"Classes, meetings, more research. The life of an assistant research professor is so exciting."

Fleur chuckled. "We're getting old and boring."

Theda laughed, moving toward the stove and the broccoli steaming there.

"How long till it's ready?" Fleur asked. "I'm starving." She settled into the overstuffed purple sofa in the living room. She didn't know if it was the dark afternoons or brisk air, but exhaustion washed over her as she leaned her head back and closed her eyes.

"Maybe an hour? I—"

The annoying whine of Blondie's *Call Me* pierced the air, startling Fleur. She groaned, regretting her choice of ringtone for her step-mother's constant calls.

"Answer it," Theda said, her voice barely louder than the chop of her knife on the cutting board.

"I don't want to." Fleur pouted and leaned back against the couch.

"Fleur." Theda stepped out from the kitchen, knife still in hand, and frowned. "She's trying. It's not fair of you to keep pushing her away."

"I didn't ask her to try. In fact, I specifically told her to leave me alone."

"You were fourteen. After fifteen years, I doubt that reasoning will hold up."

The music stopped. Fleur waited for the telltale ding of her step-mother's voicemail. Viola was persistent. No doubt she wanted to share every glorious detail from the symphony last night.

"See, she hung up. Crisis averted." Fleur smiled ruefully.

"Don't be cruel. She just wants to be part of your life, Fleur. Give her a chance."

"I do."

"One-word texts don't count." More chopping, followed by the hiss of oil in the frying pan. "Call her back. Don't be a baby."

"You're a pain in the ass sometimes," Fleur groaned, reaching for her phone. To Theda, Viola was reaching out—protecting, just as Alma did after her mother's death, but to Fleur, Vi was another vestige of her distant father's death.

"That's why you love me," Theda shouted from the kitchen.

Fleur made a face and tapped at the call button on her phone.

Viola answered on the first ring.

"I was just about to redial," she said hurriedly, her voice rising with each word. "You'll never guess what happened."

"What's that?" Fleur nestled into the sofa. From the kitchen, she could hear Theda rummaging through the cupboard. Plates clanked and shifted as she pulled one free.

"Louisa Whethermore's alarm system malfunctioned in the middle of the symphony last night! Can you believe it? Wasn't I just saying something like this would happen? I told her, too, she keeps her phone so loud—she really should just turn up her hearing aid, but she ignored me, like always. She'll listen to me now, I bet."

"Oh, yeah? Better get that fixed." Fleur couldn't care less about Viola's stuffy friend.

"It was horrible!" Viola continued as if Fleur hadn't spoken. "The alarm app on her phone went off twice before she even noticed it. Of course, she forgot to mute it. The ring was louder than the horn section, if you can believe it. Everyone turned, but she just ignored it. I nudged her three times. Three! We were in the middle of the third movement. Rachmaninoff's *Symphonic Dances*, so many church bells, it's a wonder one could hear anything. Fleur? Are you there?"

"I'm here."

"Anyway, back to the reason for my call—"

"You mean there's more?"

Fleur felt her glare through the phone.

"Don't be rude. You know I hate gossip, but that was too good not to share," Viola snipped. "What are you doing tomorrow afternoon?"

Nothing. Fleur had no plans, but she'd rather cut off her fingers one by one than tell Viola that. "Theda's giving a lecture."

It was only a harmless lie. Theda gave lectures all the time. Being an associate research professor specializing in indigenous archeology meant lots of lectures. Fleur glanced to the kitchen door, hoping Theda didn't realize she was using her as an excuse.

"I heard that," Theda shouted. "Don't listen to her, Viola."

"Was that Theda?" Viola chirped in her ear. "What did she say?"

"Nothing." Fleur glared at the kitchen.

"I said," Theda raised her voice as she entered the room, climbing over Fleur in her rush to get to the phone, "don't listen to her, Viola. She's free. My lecture isn't until next Monday."

"Did you hear that, Vi?" Fleur asked, glowering at Theda.

"I did, and I'm thrilled." Viola's voice rose. "You'll be my plus one, Fleur. Oh, this *is* exciting."

"What is?"

"The unveiling of the corpse flower. It only blooms once every seven years, you know. The botanical society is holding a séance in its honor at the conservatory. It will be delightful."

Fleur's stomach clenched. A séance? Of course, Viola didn't know what Fleur was capable of. Why should she? Her father never told Viola anything about their past. He wanted to forget, to move on. Viola didn't realize a séance was next to torture for Fleur. Atua flocked to them, their desperation tangible. Fleur shivered, her heart quickening, and glanced at Theda, noting the question in her partner's rich brown eyes.

"Why a séance?" Fleur swallowed back her fear as understanding dawned. She bit back a laugh. "Wait. Is it because it's called a corpse flower?"

"Well, of course. Why else?"

"A séance for a corpse flower?" The ridiculousness of her step-mother's reasoning was eclipsed by dread, cramping her stomach. She inhaled sharply. "OK, then."

Theda moaned and shifted off her, but Fleur held fast to her arm.

"It'll be a hoot. I'll pick you up at twelve thirty. Don't forget to wear something hauntingly morose."

"Morose outfit, got it." Fleur ignored the tremors shaking her hand as she said goodbye, set the phone down, and looked at Theda. "Well, this will be fun."

"Oh, Fleur. I'm sorry. I shouldn't have butted in." Theda's eyes glistened, and she wiped them with her free hand.

Fleur shifted into a sitting position and leaned forward, allowing Theda's arms to wrap around her. Fleur buried her face in the crook of her neck, inhaling the cocoa lotion on her brown skin. Her fingers toyed with the black curls at Theda's nape.

"It's OK. It'll be fine." And it would be. This wasn't her first, nor would it be her last brush with the unwieldy Atua. She knew better than to give them attention—no matter how extreme their screams.

"Will it?"

Fleur nodded mutely, unwilling to free Theda just yet.

"OK, then. It will be fine. Just keep your focus. I know you can do it."

"I can."

Theda nodded.

"I can," Fleur repeated, strengthening her resolve. She pulled from Theda and sniffed. "Is something burning?"

With a yelp, Theda jumped, rushing to the kitchen, and pulled the pan of sautéed onions and ham from the burner, fanning the smoke with her oven mitt.

CHAPTER
TWO

LENORA

The room erupted in light, tugging the edges of my aura, pulling me forward. Voices echoed as I tumbled headfirst into a vacuum—a void? My awareness cried out, my phantom limbs searching for anything to cling to as a burst of wind threatening to rip me apart. Whether it lasted an eternity or a moment, it ended as abruptly as it began.

I stood, shaken and angry, in a waiting room colored with the muted textures of another era. And I wasn't alone.

Beams of light, like me, were everywhere. Scattered and chatting like a ghostly cocktail party. Lifeless eyes turned in my direction as I stumbled onto the parquet floor, but no one moved. No one acknowledged my entrance.

I fluttered over to a solitary spirit, nervously flickering in the amber light.

Where am I? I asked quietly.

The spirit turned, its light coloring pale blue. *This is the Inbetween.* The spirit shifted, and I saw the shell of an old man clad in a worn wool kilt flickering within his light. His face half hidden by the thickness of his beard. His voice blossomed in my head, gruff and uneven, yet his mouth didn't move. *You're still fresh, then?*

I nodded grimly.

You get used to it. He brightened. *Just takes time. Name's Oliver.* He inclined his head in greeting.

I smiled. My name feathered into the air, then disappeared before I could catch it. Just like the rest of my memories. My light fizzled as I searched for any shred of my past—gone. All of it. Replaced with grainy photos and half-hearted smiles of someone else's life. I wanted to scream with anger. I had nothing, not even flesh.

Whoa, there. Calm down. I know it's hard.

I raised my chin as if I could defy what I had become. *Is it always like this?*

Sometimes, yes, sometimes ... no. Oliver shrugged. *The Soulkeepers know what's best. Just keep at it. Trust me, it gets easier. Right now, you're all chaos and light. Harness that anger—*

Soulkeepers?

Our Watchers. Oliver nodded as if that was explanation enough.

I don't understand. What is this place? What is a Watcher?

Oliver smiled softly, his gaze scanning the room. *The Soulkeepers manage the Tree. They take care of us even though no one has ever seen them. The Guardians speak for them.* He nodded in the direction of two spirits, more imposing than the rest, clad in indigo-blue light.

I tried to follow his gaze, but my attention was diverted by the immense canopy of branches above us. *You said tree? Are we in a tree?*

He looked back at me, his smile tilting down slightly. *Tis the Great Tree, the All-being that guides us to our next path. You don't know the Tree?*

My light tinged pink. Was this something I should know?

Suddenly his light flickered, and his smile returned. *You're from Mundad, aren't you? That would explain it. Most Atua from the second realm suffers from confusion here.*

The second realm? My head started to spin. The term was familiar, though ... I pushed through the kaleidoscope of images—unknown memories, searching for the unusual cadence. The words popped into my head in a low, gruff tenor, but the context was lost. I wanted to huff in frustration.

Oliver leaned back, his arm raised as if beckoning someone. *Maybe we start small, yeah?*

Yes, please. I smiled gratefully.

You're dead, lass. And you've chosen to remain here—

Chosen? My light flickered softly. I wasn't given a choice.

You were given a choice. We all are. To continue to the Glorious Feast of the Holy Mother Purna, or to remain, and clean up your mess, so to speak. Most continue, but a fair amount of us stay.

I pressed my lips together, my light pulsing slightly. *You chose to stay? Did you clean up your mess?*

Oliver laughed. *Centuries ago, but I keep making new ones, so they'll keep me around.*

Why?

Why not? Nothing waiting for me at the Feast. At least here I can watch.

Watch what?

Newbies like you. His light colored yellow with mirth. *This place is kept by the Soulkeepers—they're like our overlords in an ominous but friendly way. They speak to us through Guardians. See the dark, imposing spirits over there?* He nodded to the same two spirits as before.

What do they do?

Keep us out of trouble, mostly.

So, I'm here. Dead. I paused, allowing, for the first time, my light to dim. *What now?*

Oliver grinned and leaned back. *That's the fun bit. You get to clean up your mess, lass.*

If only I knew what my mess was.

Your death was not in vain. A voice, low and husky, echoed within me.

Oliver's head turned quickly, and his smile dimmed. *Ah ... I was wondering when she'd speak up.*

She who?

The Guardian yonder—she's been watching you. He nodded behind me and began inching away.

Wait—I began, but he was gone. My light flickered in frustration, or was it confusion? A myriad of emotions clamored for attention, all facets of fresh anxiety over my circumstances. I closed my eyes and willed them back. Now was not the time for a massive freak-out. First, I needed to know more ... so much more.

I turned to the indigo spirits edging the room. They were brighter, yet their features blurred. An air of authority floated around them as they watched, a stark contrast from the jittery souls lingering beside the tree. *Who's there?*

An indigo spirit turned toward me. Her light throbbed to the cadence of the voice. *We are the Guardians. Be easy. There is much to learn.*

I frowned. *Why can't I remember myself? Why wasn't I given a choice?* Questions tumbled forward, pulsing my light orange. *Who are you?*

A friend. A mentor if you'll allow me.

Do I need a mentor?

Perhaps. Perhaps you will need a friend.

What I need is answers. I blustered, challenging the spirit as it broke away from the others and moved closer.

I will tell you what I can—

The spirit broke off as a shadow crested overhead, darkening the amber light. The air cooled into something tangible and heavy, like snow—invisible snow.

You felt that. The spirit didn't ask.

Was that normal?

The light never splinters here. The Tree provides us its power. That ... was not of this realm. That was why you're needed.

What the hell was she talking about? I tried to slow my light as I would my breathing, but confusion was tinging me red. *What do I have to do with the shadow?*

That was no mere shadow. That was a swarm of Grima moving closer to the Tree.

Grima?

The world as you know it is so much more than you were ever taught. The spirit paused as if waiting to see my reaction. *You know only one realm—Mundad, but there are nine more, each unique. This Tree and its magick are the core of the seventh realm—Entomal, the Inbetween.*

Oliver mentioned that.

The spirit smiled slightly. *Oliver is one of the oldest Atua. He has seen many things. The Grima,* the spirit continued, *or Shadelings, come from the outermost realm, Qahil. They prey on essence, emotion, despair. The dead are made of these things, which make Shadelings extremely dangerous to us.*

Why? What do they want?

They want to feed. Their realm is devoid of life, so they cast out, hungry.

They're hungry? That's it?

That's enough. They will consume us all if we let them.

What about the other realms?

We are the most vulnerable, but the others struggle too. The dead are everywhere. You must take care.

So? What do I have to do with that shadow?

You remember another. She is but one piece of your puzzle. She will lead you to a tool—a Relic, which will help. Find her. She will help you rediscover yourself.

How? My light trembled at the weight of the spirit's words. None of it made any sense, and yet ... it all fit perfectly with the memories —someone else's memories that whirled within me.

Use the portals. Oliver will help. The spirit nodded to the doorways etched into the tree's trunk.

Where do I even start?

At the beginning.

CHAPTER
THREE

FLEUR

The bitter aroma of freshly brewed coffee wafted into the room. Fleur's arm brushed the vacant sheets next to her. She yawned, elongating her body as she twisted her arms over her head and sat up. Waking up without Theda's warmth didn't bode well on her nerves.

She grappled with the blankets until she grasped her oversized cardigan at the end of the bed, and slipped it over her shoulders, hugging it to her as she trudged to the bathroom. What time did she finally fall asleep last night? Or should she say this morning? Three o'clock? Not even Theda's light snores could banish the anxiety souring her stomach. Today was Viola's séance.

Fleur added a drop of toothpaste to her brush. She could handle this. She was no amateur medium. It was all part of the game. They would claw at her, seeking her attention, but she wouldn't look.

She relaxed her shoulders, glancing at her nightstand in the mirror and the deck of tarot cards resting there. Her mother trained her to respect the cards, to seek knowledge within their colorful depths. They would spread the deck out, past, present, and future—a basis for understanding her visions. As Fleur grew, the cards became more than a tool for insight. They became her guide. Her fingers itched to shuffle the small deck. A quick read would help detangle her nerves.

She frowned around the toothbrush, rubbing her eyes as the mirror wavered and her vision softened. Morning light tumbled over the running water from the faucet. Her reflection splintered.

Fleur stilled, toothbrush hanging from her lips.

Like a fist to the stomach, the vision slammed into her. She leaned over the sink, toothpaste streaming from her mouth. She spat, dimly aware of the clatter of the plastic brush hitting the porcelain sink.

The light flared and fractured. Shapes swirled. An empty vial, manicured fingers tucking between folds of leather—a purse? A woman slumped, hair swept over her face. Wind gusted, pushing and pulling, holding her in place. Vines tangled around her legs, growing longer, pulling her body into its thickly veined stem. She vanished into the leaves, their seams thick with syrup. It dripped, burning flesh—Fleur's flesh. Her hand, her arm, her back. She couldn't escape it. Fleur struggled, pushing against the vines.

She blinked, and she was in a hall. Chairs lined up in rows, facing a metal urn in a windowed alcove. A funeral. Who was in the urn? Stained glass reflected faces twisted in agony. Their screams were raw and silent. A man and a woman, two children—one cracked. Fleur crept closer, her hand outstretched.

"Fleur!" Hands gripped her shoulders, arms wrapped around her. "Fleur, honey. Wake up. Come back to me."

The smell of jasmine and cocoa butter floated around her, erasing the last of the vision. Fleur wept. Her eyes soggy with tears, her head pressed into Theda's shoulder. They rocked gently. Theda's touch was light but absolute. Fleur clung to it like an anchor. Her anchor—Theda.

"What happened?" Theda's voice was soft against her ear.

Fleur took a breath. They stood in the bathroom. The water off, and the mirror unbroken. Her toothbrush lay in the sink.

"Just a vision." She pushed away, grabbing a towel. She wiped the toothpaste from her lips and cheeks. "I guess I'm more stressed about the séance than I thought."

Theda rested her forehead against Fleur's temple. "Don't go. Tell Viola you are sick or something."

Fleur sputtered a laugh. "Yeah, right? You want Viola here? Because now that I've given in, she won't give up."

"I'll come with you."

"You need to finish your research—" Fleur raised her hand, cutting off Theda's protest. "Don't. I know your deadlines. You can't fool me."

"What was your vision of?"

"Vines wrapped around me. I couldn't move." Fleur inhaled unsteadily and shook her head. "It was nothing. I know an anxiety vision when I see one. Don't worry."

Theda frowned and stepped out of the bathroom, grabbing the deck from Fleur's nightstand. "Here."

Fleur arched a brow and grasped them, instinctively shuffling.

"Go on. Focus on the present. What does it say?"

Fleur pulled the top card and held it up. Death.

"Well, that's not good." Theda frowned.

"I'm about to go to a séance, remember? Besides, it means a new cycle, rebirth. Not death, not really." The card grew heavy in her hand. Its warmth spread over her like a blanket.

Theda stilled, considering her.

Resisting the urge to squirm, Fleur tucked the card back into the deck, her skin tingling.

"Just ... promise me you'll be careful today? Leave if you have to. Viola be damned."

"I thought you wanted me to bond with her."

"I do, but not like this ..."

"C'mon, Theda. I'm not a kid. I can manage this. Besides, it beats having to go shopping with Vi, or worse, her coming here." Fleur exaggerated a shudder. "In and out. I know when to leave. Don't worry."

"I should have let you blow her off."

"Yeah, you should have. But it's OK. I like your big heart."

Theda snorted, a laugh bubbling out. "My busybody heart, you mean."

"Same thing, love."

~

A MULTITUDE of colorful flowers lined the walkway to the conservatory. Fleur didn't know what kind, nor did she care. She wanted to get this over with.

Viola hurried beside her. "Must you walk so fast? The conservatory isn't going anywhere."

Fleur groaned inwardly and slowed her pace, careful not to notice the few Atua lingering around the entrance. "Sorry."

"What's got you so flustered?" Viola paused, forcing Fleur to stop as well, and frowned. "Have I done something? You didn't have to come, you know."

Oh, she knew. She could turn and run, but guilt stymied her excuses. Theda was right. Viola was virtually harmless. It wouldn't hurt to throw her a bone once in a while.

Besides, she needed a distraction. Her vision, the tightening vines, the overwhelming helplessness, simmered under her skin. Her visions were often vague, but her mother taught her to trust her instincts, even when every part of her wanted to run. Listen to the cards, trust the swelling in her heart, whether in fear or love. Something was brewing, pungent and powerful, and Fleur—she swallowed back the urge to groan—was on her way to a séance.

"Sorry. Sorry, Vi." She met Viola's gaze, surprised by the concern she saw in her bright blue eyes. "I didn't sleep well last night. I guess I'm a little on edge."

Viola's face softened. "Is something wrong? Is everything OK at work? Theda?"

"Oh, yeah, everything's great. I'm just restless, I guess."

"You sound like your father." Viola rested a comforting hand on Fleur's arm. "Arik puttered around the house at all hours, always fidgety. It used to drive me crazy." She sniffed. "It's strange … the things we miss."

Fleur offered her a slight smile. Viola didn't know about Arik's spirits, but Fleur knew it was his way of keeping his gift abated. Arik feared his magick would be discovered. As Fleur clamored to be free, Arik pushed his magick back. Even four years after his death, Viola never questioned his strange habits. She accepted him, secrets and all. Fleur wondered what she would do if she knew his midnight ramblings weren't a result of insomnia but how he contained his magick.

"Sometimes I catch a whiff of that sage oil he wore, and my heart speeds up a little," Fleur remarked, suddenly wanting to offer her stepmother an ounce of solidarity.

Viola groaned. "I hated that stuff, but he insisted."

Sage kept spirits away. Fleur bit her lip, remembering the bundles he created. Arik lit a smudge stick at every entrance. As a teenager, Fleur struggled with the taunts that came with smelling like charred shrubbery.

A rare streak of sunlight spilled through the ominous Seattle sky, brightening the glass structure ahead of them. The conservatory was built in 1912. Long, slanted greenhouses flanked the domed glass building. The white cedar framework had been long since replaced by sturdy aluminum. Only the stained-glass peacock window at the building's prow remained original to the design.

Viola grinned, smoothing a stray russet curl behind her ear as they moved into the atrium. A crowd of women, most dressed in the same wide-leg trousers and printed blouses as Viola, gathered around, chattering like a flock of magpies.

They shed their winter coats, handing them to the coat check at the front, and moved closer to the group. Fleur glanced down at her combat boots under the rolled cuff of her dark red plaid pants. She wore a soft boatneck black sweater and a collection of metal cuffs on her left arm. At least she decided against the studded choker. She snickered to herself, noting a few raised brows. With her height and gray hair, Fleur stood out, and she liked it that way.

"Fleur, you must meet Louisa, oh, and Esther, too. Hello, dear." Viola led her into a group of women.

Her stepmother was the youngest in the group. If Fleur had to guess, she would say most of the women here were a good decade older than Vi's fifty-seven years.

Louisa gave her a long look, her muddy brown eyes sliding from Fleur's boots to her hair. Her pressed lips tilted slightly upward. "We've heard so much about you." Her voice was nasal and strained.

Fleur shook her limp hand, resisting the urge to wipe her palm on her leg. "Nice to meet you." She could play nice.

"I assume you've heard. There was a death here yesterday." Her chin rose as her voice dipped.

"A death?" Viola gasped. "Really? And right before the séance! What are the odds?"

Louisa looked between Viola and Esther. "It's all very hush-hush. So, it must have been someone important."

"Or they're just respecting the dead's privacy," Fleur pointed out, ignoring Louisa's frown.

"Do they have any leads?" Esther asked, her gaze darting around the room, expecting the murderer to materialize at any moment.

"None. They left nary a print at the scene—the door was locked when they found the body. It's like"—Louisa lowered her voice— "they were killed by a ghost."

"That's so Agatha Christie!" Esther exclaimed a little too loudly.

Fleur swallowed a groan.

"Agatha Christie didn't write ghost stories." Louisa looked down at Esther.

"No, but it's a good mystery."

Viola looked between her friends. "Maybe we can call the spirit forth and find out what happened?"

Gods. Fleur hoped not.

"Attention. Attention, please." A man in a pinstripe blazer, his shirt opened one button too many, stood at the entrance, his hands clasped. "We will begin in a few minutes. If you would please find your seat." He gestured to the domed greenhouse at the opposite end of the atrium.

A round table sat below one of the most hideous flowers Fleur had ever seen. Was this the corpse flower? It formed a huge, six feet tall white tuber half covered in blackish purple petals.

Viola handed her a small handkerchief. "You'll need this."

"Why?"

"You'll see." Viola grinned, taking her hand.

The odor hit her like a brick the moment they entered the room. Old gym socks and Limburger cheese. Fleur pressed the handkerchief to her face. "What is that smell?"

"The flower, dear." Viola winked, grinning devilishly. "It's called the corpse flower for a reason. Smells like death."

CHAPTER
FOUR

A woman in a cream-colored blouse walked through me. I shrieked, unprepared for the onslaught of pain— millions of tiny arrows sliced my light like sleeping nerve endings coming back to life.

She wandered toward the large flower in the other room, oblivious to her invasion. I shuddered, my aura flickering in a prism of colors before settling. I took a breath, waiting for the swirl of air, only to realize ... I was dead, made of light.

I wanted to stomp my foot. Frustration tinged my light pink.

Beside me, Oliver chuckled. *Relax. Harness your emotions. Don't let them dim your awareness.*

How?

You're a prism, girl. Channel all that emotion. Use it to communicate, like those fools over there. He nodded to the table below the giant flower and the flickering spirits surrounding it. *Or do like me. I like to imagine it's a laser pointer. Use it to mess with them.*

Them?

The living. Nothing scares them more than a book falling off a table or a gentle tapping. Oliver's eyes creased as his smile broadened.

We can do that? My light brightened.

Oh, yeah. We're dead, not dull. Nothing better than a good haunting on a rainy night.

My light rippled at the thought. We could make ourselves known —the prospect tinged my light yellow.

See. Oliver nodded. *It's not so bad—being dead.*

I still don't know why we're here.

The Guardian said to start at the beginning, right? Well, this is it.

Where I died?

It was your second beginning. Makes sense to me.

The crowd gathered around the table, their chatter quieting. I studied them, their breath, their bodies in constant motion, the swirl of color curling around them. *What's with the color?*

Auras, my dear. How we tell the good from the bad. My advice? Keep away from the metallic ones. They've tasted evil. You don't want to mess with them.

My gaze drifted over the living. *Metallic?*

You'll know it when you see it. Trust me. Oliver flickered. *Looks like they're starting. That's my cue.*

Your cue?

Séances. Not my thing. Oliver's mouth tilted down as he turned to the brightly colored plant, his light filtering through the overcast sun. *Good luck, lass.*

A moment later, he was gone.

Get it together, I scolded myself, scanning the room for metallic auras. Most were blue, a twinge of orange, yellow—a few red. And one ... one stood out. Her purple aura pulsed around her. She was taller than the others, made to stand out. Her hair was gray and seemingly natural, caught in a loose bun. Her face was round, high cheekbones, brown eyes—and I knew with absolute certainty she hated the color of them. Just like I knew the scent of strawberries reminded her of home.

It was her. The woman in my head—the memories ... I cursed, my light seething. I flew around the room as if the movement could dispel my anger. I was here for her—she was the one who could help me. I calmed and fluttered back down to the tile floor. My gaze glued to the gray-haired woman in studded bracelets and combat boots.

Fleur.

CHAPTER
FIVE

FLEUR

"Try to breathe through your mouth," Viola said as she sat on the wooden chair beside her.

Easier said than done. Every time she opened her mouth, she swallowed more of the foul air. Holding the tissue under her nose, Fleur glanced around the room. She expected something grandiose and gothic. Instead, she got a smelly flower and a bunch of old ladies. No red velvet chairs, no thickly draped tapestries, or towering paintings of long-dead ancestors. No candles. Fleur peered around, noting the basic wood table and the ten chairs circling it—the corpse flower looming behind.

A woman in a flowing red cloak appeared from behind the flower. Her brown hair piled high and braided with ribbons of magenta and black. Fleur raised a brow as she sat in the vacant seat beside Viola, her hand raised, palms up as if she was summoning. Her eyes were ringed with heavy black liner. They wandered over the other nine participants, searching—probably for the most timid of the group. Fleur bit back a groan as they landed on Esther. The older woman fidgeted with her handkerchief, her gaze darting from the ridiculous crystal ball in the center of the table to the flower looming behind them. An easy target.

The woman in red held up her hands. The chatter stopped. "I am Madam Olga. Your guide to the veiled realm."

Fleur's eye twitched. She doubted Madam Olga had any idea what the veiled realm was.

"Please," Olga began, "clasp hands. Close your eyes and allow your mind to relax. I can sense the flower's magick. It has given us many spirits to welcome today."

Fleur scanned the greenhouse, noting only a couple of glimmers dancing between the manicured garden. Harmless Atua, probably regulars in a place like this. One caught her eye, brighter than the rest. A new spirit. Its light wavered, flickering from its human shape to a dusting of light. It was once a girl, young by the look of her. Fleur watched its form brighten as it struggled to keep a semblance of its old life.

Don't make eye contact. Fleur took a sharp breath. Don't let them know you can see them.

Viola squeezed her hand.

Madam Olga's voice rose. "Let us begin."

Fleur exhaled, willing her nerves to calm.

The air cooled. A chill danced up her spine, alerting her to a greater gathering of spirits.

Madam Olga chanted nonsense. Her voice lowered, becoming more guttural. Her words were a collection of consonants, hardly powerful enough to call such a crowd of Atua.

The Atua grew bolder. Fleur sensed their anger and confusion— their longing and desperation. They tripped over each other, their essence amplifying as they recognized her aura.

Don't open your eyes.

An icy finger touched her cheek, and Fleur bit the inside of her mouth. Don't move. Don't breathe.

Voices tumbled over each other, their volume increasing by the second. Fleur gripped Viola's hand tighter. The air chilled.

"Spirits!" Olga commanded, turning their attention from Fleur momentarily. "We beseech you. Is there one among us you wish to speak to?"

Fleur swallowed a groan.

"Speak to us, spirits!"

The table shook. Fleur peeked through her lashes, noting the cluster of twenty or more Atua grouped around them.

Viola gasped and squeezed her hand.

To her left, Louisa's damp palm pressed against hers.

"You!" Olga's voice dropped, and the group gasped, opening their eyes to find Olga pointing at Esther.

Esther's shoulders trembled. She shook her head, her blonde ponytail whipping left, then right. "No, no ..."

"Yes. The spirits wish to speak to you." Madam Olga nodded gravely.

What utter nonsense. The spirits didn't give a hoot about Esther. They were too busy trying to get Fleur's attention.

"Your husband ... he is here ... he"—Madam Olga's hands fluttered—"he wants you to ... be happy."

Esther whimpered.

Fleur's chest heaved as she tried to regulate her breathing. She stared at Esther. Focus, she chanted to herself. Don't look at them.

Atua swirled, her arms and neck burning from their icy fingers. She wouldn't give in, no matter the despair weighing against her. Fleur rolled her shoulders and looked at Esther.

Suddenly, everything quieted.

What was happening? Was this a trick? A new tactic to get her to lower her guard? Atua weren't usually so crafty.

Madam Olga's head rolled back, a thick moan rumbled in her throat. Her tongue lolled to the side of her mouth, her shoulders slouched as her arms dangled at her sides. Her entire body was slack.

Patrons muttered nervously, a few pushing back their chairs. Esther sobbed into her handkerchief. She had released the hand of the man next to her. Breaking the circle.

"How does this work? Is this on? Hello?" Madame Olga sat upright. Her fingers drummed against the wood, a vaguely familiar cadence.

"You!" She looked at Fleur.

Fleur glared back. Whatever this stunt was, she didn't need any part of it.

Olga's body flopped onto the table, her hands clasped in a pleading gesture. "I need your help."

Damn. Madame Olga got herself possessed.

Fleur scooted her chair back, releasing Viola and Louisa's hands. There was no point to it anymore. A spirit got in.

"Don't go. I won't hurt you. I need you," Madame Olga croaked.

Fleur glanced around her, from Viola's wide gaze to Louisa's horrified one and past to the fear etched on each face surrounding the table. Fleur smiled weakly. She looked back at Madam Olga and jerked her head toward the exit.

Olga's body went limp, her head thudding on the table as the spirit left her. It hovered over the madame in triumph. Fleur recognized the new Atua from earlier, the wisp of a girl. What was going on? No spirit had ever contacted her like this.

Fleur stood, shivering, and glanced at Viola, offering her a reassuring smile. "Well, that was ... crazy."

Olga moaned, lifting her head in confusion.

The Atua fluttered over the table. It floated beside her, its light keeping the restless horde away.

Viola raised a brow but said nothing.

"I, um, uh ... have to go. This has been ... eventful." Fleur inched closer to the door. "I'll call you later. Promise." She nodded to Viola.

Eight sets of eyes bore into her back as she moved into the atrium. The spirit stayed silently beside her. Fleur could feel its impatience but ignored it as she hurried to the coat check. She'd be damned if she was going to leave her favorite leather jacket behind.

Fleur stepped outside into the chilly winter rain and turned to the shining light beside her. "Well?"

The Atua ebbed into its girlish form, a grin brightening her face. *I thought that would get your attention.*

CHAPTER

SIX

Fleur huffed, shoving her hands in her coat pocket, her fingers closing over the smooth edges of the tarot deck nestled there, and trudged down the flower-lined path to the parking lot.

The light elongated, shaping back into the woman it once was. Long hair, curled to the center of her back, parted in the middle, heart-shaped face, almond eyes tilted slightly upward, giving her cheekbones a harsh slant. The light made her look gaunt and shadowed as it dimmed and brightened.

"Well," Fleur muttered, keeping her gaze on the rows of parked cars ahead. "What do you want?"

The Atua flickered, brightening as she floated. *I want ...* her brow creased, and she paused as if trying to remember her words. *I was supposed to find you.*

"Yeah? Why?"

To help you ... me. The spirit cursed and disappeared.

Fleur snickered, knowing the fresher the Atua, the harder it was for them to communicate. They still believed they were flesh, that they had control over their own minds, but Fleur had seen many new spirits stumble, grasping at their old life, begging for control. Those that fought it ended up tormented. They were the spirits hugging the séance table, despair perfuming the surrounding air.

"I got that part. Why?"

I'm supposed to find you. You'll help me find—

"You want me to find out who killed you?" She was too old for this. Years ago, she thought of herself as a crusader, righting the wrongs that brought the Atua into the Inbetween—not that she was ever any good at it. But she had problems of her own now.

Well, yes. That. But also a Relic—

"Relic?" Fleur's heart skipped. She closed her eyes, fighting the chill settling over her.

A tool the Inbetween needs to—

"No." Her eyes flew open and she shook her head vehemently.

No? What do you mean? No?

"It means I can't help you."

But you must!

Fleur's brow furrowed, and she looked away from the spirit. Searching for Relics wasn't a part of her life. Until her mother died, Fleur was only aware of their existence, not the part her family played or her mother's promise to the Goddess Hemsut.

Her mother was a powerful seer. Not only could she read the future and speak to the dead, she could also sense magickal warmth in an item. It was this gift that caused Hemsut to seek her out, begging her to find the Relics. Begging? It was more like coercion. Hemsut wasn't known for her kindness. When Fleur began showing signs of inheriting her mother's gift, her parents tried to hide it from the goddesses—as if that was possible.

Like everything else in her life, that had not ended well.

Fleur continued down the sidewalk, her gaze on the cars ahead. She *really* didn't have time for this.

I know who killed me.

The spirit was clearly changing tactics. "Who?"

The spirit moaned, her light dimming. *I don't remember.*

"How did they kill you?"

Poison. I think.

"So, what? You want me to find them?"

The spirit frowned. *Why can't I remember?*

"It happens." Fleur shrugged. "The Inbetween must have a reason, usually because you're needed for something other than your own revenge, so they eliminate your memories."

They have no right to do that.

"You're dead. Free will is no longer an option."

Fleur paused at the exit of the parking lot. She couldn't walk home. Damn. She should never have let Viola drive.

Will you help?

Fleur pulled out her phone and opened a rideshare app, typing in her address. She didn't want to help the Atua. Hunting her killer was one thing, but to get involved with the Relics—to pick up her mother's promise to Hemsut, the one thing she swore never to do—that was quite another. No. The spirit would have to find another way.

Fleur turned to the spirit, ignoring the wide, hopeful eyes peering up at her, and shook her head. "Look. I'm sorry you're dead and all, but I don't do this anymore."

What? What do you mean? You're a medium, right? This is your thing.

"Nope. I have other things now. Sorry."

But ... The Atua dimmed, its light wavering as it tried to compose itself. *No. I won't accept this. I was told to find you. You have to help.*

Fleur groaned and turned toward the gray sedan, pulling up to the curb. She moved swiftly, ignoring the light clinging to her coat tail. She didn't have time or resources to solve some poor ghost's death. She was no investigator—hell, she wouldn't even know where to start. She pulled open the car door and greeted the driver. "Paul?"

He nodded. "You Fleur?"

She climbed into the back seat, slamming the door before the spirit could figure out how to maneuver its light into the car. "Yup. Let's go."

Please. I need you.

Damn. Fleur glanced behind her. The light fluttered, growing smaller with each press of the accelerator.

Please ...

No. No, she didn't do that anymore. Once—when she was young, rebellious, and stupid—she gave in. She offered the spirits aid, and the Atua gave her the rebellion from her father she desperately needed. But that ended poorly. Fleur pulled the tarot cards from her pocket and shuffled absently, the rhythm drawing the tension from her arms. No. This was for the best.

The spirit's voice faded the further away they moved, but the longing stayed. Fleur held her breath as she exited the car, a small irrational part of her glanced around the street worriedly. She knew the spirit couldn't follow, not without an agreement between them, but her stomach clenched anyway. Atua were wily creatures, and she knew better than to trust them to follow the rules. She glanced up to the window of her fifth-floor apartment and caught Theda's silhouette hunched over her computer. Fleur released a shaky breath and let herself into the building.

Theda bent over her keyboard, her focus so great, Fleur tapped on the edge of the table to get her attention.

"Oh!" Theda jumped and leaned back in her chair. Her curly black hair held back with a bevy of pencils and a lone pen. A few escaped tendrils framed her face. She toyed with one—curling it around her finger. "You're back."

Fleur wondered if she could tell how badly everything went. "Yeah, uh ... funny story."

"Is this about the madame from the séance singling you out?"

"How do you—" Fleur frowned. "Viola called, didn't she?"

Theda pushed back her chair. "Wanna tell me what happened?"

Fleur moved to the sofa, landing with a thud against the plump cushions. Their apartment was small and musty, one of the Tudor-Gothic buildings littering the east side of the city. She liked it because it kept most of its original ambiance, from the extravagant lobby decked out in faded art deco to the blanket of ivy covering the western wing of the building. It suited her—them—Fleur smiled at Theda.

"Some Atua possessed Madame Olga to get my attention."

Theda's gaze narrowed, her jaw dropping slightly. "No."

"Yup. She wants my help to find her killer." Fleur rubbed her eyes and leaned further into the cushions. She wasn't ready to even think about the spirit's other request.

"Well? Where is she?"

"I said no."

"What? Fleur." Theda stood, moved over to the sofa, and settled in beside her. "Why would you say no?"

"Seriously? Do you understand how much of my time the spirit would consume?" She raised her hand as Theda opened her mouth. "No, not just my time—*our* time. Time I would rather have with you. Alone. Without a nosey ghost begging me to help every five minutes."

Theda scooted closer, resting her head on Fleur's shoulder. "I'm not like him, you know."

Fleur inhaled and fisted her hands in her lap. "I know. You mean more."

"Then help the spirit."

"No."

Theda pressed a kiss to Fleur's cheek, lingering until Fleur wrapped her arms around her. "I know you've been repressing this part of yourself, and you don't have to. Fleur ... I'm not going anywhere. I know who you are. I see you." She kissed her jaw, scattering tiny kisses down Fleur's neck. "I accept you."

Fleur's nerves, already raw and exposed from the séance, tingled under Theda's fingers. How long had she longed to hear those words before Theda found her? How often had she changed to fit into the mold required, but never the one she needed? "Not fair."

"What?" Theda hummed as she pressed her face into Fleur's neck.

"You. Using your wiles on me."

"Think about it. A soul needs help, and you're turning away from them. Why?" Theda pulled away and fixed Fleur with a hard stare. "Because you're scared." She waited for Fleur to deny it and held up her hand, mimicking Fleur's earlier action. "I thought you were better than that."

"Maybe you thought wrong." The words soured in her throat. "It's not about a soul needing help. It's about us. Spirits are needy bastards." Needy and cruel, Fleur closed her eyes, fighting off the memory of the last Atua she engaged and her own naivete. "The spirit can handle herself."

Theda laughed. "I call bullshit on your tough girl act." She leaned closer. "What would Alma say?"

Fleur leaned forward, rubbing her hands over her face. Leave it to Theda to pull out the big guns. Dammit, she should have known. Alma Okan was a force to reckon with. She held tight to the belief that everyone deserved help and a safe harbor—even Fleur. "You wouldn't."

"Try me." Theda raised a finely curved brow. "The spirit sought you out, Fleur. It possessed a woman to get your attention. The least you could do is try."

Fleur inched forward on the sofa and sighed. "Do you understand what that means, Theda? Like, really understand? The spirit will be a part of our life until I complete their request. We will be haunted—I mean that literally, OK? Is that something you're willing to allow?"

Theda grinned. "Truthfully, I think it will be exciting."

"Shit, Theda. I'm not joking."

"Me either. Do it. Help the ghost."

"You sure? Like, absolutely positive?" Fleur grasped her hands and rested her forehead against hers.

"Yes, Fleur." She pressed her lips on Fleur's, kissing her deeply before pulling away. "I am."

CHAPTER

SEVEN

FLEUR

Fleur frowned as she parked the Subie in the lot outside the conservatory. The spirits were waiting. At least twenty hovered around her car, frosting the windshield. Fleur took a deep breath and pulled the collar of her coat tighter, knotting the scarf at her neck. She didn't want to step into the horde of dead brimming with requests.

The crowd of spirits shuffled back, their light dimming as another, brighter Atua moved forward. Fleur watched, stunned, as the young girl from earlier pushed back the others, giving her room to breathe.

Fleur opened the car door and carefully emerged, her gut screaming at her to run.

You came back. The spirit fairly beamed.

"Yeah."

So, you'll help me?

"Maybe." Fleur studied the shimmering face of the Atua and turned to the conservatory's entrance. "Where did it happen?"

Back there. In the orchid house. C'mon. I'll show you.

The spirit flickered and danced over the damp gravel path around the building.

Fleur quickened her pace, her gaze leveled on the corner of the building and the smaller one coming into view. Something the spirit said earlier nagged at her. She bit her lip pensively as they drifted closer to the smaller greenhouse. "So, you were supposed to find me?"

The Atua paused, her light flickering. *I have no memories. Nothing. All I see are your memories. I don't know why. Then I saw you at the séance—*

"My memories?" Fleur stopped walking and faced the ghost. "What do you mean, *my* memories?"

The spirit brightened in the misting rain. *I know you're a long way from home. I know about your exile and how betrayed you felt. I know about Evirdahl and the other realms—*

"Stop." Fleur wanted to cover her ears. She wanted to run. Only Theda knew about Evirdahl, about her home, about her sadness. How could this creature? "Who are you? Is this a trick? Only my uncle has the power to usher an Atua here. Did Axel send you?"

The spirit shook her head. *I know your history, Fleur. I was dead. Life left my body, and I just knew. I know you better than I know myself.*

Breathe, just breathe. Fleur had heard of such a thing. Her mother told her stories when she was small, but Fleur never thought it would happen to her. Why would it? She was a nobody, a paltry medium and half-assed seer. She was of no use to anyone. Why would the Inbetween do this to her?

"What's your name?" Fleur asked.

The Atua dimmed, her eyes drifting down. *I don't know.*

Well, damn. So much for a starting place.

"You don't know your name? Do you know anything other than that you were murdered in the orchid house?"

It was hard enough just remembering that.

Fleur groaned and began walking, the Atua fluttering next to her.

This was ridiculous. If the damn spirit couldn't remember anything, how was she supposed to help her? Guilt nudged at the tightness in her stomach. The spirit couldn't remember because they replaced her memories. Fleur never thought the Inbetween was a kind place, but she didn't believe they were cruel. She'd seen her share of ghosts left behind—the ones offered entrance into the Tree but remained, and the regret they felt after. It was a one-time offer. Stay or go. Those that went … well, Fleur knew little about what happened to them, only the lore handed down of the Glorious Feast at the table of the Tree Mother, Purna. But those who stayed—Fleur knew their agony as if it were her own.

"OK." Fleur pulled open the greenhouse door and crouched under the crime scene tape. The heat slammed into her. Thick enough to cut with a knife. "We'll start with what we know. Where did you die?"

The spirit floated around the tall stems, and colorful blossoms scattered over the metal shelves and tables. The air was sickly sweet, and sweat beaded at Fleur's nape as she followed the light.

Here? No. Here? This seems right. The spirit paused at the end of a wooden bench. *I sat here.*

"Were you with anyone?" Fleur circled the tight space.

The Atua flickered and dimmed. *Maybe?*

The greenhouse was empty. The room grayed as the clouds darkened. String lights decorated with Edison bulbs hung from the metal rafters, brightening in the dim afternoon light. Fleur studied the bench. The skin at her nape tingled. She ran a hand over the smooth wood, her gaze following the swirl of wood grain curling around the seat. Breath built up in her chest, tightening her lungs. She gasped, her attempts to fill her lungs futile. Her eyes shot up, finding the spirit in the amber light.

"Your lungs collapsed." Fleur gasped, crouching closer to the bench. She wheezed, leaning closer despite the burning in her chest.

Pain shot through her, bursting from the pit of her stomach. She doubled over, groaning.

What's happening? Are you OK?

Fleur waved her hand at the spirit, dismissing her worry. "Just give me a minute," she rasped as she closed her eyes, allowing the vision to take shape.

It was midday; the greenhouse wasn't busy yet. A few patrons lingered around the lavender petals, chattering with each other. They moved on, passing through the room, all but one—the girl stumbled toward the bench. Long auburn hair curled down her back, veiling her face as she hung her head. Fleur moved closer to her, taking in her dark blue jeans and leather booties. She wore a cream lace blouse and clutched her jacket in her hand. She dropped it as she fell back on the bench. A thick sheen of sweat flushed her pale skin. Her pupils enlarged. She blinked rapidly as if trying to wake herself up. The girl heaved and gasped—choking. Fleur inched closer. She was dying. The girl clutched at her chest, her body wheezing.

The vision faded. Fleur inhaled, reassured by the swirl of air filling her lungs. A veiled face—just like in her vision. Death.

Fleur bit her lip to keep from screaming and closed her hand closed over the cards in her pocket. Focus, breathe, she told herself as she shuffled, turning her gaze on the spirit, a tangle of faded lace hidden within the folds of light. "You died here. Your lungs swelled, your heart stopped, and you suffocated."

What poison does that?

"There are a few, belladonna, hemlock, jimsonweed, strychnine—"

Rat poison?

"It's easily accessible. Hell, half the stuff in our houses will kill us."

Did you ... The spirit wavered. *Did you see me die?*

Fleur nodded, looking at the cards in her hand. Her intentions focused on the vision still tingling beneath her skin. She lifted the top one. The Chariot.

What's that? The spirit hovered over her shoulder. *Does it tell you anything?*

Drive, intensity ... control, Fleur frowned, filing the meaning away. The card implied the spirit knew more about her death—at least while she was alive. "Tell me what you remember."

Nothing really. I remember the janitor finding me ... He called the police. There were people everywhere. They moved through me and hovered over me. I didn't know who I was—I still don't. Then the crowd shifted, and I saw—

Fleur raised a brow. "What?"

I was a vapor, a mist—and I suddenly couldn't breathe. The spirit looked Fleur in the eye and drifted closer. *I didn't need breath. I had nothing but emotion left. Emotion, confusion, and you.*

"Me?"

Just what I said before. I didn't know myself—whenever I tried to remember, I saw you, but not this you ... The spirit blinked at her. *A younger you—you as a little girl.*

"So, you thought you were me?"

No, I knew I wasn't. I saw your life like the faded reels of an old movie.

Fleur snorted and rolled her shoulders. "Sounds boring."

Something scraped the concrete floor, gritty and low—a welcome interruption. Fleur turned, glancing around at the empty greenhouse. "Hello?"

Like nails on a chalkboard, the sound increased.

The Atua faded, her glimmering eyes wide with worry. *Someone's here.*

The air cooled, her breath puffed like a seeded dandelion.

Not someone, something. Fleur's skin rippled with goose flesh as her hand crept upward to the slender key at her neck. To most, it was unremarkable—small, rusty, and round, a faded goddess symbol etched on the bow, its teeth dull with age, but to Fleur, the ancient key was a talisman, given to her by her mother, infused with her own spirit. It was all Fleur had left of the woman who gave her life.

She inched down the back row. Brushing against the staunch orchid leaves, Fleur pressed closer to the edge of the narrow walkway. A yellow moth fluttered near her, its wings broad and laced with black, tapering to a swallow-like point. Its movements were frantic as it fluttered from flower to leaf before landing on the shoulder of her jacket.

Fleur turned to the darkened space ahead. The scraping sound gritted over the concrete to her left, closer this time. She turned, bracing herself.

The shadows moved, curling away from the dimly lit corners, splaying their wispy limbs over the rows of flowers. Searching.

Fleur held her breath, inching back as the Grima's smoke seeped closer. It couldn't kill her, but one brush of its sooty fingers would feed on her despair and pull the sadness Fleur buried deep to the surface. She took another step back, then another, trapping herself between the Shadelings and a dead end lined with spades and trowels. Fleur clutched the key at her neck tighter. Its warmth pulsed beneath her fingers.

A black spot opened between them, rippling with sparks. It beckoned the Shadelings, tugging at their smoke. It grew as the creatures drifted closer. Breath held, she watched the darkness devour them until only a watermark remained.

Fleur straightened, rolling her shoulders back and tilting her head, listening. Nothing but the dull roar of the ventilation system. "You can come out. It's gone." She released the key around her neck.

The moth fluttered around her. Its yellow wings brightened before dissipating into light. The Atua elongated into a semblance of her living form and turned worried eyes to Fleur.

Fleur narrowed her eyes. "You can shapeshift?"

I don't know. I was staring at the bench when suddenly I was heavier, filled with color. I tried to tell you, but you couldn't hear me.

Fleur pressed her lips together and looked back at the watermark. "Grima, or Shadelings, as my father called them. They've gotten bolder." She eyed the spirit. "Fresh spirits taste better than old ones, I guess." Her words were harsh, but the Atua needed to understand what was out there. Being dead didn't make you safe.

The spirit nodded. *They're in the Inbetween too.*

It wasn't surprising. In the millennium since the sheath's destruction, they've begun spreading out, invading other realms. She had seen a few here but never so close.

The glass door to the greenhouse rattled. Fleur swung around, her hand grasping her key necklace as the Atua glimmered brightly, transforming into a moth once more.

A greenhouse attendant pushed the door open on a long creak. He wore the typical conservatory uniform of a green long-sleeve polo shirt and khakis. His face creased with laugh lines above his shaggy brown beard. He caught Fleur's eye. "You can't be in here."

Fleur released the key, her shoulders relaxing. "I got lost."

He narrowed his gaze. "You don't seem lost. Didn't the police tape tip you off?"

He wasn't buying her story. Fleur frowned. "I heard a girl died here."

His eyes narrowed. "Are you one of those reporters? We don't want any of you poking around. Leave it in peace."

"Reporters? No. I'm from the séance earlier." Fleur cringed at her words. Séances were just reporters for the dead, snooping where they didn't belong.

"Can't get enough, eh? The poor girl hasn't had a moment of peace since she died. Such a shame, people just can't leave it be." He looked pointedly at her.

Fleur ignored the accusation in his eyes and pressed on. "Why? Who was she?"

"Don't you read the news?"

Fleur knew the realm was a mess. She didn't need someone else clogging her world with their opinions. She shook her head and waited.

"Lenora Khade, last surviving heir of Rodney Khade … Khade Securities?" He stared at her, waiting for recognition.

Rodney Khade. Why did she know that name? Fleur searched her memory, latching on to a conversation with Viola. Rodney Khade, the rich finance guy who died in a car crash a decade ago. Fleur's gaze flickered to the yellow moth fluttering beside her. Oh, *that* Rodney Khade.

"His daughter, you said?"

The attendant nodded. "Found her right there." He pointed to the bench. "Poisoned, they say. It's a shame. The whole family's wiped out now. Rodney, his wife, and son in the car crash, and now the daughter." He crossed his arms over his chest, nodding to the door. "You got what you came for?"

Fleur thanked the man as she made her way toward the exit. The moth—Lenora—landed on her shoulder as she moved onto the walkway leading toward the main greenhouse.

The Atua flickered, her eyes downcast as she reshaped her light. *I don't remember that.*

"Lenora Khade." Fleur paused and looked at the Atua with fresh eyes. She'd seen a few pictures of her in the society pages Viola loved. It fit with the girl in her vision. Damn. Lenora Khade? The spirit before her seemed muted and limp compared to the woman she once was.

Will you help me? Please? Lenora's eyes widened, and Fleur could swear she saw tears in their corners.

A rebirth. The start of a cycle. Fleur cursed her vision for the millionth time. The image of the family etched in stained glass blossomed in her mind—the cracked glass. It was Lenora, tangled with vines.

Grima and a shapeshifting, amnesiac heiress all in one afternoon. Fleur bit back a curse. "I'll help you find your killer." She narrowed her eyes at the ghost. "As for your other request—"

The Relic? The Guardian said you could help me find it. They need it to—

"I don't care. The realms tossed me out. Why should I help them now?"

All the realms? I thought it was just your home—

"They're all the same." Even as she said it, Fleur could taste the lies in the back of her throat. They weren't the same. Fleur knew better than anyone the realms' histories, but the truth, the anger she'd wrapped around it and hidden deep, wasn't something this spirit deserved to know.

Lenora considered her, her light pulsing softly as she studied Fleur, from her messy bun of gray hair to her scuffed boots. Fleur wanted to squirm under the scrutiny but instead crossed her arms over her chest and glared ... waiting.

OK. Once we've found my killer, we can revisit my second request.

Fleur frowned. "I don't think you have the leverage to make that deal, Lenora."

I've been told I can haunt the living, although I haven't tried it yet ...

A threat? Fleur blinked. That was unexpected ... and intriguing. She sighed and shook her head. "Fine. I guess I should introduce you to Theda," she said, ignoring the smile brightening Lenora's light.

"Wait. Wait. I don't understand. She remembers nothing?" The moth settled on Theda's fingernail. "Spirits can shapeshift into physical beings?"

"It's rare—both things. My father told me about it, but until today, I've never seen it. And as for the memory thing ... The Inbetween decides what is done with you when you die. Soulkeepers usually give the dead a choice, but not always."

"She lost her memories but gained yours?"

Fleur shrugged, watching as Lenora fluttered into the air and brightened, elongating into her spirit form. Theda's eyes widened as the moth vanished.

Tell her who I am. Maybe she knows something.

"She wants me to tell you she's Lenora Khade. You know, that finance guy's daughter."

Theda tilted her head slightly, searching the room before her gaze landed on Fleur. "I know of her. Everyone does. Socialite artist, philanthropist. She gave most of her proceeds from her art to local charities if I remember correctly."

Fleur snorted. "A regular Robin Hood."

And what's wrong with that? Sounds like I was a lovely person. Lenora scowled slightly, then nodded at Theda. *Ask her if she knows about my family.*

"She knows what everyone knows."

Just because you don't care doesn't mean she's the same. Ask her, please.

Theda lifted a brow, watching Fleur's interaction. "Anything I can do?"

"She wants to know if you know about her family."

"Barely. The Khades were very private. The media only posted Annibel and Rodney at events his company hosted. I didn't even know they had kids until the crash."

Fleur glanced at Lenora. "Sound familiar?"

Lenora's light dimmed. *No.*

Fleur yawned and squinted at the clock. Almost eight. Ordinarily, Fleur was a night owl, but tonight … Her muscles ached from unwanted tension. She turned to Lenora. "Well, we'll check it out. I said I'd help, so I'm going to help."

Lenora grimaced. *I don't know where to start.*

"We'll head over to the Khade place tomorrow. See what we see."

"You can't just waltz into a place like that," Theda remarked. "Maybe start at the mortuary. See if anyone claimed Lenora's things yet. I'm sure she had a key."

"Good point." Fleur grinned. "See? This is why I keep you around."

Theda laughed and moved to sit beside her on the sofa. "I thought it was for my quiche."

Fleur pressed a kiss onto Theda's cheek, her fingers caressing her nape. "That too."

CHAPTER
EIGHT

LENORA

My name was Lenora Khade. It was strange and heavy, a string of foreign syllables on my tongue.

I chanted it to myself, elongating the vowels until it felt more like a name than a grouping of letters. My name. A small piece of me. A child I gathered close, prepared to give my life for.

I watched Fleur and Theda retreat down the hall into their bedroom. There was so much more I wanted to ask, like why was she set against finding the Relic? Fleur hoarded her answers, unwilling to give me the freedom to ask. The questions nagged, dimming my light.

Patience, I told myself. This was just the beginning. Fleur agreed to help. That was something. Now I just had to gain her trust—as if that would be easy.

I glanced around the room. Compact, with a large purple sofa and bay window. Terracotta pots littered the windowsill. I floated closer, inspecting the delicate plants' curled arms, luring unsuspecting gnats with their nectar. I straightened, wondering why Fleur had so many carnivorous plants. A few of the tall, veined, purple pitcher plants stuck out from the cluster of sundews, their mouths open wide. Waiting.

Just like me.

My light pulsed. I longed to melt into the sofa behind me, but I was vapor, a beam of light clouded with fog. I folded my arms over my chest—but there was no chest, nothing solid to hold. I was light, and yet I could still feel the phantom sway of my arms, the thud of my heart. I pressed my hand to my chest and waited. Was my mind playing tricks on me? I pressed harder. No. Nothing. Just light and wishful thinking.

I missed the heaviness and tingle of life.

I faded, drawing the darkness around me like a curtain, and appeared in the amber light of the Inbetween and its colorful lobby of doors.

The Lobby—the waiting room of the dead. Heavy curtains draped tall vaulted windows, patterned with brightly colored geometric shapes. Triangles and trapezoids fighting for space on a cream background. At the center of the circular room, surrounded by atomic-age luxury, was a colossal tree. It was ... startling—the whole place settled between heavy branches like a bird's nest. I didn't know what I expected death to look like, but I doubted it was an elaborate treehouse. Branches loomed above, chandeliers hung from their boughs, and round, disc-like lights that looked more like a spacecraft than a light fixture. The tree's truck encompassed the center, its ragged bark peeled away to reveal dozens of doors—our gateways to the living.

I drifted around the tree, dodging the few spirits emerging from the core. Some shone brightly—new Atua, like me, while others dimmed, their light faded with age and neglect.

I didn't know what to do. I was tethered to Fleur in a way I barely understood.

Fleur, a creature from a different realm. A place of magick, where her ability to speak with the dead was common, where fey creatures controlled the elements and time passed slower. Where the sky wasn't clogged with fumes or chemicals, and only the repercussions of spells and bloodshed darkened the soil.

No wonder she left.

But she didn't leave of her own free will. Her tribe forced her out —they forced a seven-year-old girl into exile over a vision she couldn't control. A vision of death, of change, of the loss of their queen. Her father smuggled her through a magickal veil and settled here.

I knew all this and struggled to remember the color of my eyes.

Patience, Lenora. A voice, low and husky, echoed in my mind.

Patience? I asked, doubt tinging my light. *I don't know if I have enough patience for Fleur.*

The Guardian's light colored yellow with mirth, quickly, like a hidden smile. *She will help.*

She said no to the Relic ... I paused, realizing I was advocating for something I didn't actually understand. *You said it was a tool, something to stop the Grima. But what is it?*

Many centuries ago, long before even my own birth, the realms were in distress. Raiding parties from the outer realms invaded the more fertile core, pillaging our resources—and creatures. Despite our offenses, the invasions continued until the Trinity Goddesses took matters into their own hands, crafting a protective sheath and instilling within it the magick of each realm. That magick was given to the goddesses as gifts, trinkets instilled with a glimmer of each chieftain's magick.

Trinity Goddesses? A small shudder raced through me. I'd heard mention of the trio in Fleur's memories but struggled with the lore. I wondered if I was raised in a spiritual home—my light flickering slightly.

Our trinity—maiden, mother, crone, so to speak. They watch out for us, guide us on the tapestry of life. Hemsut, the weaver of destiny; Oya, the lightning bearer, our warrior; and Gula Bau, the healer, our nurturer. They wove the realm magick into the sheath, keeping us all safe.

So ... the Relics are the trinkets given to the goddesses?

The Guardian's expression softened slightly, and she nodded. *When the sheath was destroyed, the Relics were drawn to the one realm without magick—Mundad.* The spirit's light tinged pink, and she looked away. *Fleur is stubborn, but she will help. Give her time.*

I didn't know if I believed her, but I was willing to try. I was dead. What else did I have but time?

CHAPTER
NINE

FLEUR

Fleur rested her chin on her palm, squinting at the screen, and tried, for the third time, to finish cataloging her uncompleted stack from Friday. Usually, Sunday meant the university library was closed, but finals loomed over the upcoming holiday weekend, offering extended hours for the next few weeks.

Only a handful of students lingered at the room's long oak tables. Lenora floated around them, peeking over their shoulders and twisting over the tables. She drifted up to the vaulted ceilings, her form shimmering in the hazy sunlight. Fleur ignored her and rubbed her eyes, blinking at the computer screen.

Her phone buzzed in the pocket of her black jeans, startling her. Viola had called three times already. Fleur groaned, ignoring the persistent buzz.

She's just going to keep calling. Lenora fluttered closer, her voice blossoming in Fleur's ear.

"How do you know?" Fleur whispered, ducking her head.

How do I know anything about you? I just do. Just like I know you

56

broke your wrist falling from ... Lenora paused, her brow furrowing. *Birdy's treehouse—*

"Stop." Anger flashed red behind Fleur's eyes. "Just stay quiet."

You'll have to tell me someday, you know.

"No, I don't. Please, go to the Lobby."

The Lobby is just a bunch of sad spirits wandering around.

Fleur gestured with her pen toward the rows of study tables. "As opposed to this?"

Lenora frowned. *Good point.* Her light flickered once before she vanished.

Fleur scowled at the computer screen. Did Lenora think she just wandered the earth looking for spirits to help? She had bills to pay. Fleur wouldn't risk her well-earned seat behind the circulation desk to solve a murder. She flipped through another book, tracing its spine with her finger, then recording the title on the spreadsheet open on her screen. Lenora and her killer could wait until she finished work.

Her phone vibrated again.

Viola wasn't giving up.

Fleur removed her phone from her pocket and glared at it as she set it on the desk. After Arik died and the bookstore he had so lovingly crafted out of a pile of used tomes had passed to his former business partner. Viola found herself alone and jobless. Sure, Soren offered to keep her on, but to Fleur's surprise, Viola struck out on her own. Fashioned a new life for herself from her small inheritance.

Viola got a job as a bookkeeper at an insurance firm and began frequenting a woman's group composed of widows looking for companionship. That's how she met Louisa, and the rest, as they say, is history. Fleur knew she was hard on her stepmother. She couldn't help it. The more Viola tried to befriend her, the more Fleur retracted. She didn't need Viola, but as Theda pointed out, Viola might need her.

Fleur unlocked her phone. Five missed calls and one message.

Fleurie, dear. Where are you? Is everything OK? I talked to Theda. She said you just needed some time. I'm sorry about the séance. It was foolish of me not to see how sensitive you are. Please call me.

Fleur tapped reply and stared at the blinking cursor for a minute before typing on the miniature keyboard. *Don't worry. Everything is fine. No need to apologize. Will call you soon.*

That done, Fleur hunched over her computer, skimming the spreadsheet. She blinked, willing the words to focus. It was no use. Her mind was miles away.

She minimized the sheet and opened the computer's search engine, typing *Rodney Khade car crash 2011* in the search bar.

Results populated the page, from tabloids offering the sensational to *The Seattle Times'* crisp bullet-pointed facts. Sunday morning, Rodney was driving. His blood was clean of alcohol, unlike his wife's. Annibel was far from sober. A photograph of the Khade family filled the screen. Rodney and Annibel were smiling, hands clasped, two beaming children grinned at their sides. They looked happy. Fleur stared at the picture, searching the clean lines of Rodney's face for any trace of sadness, of stress, and found none. No one was that content. They were young, his company was taking off—this was the moment when everything connected before Fate plucked his thread.

Fleur pointed her cursor at Annibel. There wasn't much on Annibel Khade, nee Alen. She was a teacher before she met Rodney through a mutual friend. Theda was right—the Khades had almost no social media presence until their death. Fleur reopened the page on the crash.

The family was driving north toward Bellingham. Visiting Rodney's business partner's newest property, according to one article. Dugal Griffin dropped several million on his water view estate. Money that, according to another article, he didn't have.

Fleur clicked on Griffin's name.

Dugal Griffin, born in 1972 in San Fernando to hedge fund financiers Fredric and Patricia Griffin. Fleur scanned the Wikipedia article. Typical rich kid stuff ... private schools, private universities. His parents divorced when he was nine. Fleur frowned, scanning past his illustrious schooling. An old photo scrolled onto the screen. A group of ten khaki-clad archeologists at a dig site in Turkey circa 1996. The picture was grainy. No matter how much Fleur zoomed in, the group's features were blurred. The text said Griffin was the second from the left. She studied the hazy figure, one arm around a smaller woman's shoulders, the other cradling a book. A regular Indiana Jones.

Rolling her eyes, Fleur closed the window and resumed her search of the Khade crash.

A pickup struck their car head-on. Rodney would have known Highway 11's tight curves and steep drops into Puget Sound, but that didn't stop him from accelerating well over the speed limit. The pickup hit them on one such curve, causing the car to spin out, crashing through the guardrail and into the rocky depths below. Fleur shuddered. No one could have survived that kind of crash. Both Rodney and Annibel died at the scene, but their son, Edgar, twelve, was rushed to Harborview Medical only to die a brief time later from internal bleeding.

Fleur typed Lenora Khade into the search bar, arching a brow as a large collection of photographs depicting a young, heartbroken Lenora at her parents' funeral came into view. After that, Lenora became a regular addition to the weekly gossip rags. She inherited the whole of her father's estate in trust until her twenty-first birthday. Until that day, Griffin managed her money, making her his ward.

As Lenora grew, so did her exposure. Photos of her laughing at cocktail parties or grinning into the camera on various social media pages eclipsed actual articles. Lenora became quite the party girl. Fleur scrolled down her Instagram page, noting the faces that popped up regularly. A young Asian man, mid-twenties with a shock of black hair and a wide smile, stood beside her in almost every picture, one arm draped over her shoulders, Lenora leaning toward him, her hand on his chest. A boyfriend? Aside from him, her art littered her Instagram page, as well as multiple aged family pictures hash-tagged "never forget."

Fleur squinted at the image of Lenora at a charity function. She held up a painting, the canvas's size dwarfing her slight frame, splattered in color. Broad brushstrokes curved into the outline of a face. A boy, his brown hair cropped short and wavy, his smile huge, dimpling his cheek. This must be Edgar, Lenora's brother. Fleur minimized the screen and pulled up the family photo. Same boy. The pudginess of youth clung to his face—he would never lose that innocence.

The edges of her vision blurred, and Fleur blinked, pulling back from the screen. She looked around, focusing on the chain of each chandelier. Her stomach cramped, pain lanced through her, and Fleur doubled over in her seat.

Dammit, no. Fleur bit back a moan. Not here.

The room swam as she choked on a sob, covering her mouth with her hand. Except for the rustle of pages and tap of keyboards, the room was silent. Fleur pushed back from the desk, looking at the exit and her coworker sitting at the desk beside it.

Focus on the door. The vision pooled behind her eyes, causing bright yellow spots in her vision. Fleur bumped into a cart overfull with books and winced. Lindy looked up from his desk, watching with hooded eyes as Fleur moved toward him.

"Break time already?"

"Just"—Fleur clutched her stomach—"watch the front for me, OK?" She didn't wait for a response as she pushed through the swinging door and into the hallway.

She barely made it before the vision pushed through. Fleur stumbled through the bathroom door and hunched over the sink.

Darkness bathed the room in impossible shadows. A streak of light in the distance. A streetlamp. Her feet crunched over gravel as she moved toward it. The light was amber and warm, tanning her pale flesh. Fleur looked up. The bulb was a shard, a quartz stone? No. Amber. Hands pressed against it, small hands—a child's hands.

Fleur lifted her hand, her fingertips brushing the heat of the amber —magickal heat. A shudder wracked through her, chattering her teeth, and she pulled away. The light flared, then vanished. Fleur stumbled backward as a sweet wind blew across her face. Music. Low, mournful, and familiar. Fleur shifted blindly, her hands outstretched, searching for the source.

Footsteps tapped toward her. Lenora appeared flushed with life, her hands gripping another, darker form. She laughed, her body buoyant with joy. Fleur reached for her as Lenora slipped away. A low chuckle split the air to her left. Fear laced through her. Fleur stilled, her body taut.

A man with long black hair wrapped with a ribbon of leather at his nape. A flash of light illuminated the sky, bringing his face into focus—square jaw, clean, sharp cheekbones, deep-set eyes—ice blue, glinting in the dim light, broad shoulders tapered into a long torso. Another flash revealed his cane. Its head was a wooden bulb, a symbol etched on the dark burls. The crescent moon embracing the eye of the sun—the goddess symbol. The man's lean fingers caressed it. He tilted his head and smiled. Fleur's skin crawled, and she stared, transfixed, at the light touch of his fingers against the sacred symbol.

She couldn't move. Wind slapped her back, piercing her with dread.

She knew the goddess emblem like she knew the color of her own eyes. Moon, eye, and sun born of three goddesses: Oya, Gula-Bau, and Hemsut, who crafted the sheath, branding the Relics held within with their mark.

Reality crashed into her with the whirl of a toilet flush. Her hands clutched the porcelain sink, and she heaved, vomiting her breakfast muffin into the bathroom sink.

CHAPTER
TEN

LENORA

I suppose the plush wall-to-wall beige carpet, exposed limestone walls, and tufted club chairs scattered around the Lobby were designed to comfort, but they seemed more like artifacts than home to me.

The chairs looked comfortable, velvet, and well loved. Spirits were composed of light, not bone. I couldn't imagine why the Lobby had endless seating—if no one could actually sit—until I tried it. Maybe it was the need to cling to the familiar? To rest our phantom limbs? The reasoning didn't matter, only the ability to sit and recline as if I was whole again.

A group of spirits floated across the room, their voices like distant echoes seeping into the lush interior. They knew who they were. They basked in memories like the sun warming their skin. Not me. I had nothing but facts, a name, and a purpose.

If only I could remember what it was.

The Guardian spirit, who had spoken to me before, inched closer, her light brightening. I glanced up, prepared to remind her to mind her own, when I noticed her face for the first time. Unlike the others, her features were defined. Her hair had been long in life, fringe feathered her forehead above wide upturned eyes, a broad nose, and a narrow pointed jaw. No mouth. Guardians spoke in light, drawing out emotion and thought with their luminescence.

You must return. The Guardian's eyes, dark and bottomless, looked frantic.

I just got here.

The Grima grow closer daily. You must return, she repeated.

Why don't I remember myself? I asked her, trying again to get a few answers. *And why Fleur? Why replace my memories? What's so special about her? Aside from the obvious.*

Like us, you were chosen. You must respect the honor.

I didn't ask for such an honor.

The Soulkeepers know best.

So, I'm what? A Guardian in training?

No. You are a companion spirit, Lenora. An honor born of sacrifice.

Sacrifice? What sacrifice? My light rippled.

Fleur will aid you. You have only begun your journey. The Relic is closer than either of you know.

I hate when people talk in riddles.

The Guardian's light tinged orange with mirth. *You'll get used to it.*

The branch closest to me shook as if ruffled by a light breeze, and I glanced down. Its leaves glinted and flickered. I rose, following the glowing leaves to the heart of the tree.

Go. Fleur needs you.

What about you? I wasn't ready to end this conversation.

The Guardian's eyes crinkled. *I'll be here when you return.*

CHAPTER
ELEVEN

FLEUR

Fleur fumbled with her cards, her chest heaving. The vision was powerful, soaking her skin in sweat. Images flashed—stained-glass windows, a family of four, one child cracked, and now this man and his cruel smile ... and Lenora. Another shudder racked through her, and Fleur rested her head against the cool tile of the bathroom sink.

She gripped the cards, their weight relaxing her fingers.

A toilet flushed in the stall behind her. Fleur shuffled the cards one more time, flipping the top card over. The Emperor—reversed.

Abuse of power, cruelty ... and he had a Relic.

No. No. No. It wasn't possible. Didn't Arik tell her this realm was mundane and pure in its timidness? But ... her head throbbed. Magick was drawn to the ordinary. This was no coincidence.

Fleur coughed as the urge to gag overwhelmed her again. She inhaled, pocketing her cards. Focus, she chanted silently, her mind sliding over the long vowels as her breathing calmed. She didn't have any paper. Damn. She needed to sketch the man—the emperor of her vision.

A woman washed her hands in the sink next to her, and the pen fixed behind her ear. Fleur cleared her throat.

"You, OK?" she asked, meeting Fleur's gaze in the mirror.

Fleur flushed and glanced at the sink. She had done her best to clean the remains of her muffin, but the putrid smell lingered. "Yeah, I'm not great with gluten," she lied.

She nodded. "Me either."

Fleur's gaze flickered to her hair. "Can I borrow your pen? I just remembered something ...," she trailed off.

"Oh! I forgot that was there." She pulled the pen out. "Go ahead. It's the library's anyway."

Fleur clutched the pen, the bold purple and gold university lettering wrapped around it. "Thanks."

The woman nodded. "Try some coconut water. It helps me."

"Electrolytes, got it." Fleur pasted on a smile as the woman pulled the bathroom door open and slipped into the hallway.

Fleur yanked at the towel dispenser and flattened a heap of paper towels on the counter. She had to be fast—she was losing his image. She drew the line of his jaw, then scratched it out. Was it square or round? Damn. She drew an inverted triangle. His shoulders were broad, she remembered, but his eyes? Fleur sketched everything she could remember onto the towel. An impression of the cane's head fluttered over her memory, and she drew the rounded top, the emblem etched on its side.

Her sketch was horrible, but it would have to work. She was no artist. Maybe Lenora would understand?

Lenora appeared, her aura tinged red as if she could sense the residue of chaos swirling around her. She studied Fleur, her light calming. *What's wrong?*

"Nothing—a vision, that's all," Fleur responded to the paper towel on the counter. "Does he look familiar?"

Lenora narrowed her gaze and drifted forward. *Should he?*

Fleur wanted to throw her hands in the air. "How should I know? This is your death we're investigating."

Lenora peered down at the drawing, her light dimming. *Maybe? It's not a great likeness, is it?*

"Hey." Fleur snatched up the towel, folded it into a square, and stuffed it in her pocket. "We can't all be Van Gogh."

You drew that?

"So?"

Lenora shrugged. *The cane feels familiar, but I don't know why. What is that symbol you drew?*

Fleur drew in a breath. Gods. She didn't want to talk about the damn Relics. "The goddess symbol. Each Relic was branded with it," she muttered.

Lenora's light brightened. *So that man has one? Is that what that means? And he's tied to my death?*

"I don't know. My visions aren't super accurate ... but, yeah ... maybe?" *Dammit,* Fleur cursed silently.

So? What are we waiting for?

"It's a crappy picture of a random guy. Not like I can just go showing it around and get answers. We focus on your death. Remember? That was the agreement." Fleur frowned down at the drawing.

Fine. What now?

Fleur glanced at the clock on her phone. She was in no mood to finish her shift. "We've got a morgue to visit."

THE ACRID CHEMICAL scent of Lysol barely masked the cheesy-sweet odor of death. Fleur wrinkled her nose. It was easy enough to sneak past the nurse at the information desk, as well as the morgue assistant staffing the outer reception in the hospital basement.

Lenora's moth was a great distraction. Who wouldn't focus their attention on the yellow tiger moth landing on their computer screen? Worked like a charm. Fleur grinned as she tiptoed past the now empty desk—the distracted attendant following Lenora down the opposite hall.

Two gurneys sat side by side, bodies covered with white sheets ready to be autopsied. Metal doors, each holding a newly refrigerated body, covered the back wall. A steel shelving unit flush with cubbies lined the side wall. The dead's personal effects, she assumed. Lenora's wouldn't be there. Fleur cringed as the realization struck and cursed herself. Lenora Khade was still an active police investigation. Shit. That meant seeing Javier. That did not bode well at all. Their breakup wasn't exactly amicable.

Well, did you find it? Lenora materialized opposite the two gurneys. She glanced at the bodies resting there, her expression troubled.

"No." Fleur examined the names on the metal doors. Maybe she'd get lucky. Maybe she wouldn't have to involve Javier. "Your stuff isn't here."

What do you mean?

"I'm an idiot, that's all. You're an active investigation. All your belongings are in police custody. Not here."

So, let's talk to the police. Lenora reasoned, drifting toward the door.

"Wait, a minute ..." Fleur touched the label on the door beside her, *Lenora Alen Khade.*

I'm in there? Lenora's voice shook even as she inched forward.

"Seems like. Wanna see?"

NO.

Fleur chuckled and released the latch. "There must be a copy of the report somewhere ..." She spied a computer cluttering the desk in the room's corner. "Keep a lookout, would you?"

Lenora nodded once and hurried back into the vestibule. Fleur didn't blame her. The morgue was creepy, living or dead.

The computer was password protected. Fleur scanned the cluttered desk for personal details. The coroner was older, maybe in his late fifties, if the picture pinned to the corkboard above the desk was any sign. Married, two kids. Birthdays were common passwords, but something about the picture made Fleur hesitate. She inspected the woman next to him. The image blurred. Pigments of color swam and multiplied until Fleur saw only varying shades of blue. The woman's name was Peri, short for Perita. A word spilled into her thoughts like a wave. Periwinkle. The blue darkened and stretched, outlining the photo and the small red numbers in the corner.

0704

That's it.

Fleur tapped on the space bar and brought up the welcome screen, her fingers roaming the keyboard.

PERIWINKLE0704

The computer flared to life. Fleur grinned, pleased she hadn't lost her touch.

Finding the right file was simple. The coroner was hardly a computer mastermind. Current files were all organized by last name on his desktop. Fleur clicked on the files labeled Khade.

Fleur's stomach clenched as an album of pictures graced the screen. Lenora, pale and lifeless, splayed open on the examination table, her torso a single bleeding wound. Fleur wiped her eye. She wasn't crying—the disinfectant made her eyes burn.

Cause of death: complete respiratory collapse; depression of the central nervous system, brought on by the ingestion of Atropa belladonna (deadly nightshade).

It sounded so archaic, like something from Shakespeare.

Fleur bit her lip and scanned the page, looking past another collection of pictures detailing Lenora's stomach contents, and noticed a footnote. A chemical analysis showed alkaloids in the lining of her stomach. Fleur read the statement again. Toxicity levels like that couldn't come from a single dose.

Lenora wasn't poisoned and left to die in the conservatory. She was killed slowly. That meant her killer had to be someone close to her, someone in her household.

Fleur groaned and pushed away from the computer.

She would have to talk to Javier.

CHAPTER
TWELVE

FLEUR

T he cracked leather of the Subie's headrest pulled at Fleur's hair as she moved, but she ignored it. Just as she ignored the rain splattering her windshield and the flash of lights as a sedan pulled into the parking spot beside her.

What are you waiting for? Lenora brightened in the passenger seat.

Fleur stared at the blank screen of her mobile phone, her fingers clutching the plastic case. "Just give me a minute."

Why? I thought you said you knew someone who could help?

"I do ... It's complicated."

Why?

Fleur groaned and rolled her eyes. "Don't you know everything about me?"

Lenora flickered. *I know your past, not your present.*

"Figures."

What does that mean?

"I guess the Inbetween didn't think my relationship status was important to our cause."

Lenora shook her brain and dimmed. *Theda surprised me.*

"Why? Because she's a woman? Or because she's Black?" Fleur bit out the words.

Lenora glared. *Because I didn't expect her to know about me.*

Fleur took a breath. "Yeah, right."

I didn't. Lenora brightened, her aura coloring red. *Don't assume you know me. I don't care who you love.*

"I don't keep secrets from her."

Good. Lenora faded back to white and nodded. *I like her.*

"What's not to like? She's brilliant, beautiful, and has the patience of a saint."

Enough to put up with you, at least.

Fleur's gaze shot to Lenora's, and she smiled.

So, what's the problem?

She sighed and turned from Lenora. To give her worried voice made it real, tangible, and she didn't need to give Javier that kind of importance. Not that he'd care, not that he even remembered how his words hurt her, cutting her to the quick.

"Before Theda, there was Javier," Fleur said, looking down at her phone, not sure how to continue.

I thought you were gay.

"I don't love gender. I love people. Javier was one of those people for a time."

What happened?

"Lack of trust, I guess."

Lenora brightened and leaned forward.

Words she hadn't spoken aloud in an age tumbled forward, but she hesitated. "We didn't fit together, that's all."

Lenora huffed, her light dimming in disappointment. *Fine. If you won't tell me, we could at least get a move on. Call him, or I'll give him a haunting like he's never seen.*

Fleur grunted. She doubted any ghost could scare Javier, not after their last encounter.

"My father kept his talent for speaking to the dead a secret, and he taught me to do the same," she began, the words pulsing to the surface. "I was young and wanted to please him, but my abilities were bigger than his, harder to conceal. It drove a wedge between us. Spirits don't like to be ignored. I thought I could do some good. But the toll was greater than I expected. When Javier and I met, I thought maybe my father was right. It was better to stop."

I get it. You didn't tell Javier, did you?

"But he found out."

How?

"How do you think?" Fleur narrowed her eyes and nodded to Lenora's wisp of light.

You can't blame the spirit for that. You're the one who kept it a secret.

Fleur scoffed. "Not this spirit."

Lenora rolled her eyes. *So? How long has it been since you two talked?*

"Five years, give or take." Fleur unlocked her phone, glancing at the assortment of apps gracing the home screen. Last time she saw Javier was at her father's funeral. He brushed past her, nodding to Theda, his eyes taking in her arm draped around Fleur's shoulders, and embraced Viola before moving past the small group of mourners and onto his car. He hadn't joined the gathering at Viola's house or offered her any warmth. Fleur's stomach soured at the memory.

Lenora flickered eagerly. *I bet he answers.*

Fleur shook herself and opened her contacts. She bet he wouldn't.

Maybe she should just text him? Make it less formal, less needy, give him an opportunity to ignore her if he wanted.

C'mon, Fleur. We need this.

Dammit. Fleur tapped on Javier's number, cursing herself for not deleting it years ago.

Voicemail. She knew it.

"Uh, hey, Jav, it's Fleur. I know it's been a while, but I need … well, I'm hoping you can help me with something, um … something I need help with." She cringed. Shit, she sounded like a moron. "Anyway, please gimme a call. Or not. Up to you."

She hung up and dropped the phone back into her lap.

Smooth.

"Shut up."

FLEUR DROVE to the East Precinct, anyway. She knew it was a long shot. Javier wouldn't call her back, which meant she'd have to figure out another way of getting into the evidence locker.

Fleur parked at the far end of the lot. The Subie idled, its frame vibrating. Her hands still gripped the wheel as she took a deep breath, then another. Javier would be at his desk, facing the reception area—he'd see her the moment she opened the door. Unless he had moved, which was possible. Maybe he had even moved precincts or changed cities. The thought calmed her. Hell, he could have moved to a different state altogether.

Let her be that lucky. Please.

A knuckle rapped against her window.

Lenora brightened beside her.

Fleur released a breath.

Another knock on her window.

At least the rain had let up.

Fleur turned, her hand moving to the window crank on her door.

The man hadn't changed an ounce.

Javier pulled up the collar of his wool jacket and looked down at her. She guessed he had gotten her message.

Fleur rolled down the window, allowing her nerves to calm with each motion. "Hello, Torres. Didn't think you'd listen to my message."

"Curiosity got the better of me." He took a step back, his eyes on the hood of her car. "Surprised this jalopy hasn't died on you yet." He winced over his choice of words, then frowned. "Not that death would stop you."

She gritted her teeth and tried to play nice. "Good to see you, too."

His brows narrowed, furrowing his forehead. His brown hair was shorter than she remembered. He had a beard now; it curled around his jaw, neatly groomed. He pushed his glasses up his nose, smudging the clear frames with his damp fingers. Same brown eyes, same golden tawny skin, same hard expression.

"What do you want, Fleur?"

Beside her, Lenora moaned at the bite in his voice.

Fleur cleared her throat. "I'm, uh, looking into something—"

"More ghosts?" He peered through the window. "Plan on unleashing them on me again."

"I didn't unleash anything on you, Javier."

"My scars say different."

"It wasn't my fault you freaked out and put your hand through a window."

"I wouldn't have freaked out if your ghost hadn't attacked me."

Fleur gritted her teeth. "How many times do you want me to apologize? Huh? I didn't know who he was, OK?"

Had she known the Atua that confronted her in the precinct parking lot was the man who killed Javier's brother, Fleur would have never engaged with him. But she didn't, and Javier never forgave her for that. Never forgave her for any of it.

He pressed his lips together in a frown.

A spirit attacked him? Is that possible? Can I do that?

"Not now, Len—," Fleur hushed.

"I knew it." Javier's eyes narrowed as he stepped away from the car. "You haven't changed."

Fleur opened the door and stepped out, zipping up her leather jacket against the chilly wind. "I wouldn't have come here if I didn't need your help."

Javier shook his head. "No. Whatever you need—I won't be a part of it. I thought maybe you'd changed. But, no. You don't care about me."

Fleur stuffed her hands in her pockets, unsure how to answer that. She always cared, but he just made it so damn difficult. It wasn't like she could just turn off who she was. She tried, and it backfired. "That's not true."

"Could've fooled me."

"Forget it. This was a stupid idea." She pulled the car door open, then turned back. "I tried to be different. I'm not. This is me. I can't control the spirits in my periphery any more than I can the living—I didn't know. OK? And as soon as I found out, I did what I could to minimize the impact. I opened up to you. I did what I could to help."

Javier laughed bitterly. "It took a ghost taking the shape of my dead brother to get you to understand? Maybe you should have tried harder?"

"I'm not all-powerful. And he was stronger than I suspected. I messed up. Is that what you want to hear? But when I tried to explain … You rejected it—me. I thought, after all this time …" Fleur trailed off and studied the hard angles of his face, the ice in his eyes. "No. It was a dumb idea. Forget it." She got back in the car.

"Dammit." Javier's expression softened. "Fine. What do you want?" he asked again.

"Nothing."

"You contacted me after years of silence to yell at me in a parking lot?"

"I'm not yelling."

"Fleur." He ran his hands through his damp curls, pinning her with a knowing stare.

"Fine. I needed some info on Lenora Khade's murder."

He whistled and shook his head. "That's a pretty sensitive case."

"But you're working on it." Fleur didn't ask.

"Why that case?"

She shrugged, ignoring Lenora's light brightening in the seat beside her.

Tell him.

"Just curious."

Javier braced himself against the roof of the Subie and leaned in. "You have a ghost in here, don't you?"

"So?"

"Is it Lenora Khade?"

"What do you care?" Fleur began rolling up her window, edging out his fingers.

He knocked on the now-closed window, but she only glared.

"I can't help you, Fleur," he exclaimed, shaking his head as he backed away from her car.

Can't or won't, it didn't matter. This was a horrible idea.

What do we do now?

Fleur glared at Javier's back and put the car in gear. "Plan B."

What's plan B?

The Subaru whined as she rolled into traffic, the rain renewing its tapping against her windshield. "I'm not sure yet."

CHAPTER

THIRTEEN

FLEUR

It wasn't always called Khade House. Until Rodney Khade purchased it in 2003, it was just another fancy house gracing the western shores of Lake Washington. One of the few remaining Carpenter Gothic homes left in the city. Its tall, arched windows faced the lake, their curvature at odds with the square board-and-batten siding.

Fleur eyed it from across the street. It reminded her of the house in *Psycho*—all hard edges and dark corners. The house sat back from the road, surrounded by wrought iron fencing and a tall, curved gate. A security box fixed to the side, half hidden by ivy.

Her eyes wandered over the fence and the cameras on every third post. This was no cheap security system. Fleur frowned. She could try breaking in. How hard could it be? A light moved on the side of the house, highlighting a dog-like blur—motion sensors and a dog. Damn.

Fleur hated dogs.

Lenora flashed beside her. *That's my house?*

"Yup."

It's so ... big. How do we get in?

"No idea." Fleur shook her head. "That's beyond my skill level."

Maybe if you talk to Javier again—

"No."

Fleur swore she heard Lenora huff.

You're being ridiculous. What if we—

"Stop it, Lenny. I will not grovel at Javier's feet. You heard him. He said no."

Don't call me Lenny.

"Why not?"

Want me to call you Fleurie?

"Point taken." Fleur pressed her lips together and turned back to the car.

There must be an easier way around the security system. Maybe the roof? It held a slight slant, lined with the gingerbread-type gables found in most Victorians. Fleur smiled. Gables meant it was easier to climb if needed. But how to do it without setting off the alarms?

"Hello there! Are you a reporter?" a voice rang out behind her.

Fleur turned, a lie gathering on her tongue.

"Of course you are. Who else would you be?" the voice continued, growing louder as a woman in her mid-forties appeared from behind a row of cypress trees. "I knew you'd want to talk to me." She smiled, revealing a set of bright white teeth at odds with her overly self-tanned skin.

Fleur frowned, taking in the pale pink jumpsuit and padded sneakers. They looked designer, but Fleur knew little about fashion outside of a thrift store. The woman tucked her shoulder-length brown hair behind ears covered in a row of gold hoops, each one longer than the last and just as shiny.

"Why would I want to talk to you?" Fleur raised a brow, noting Lenora's light brightening.

Maybe she knew me?

"Well, I live here, of course. Across the street from that poor girl." She pointed to the red-shingled ranch house behind her and leaned in, pressing the back of her hand to her cheek as if revealing a secret. "I knew her, you know."

"Oh, yeah?"

She straightened, her red lips curling, and fluttered her lashes—Fleur blinked to keep from staring at the length of them. "She was a delight, pity about all the tragedy."

Fleur cleared her throat and tilted her head. "And you are?"

"Oh! Forgive me, Poppy Albright, mindfulness coach and healer." She pulled a business card from the pocket of her fitted pink hoodie. "Lenora was a troubled soul. I often tried to help her. She was struggling, I'm sure of it."

"What does a mindfulness coach do?" Fleur asked, pocketing the card.

"I help one focus on the here and now through breathing exercises and meditation." She stepped closer. The scent of sandalwood and lilies wafted around them. "Finding the right mantra can renew our consciousness. Creating an awareness of your surroundings is the first step to rendering positive vibes." She nodded.

"So, you, ah ... what? Teach people how to meditate?"

She nodded. "Stress, childhood trauma—it can overwhelm us, keep us from seeing the now."

Fleur bit her lip, a theory forming. "Did you help Lenora?"

"She was a complex being, but I did my best." Poppy blinked her long lashes.

"You two were close?" Fleur persisted, noting how Poppy hedged the question.

Lenora's light brightened as her gaze narrowed. *Something doesn't feel right about this.*

Poppy nodded. "As much as I could be to such a tortured creature."

"Tortured? How?"

Poppy's hand fluttered over her heart, and she exhaled. "You know of her family's deaths? She was the sole survivor. Can you imagine the guilt and longing she must have been feeling? To be all alone, no one to care for her."

"Except you, of course," Fleur replied sardonically.

Poppy smiled. "Of course."

"What about her staff? Her friends? Her guardian?"

"Oh, they were just using her. She was an innocent soul with too much money. Predators, all of them."

Fleur raised a brow. "But not you?"

"I'd never," Poppy swore, her face flushed. She turned, her gaze raking over the sidewalk. She frowned and jerked her head to the shape of a man walking toward them. "Unlike that one."

Fleur turned toward the young man hurrying up the sidewalk. He wore a faded blue plaid coat and a pair of brown corduroy trousers. Tousled black hair above a pair of narrow brown eyes. "Who's that?"

"Just another leech." Poppy sniffed and stepped away. Her eyes flickered back to Fleur. "I'm late for another session. Call if I can be of help, won't you?"

Poppy turned, her pink silhouette disappearing as quickly as she came.

Something's off with that woman. Lenora stared at Poppy's cream stucco rambler. *I doubt we were as close as she says.*

"Why? Because she said you were troubled?"

No, because her aura was almost metallic.

"What does that mean?"

Deceit. Falsehoods. Lenora shrugged. *She was lying.*

"Hey! What are you doing?"

The voice startled them. Lenora brightened, her eyes widening as the young man moved closer to them.

"Sightseeing," the lie tumbled forward.

"Oh, yeah?" He paused in front of her and tilted his head. "At Khade House?"

"I like old houses."

He considered her, his gaze sliding over hers to focus on the house in the distance. "Are you a reporter?"

Fleur shook her head. Something about him tugged at her memory. "No. Why?"

"I saw you talking to Poppy. She's been hunting for reporters since it happened." He frowned. "Whatever she told you—don't believe her. The woman would sell her soul to get followers."

"She's on the socials?"

He rolled his eyes. "Wants to be an influencer. She was always hounding Lenora to promote her coaching thing." He paused. "What'd she say?"

Fleur shrugged. "Nothing much."

I knew it. She didn't know me. Lenora fluttered. *But he does. Ask him.*

Fleur narrowed her gaze at him. "Do you live nearby?"

He nodded to the wrought-iron fence. "I used to live there."

Lenora brightened and drifted closer to the man. Her aura flickering yellow. *Ask him if he knew me,* she insisted.

"So, you knew Lenora?"

He nodded again, pressing his lips closed.

Fleur gritted her teeth and pressed on. "How?"

"How do I know you're not a reporter?"

This man was infuriating. "You don't."

Fleur. Please. Lenora moved to stand beside the man, her face turned to his.

It occurred to Fleur that she *had* seen this man before on Lenora's Instagram account.

"You were her boyfriend, weren't you?" Fleur asked, nodding to the gate. "You two lived here together."

Lenora brightened, her translucent hand covering her heart. *What?*

The man crossed his arms over his chest and leaned back on his heels. He regarded her, then sighed. "You really didn't know who I was, did you?"

Fleur arched a brow. "Should I have?"

"If you were a reporter, you would have."

"Well, that solves it."

Ask him his name and how we met—oh! And if we were in love. And what I was like—

Fleur offered her hand, hoping to cut off Lenora's tirade. "Fleur Harkyn."

He shook his head and relaxed his stance, grasping her hand in his. "Takeo Sato, but everyone calls me Sato."

"You don't seem upset."

"You don't know me enough to make that call."

Touché.

Fleur grinned. "Withdrawn. Sorry."

Lenora brightened, inching closer to Sato, her aura turning orange with excitement.

"So, what was she like?" Fleur gave in and watched Lenora's light flare.

Sato pushed a rock around with the toe of his black sneaker, clearing his throat before looking back at Fleur. "She was radiant."

Lenora shimmered gold.

"I know that sounds dumb, but it's the best way I can describe her. Radiant, like the sun. I don't understand why anyone would hurt her like this. She was so kind to everyone."

According to the toxicology report, she wasn't kind to everyone. "No one is that kind. Did she have any enemies?"

Lenora ingested small doses of belladonna. A live-in boyfriend would have had that kind of access.

"Enemies? What are you, a cop?" Sato tensed.

"I'm not a cop, or a reporter, promise. I'm just a … uh, friend."

"Yeah? You don't look like any of Lenora's friends." He gestured to Fleur's gray hair, purple eyeliner, and black leather jacket. "Where did you meet her?"

Fleur looked him in the eye. "Botanical Gardens in Volunteer Park."

Sato released a shaky breath. "She loved the gardens." He blinked, turning his face away. "That's where they found her, you know."

Lenora fluttered closer to him, her hands clutched over her heart. *Tell him I'm OK.*

Fleur groaned. "Take it easy. I'm sure she's fine."

"Fine? She's dead, lady." Sato took a step back, his gaze narrowing.

"Then she's better off than us."

A flash of blue light broke through the overcast sky, followed by the squeal of a police siren. Fleur turned and cursed.

"Not a cop, huh?" Sato snorted, his eyes on the blue sedan behind them.

Javier stood on the sidewalk beside his unmarked SPD car, frowning.

Dammit, why? Fleur looked back at Sato. "I'm not. He's just an old ... associate."

Sato took a step back and stuffed his hands in his pockets. His body hunched as if defending himself from an invasion.

"Thought I'd find you here." Javier sauntered up to them, his shoulders back in mock confidence.

Fleur glared. "I thought you couldn't help."

"I can't." He glowered. "This is an active investigation."

"So, why are you here?"

"I'm not an idiot, Fleur. I knew my denial wouldn't deter you."

Anger flared in her breast. "This is a public sidewalk, Detective."

Javier shrugged once and turned to Sato. "Is this lady bothering you, Mr. Sato?"

Sato shook his head.

Lenora's light twitched and colored blue. *Told you to talk to Javier.*

"Shut up, Len," Fleur muttered under her breath.

"Len?" Sato's head spun toward her, and he took a step closer. "Did you say, Len?"

Shit.

"Oh yeah, didn't she tell you?" Javier nodded to Sato. "Fleur is a medium. Ghosts everywhere."

"You can speak to Lenora?" Sato's voice hitched.

Fleur's gaze flickered from Javier's smug face to Sato's expectant one, and she swallowed back a curse. "Yes. I can speak to Lenora."

Sato looked around them, his cheeks flushed. "Is she here?"

"Yes. She's here." She held up her hand, palm out. "But she remembers nothing. Not you, not this house, not her death—not even herself. Nothing."

"Shit. Really?" Sato shook his head, then narrowed his gaze at her. "Then how do you know it's her?"

"Little thing called the Internet. Ever heard of it?"

"You could be lying." Sato crossed his arms over his chest.

"I could be." Fleur shrugged. "But I'm not."

Javier grunted.

Lenora beamed. *His aura is pale yellow—it was gray before. He's suspicious—that means he cares.* Her light flushed rose.

Sato studied the air, his eyes darting from Fleur to the space between them. "Where is she?"

Lenora's light ebbed and faded, shrinking into the delicate yellow wings. She fluttered around them, landing on Sato's shoulder.

Fleur sighed. "On your shoulder."

Sato stilled and turned his head to the flutter of yellow. "A swallowtail?" He sniffed and raised his head, glaring at Fleur. "How did you know?"

"Know what?"

"Len had a thing for moths. How did you know?"

"I didn't." Fleur rolled her eyes. She didn't care if this kid believed her or not.

Sato looked back to Lenora, fluttering on his shoulder, his eyes widening. "No shit?"

"No shit."

A laugh escaped Javier, and he shook his head. "You've got to be kidding me."

"Just because you don't understand it doesn't make it less true, Detective," Fleur asserted, ignoring his snort.

"I think I've had enough of the ghost world today." Javier frowned. "Sato, you'd be wise to leave this alone. Nothing good will come of it."

"Yeah?" Fleur countered. "Then why are you here?"

"To keep you from getting into trouble." He nodded at the house across the street. "You forget, Fleur—I know you."

"No. You *knew* me. Big difference." She turned, her hand grasping the keys in her pocket. Enough was enough. Fleur moved back to her car.

"You're leaving?" Sato asked as he caught up to her. "Can I come?"

"Why?"

Sato shrugged and looked at Lenora.

Fleur huffed and jerked her head toward the Subaru. "Sure—"

"Yeah?" Sato grinned, the corners of his eyes crinkling.

"Why not? Maybe you can answer a few questions for me?"

"Taking in stowaways now?" Javier asked, his mouth crooked into a half smile.

"What do you care?" Fleur unlocked her car and pulled open the door.

"Wait a minute."

Fleur turned. "What?"

Javier cleared his throat and leaned against the Subie. He almost looked contrite—almost. "About before ..."

Fleur crossed her arms over her chest.

"Maybe we can help each other out?"

"Oh, yeah?"

His shoulders drooped. "The case is ... at an impasse. And I thought maybe we could share information."

"I don't have any information."

"No"—he shrugged—"but you have Lenora."

She didn't think. It was all reaction, all emotion, and the moment Fleur's fist hit Javier's cheek, she knew it was all worth it.

CHAPTER
FOURTEEN

FLEUR

Holding cells smelled like urine. Well, at least this one did. Fleur crinkled her nose and shifted on the metal bench.

She shouldn't have hit him. Striking an officer was never a good idea, but just thinking about Javier's smug face made her want to hit him again. She was an idiot to think he'd help. Fleur grimaced and hung her head. He wanted to use her, not help her. Javier was an asshole.

He wasn't always. Old Javier would have listened, offered a few bad jokes, and helped her solve this infuriating problem. This Javier ... was angry. She couldn't fault that. Sure, she could have done a few things differently, like be honest and keep a spiteful spirit away, but if she learned anything, it was she was right to keep her secrets. Her biggest mistake was telling him. She was careless. A mistake she wouldn't repeat.

How long had she been in here? Did he think letting her stew in this cage would change anything? Fleur huffed and crossed her arms over her chest.

I've never been to jail before. Lenora glowed beside her. *Is it always like this? At least, I don't think I've ever been in jail. I feel like I'd remember if I had a criminal past.* Lenora drifted around the cell, hovering over the woman curled in the corner. *Do you think she's all right?*

Fleur studied the woman's thin frame. The frayed hem of her stained hoodie hung over a pair of grime-covered jeans. Fleur frowned. A dry place to sleep was a temporary solution. She needed a place to get back on her feet and a few square meals a day. She needed care, not punishment. Who knew what circumstances led her to this point?

The woman moaned, twisting on the bench.

"Hey." Fleur leaned forward. "Hey, are you OK?"

The woman grumbled and sat up. Tangled blonde hair fell over her face. "Let a girl sleep."

"Sorry." Fleur sat back, watching Lenora drift around the room.

The woman slouched back into the corner. "I'm always OK. It's not a choice."

"What's your name?"

"Why should you care?" She waved at the officers passing the doorway beyond the cells. "They don't. I'm just another faceless vagrant."

The nameless horde—what so many see when they pass the tent cities and poverty-stricken struggling in the parks where their children used to play. But they weren't nameless—An arrow of anger pierced Fleur's skin. They had as much value as the judgmental faces turning the other way.

"I'm Fleur." She stretched out her hand, leveling the field.

The woman studied her with round, sunken eyes.

Fleur waited, her hand outstretched. She'd wait all day if she had to.

"Reva." The woman's fingers were rough with callouses, but her grip was firm.

Fleur smiled. "Nice to meet you, Reva."

Reva snorted and pulled her arm back. "What're you in for?"

"Assault."

Reva's eyes roamed Fleur's curvy form. "You?"

Fleur shrugged. "The detective ticked me off."

"A detective?" More laughter. "Girl, you'll be here a while."

What does she mean, a while? What about Sato?

Fleur shook her head, hoping Lenora would quiet, and turned back to Reva. "What's your story?"

"You really want to know?" Reva narrowed her eyes, waiting for Fleur to nod. "I got tired of being my husband's punching bag, so I left. He froze our accounts—tried to force me back." She shrugged, her face tilting to study the grime under her fingernails. "I used to get manicures, you know that?"

"What'd you do to get here?"

"I existed."

"Your husband took everything? What about family? Friends?"

"I don't want anything from them—told me it was all in my head, that I should just apologize and play nice. Hell with that. He crushed me. Everything he touches turns to dirt."

"You tried a shelter?" Fleur knew of a few reputable ones.

"You know how hard they are to get into?" Reva huffed, pulling her hoodie tighter around her narrow shoulders.

Theda's aunt wouldn't turn her away. "Try Jubilee, on 18th Avenue."

"No way I'll get in."

"Just try it, OK? Ask for Alma."

Reva laughed bitterly. "Oh, yeah? You think they'll help me? What are you? Some kind of fairy godmother?"

"Hell, no. My partner calls me a busybody."

"They're right. Leave it alone."

"Fleur Harkyn," the officer's low timbre rumbled into the cell.

Fleur stood. "Here."

"Let's go." Keys rattled against the metal bars as he opened the door.

Finally. Lenora brightened and slipped past the officer.

Fleur looked back to Reva. "Alma at the Jubilee Shelter." She nodded once. "Can't hurt."

Reva snorted.

"C'mon, I don't have all day." The officer opened the door wider and glared at her.

The door slammed closed behind her.

Fleur followed the officer into the processing area and waited as they handed her back her belongings. The uniformed officer behind the screen laid out her purse, its contents itemized into separate plastic bags. Fleur dumped it all together and moved toward reception. She'd check it later.

Theda stood beside Javier in the waiting area. Her arms folded in front of her, creasing the folds of her plum-colored wool wrap into a deep V. A frown tilted the corner of her mouth. Fleur bit back the urge to rush forward, to embrace her warmth and forget the last few hours ever happened. Theda's gaze slid from Fleur to Javier, her frown deepening as she took a step back, distancing herself from him.

Fleur's limbs slowed as she neared. A tinge of jealousy flushed Theda's brown skin. Fleur's nerves fizzled, and remorse curled her stomach. Damn. Fleur cursed herself for not realizing sooner how this would play out.

"Are you ready?" Theda's words were soft and biting, her body taut.

Fleur nodded. "Yeah." Excuses scattered over her tongue, but she swallowed them down.

Theda nodded and turned toward the entrance. Fleur jogged beside her.

"Before you go," Javier ventured, his jaw red, the remains of her fist. "Can I have a minute?"

Fleur stilled, her arm reaching out to stay Theda, tugging on her wool sleeve, earning her a glare.

Beside her, Lenora glimmered, her eyes wide with excitement. Fleur didn't blame her, but now wasn't the time to pepper Javier with questions he wouldn't answer.

"What?" Fleur grasped Theda's hand, pulling her into the conversation.

Javier's gaze flickered between them. He cleared his throat again and ran a hand through his hair. "I was out of line before."

"You think?" Fleur snapped, unwilling to give him the inch he wanted.

"Doesn't mean you were right to hit me, but ..." He pressed his lips together, searching for words. "I shouldn't have proposed a collaboration like that."

"No, you shouldn't have." Fleur clenched her jaw, hating the words that bubbled forward. "The case is at an impasse? What kind of impasse?"

His gaze darted from desk to desk, over the scattered uniforms lingering around them, and he jerked his chin to the entrance.

Fleur sighed and linked arms with Theda. "This ought to be interesting," she whispered as they followed Javier out of the station.

Theda glowered. "Did you have to get *him* involved?"

"I've got nothing but an amnesiac ghost and her puppy of a partner. I need something concrete." Fleur shrugged. "Necessary evils and all that."

"Fleur ..." Theda trailed off and looked away, her gaze following Javier as he moved outside, past the line of police cars.

Theda knew about Javier. She knew his rejection sliced into the delicate flesh of Fleur's heart. Fleur loved Javier once, but it was smaller, less whole than the love she had for Theda. Fleur understood her anger and uncertainty, but it didn't make it easier. She paused and faced Theda. "He wasn't my first choice, but ..."

Theda shook her head and looked down, examining the toe of her loafer. "I get it. I do. But, c'mon, Fleur. What were you thinking?"

Fleur shrugged, knowing there was no suitable response. "I wasn't."

"Obviously."

"You told me to help the ghost, Theda. I warned you this would get intense—"

"This isn't just intense, Fleur. You hit a cop. It doesn't matter how much baggage you have with him. You can't do that." Theda took a breath and looked back to where Javier stood waiting.

Fleur leaned into her, pressing her forehead to Theda's. "I know. I just ... snapped. I'm sorry, Theda."

Theda closed her eyes and leaned in, a strangled laugh escaping. "You scared the shit out of me. Don't do that *ever* again."

"I promise." Fleur kissed her cheek.

I wonder if Sato loved me like that. Lenora drifted beside her. *Like you love Theda. I wish I could remember him.* Her voice lowered. *I wish I remembered anything ...*

Fleur sighed and shoved her hands in her pocket, her fingers curling around the sketch she made earlier. She was still no closer to understanding it or the rest of the vision. The goddess symbol unfurled in her head, and her body tensed.

Out of the corner of her eyes, Fleur spied the Subaru parked at the end of the lot, a dark shape leaning against the hood. Sato straightened when he saw them appear but paused. She'd have to ask him how he and her car ended up in the precinct parking lot when her keys were in her purse. Sneaky devil.

Irritation flushed Javier's face as they stood before him. Lenora fluttered from Javier's shoulder to Theda's as if she could sense the distrust.

"Took you long enough," he ground out.

"So? What impasse?" Fleur asked, ignoring his remark.

"Toxicology report shows alkaloids lining the victim's stomach, consistent with a more gradual death than we thought." He paused for dramatic effect. Lenora fluttered to Fleur's shoulder and stilled.

"She was being poisoned," Fleur repeated. Javier didn't know she had already read the report, and she preferred to keep it that way.

"Right. But Lenora lived alone. About six months ago, she dismissed the housekeeper—"

"Housekeeper?"

"Opal Barlow. Worked for the Khades for nineteen years, lives in Maple Leaf with her husband, no kids," Javier recited, swiping his hand over his phone.

"Have you questioned her?" Fleur asked.

"I'm not some rookie, Fleur. She was heartbroken but couldn't tell us anything useful. Knew Lenora since she was six. Hired on after Edgar was born, she was half childcare worker, half housekeeper for most of the kids' childhood."

"What about the boyfriend? He lived there, too, right?"

"Wrong. Address is with a cousin in Beacon Hill. Sato and Khade dated for five years until she went dark. One day she was living it up. The world toasted her as its social media darling; the next, nothing."

"Did you search the house?"

Javier rolled his eyes. "Of course we did. Found nothing out of the ordinary. Tech is examining her laptop and security footage as we speak."

"What about a diary or something? Lenora seemed like a girl who kept one of those."

Javier shook his head. "Nothing."

"What about her social media?" Theda offered. "Have you cross-referenced the images? There may be a pattern? Maybe someone or someplace you could use to understand why she went dark."

"We did. Nothing unusual."

"So ... what?" Fleur couldn't keep the bite out of her tone. She thought about the Google search she had done earlier, cursing herself for not paying closer attention to the dates.

"So, nothing." His gaze flickered to Lenora's yellow wings. "It was wrong of me to assume you would want to help."

"Oh, stop it, Jav. You knew that's why I reached out, and yeah, I wanted to. But I won't let you use Lenora or me. You crossed the line with that."

"Yeah, I know." Javier touched the bruise on his cheek and grimaced.

Fleur rolled her eyes. Dammit. "If I discover something, I'll let you know, OK?"

Javier grinned. "I'd appreciate—"

"Wait." Fleur held up her hand. "This isn't out of the kindness of my heart. If you want my help, you'll need to hand over Lenora's personal effects."

"You know I can't—"

"Then there's no deal."

"Fine." Javier frowned, shoving his hands in the pockets of his jeans. "I'll see what I can do."

Fleur straightened and held out her hand.

Javier clasped it and sighed. "Don't make me regret this."

CHAPTER
FIFTEEN

LENORA

Watching Sato talk about me was heartbreaking, not because we were two souls cut down, but because I didn't know who he was, and I wanted to.

I fluttered beside him. He sat on the armchair across from the sofa in Fleur and Theda's cramped apartment, staring at the carnivorous plants on the windowsill. He looked uncomfortable, as if he regretted his decision to come.

Fleur sat beside Theda on the sofa, her legs tucked under her. The room was silent, both parties waiting for the other to begin. I drifted around them, my light illuminating their faces in the dimly lit room —light that only Fleur could see.

I drifted over the windowsill, my aura coating the sundew's unfurled arms, triggering them. How was that possible? I was intangible, and yet the plant's limbs curled as if a fly had landed on them.

"You're not imperceptible," Fleur said, noting my inspection of the sundew's arm. "The plant can sense the movement in the air." She shrugged.

It's like a warning system?

"Are you talking to Lenora?" Sato asked, turning from the windowsill to Fleur.

"Who else?"

Sato flushed and leaned back in the chair.

Theda shifted, scooting to the edge of the sofa. "Anyone want a drink?" She glanced around before rising. "Wine?"

"Gods, yeah."

Sato shook his head. "Do you have beer?"

"No."

"Oh, then yeah, wine's fine."

I drifted closer to Fleur and studied him. Javier said I was poisoned gradually. Only one person was close enough to me to pull that off. But Sato didn't feel like a killer.

"All right. Spill it. What didn't you tell Detective Torres about Lenora?" Fleur cut to the chase.

"What do you mean?" Sato narrowed his eyes.

Fleur sighed and leaned forward, accepting the glass of wine Theda held out to her.

A sudden urge to touch the glass, to feel the weight of the burgundy liquid slide around it, overwhelmed me.

"How long were you and Lenora together?" Fleur asked, sipping her wine.

"Four years."

"How'd you meet?"

"At a club?"

"What kind of club?"

"A dance club in Pioneer Square."

Fleur narrowed her eyes.

Sato sighed and rubbed his hands over his eyes before reaching for the glass Theda set on the coffee table in front of him. He gulped the wine down, making a face as he set the empty glass back on the table.

"Why the third degree?" he asked.

"Why'd you hotwire my car?"

I glided closer to him, waiting.

He flushed and straightened in the chair. "I was wondering when we'd get to that."

Theda sat, sipping her wine.

Fleur didn't say a word.

Sato groaned. "Fine. Yeah, I wired it. I watched you hit the cop, and I was like, oh, shit, I'm going to lose my chance to talk to Len. I didn't think. Your car door was open—sweet suicide doors, by the way. It's not like I broke in or anything."

"Talking to Lenora was that important to you?" Theda asked. "Why?"

Sato shrugged. "I didn't get to talk to her before ... it happened."

"What would you have said?"

"That's none of your business."

"C'mon, really? You think you can talk to her without me?"

Sato remained tight-lipped.

"This is getting us nowhere." She paused, studying Sato. "Lenora doesn't remember you. She asked me to help her, but all I've got are dead ends and a headache. Either you tell me something useful or get out. My patience is at its end."

Theda placed her hand on Fleur's arm.

"I wanted to apologize. OK?" Sato muttered.

Was this a confession? Could this be that easy? I hovered closer, his aura warming yellow, then blue with conflict, and I knew he believed he was at fault. My instinct flared. Sato didn't kill me.

"Why?"

"For not protecting her. For getting angry when she kicked me out." His voice was thick. "We argued. She told me she wanted me out, that it was for my own good. I shouldn't have listened. I should have stayed." He searched the room with strained eyes, looking for me. "I'm sorry I didn't fight for you, Len."

I wished with all my might I could remember him.

"How do we know it wasn't you?" Fleur arched a dark brow and leaned back.

"Didn't you just hear me? I loved her."

"Yeah, but you just said she kicked you out, and you were hurt. Sounds like motive to me," Fleur pressed.

Sato swore and straightened in his chair. "Look, I didn't kill Lenora. I would never hurt her. Yeah, I was upset. Who wouldn't be? I did everything I could to help her, and she broke up with me. I was bitter, sure, but I loved her." He glanced between Fleur and Theda, his aura coloring blue with loyalty. "If she broke up with you, would you kill her?"

I flickered at the bite in his tone and inched closer, as if I could somehow calm him. This man—this stranger—cared for me, maybe even loved me, and I ... my light dimmed, I had no memory of him. *Fleur. He's telling the truth.*

Fleur ignored me, shaking her head at Sato. "Not the point."

"It's totally the point. Don't accuse me of something unless you have proof," he sneered, folding his hands together in his lap.

Theda set her wine on the table and looked between them. Waiting. Could she sense his truth too? She didn't look convinced of his guilt, not like Fleur.

Tell him it wasn't his fault. He didn't kill me.

"Lenora said it wasn't your fault."

Sato released a strangled laugh.

Ask him why I sent him away? What did I say? How did I act?

Fleur took a sip of wine and looked from me to Sato. "Wanna tell me what happened the day Lenora broke up with you?"

"Not really."

"That's not the right answer."

Theda leaned forward. "Please, Sato, if you want to make amends with Lenora, help us."

I hovered over the sofa. Waiting. My light beaming pale pink. I wanted to scream. The urge to shake him throbbed within me. I needed more. I needed to know who I was.

Instead, I flickered. Another drawback to being made of light.

"I thought we were good. We had arguments, sure, but nothing big, nothing that would make her send me away. And things had been quiet. I started school in the fall—community college, wanted to get my computer science degree. Len encouraged me. She knew my background. She knew what I wanted to accomplish. She was my cheerleader, my rock."

"What about your background?" Fleur asked, sipping her wine.

"I have a record, juvenile stuff ... computer fraud, nothing bad, but enough to close doors, right? Lenora helped me. She opened a few windows. Introduced me to her father's old partner, convinced him to take me on once I finished my degree. She wanted me to clean my slate, said Griffin would be the best person to help do it."

"What'd you do? Try to hack the NSA?"

"Something like that." Sato leaned back. "Anyway, things were good. Until they weren't. It started with the trash. I figured it was just raccoons, but Len worried. It was crazy. But it continued for weeks. Then she found the mailbox open. Someone had resealed two of our letters. That freaked Lenora out. She was sure she was being stalked." He frowned. "Maybe she was? Maybe this is part of that? I should have tried harder to understand. Things were dying down ... until the face in the window."

"What face?" Fleur leaned forward, her body tense.

Sato shrugged. "I dunno. Never saw it. I just got the call from Len. She was in a full-blown panic. It took me forever to calm her down. She said it was pale, with enormous eyes. Lenora swore it was a ghost."

He paused and took a breath. "After that, things were different. She was distant, stopped hanging with our friends, started reading all these books on witchcraft and the supernatural. She wouldn't talk to me. The panic stopped, replaced with determination to solve whatever mystery she had in her head. I didn't know what to do. I went to see Griffin, thought maybe he'd know what was wrong. At the time, I thought, hell, it's a long shot, but maybe? A week later, she kicked me out. And now she's dead." He hung his head.

His words flared within me, and I knew I had discovered something. Certainty washed through me, followed by anguish. But what? What was I looking for? And why? I sent everyone away, isolated myself because I discovered something—but what? Frustration splintered my light, mingling with the racing anxiety. Terror rippled, tugging at my memory. I closed my eyes, probing the darkness for any shred of color. Whatever it was—it changed everything.

It got me killed.

"Shit," Fleur breathed. "You think she knew she was going to die?"

Sato lowered his eyes, focusing on the tips of his shoes.

Theda inhaled and set her empty glass on the table. "What did Griffin say?"

"Said I was imagining things, that Lenora was given to fits of fantasy, and I should just let it play out."

Was I being haunted? My light dimmed and flickered lowly. Was that a precursor to my death? Is that why the Inbetween erased my memories, replacing them with Fleur's fractured history? The thought pressed against me, cracking my facade like glass—I had known I was going to die. How was that possible? Why? Did I just let it happen? How could I do that? Panic webbed, racing through me. My light flickered in a frenzy color. The room blinked in dull gray like a reel stuck in a projector. It skipped and flapped, film bubbling over the heat of the bulb until the entire world was white.

CHAPTER
SIXTEEN

FLEUR

They lay in silence, their bodies intertwined, their breathing in unison. A beam of light from the streetlamp outside shined through the shuttered blinds coloring the opposite wall gold.

"Do you think Lenora's OK?" Theda asked.

Lenora's sudden disappearance had startled Fleur. The Atua was obviously shaken by what Sato said, but Fleur had never seen a spirit flare yellow with such fear—the entire room exploded in bright golden light, blinding her. It wasn't so much Lenora's exit that bothered her. It was the skip of her own heart, the strangled breath she struggled to release, as if Lenora's dread was her own, leaving Fleur shaken, gasping for air.

"I don't know. I've never seen a ghost have a panic attack before." Theda's breath warmed her cheek. "I thought she attacked you."

The room had erupted. Theda was by her side in an instant, her hand drawing slow circles over her back to calm. Sato raced to the kitchen, opening cupboards until he found a glass, water sloshed over the side as he raced back to her, thrusting it into her hand. Fleur was shaking too much to drink. Her body struggling to take in the panic Lenora left behind.

"I doubt Lenora has any idea what happened. Her only thought was to run."

"Is that what you felt?"

Fleur nodded. "Terror. Lenora was terrified." She took a deep breath. "She was spiraling—no, I was. It was like wind slapping my skin, and I was paralyzed with fear. I've never connected to a spirit like that. It was as if I *was* Lenora."

"How is that possible?"

Fleur didn't know. Their connection was unexpected. She exhaled a shaky breath and tried to still her heart. Lenora was safe. She could feel her thrumming like a second heartbeat.

"She'll return when she's ready."

"Do you think she remembered something?" Theda wondered.

"If not a memory, then an emotion tied to Sato's words."

Theda seemed to consider that. She smoothed Fleur's hair under her chin, her body tensing with a problem she couldn't solve.

Dread pooled in Fleur's stomach, mingling with longing. Her father would know what to do. Fleur wished he was here. She sucked in a breath and closed her eyes. To say she was estranged from him was an understatement. Fleur pushed away from him, loathing his need for normalcy. Didn't he understand she would never be normal? She tried. So many times. Her gifts wouldn't be ignored. But Arik was determined to ignore them, blinding himself to his daughter. And Fleur hated him for that.

Just as she hated how much she needed him right now.

Arik didn't linger past death. He chose the Inbetween and followed the amber light into the Great Tree's core. By the time Fleur arrived at the hospital, his body was a husk, and she had lost her only chance to say goodbye.

Fleur released a shaky breath and rubbed the tears from her eyes. Enough. Arik was gone. Dead from the heart defect he had kept secret from her, robbing her of yet another part of himself. Dwelling on the past wouldn't help her. She needed answers, not memories.

"Do you think there's anything to this stalker stuff?" Theda murmured, her breath warm in Fleur's ear.

"It's the most logical place to start, right? Lenora was well known. It would make sense. A follower on Instagram? Maybe someone who knew her rituals enough to poison her?"

"Seems like a stretch—I mean, if you were obsessed with someone, wouldn't you want their death to be personal—like a stabbing? Poison is a distant death."

"Yeah, but she was poisoned slowly. That's personal."

"Sounds like a vendetta."

Who had a quarrel with Lenora? And why? Jealousy? Betrayal? Lenora's Instagram page flashed in Fleur's mind. Something about her face. Crowds hovered around her, but she ignored them. No, it wasn't something Lenora did, but maybe something she didn't do.

"I need to speak to her neighbor again."

"Who?"

"The mindfulness coach, Poppy. There's something there. I can feel it."

"You think she saw something?"

"She was lying, Lenora sensed it, and she seemed pretty keen on exposure. I'm willing to bet she saw something but wants her fifteen minutes."

Theda tightened her arms around Fleur and blew out a breath. "Lemme guess, you want to poke the sleeping bear a little?"

Fleur grinned. "Could be fun."

Theda groaned.

"We need to talk to Dugal Griffin, too. Maybe he knows something that will shed some light on what Lenora was doing?" She paused, the list of characters racing through her mind. "And the housekeeper."

"Don't forget Khade House."

"I need to find the key and the security code. That place is wrapped tighter than one of Viola's Christmas presents."

Theda giggled. She tightened her arms around Fleur. "Just be careful. I know you, don't go stepping on toes. You need these people to trust you."

"You make me sound like a bull in a china shop."

Theda laughed. "If the shoe fits ..."

"Rude." Fleur lifted her head, pressing a kiss to the side of Theda's neck.

"What about your connection with Lenora?" Theda asked.

"What about it?" Fleur hissed, then softened her tone. "I'll worry about that later."

"Later might be too late," Theda replied, shifting to meet Fleur's gaze. "What if this is something dangerous?"

Fleur moaned. "Please, Theda ... I can't, OK? Let's focus on what we know, not what we don't."

Theda tightened her arm around Fleur, her breath shallow. "Why'd you go to Javier?"

Fleur closed her eyes. She knew this was coming. "He's a cop. I needed Lenora's stuff."

"We could have done it together."

"I know. I just ... didn't think. Lenora and I were in the morgue, and I realized her stuff was in custody, and I called him. I didn't want to."

Theda stilled. Fleur could hear her brain clicking. "I don't like this," she said finally.

"I tried to warn you—"

"I know, OK? I know you did, but I didn't think it would escalate like this."

"What's upsetting you? That Javier arrested me or that I called him?"

"Both? One leads to another, right? If you hadn't called him, you wouldn't have punched him ..." She shook her head. "I don't know how I feel, Fleur. I'm angry and scared."

"Do you want me to stop? 'Cause I'll stop. Just say the word." Fleur twisted around to face her. "You matter more than all this."

"I don't know." Tears welled in Theda's eyes. "I-I just ..." She took a deep breath and rested her head against Fleur's. "No ... no, I told you to take the case, and I meant it. If you can help Lenora, then you should finish it."

"That means more Javier and more ghosts."

Theda nodded, wiping her tears with the back of her hand. "I know. It'll be OK. I promise."

"Oh, Theda ..." Fleur tightened her arms and lifted her head. "You don't have to be OK with it. It isn't fair of me to even ask you to try—"

"No. I told you to start this. This is on me. Don't make it easy on me." She sniffed. "This is you. I know that. You've been upfront about it from the beginning. I see you, Fleur. I see how alive you are with Lenora ... and, well"—she shrugged—"maybe there's a petty part of me that's jealous. Then you brought Javier into it ... and I just—"

"I know, Theda."

Theda sighed. "I'll be better."

"Don't." Fleur kissed her, allowing her lips to linger, basking in the sweetness of her breath. "Just be you. I need you, not them. You're my anchor."

Theda smiled. "I love you."

Fleur tangled her limbs with Theda's and tucked her close. "I love you more."

SEVENTEEN

FLEUR

Viola wove between tables, her hands fisted, brushing her raincoat as she moved. The rubber soles of her galoshes sloshed and squeaked over the polished hardwood, causing a myriad of students to lift their eyes in annoyance from the books and computer screens littering the tables.

Fleur scowled. She should have responded to her stepmother's last message. Not that dealing with an asshole ex, a temperamental spirit, and her irritating boyfriend was a valid excuse for Viola.

After a considerable amount of groveling, Lindy had agreed to cover her half day. Fleur owed him one—she would owe him more by the end of this investigation if she wasn't careful. Concentrating was pointless. She'd be better off working on Lenora's history, not cataloging manuscripts.

"Well," Viola huffed. She stood arrow straight, her arms folded over her bosom. "Did you think I had nothing better to do today than drive all the way here to make sure you weren't dead?"

"Nice to see you too, Vi." Fleur smirked.

"I know you're a busy woman, Fleur. But the least you could do is send me a thumbs up every so often." Viola leaned over the desk and lowered her voice. "I was worried—you ran out of the séance so fast, I didn't have time to check on you. What happened?"

Fleur frowned, her gaze darting around the reading room. This wasn't the time or place to have this conversation. "I'm fine, Vi. Just a little shaken. That madam was very convincing," she lied, praying that would be the end.

Viola straightened and smiled. "She was, wasn't she? I told Hiram she was worth the money. He can be such a stickler about those things. We wanted to do it right, for the corpse flower, you know," she added with a nod.

"Of course."

"But why did Madam Olga say she needed you? Were you part of the ruse? I told Esther you were, but ..." Viola paused, blinking innocently up at her. "It was all so strange."

Fleur shrugged. "Séances usually are."

"Don't be snippy. Something bothered you. Don't tell me it didn't because I saw your face, Fleur Agathe Harkyn—and I know what I saw."

Fleur cringed at her full name and blinked at the tiny woman in front of her. Viola was a force to be reckoned with when needed, and apparently, she thought Fleur needed it. She opened her mouth, prepared to repeat that it was nothing, then closed it. The urge to tell Viola the truth, to see if she could handle knowing what her husband and Fleur were—to have someone other than Theda on her side was overwhelming. Fleur swallowed her words, knowing it was fruitless. Viola would never believe her. She didn't want another parent to turn from her.

She stared at Viola with wide eyes, pleased that Viola cared enough to worry.

"I'm fine, Vi. I don't know why Madam Olga singled me out. I left because"—she paused, her eyes softening—"I thought she'd try something with Dad like she did with Esther's husband."

Viola released a ragged breath. "Oh, honey ... I hadn't thought of that."

"Weren't you worried?"

Her stepmother shook her head. "Arik would never bother with someone like Olga. And if he did, I'd know it was because he missed me. That wouldn't be so bad."

Fleur's brow furrowed at Viola's words. "What do you mean, wouldn't bother with Olga?"

Viola stared at her as if picking which words to use. Was it possible she knew something? Had Arik told her? Had he broken his internal vow and told his wife the truth? Fleur held her breath.

"He had no patience for ... mumbo jumbo. I believe he called it."

Of course not. Arik may have loved Viola, but not enough to share all of himself with her. Hell, he didn't even share with his own daughter.

A shadow fell over her desk, followed by the thud of a small cardboard box against the raised wooden counter. Fleur frowned and turned from Viola, prepared to give the owner a piece of her mind.

"Javier!" Viola gasped, her voice raising as she turned toward him, her mouth curled into a smile. "Whatever are you doing here?"

Great. Fleur cursed. When it rained, it poured. "Yeah, Jav. What *are* you doing here?"

"Hiya, Viola." His smile bloomed as he wrapped her in a quick hug. "Been a long time."

"And whose fault is that?"

"I know, I know. I've been busy. A detective's work is never done."

Fleur rolled her eyes.

"Detective? Congratulations." Viola beamed as she turned to Fleur. "Did you hear that, Fleur?"

"Yeah, Vi. I heard."

"Well. That's just lovely." Viola paused, looking between Fleur and Javier. The wrinkle between her eyes deepened. "So, I gather you two have buried the hatchet?"

"That's one way to put it." Javier nodded to the box. "Fleurie, here, is helping with one of my investigations."

Fleur glared. He knew she hated that name. And what was he doing, spilling all the news to Viola? He knew she couldn't leave well enough alone.

"What?" Viola grinned, her worry lines smoothing. "That's wonderful. I'm glad to see you getting along again. What does Theda think about all this?"

"Theda's helping too," Fleur added. She turned to the box, her hand reaching for the flap. "Is this what I asked for?"

Javier nodded but kept his attention on Viola. "How are you? I heard you're working for an insurance company now—didn't want to stay at the bookshop?"

Viola's smile dimmed. "No, no ... it was time for something new. Arik would have wanted it that way."

Arik would have wanted her to stay at the shop, but Fleur knew how hard it was for her. Fleur didn't fault her leaving. She would have done the same.

Javier nodded. "Well, I'm glad you're taking care of yourself— and Fleur too."

"Someone has to."

Fleur repressed a groan.

Javier cleared his throat.

"Oh, well." Viola grinned at them. "That must be my cue." She turned to Fleur. "I'll see you and Theda on Thursday."

"Thursday?"

Viola frowned at Fleur's blank expression. "Thanksgiving?"

Fleur smiled half-heartedly and stifled a groan. Damn. Already? "Right."

"Alma's making her green bean casserole. Tell Theda I'm looking forward to her yams. They really are delicious. I don't know how she does it." Viola beamed, then turned to pat Javier on the shoulder. "You're welcome, too."

"Oh, thanks, Vi, but until I close this case, I'll be eating out of takeout boxes."

Viola shook her head. "Don't work too much. You're still young."

Javier laughed. "It was nice seeing you, Viola."

"Stay safe, Javier." Viola turned to Fleur. "See you Thursday."

Fleur pasted a smile on and nodded. "Yep. Bye, Vi." She waved.

Javier waited until Viola was out of earshot. He turned to Fleur. "Do you have any idea how hard it was to get this?"

"Probably not as hard as you'd have me believe." Fleur frowned and reached for the lid.

Javier pulled the box away. "Not so fast. I held up my side. Now your turn." He lifted a brow.

Fleur frowned, glancing behind her. Lindy sat at his desk, chin cradled in his hands, eyes on his computer screen, his thinning head tilted toward her—listening. He'd peppered her with questions when she arrived this morning, pleased to see she had recovered from her stomach ailment. Lindy looked up, as if sensing her gaze, and frowned.

"Not here." Fleur turned back, waving her hand at him. "Leave the box, and I'll call when I'm done."

"Oh no, nope—this box doesn't leave my sight." He glanced behind her. "I'll wait for you in the parking lot. When are you finished?"

Fleur glanced at the clock. "Ten minutes."

He nodded, tucking the box under his arm as he turned back to the exit.

Fleur swiveled her chair to Lindy. "So?"

He glanced up. "So what?"

Fleur shrugged. "Ask. I know you want to."

"You really working for the police?"

"With, not for. And yes, Javier is a friend. He's helping me with something."

110

"Helping you? With what?"

"Death of a friend."

Lindy narrowed his eyes, leveling their steel gray in her. "You don't have friends."

Fleur met his gaze. "Rude."

"What are you up to, Fleur? Is this about yesterday? Was that food poisoning? You seemed fine when you left. And who were you talking to in the bathroom? You know how it echoes. I watched the hall. One student came out, but you kept talking."

"Is it a crime to talk to myself?"

Lindy scratched his chin. He didn't believe her, but whether that was a trust issue, or his own desire to stir up trouble, Fleur didn't know.

"I don't carry full conversations with myself," Lindy pointed out.

Fleur shrugged. "What can I say? I'm odd."

Lindy snorted.

"Thanks for helping me out this afternoon, by the way."

Lindy shifted his gaze over her shoulder and nodded. "If you want me to help next time, you've got to tell me what's going on."

"What do you care?"

"Humor me."

Fleur tilted her head. "Maybe."

"So, who's your dead friend?"

Fleur expelled a breath and threw her hands in the air. "Gods, you're a pain."

Lindy's frown deepened. "Don't you have work to do? You're not off yet."

Fleur wrapped her messenger bag over her shoulder and pulled open the library doors. She peered up at the overcast sky. Dark clouds, their bellies bulging with rain, draped over the landscape. A shiver raced over her, and she tugged at the collar of her leather jacket, wishing she remembered a scarf.

The dreary sameness of a Pacific Northwest winter was a comfort. She longed for the dark swell of clouds on the brightest of summer days and reveled in them during the long winter nights, but today, Fleur felt only irritation.

It could have been Viola's visit, Javier's appearance, or Lindy's nagging, but it wasn't the people present in her bubble that irritated her. It was the absence of one.

Lenora.

Javier leaned against a concrete planter at the base of the stairs. She moved toward him, willing her legs to move slower than her racing heart commanded. Fleur needed what was in the box if she was going to make sense of Lenora's death, needed to know what Lenora knew, understand what drove her to alienate herself.

She didn't know when she began to care about the blasted spirit. She was still a nuisance, demanding more of Fleur's time than she wanted to give. Part of her felt guilty. Fleur ignored that part, or tried to. It wasn't her fault that the Inbetween replaced Lenora's memories with her own—and they didn't even give her all of them, just her childhood, her family, her regrets.

Maybe that was all the Inbetween needed—memories of her time in Evirdahl and her mother's search for the Relics.

Dammit. Fleur could almost smell the scheming. Someone in the Inbetween had a sick sense of humor. Well, they could scheme all they want. She didn't have to help. Once she found Lenora's killer, it would be over, and she could move on with her life.

Javier crossed his arms over his chest, hands tucked into the fold of his elbow for warmth. He arched a brow as she approached, straightening his spine.

"Well?" he asked.

"Well, nothing. I'm still working on it."

"Seriously? How hard is it to manipulate a spirit?"

Fleur scowled. "It isn't about manipulating, it's about coaxing, and Lenora doesn't remember enough to coax anything."

"You said that before. She's an amnesiac ghost?"

Fleur nodded. "Like I said—I'm working on it."

"Well, what *do* you know?"

"Not much more than you. According to Sato, she got scared. Someone went through their trash, stole their mail. Lenora thought someone was stalking her—"

Javier frowned. "Stalking her? We found no evidence of that. Nothing on the security footage—" He shrugged. "It's not the best security system—it's basic, something anyone could get on the Internet. Too many blind spots. Sato said nothing about it, and there's no police report."

Fleur made a face. "Just because she didn't make a report doesn't mean it didn't happen. She was Lenora Khade—she probably didn't want the publicity. Think about it. The media would have a field day."

"Noted. Anything else?"

Fleur shrugged. "It was around that time that she dropped off social media, dismissed her housekeeper, and started researching."

"Researching what?"

"Witchcraft, talismans, Relics—hocus-pocus stuff. I don't know why."

"Talismans, huh?" Javier expelled a long breath. "That's something, at least." He nodded to the box. "Maybe you can make something of this."

Fleur pulled off the lid and peered inside. "That's it?"

"That's all she had on her."

Fleur rested her arm on the edge of the cardboard and surveyed the contents. She pulled a pair of latex gloves out of her bag and tugged them on before reaching inside. There must be something useful here. Only a quarter of the box was full, each item wrapped in plastic, marked with the chain of command. Fleur pulled out an iPhone. The screen was cracked, as was the lining—it must have fallen on concrete. Maybe when she died? Had she been trying to call for help? Fleur pressed the power button. Nothing happened.

Under the phone was a worn paperback copy of Jane Austen's *Persuasion*. The cover was torn in the corners, and the spine broken in multiple places. It was well loved, read hundreds of times. She opened the plastic bag and pulled the book free.

"Don't—" Javier cut off, knowing it was useless.

Fleur ignored him and flipped through the stained and marked pages. Lenora liked to take notes. No, not just liked—she marked the book beyond an inch of its life. Passages highlighted and underlined. Asterisks noted thoughts, feelings. She highlighted Anne Elliot's journey to Bath and scribbled a series of numbers into the margin. Fleur flipped ahead, noticing more numbers asterisked at the pivotal points in the story.

Fleur closed the book, tucked it under her arm, and looked back at the box. She drew out a USB drive and pulled off the bottom. It seemed intact—

"It's corroded. I tried opening it, found a virus."

Fleur lifted her eyes to his. "Did you have tech look at it?"

"Of course."

"And?"

"Things like this take time, Fleur."

"So, that's a no."

Javier ran his hand through his hair. "They found nothing."

Fleur snorted, ignoring Javier's protest as she pocketed the drive. She bet Sato would have better luck.

"What's this?" Fleur held up an iron mandala. It was heavier than she expected and small, about the size of her palm, with a deep groove in the center. A smaller version of the wind spinner in Viola's yard. Fleur turned it around, examining the small etching on the back. She sucked in a breath. Crescent, eye, sun—another goddess symbol. Fleur's fingers curled around it, noting the cool metal. It wasn't a Relic, which made the symbol more curious. Why would Lenora have this? What the hell was going on?

Javier shrugged. "Looks like a wind chime."

"Smart-ass. Why would she have something like this on her?"

"How should I know? Maybe she liked it? It's just a spinner. My mom has one."

Fleur nodded to the remaining lipstick tube and a small tin of mints in the box. "None of this is *just* anything." She held up the wind spinner. "Look at it. Have you ever seen one so small? I haven't."

"What? You think it poisoned her?"

"Maybe?" She winced at his tone and ran her finger over the rough iron edges.

"The poison was ingested."

She glanced back at the box. "Yeah? So, how do you eat mints?" Fleur asked, holding up the small red and white tin, her patience wearing thin.

Javier just glared. "Well, she didn't eat the spinner."

Fleur snorted and looked back into the box.

Bingo. Keys. She smiled, jingling the key ring between her fingers.

"Oh, no, you don't. Police property."

"Don't you want my help?"

"Dammit," Javier cursed. "Fine. But I'm coming with."

"Of course, I wouldn't have it any other way." Fleur smiled sweetly as she tucked the book and the wind spinner into her bag. "But I'm driving."

EIGHTEEN

FLEUR

J avier hunched in the passenger seat of the Subaru 360, his knees pressed against the dash, his arms folded over his chest. His six-foot frame barely fit in the cramped car. Fleur shifted in her seat, her shoulder brushing against his with every move. She scowled, turning left into the driveway of Khade House. She stopped in front of the security box.

Yesterday the house looked cold and vacant. No lights brightened the arched windows, the only movement a flash of dog fur out of the corner of Fleur's eye, but now ... Fleur eyed the sprawling Gothic Victorian beyond the ivy-covered gate. Its beige siding throbbed with aura. A chill crawled up her spine, and she exhaled, her breath a puff of smoke in front of her.

Fleur turned to Javier. "Maybe you should wait in the car for this one."

He snorted and shook his head. "We do this my way, or we don't do it."

Fleur considered him, his tense shoulders, his arched brow. She didn't want another argument. "Fine. What's the code?"

"091503," Javier recited, looking at his phone. "The date they bought the house."

Fleur pressed the numbers on the keypad and waited for the gate to slide open.

The house glowed purple, pulsing brighter as they inched closer. Fleur's brow wrinkled as she studied the building. Atua littered the yard, their light pale white. The pair stood frozen, eyes on the house and the evil lurking inside.

Fleur bit her lip and eased off the brake, letting the Subie roll forward.

"Hello!" The breathless singsong greeting drifted through the window.

Damn. Poppy. Fleur pressed the brake and frowned. She had hoped to question her again without the police. She glared at Javier. "Let me manage this, OK?"

He frowned. "Which one of us is the cop?"

"Oh, shut it." Fleur rolled down her window the rest of the way and waved at Poppy, jogging up to them. "Hello."

"I was wondering if you'd come back." Poppy leaned down and grinned, revealing her set of gleaming white teeth. "We didn't finish our conversation the other day. Oh, and this car! It's just adorable and so old. You must have a strong solar plexus." She nodded.

Fleur swallowed back a biting response and broadened her smile. She didn't know what the hell a solar plexus was, but she doubted it had anything to do with cleaning a carburetor or redistributing a fuel line. She didn't rescue this car; it rescued her. Fleur caressed the steering wheel. The moment she saw it, she knew this old beast was perfect. It took months to get it up and running. Even now, a decade later, it chugged and puttered around the rainy Seattle side streets a breath away from breaking down.

"Yeah, she's a good little car." Fleur cleared her throat and opened the door, untangling her limbs as she moved beside Poppy.

"Sure, if you like breaking down every fifty miles." Javier climbed out of the car.

"Oh!" Poppy exclaimed. "I didn't see you there. How did you fit inside?" She tucked a strand of chestnut hair behind her ear and lowered her lashes, smiling at him.

Fleur suddenly wanted to gag.

"Pure inner strength," Javier replied, his lips twitching.

"I can tell." Poppy took a step closer. "Poppy Albright, and you are?"

"Detective Torres."

"Oh, a detective. Pleasure to meet you."

Fleur pinned him with a glare before turning back to Poppy. "Have you seen anything strange around here?"

"Like what?"

"Like anyone rummaging through the Khade's trash or trespassing, maybe climbing the gate? Anything out of the ordinary?"

"Oh! Do you think the murder happened here? Was it a dump job? I watch *CSI*—you know. It could be." She nodded thoughtfully. "It really could be."

"We're still investigating that," Javier cut in.

"Did you ever see anything unusual?" Fleur asked again.

Poppy adjusted the hem of her pastel blue jacket and straightened her shoulders. "Why? Do you think they're still around?" She paused, her blue eyes widening. "Am I in danger?"

"No." Fleur shook her head. "Nothing like that."

"Lenora would have told me, I'm sure of it. But no, she never uttered a word." Poppy sighed and gestured to the house. "The poor thing was so alone here. You know, I think if it wasn't for me, she would have never found her calling."

"Her calling?"

"Her art, of course. She was brilliant." Poppy laughed, pressing her hand to her heart. "And I'm not one to brag, but it was our sessions that changed everything, brought painting back into her life."

Fleur gritted her teeth. The woman really was too much. "You were her inspiration?"

Poppy let out a cackle and threw her head back. "It's kind of you to say. I tried, I really did."

This was getting them nowhere. Fleur turned, catching Javier's eye, and waited.

"You saw nothing unusual?" Javier persisted.

"If I had, I would have reported it, Detective."

Javier nodded. "You said you and Lenora were close?"

"Oh, yes." Poppy nodded. "Until her boyfriend came around. He never cared for me." She narrowed her gaze on Fleur. "You should look into that one. He was only after her money."

"We're looking into *everyone*," Fleur assured her. "Don't you worry."

"Good. Good." Poppy blinked, dropping her gaze and taking a step back. "Now, I really must dash. I have meditations to conduct."

"Thank you for your time, Ms. Albright." Javier nodded, folding his arms over his chest. "We'll be in touch."

"Yes, of course." She waved and turned, moving back into her own yard.

Fleur shook her head and turned to Javier. "That woman is lying through her teeth."

"Doesn't mean she did it."

Fleur opened her car door and climbed in, glancing at the house. A shiver pierced her spine. The spirits hadn't moved, lingering in the purple half-light of the faded garden. She turned to Javier as he folded himself back into the Subie. "Doesn't mean she didn't, either."

CHAPTER
NINETEEN

LENORA

Everything had changed.

This wasn't some run-of-the-mill murder. Suddenly finding my killer or some damn Relic seemed insignificant compared to the possibilities—I *knew* something about my death.

My light flickered and dimmed. A spirit clad in indigo light paused beside my chair. The Lobby was bustling with lost souls seeking aid, looking to right their wrongs—mocking me with their purpose. The whole stinking lot of them hummed with need.

I was a mess when I returned from Fleur. I burst through the gate, my frenzied glimmer lighting the tree bark yellow with fear. The Guardians took me in hand, settled my nerves, listened to my prattling. They cooed words of solace, dimming my light until the unwanted panic had subsided.

Until only a wisp of confusion remained, cloaked in fury.

I knew I was going to die. It shouldn't shock me—but it did, accompanied by the overwhelming knowledge that whatever I discovered had gotten me killed—that I let it happen. Why would I do such a thing?

Questions, and still more questions. I didn't know enough about myself to answer them. I didn't know what kind of music I liked or whether I could ride a bike.

All I knew was Fleur. And I hated it.

It wasn't fair.

The Guardian hovered beside me, her light steady, her presence comforting.

I peered up at her, wishing she had a name, something tangible for me to cling to. Need brightened my light.

Names are worthless social constructs. We have no need for them here.

But you have one, don't you?

The Guardian flickered. *You seek normalcy. But nothing was ever normal. All beings are one. Normalcy is merely a need for the familiar. It is dangerous.*

You're the same as the others? As me?

Yes. We are the All-being—one soul stretched and broken, each of us seeking to return to what we have lost. To ... gather our pieces. You are part of me, just as you are part of Fleur.

Then why the hierarchy? Why Guardians? Companions and the rest? Why steal my memories? Fury sparked within, and I blossomed bright red.

Need.

Need?

Every soul has a purpose. Although we are one in the Inbetween, our collective pulse is too broad for what is needed in the realms. Therefore, we follow the need.

My light flickered.

You will learn, Lenora.

If I have a name, you must have one too.

I did.

What was it?

The Guardian's light dimmed, her vestige lowering until her translucent gaze met mine. *I was called Ellory in life.*

I brightened. *Thank you.*

We need you, Lenora. Fleur needs you. Find your killer. Find the Relic. It is the only way ... Ellory's echo trailed off.

I followed her toward the tree at the center of the room. The air was cooler. A thin web of darkness pierced the higher branches. I looked up as they unfurled around me, their leaves flickering bright green, leading to the gate.

Ellory paused, her light darkening. *You feel it too.*

The Grima?

Some creatures want to destroy, we cannot allow that. You must work with Fleur. Your threads are intertwined. Solve your mystery soon.

It would go faster if I had my own memories, you know. Why erase them in the first place? You say only I can find the Relic needed, that I need Fleur—why? Wouldn't my memories help?

Your death is unfinished. Your memories clog our purpose. It was necessary.

Necessary? Anger singed my light red.

Please, Lenora. Temper your rage. Ellory's eyes softened, and I imagined her smile. *You'll understand soon enough.*

Why can't I understand now?

Ellory's light brightened and faded like a long sigh. *Your threads are tied to things you need time to understand. Words are not enough. You must find your path first.*

But ... I knew I was going to die. Accepted it even—isn't that something? Wasn't that my path? Why take it all away?

Destiny is rarely as simple as we hope.

Destiny? The words soured in my ears. My light flared, and I knew, somehow, that in life, I put little stock in fate.

Go, you are needed.

But I need more answers ...

And you will find them. Have faith in yourself, Lenora. Ellory smiled softly, nodding toward the tree. *Go. Find them.*

I frowned and rose off the chair, my anger dissolving with each movement.

Good luck, Lenora.

CHAPTER

TWENTY

FLEUR

They inched up the driveway. Khade House loomed before them, faded and forlorn in the overcast sky. Fleur grasped the wheel until her knuckles whitened, her eyes on the scattered Atua. A groan escaped, and she bit her lip. First Poppy, now this.

"What?" Javier glanced at her, his hand on the door handle as they came to a stop in the circular drive.

"I *really* think you should stay in the car, Jav."

His eyes narrowed. "Why would I do that?"

Fleur rubbed her eyes and shook her head. Did he have to be so impossible? "Just trust me."

Javier choked on a laugh. "I'd rather take my chances."

Fleur opened the car door. Bracing herself, she turned to look at the scattered Atua in the Khade garden. They would sense her if they hadn't already. Atua's ability to sense a medium was uncanny, and Fleur steadied herself against the onslaught of helpless demands and piercing wails.

The spirits didn't move.

"Why are you just standing there?" Javier stood beside her. His hands tucked into the pockets of his coat. He surveyed the lawn, overgrown and green, then the juniper and cedar-filled flowerbeds lined with flowerless rhododendrons. Skimming over the vapid wisps of light all turned to the house.

A dog barked.

The spirits didn't budge.

A flash of fur, caramel and wet, bounded over the western side of the house. A tangle of limbs raced toward them. Fleur tensed, took a step back, and raised her hands. The giant pug-faced beast skidded to a stop, drool spilling from the corners of its mouth.

It barked, snarling as it stood its ground between them and the front porch.

"Easy now." Javier moved out in front, his hand leveled, palms out. "You remember me? Easy, easy ..." His hand hovered over the space between them.

Fleur tried to calm her breathing, pushing back the panic until her heart beat steadily once again. Javier waited, his hand stable. The beast snorted, his muscles relaxing as it extended its nose, sniffing his fingertips.

"There's a good girl," Javier cooed. "Who's a good girl?"

Fleur rolled her eyes. "You know this dog?"

The beast licked Javier's hand and whined, leaping on him with apparent joy.

Javier rubbed the dark fur between the dog's ears. "She's such a clever dog, aren't you, Nova? You're just protecting your home, yeah? Such a good puppy."

Javier was ridiculous around dogs. Fleur eyed the beast. "What is she? It looks like a bulldog and a horse had a baby."

"She's a bullmastiff. Nova, here, tried to attack my team when we searched the house the first time. It took a while to calm her down. She was pretty scared. Thankfully, we had the K-9 unit with us. They were a tremendous help. I thought Sato took you with him?" He ruffled Nova's fur. "How'd you get back here?"

Nova turned her big brown eyes on Fleur and pushed her nose against her leg. Great, she was going to have dog snot on her black jeans. Fleur frowned and patted the dog's head. "Hi, doggy ... er ... Nova."

Nova pushed again, drool spilling onto Fleur's boots.

"All right, dog. That's enough." Fleur took a step back and shook her foot.

"She's just a puppy, Fleur." Javier grinned. "Drool never killed anyone."

Fleur shook her head and turned to the front porch. The Atua's blank stares ate at her. She didn't have time to play with a damn dog. She turned her gaze back to the house, scanning the upper floors. Something was there. Waiting.

Lenora's key weighed heavily in her pocket. She clutched it, sliding the ring over her index finger and cupping the keys in her palm. She ignored the fading light of the Atua on the porch, angling around them. Her heart pounded harder with each step.

Javier held out his hand, waiting for her to drop the keys, but Fleur shouldered past him and unlatched the door herself.

"Wait." He touched her elbow, handing her a pair. "Gloves."

Fleur frowned and pulled them on, unwilling to admit that, in her unease, she had forgotten.

They moved into the entryway. The air was heady with lavender. The fragrance stung Fleur's eyes and coated her throat. She coughed, glancing at Javier, surprised to find him unaffected. She looked around the room. Polished hardwood floors covered in patterned rugs branched from left to right, welcoming them into the living room or library, a narrow hallway extended behind the large, curved staircase ahead. The entryway itself was the size of her apartment. Fleur inhaled, trying not to gag on the sweetness.

Gray light streamed in through the windows, arching and tilting over furniture covered in cream-colored sheets—remains of a life half lived. Fleur moved into the living room. The room thrummed like a heartbeat, ebbing purple and gray. She paused. The delicate strain of piano circulated through the air, soft and melodic, almost an afterthought.

"Do you hear that?" she asked, tilting her head.

Javier looked up from the book in his hand. "What?" He set the book back on the windowsill and moved closer to her.

The music grew bolder, thickening with each crescendo. "That? Piano?"

Javier studied her and shook his head. "Dammit, Fleur."

Her gaze snapped back to him. "What?"

"Ghosts, right? That's why you wanted me to stay in the car?"

Fleur shrugged. "I told you to trust me."

Javier sucked in a breath. "So, what now? You hear music? Is it like a big deal? Should we find it?"

"Strings, an orchestra"—Fleur tilted her head and turned from the room, following the sound into the entryway—"trumpet, now."

The room tinged red as the music dimmed. Fleur paused at the base of the stairs. The walls rippled, wainscoting splashed against the floral wallpaper like a wave on the sand. She glanced back to Javier. "Tell me you saw that."

He shook his head. "Nope. This is on you now—ghosts are your department, not mine."

Violin and oboe harmonized, pulling her away from the rippling walls. Fleur followed it, ignoring the squeak of Javier's shoes on the floor. Her gloved hand slid over the banister. The smooth wood gleamed and shuddered. She looked down, unable to move. The wood whorled, its grain darkening with sap. Blood-red sap. Sap she knew from another time, in another world—Fleur shook her head and released the rail. It curled around her arm, tugging her toward the landing and a harmony of flutes.

Her feet tripped over themselves in her rush. She heard Javier curse. Her heart pounded in her ears, and her breath hollowed in her chest. The carpet on the second floor cushioned her feet, propelling her toward the door at the end of the hall—the only door cloaked in stillness.

The attic.

Fleur knew with each thump of her heart that whatever the house wanted her to find was beyond that door.

Downstairs, Javier shouted her name. His voice was cavernous and low, like a memory of something other, a dream she couldn't pull out of.

Fleur's hand grasped the doorknob. She didn't recall reaching out or how the distance between her and the door faded. She only knew she needed to turn it.

The lavender aroma faded, replaced with something more pungent and acidic.

Fleur turned the knob.

The door swung open as if pushed by a gust of wind. Before her lay another set of stairs anchored by warped beadboard walls on either side. Fleur touched the wood. It was dormant. The stairs opened up to a wide room covered in rugs and wood-paneled walls. High vaulted ceiling sloped over narrow, arched windows. A well-worn sofa sat to one side opposite a red brick fireplace. A painting of a boy—the same painting Fleur saw in Lenora's Instagram—hung above a mantel littered with candles. Opposite the seating area was an easel, canvas covered with a white sheet. Paint splatter covered the surrounding floor. Behind the easel sat a cluster of canvases, leaning against the wall at various angles, weight distributed.

Fleur moved to the canvas. The music blossomed. She jumped, catching herself before tripping over the layered carpets lining the floors. This was Lenora's studio—her home. Fleur glanced at the mattress pushed to the side, covered in a lilac satin duvet, a pile of pillows scattered around it. Lenora confined herself to the attic, closing herself off from the memories of her family below. A crash of tympany grew, vibrating over the swell of woodwinds like a storm. She touched the white sheet. Music throbbed, begging for an audience.

The sheet brightened as she grasped it. Fleur held her breath as she tugged it from the easel.

The canvas was blank.

Music blared. Her blood hummed with melody, the whine of trumpets screeched in her ears. Violins cried, weeping over the stains of French horns as she searched the empty canvas—it wasn't the canvas she was meant to find, but something else, something nearby. She slid her hand over the rough surface, over the corners, and under the seams. Following the crescendos until her fingers scratched the edge of a small, thick piece of paper.

Fleur pulled the paper from the seam of the canvas.

The music stopped as abruptly as it began.

She looked down. It was a ticket stub. She turned it over, dread trickling down her spine. A ticket for Rachmaninoff's *Symphonic Dances* at Benaroya Hall on November 18—the same symphony Viola attended.

Lenora was at the symphony the night before she died.

Fleur studied the stub—there had to be more to it. She turned it over, her eyes alighting on the blue ink-pressed letters in the bottom left corner. *DG1085*—the edge was torn. She ran her finger over the frayed fibers, noting an ink smudge above the tear. She doubled over, the edges of her vision blurred, her stomach cramping as the vision unwound around her.

The dark-haired man was speaking to another, smaller man—blond hair cropped short and a long oval face. His features blurred. The image faded, replaced by another. The blond man stood in front of a shadowy building. Keys jingling in his hand. Raincoat pulled tight against the gale. Light flickered and elongated. Fleur blinked. *I followed him.* Lenora, alive, materialized beside her, then faded. *I needed to find—* adrenaline flooded Fleur, followed by panic.

Her shoes slapped against puddles as she got out of the car. Fleur shuddered, her eyes darting between warehouses. He went into the one on the left. Locked. She would have to climb. She pulled herself up, her coat caught on the wood from a splintered crate. The fabric ripped. Fleur could smell the damp wood and mold. *My fingers were sticky with tar—no, mud ... I wiped them on the front of my raincoat.* Lenora's voice echoed as Fleur pulled herself over another crate. This was it.

The last piece of the puzzle ...

Fleur's breath hitched in her chest as she steadied herself on the crate. A dim light flickered beyond the glass. She squinted her eyes, pressing her nose to the glass of the warehouse window. Images flickered, a cyclone of color and sound. Her heart froze in her chest.

"Fleur!"

Fleur coughed. She bent over, her chest heaving as the last of the vision faded. "Up here."

She pulled a tarot card from her pocket—no time to shuffle; the cards knew what was needed. Wheel of Fortune—a turning point, destiny. Whatever Lenora saw turned the tide for her. Fleur blinked and shoved the card back into her pocket. Confirmation Lenora was on the right track.

Fleur looked at the ticket stub. Lenora had doodled a crescent moon above the writing. Damn it. There was no escaping the connection—even the cards were telling her to stop ignoring it. Fleur sucked in a breath. The dark-haired man's cane, the wind spinner—and now this stub. All marked with the sacred symbol. Another reference to a Relic. Fleur shook her head. It shouldn't be possible. Was there something bigger tied to this? The Goddess of Fate wouldn't be so obvious, would she?

Fleur needed to focus. The supposed Relic could wait. She had no evidence other than her visions, and Fleur knew better than to rely wholly on them. She needed facts. What had Lenora seen in the warehouse? Her emotions—validation, grief followed by a surge of hope. Hope so potent, Fleur thought her heart had exploded in her chest. Fleur coughed again and took a deep breath, allowing her lungs to expand with the attic's dusty air.

"Fleur," Javier exclaimed as he bounded up the stairs, "guess who

—" He rushed to her, draping his arm over her hunched shoulders. "Are you OK? What happened? Was it the music?"

Fleur held up the ticket stub. "It wanted me to find this."

Javier took it from her. "The night before she died."

Fleur nodded. "See that?" She pointed to the scribbled letters and the torn corner. "Any ideas?"

"DG, huh?" He scratched his cheek. "Could be Dugal Griffin, but he was out of town on the eighteenth."

Fleur exhaled another breath, allowing reality to settle back into her bones. "What if he wasn't?"

"Nah, his alibi checked out. His flight from Dubai didn't get in until the twentieth."

Fleur straightened her shoulders, rolling back the stiffness. The music was gone. She moved to the window, staring at the now-empty garden. Whatever was holding the Atua had released them. She crinkled her brow, noticing a flutter of yellow out of the corner of her eye.

A yellow tiger moth landed on Javier's shoulder. A strangled laugh escaped as relief washed over her.

Lenora was back.

"Why are you looking at me like that?" Javier frowned, following her gaze to his shoulder. He gasped and slapped at the moth.

Lenora flickered and brightened as she shifted into her spirit form. *He doesn't like spirits, does he?*

Fleur laughed. "Calm down, Jav. She won't hurt you."

Lenora drifted around the room, her light warming as she took in the books and photographs on the shelf beside the mattress. *This was my home—my things?* Her voice was low, laced with sorrow.

"Are you alright?" Fleur asked, glancing at Lenora.

"I don't think I'll ever get used to that," Javier said, taking a breath.

"Not you." Fleur turned to Lenora, setting the book back on the stack.

I'm working on it. Sorry I vanished. I had some things—

"No worries, I get it. I'm glad you're back."

Fleur plucked a book on Egyptian mythology from the floor and flipped through it. Lenora had marked the page on Hemsut, the Goddess of Fate. Hemsut was one of the sacred trinity, the crone and weaver. Had the goddess revealed herself to Lenora? But why? What connection did Lenora have? Fleur glanced at the stack of books beside her: Greek, Roman, Sumerian, Inuit, and Mayan mythologies. Her mother taught her there were no coincidences, but this? This had to be … Fleur narrowed her gaze on the spirit.

Lenora beamed, her aura tinged orange as she drifted around the room. Her light trickled over the half-finished canvases and unmade bed. She paused beside a low wooden bookcase, studying a photograph. *This guy looks like the man in your drawing, Fleur.*

Fleur moved closer, a chill racing through her. She picked up the framed photograph and blinked. It was him. The black-haired man with the sinister smile and rounded cane. They stood in front of a waterfall—Multnomah Falls? Lenora smiled at the camera, but the man's gaze was off as if something more important had captured his attention. She shuddered and held up the photograph.

"Who is this?" she asked Javier.

Javier glanced up. "You don't recognize him?"

"Who is he?"

"That's Dugal Griffin. Lenora's guardian."

CHAPTER
TWENTY-ONE

FLEUR

S ato stood at the base of the stairs in the entryway, Nova camped at his feet. His plaid flannel jacked was damp and hung over his narrow frame. He ran a hand through his thick black hair and eyed them.

"What are you doing here?" Fleur asked as they descended, noting the key in his hand. "I thought you didn't live here anymore."

"I don't." Sato shrugged. "Nova got away from Ayame this morning. Figured she'd come here."

"Ayame?"

"My cousin. I live with her and her husband."

Javier nodded to the key in his hand. "Then why do you have a key?"

Sato tucked the key into his pocket. "Is it a crime to keep one?"

Fleur frowned. If she had known he still had his key, she wouldn't have needed Javier. She touched the leather flap of her messenger bag, feeling the outline of Lenora's book just below the surface. No, she needed to get Lenora's belongings. She wondered if the book would spark anything in Lenora or Sato—or maybe the USB drive? Fleur studied Sato, taking in the lifted chin and narrowed gaze.

She turned from them, allowing her gaze to drift over the rest of the house. Fleur moved toward the library. The lavender fragrance had vanished with the music—a connection that escaped her. She flipped the switch, and the walls of books illuminated. The room was dusty and unused. Shelves lined three out of four walls, tall and filled with volumes. Philosophy, mathematics, there was an entire shelf devoted to religion and another to music theory. A quartet of leather chairs gathered beside the windows on the west wall, covered with ivory sheets. She moved to a bookshelf, her gloved finger leaving a trail in the dust.

"Not big readers, huh?"

Sato had followed her in, Nova at his heels. "Lenora loved to read. This was her favorite room until …" He paused, crouching down to scratch Nova's ears. "When she let Opal go, she covered everything. I helped her move her stuff into the attic. Said it was safer up there."

"Opal's the housekeeper, right?"

"She was more than just a housekeeper. She and Len were tight." Sato's voice tightened.

Lenora brightened and floated to Fleur's side. *Can we talk to Opal? She would know me … and Edgar. She might know what happened.*

Fleur looked back to Javier. "Where's Opal now?" A housekeeper would know the ins and outs of a place like Khade House.

Javier narrowed his eyes. "I told you we already spoke to her."

"And I'm telling you, I don't care. Where is she?"

Javier clenched his jaw. Fleur could practically hear his teeth grinding.

Sato nuzzled Nova's damp fur and kept quiet.

"Fine," Javier said. "I'll message you the address. But"—he pinned her with a stare—"you didn't get it from me."

Fleur grinned. "Of course not." She turned, catching a blur of movement in the window.

Lenora drew closer, her light flickering. *Fleur ...*

Fleur glanced to Sato, Nova's leash clasped in his hand, then down to the dog, panting at their feet.

Something was in the yard, watching them. "Did you see that?"

Lenora shimmered beside her. *A face ... another spirit?* She shivered, as if her phantom muscles remembered the fear.

Javier shook his head. "More ghosts?"

Fleur shot him a glare and wandered closer to the window. It could be the Atua, but the foreboding sensation that lingered over the house was gone, as was the telltale glimmer in her peripheral. No, this wasn't a spirit.

She peered out the window, her gaze raking over the green lawn peppered with flowerbeds, until ... there! At the back of the house, a flash of blue.

Fleur raced from the room, ignoring the exclamations following her through the entryway and down the porch stairs. A face in the window—pale with wide eyes—isn't that what Sato said? Lenora thought she was being haunted, but what if it was something else— something simpler?

Around the corner. Lenora's voice was breathless in her ear.

Fleur raced around the house, her eyes on the strip of blue. She lengthened her stride, her chest heaving as she closed the distance. She turned the corner—nothing. Damn. Fleur jogged around the kitchen garden toward the back gate leading to the alley and the old converted carriage house.

Lenora wavered, her light fading as she wove through the fence. *It's getting away. Hurry!*

She paused, listening.

The sound of gravel crunching shuffled ahead.

Fleur rushed forward, tripping toward the gate. She flung it wide and raced through.

A shape jogged toward the end of the ally, turning the corner onto the main street before Fleur could catch up—a shape in pale blue.

"Shit." Fleur gasped for breath. She leaned over, hands on her knees, and coughed. She really should work out more.

Damn. It's gone. Lenora materialized beside her. *Was it a Shadeling?*

Fleur shook her head. "No—she was alive." Of course. Why didn't she guess this before? Lenora wasn't being haunted, at least not by spirits.

She?

"I'll give you one guess."

Lenora flickered red with anger. *You mean—*

"Well?" Javier shouted at her from the gate. "What was that?"

Fleur turned, eyeing the three of them waiting for her. "The face in the window ..."

Sato's eyes widened. "Yeah?"

She gestured to the end of the alley. "Did you check out the neighbors?"

Javier scratched his beard and glanced around. "Anyone in particular?"

Fleur stuffed her hand in her pocket and felt the sharp corner of a business card. She grinned, handing Javier the card. "Have you considered hiring a mindfulness coach?"

SHE HAD THREE LEADS. Fleur stared at the blue-inked names in her notebook.

Dugal Griffin.

Poppy Albright.

Opal Barlow.

She bit back a smile, she'd only been on this case for two days, and she already knew more than the police. Javier must be seething.

Well, to be fair, she had her vision of Dugal and the blond man to work with, something she should have told Javier about. And she would—after she did a little investigating of her own.

But who to start with? As the housekeeper, Opal would have insight into Lenora's life. Insight they needed but it didn't make her a suspect. Poppy was up to something. Fleur added spy to her mental list of Poppy's traits. Was she spying for someone or just a typical nosy neighbor? What if Poppy was spying for Dugal? They would have crossed paths at some point, right? Fleur crinkled her brow and made a note to ask Javier about Dugal's involvement in Lenora's life. Then, there was the goddess symbol, on the spinner, on the cane— Fleur's brow crinkled. Relics. Dammit. No. It wasn't possible. Focus on facts, on what's tangible, not fairy tales.

That's the problem. The Relics and their history were true and real, no matter how much Fleur wished they weren't. Her mother died searching for them, died protecting her from the burden she shouldered for decades. Fleur struggled to dismiss that.

Javier had returned to the station after Fleur's little jog around the house, promising to look into Poppy's alibi and history. Fleur wondered if he had found a connection. Poppy was too convenient a lead, but sometimes the most obvious possibility was the right one.

"I can hear your gears turning," Theda murmured, twisting her head from its perch on Fleur's shoulder to look up at her. "Wanna share?"

Fleur grinned. "Oh, it's nothing. Just thinking about the case."

Theda folded a ribbon between the pages of her book as she closed it. "Go on, tell me."

"What?"

"You're restless with thought. I know what that means." Theda sat up and crossed her legs under her. "Let's have it."

Fleur frowned. "We need to talk to Dugal Griffin," she decided, realizing that of all the suspects, he was the most ominous.

"And how do we do that?"

Something in his online bio nagged at her. Fleur bit her finger-nail, allowing the articles and speculations to twist around her thoughts. "We'll make an appointment," she announced, an idea dawning.

"Right. Like he'd see us," Theda scoffed, shaking her head.

"He would, if ... and hear me out, OK? If he was being interviewed by an associate research professor about his archeological finds ..." Fleur paused and looked at Theda. "Eh? Think about it—he's obsessed with archeology, right? We could set something up about whatever his most recent find was—*you* could set something up ..."

"Whoa, there, Sherlock. I'm just an associate, not the real deal—"

"Yeah, but you've got a paper published and another one in the works. I bet he doesn't even notice, right? Think about it. He's a billionaire, spending all his free money on digs, looking for who knows what, and all the media focuses on is his dead partner's company. He's hungry for attention—especially if it's attention focused on him, not Khade Securities." Fleur faced Theda. "It'll work. I just know it."

"So, we go interview him, then what? You ask about Lenora? He'll see through us in a heartbeat."

Fleur shrugged. "Then we'll know he has something to hide." Fleur shook her head as Theda protested. "Don't worry. We'll make it look real. Besides, maybe he has something you could use in your paper."

"I doubt he knows anything about submerged Aboriginal land-scapes," Theda muttered. "Besides, didn't Javier say he was out of town at the time?"

"So? Maybe he had someone do it for him?" The image of the blond man blossomed in Fleur's mind. "A guy like that has dozens of nefarious people on his payroll. Besides, we need to know what his relationship with Lenora was like."

Theda glanced around the room. "And what does Lenora think about this?"

Fleur shrugged. "I don't know yet. She's been absent since the encounter with Poppy at Khade House. Probably—"

I'm not gone, just quiet. Lenora's voice echoed in Fleur's mind.

"Quiet? Since when are you quiet?" Fleur asked, lifting a dark brow and smirking at Theda.

It's not a crime to listen, is it? I just needed a minute to myself.

"I guess she's back?" Theda asked, setting her book on the coffee table.

"She never left, just faded, I guess." Fleur glanced back at Lenora's shimmer opposite her. "What do you think of our plan?"

Seems solid, but considering my lack of memory about the man, I can't give any input. Lenora paused, her light brightening. *I'm curious about our relationship, but there's a kind of ... I don't know—hesitancy? Caution? Something bothers me. I just don't know what.*

Fleur studied her rippling aura. Lenora was usually eager to rediscover her life, that she hesitated this time spoke volumes. "How so?"

Just ... be careful.

"What is it?" Theda asked, following Fleur's gaze, her brow wrinkling. "What's she saying?"

"She wants us to be careful." Fleur frowned. Of course, she'd be careful. Dugal Griffin was a powerful man and powerful men almost always had secrets.

CHAPTER
TWENTY-TWO

FLEUR

K hade Securities occupied the top floor of a windowed skyscraper at the corner of 2nd and Marion. Fleur paused as the elevator door swished closed, her hand reaching for Theda's beside her. She took in the creamy white marble floors polished until the striations of gold gleamed. Florescent bulbs beamed from the glinting wall sconces scattered around the stark white walls. Theda squeezed her hand and stepped forward, the heel of her loafers clicking on the sterile floor. A rounded receptionist's desk stood tall and pale at the center, surrounded by a cluster of black leather club chairs.

A shudder rippled down Fleur's spine, and she released Theda's hand. The chill seeped into her clothes, working its way over her shoulders. She pulled the collar of her leather jacket closer, wishing she had worn her hair down—anything to melt the ice creeping up the back of her neck.

"Ready?" Theda whispered as they approached the desk.

"Are you?"

Theda nodded, rolling her shoulders back and straightening her spine as she stepped up to the desk and peered over the counter.

A man dressed in a pressed shirt and tie smiled up at them. Fleur studied his brown coif of combed waves heavy with styling product and tried to regulate her breathing.

"How may I help you?" he asked, his smile waning as he took in their casual attire.

"We have an appointment with Mr. Griffin. I'm Theda Okan, from the Indigenous Archeology department at the university."

The receptionist glanced at the small computer screen mounted on the inside of the cubicle. "Ah, yes—the article on his latest dig?" His brow furrowed before looking up. "You're early."

"Yes," Theda said with a slight nod.

"Mr. Griffin is on a tight schedule."

Was he scolding them for being early? Fleur bit back a frown and tried to look disinterested.

The man looked from Theda to Fleur. "I wasn't aware there would be two of you. Mr. Griffin won't like that."

"Ms. Harkyn is my assistant. That isn't a problem?" Theda sounded more impressive with each syllable.

The receptionist's mouth tightened into a thin line as his fingers moved over the touch screen. "I'll inform him of your arrival. Wait over there." He nodded in the general direction of the leather chairs.

Theda smiled. "Thank you."

Fleur shuffled over to the waiting area. She wished she had Theda's poise as she perched at the edge of the uncomfortable leather chair. Fleur mimicked Theda's straight back and folded hands, hoping she looked convincing.

The wall beside the receptionist's desk opened, and a woman in a navy pantsuit appeared. Her russet hair was pulled back in a bun, making the softness of her cheeks more severe. She didn't smile, just crooked her hand in a silent gesture.

They stood, following the navy suit beyond the hidden door, past offices and conference rooms branching off from the narrow white hallway. The further into the department they went, the heavier the silence grew. Bodies swathed in muted colors bent over desks and murmured into phones, and yet the dim of sound never extended past their closed doors.

"Why is it so quiet?" Fleur couldn't help but ask.

The woman turned her head. "Mr. Griffin prefers a peaceful workspace."

Theda elbowed her and shook her head.

The navy-suited woman paused in front of a set of black double doors at the end of the hall. She rapped her knuckle against the wood, her gaze shifting from Theda to Fleur, a frown curling the corners of her mouth.

"Enter," a voice boomed, deep and husky.

She pushed open the door and swept into the room, motioning to them as she spoke. "Ms. Okan and Ms. Harkyn."

Dugal Griffin sat behind a long glass desk. Black hair tied at his nape with a strap of leather highlighted his wide expanse of forehead and the crease between his brows. His head snapped up at their names, revealing a pair of deep-set ice-blue eyes.

Fleur's breath caught—the emperor reversed. Just like the tarot card she pulled after her vision. A person of authority who abuses power, who leaves one helpless. She exhaled and pasted a benign smile across her face, inching forward, Theda at her side.

"Harkyn?" he repeated, elongating the hard vowels of her name.

Fleur nodded, resisting the chill his voice left over her. Cold hail pelting her flesh.

"The assistant, sir," the woman explained as she backed toward the door.

Dugal nodded and leaned back in his chair. He reached for something, his fingers splaying over a rounded wood surface. His cane. Fleur studied it, the slender curve marked with the stained burls. She wanted a closer look. Was the goddess symbol etched into the side?

He gestured to the pair of chairs opposite him. "Sit, please. It isn't often that I have such exciting visitors." He stared at Fleur.

Fleur met his gaze, fighting the urge to squirm under the scrutiny.

"Thank you," Theda said, pulling a notebook from her messenger bag.

Theda hadn't slept the night before. They practiced the scenario all night until Fleur, energized by their third pot of coffee, had pointed to the clock. Now Fleur watched Theda recline in the office chair, her pen poised over the ruled pages of her book, awed that this was the same woman who fretted so ardently hours before.

"Do you mind if we record this?" Theda nodded at Fleur, fumbling with the recording app on her phone.

Dugal shook his head. "I would rather not."

Fleur lowered her phone and switched it off, ignoring the warning racing up and down her spine. Like the lobby, the room's chill was almost tangible. She offered him a weak smile and pocketed her phone.

"Now, Ms. Okan, I suspect you'd like to hear about the last of my finds, yes?"

Theda nodded. "First, we'd like to offer our condolences on your ward. We heard of Ms. Khade's passing. It must have hit you hard."

Fleur bit back a smile. Theda was flawless.

Dugal blinked—as if processing her words—before shifting his gaze to Fleur again. "Yes. Thank you. It has been an emotional time."

Fleur lifted a brow before she could help herself.

Be careful, Fleur. His aura's metallic. Lenora gasped in Fleur's ear.

They had decided that Lenora's presence was too much of a distraction for Fleur. That Len was speaking to her now meant the spirit sensed something—maybe even the same cold detachment Fleur herself was fighting.

"Were you close with Ms. Khade?" Fleur asked, unable to stand the silence.

Dugal narrowed his eyes at her. "Of course. She was my ward, the daughter of my late partner. She will be missed." His voice belied any sentiment he may have hoped to convey.

"It must have been a shock—the news of her death, I mean. Were you with her at the end?" Fleur continued, ignoring Theda's frown.

"No. I was attending to business overseas." He scowled, his gaze slipping past them to the bookshelf behind. "Now, if you'd like to—"

"Business where?" Fleur interrupted, enjoying the frustration in his tone.

"I don't see how that concerns you." His words were smooth. "Is there anything else about my former ward I can help you with, or may we continue?"

"Who do you think did it? Poisoned her? Did she have any enemies?" Fleur persisted.

"I don't have the faintest idea. Lenora's life was her own. I didn't meddle in her affairs."

"But you must know something? She was in your care. You must have been close?"

"As I have said. Lenora and I had a distant relationship. I maintained her upkeep but left her to her own devices. Her death, and the consequences of it, are not in my purview."

Theda cleared her throat, drawing Dugal's attention. "Please tell me about your interest in Indigenous culture. Where did it stem from, and will you be donating your finds to the museum?"

Dugal straightened in his chair. A slight smile creased the corners of his mouth as he tented his fingers in front of him. "My love of history came, like most, from my love of books," he began. "In order to understand our future, we must understand our past ..." His words, trite and unimaginative, clustered together until all Fleur could hear was a dull hum. She didn't care about his passion for archeology, but their premise worked.

As Theda prodded, Fleur's gaze wandered around the room. She tried to keep an air of interest, but the low cadence of his replies left her feeling restless. His office was large and narrow, with two walls of windows facing the door. His desk backed up to them, casting his features in shadow. Leather chairs clustered near the bookcases behind them. The skin at her nape tingled, drawing her gaze to the glass display on the center shelf of a bookcase.

It was a small case, a glass dome over a dark mahogany base surrounding a rather ordinary-looking conch shell.

But the shell was far from ordinary.

Its warmth wove around the cool air like a spider crafting its web, tugging at the fine hairs of Fleur's arms. Magickal warmth.

Fleur's fingers tightened on the arm of the chair, sweat beaded on her forehead.

The bastard owned a Relic.

How was that possible?

The strains of the lullaby slithered through her mind. Her parents, her mother, the impossibly tall stone walls of their family home. The gentle rhythm of her mother's voice flooded Fleur's mind, blocking out the low hum of Dugal's words. Rhyming couplets danced in her ears. *The sixth protected flesh of its own, hungry for breath* ... The words blossomed on Fleur's tongue, and she turned, pretending to adjust her coat.

It was just a seashell. Its sharp edges dulled by time.

She stood, compelled by the lure of warmth, and drifted to the bookcase. Her eyes on the conch shell. Fleur peered into the glass case, searching for the goddess symbol.

There. Under the pale pink curve, pierced by a needle. The crescent moon embracing the sun's eye.

Son of a—

Fleur looked up quickly. Dugal's gaze rested on her, curiosity brightened in his eyes. Theda cleared her throat again.

"Do you recognize it?" he asked Fleur, Theda's question forgotten.

Warning bells rang in her ears, and Fleur shrugged. "Should I? It's just a shell."

Dugal pressed his lips together and straightened, his gaze boring holes into her.

Fleur met his stare. She'd be damned if she looked away first.

Dugal's lips curled, and he leaned back, interlacing his fingers on the desk in front of him.

What kind of game was this? Did he want her to admit knowledge of the Relics? Why? And how the *hell* did he know? Fleur folded her arms over her chest and looked back at the shell.

Svinnka, the sixth realm, whose population fled millennia ago when the once dormant volcanos beneath the oceanic realm's surface erupted, poisoning the seas that were home to so many. The Svinkraken, squid-like warriors, fled to Evirdahl seeking sanctuary. They were one of the first tribes of invaders to cross the veil, setting the precedent.

In her mother's stories, it was once a piece of armor worn by the Svin chieftain. The conch was a blood Relic. A single drop of the victim's blood triggered its magick, and in a matter of seconds, they would drown in their own breath.

"Where did you find it?" Fleur asked.

"Antarctica, I believe. One of my first expeditions. It's a fitting memento, don't you think?" His gaze softened. "But I'm sure you've seen more impressive *Relics*."

Fleur's gaze flew to his face, locking her eyes on his. "It's just a shell." She struggled to keep her voice steady.

Dugal Griffin smiled. "Yes, Ms. Harkyn. It's just a shell."

He was toying with her. Fleur blinked, breaking his stare, and glanced at Theda, pleading with her to wrap it up.

"Thank you for your time," Theda said as she folded her notebook back into her messenger bag.

Fleur moved back to her chair and fumbled with her handbag. It slipped, landing on the floor with a thud, jostling her tarot deck—a card fell out. She scooped it up, concealing it in her hand, and offered Griffin a weak smile. "Yes, thank you. You've been helpful."

"One question, if you don't mind?" Dugal asked, nodding at Fleur. "Did you know Lenora?"

Theda stood, stepping closer to Fleur. "Of course not."

Dugal shrugged. "You're quite curious about someone you've never met."

"Her death was a pretty sensational story. Of course, we're curious," Fleur replied, trying to sound nonchalant.

"Yes, it was." Dugal looked lost in thought, his gaze flickering over Fleur's face, leaving a trail of ice in its wake.

"Thanks again for the interview," Theda repeated, securing her purse on her shoulder.

Fleur fastened her eyes to the door, smiling weakly as Theda caught up to her, and they reached for the door handle together.

"Goodbye, Ms. Okan, Ms. *Harkyn.*" His voice rose as he spoke her name.

Fleur glanced back. Dugal stared at her. He nodded, and she knew, without a doubt, he not only knew what he had—he knew who she was.

Fleur couldn't shut the door fast enough. She gripped Theda's hand, urging her forward as they moved toward the lobby. Her fingers clutched the tarot card. She wouldn't look—not yet. They didn't speak in the elevator, nor in the first-floor lobby, despite the question in Theda's eyes.

Fleur needed fresh air. She needed the frigid breeze to rid her of the stagnancy of that office. As they stepped onto the street, Fleur released a ragged breath.

"What?" Theda grasped her arms. "What the hell was all that?"

"He knows ..." Fleur squeezed her eyes shut and expelled a long breath.

"Knows what? Fleur?" Theda wrapped her arm around her. "What happened?"

"He knows about the realms, Theda. He knows who I am and what my family can do."

"But ... how?"

Fleur shook her head, wishing she could shake off the residue of Dugal's stare. "I don't know."

"How do you know?"

"The shell. It's ... special."

Theda leaned back and met Fleur's gaze. "Special, how?"

Words escaped her. Fleur swallowed and looked down, unsure how to continue. She knew she needed to tell Theda the truth, tell her about the Relics and her mother—her ability to sense them, but what if ... No. Fleur gave herself a mental shake. Tell her the truth.

"Each realm crafted a Relic infused with magick. Once, they were a part of the defensive sheath that protected all realms from each other. When the sheath was destroyed, those Relics were drawn here. To Mundad ..."

Theda nodded slowly, processing Fleur's words with what she already knew. "But ... How do you know that's a Relic? It could just be a dumb shell."

Fleur inhaled and looked up. "My mother was gifted with the ability to sense the magick in an object, and I inherited that trait."

"So, you felt it was a Relic? What does it feel like?"

"Heat. Like my blood is boiling."

Theda studied her, her gaze moving from Fleur's eyes to the curve of her jaw and back again. Did she believe her? Fleur didn't know what to do if she didn't. Finally, Theda nodded, her shoulders relaxing. "So. What do we do?"

Fleur bit her lip and stuffed her hands in her pockets, willing her heart to stop pounding. "There's more ..."

Theda folded her arms in front of her and waited.

"Lenora didn't just want me to find her killer. She also said the Inbetween wanted me to find a Relic to help them with an oncoming invasion. And ... and I said no."

Theda sucked in a breath. "Why would you say no?"

"Because I saw what the goddesses did to my mother when she betrayed them—" Fleur broke off, suddenly unable to find the right words.

"How did she betray them?" Theda's voice was calm, her questions methodical, as if she was in a thesis discussion.

"My mother hid my abilities from Hemsut. She didn't want me to be under the goddess's thumb the way she was."

"And now?"

"Now ... I'm the last of the seers. My mother's commitment to the Relics fell on me when she died—but I won't do it. I won't." Tears welled in Fleur's eyes, and she blinked them back, her hands toying with the tarot cards in her pocket.

Theda nodded, her gaze softening as she stared at Fleur. "I don't think you have a choice anymore, love."

She was right. Dammit. A tear fell from the pool and slid down Fleur's cheek. She sniffed and wiped it away with the heel of her hand. She hated that Theda was right. Hated it with all her being. "I need to think." She pulled the tarot card from her pocket and cradled it in her hand.

"Go on ..." Theda nodded encouragingly.

Fleur turned it and froze.

"What?" Theda asked. "What's wrong?"

Fleur held up the card, unable to hide the tremor in her hand. The Tower.

Theda eyed the flames depicted on the card. "That doesn't look good."

"It's the only card with the same meaning from both sides. Catastrophe, sudden change—destruction. So, no. It's not good."

Theda linked her arm through Fleur's and maneuvered them down the hill to the Subie. "What do we do?"

Fleur unlocked Theda's door and held it open. "I don't know."

"He's involved with Lenora's death. He has to be. Why else would the Inbetween tell her about the Relic and you?"

"It's something to consider. But I need to think. We have no evidence, just my vision, a tarot card, and Griffin's unpleasant demeanor. The Relic could be a total coincidence." Fleur cringed even as she said the word.

"So, we focus on finding her killer. Dugal isn't off the list, though."

"Definitely not. But first, we need to eliminate the rest." Fleur shuddered. "Ugh. I need a shower after that interview."

Theda chuckled. "You and me both." She paused and leaned back in the seat, waiting until Fleur settled behind the wheel. "You think he'll be pissed when there's no article?"

"I don't care. Do you?" Fleur started the car, letting the engine idle as it warmed up.

Theda sighed. "Hell, no. Let's go home."

CHAPTER
TWENTY-THREE

FLEUR

Fleur wrapped another blanket around her shoulders and pulled the sleeves of her wool sweater over her hands. She didn't think she'd ever be warm again. She sunk into the cushions of the sofa and stared at her computer screen.

How the hell did Dugal get a Relic? The question danced around Fleur's head, twisting into a tangle of knots. He knew what it was, but ... how? The realms were hardly common knowledge here. The other nine had gone to great lengths to hide from this realm, afraid of what the magickless would do to them. Jealousy is a powerful motivator.

Lenora shimmered beside her, bright with questions Fleur wasn't sure how to answer. Truth, her brain screamed at her—tell Lenora the truth, but Fleur hesitated. It wasn't that she didn't trust Lenora—it was the Inbetween's request that bothered her.

Baby steps. Fleur told herself. "Dugal is a piece of work."

You don't have to shield me, Fleur. I was there, listening in.

"What?" Fleur glared at the spirit. "I thought we decided you'd stay out of this one."

You decided. Not me. Lenora's light flickered. *He has a Relic.*

Dammit.

"Did you tell your Guardian friend?"

Not yet. I wanted to talk to you about it. What does it do?

"What is she asking?" Theda sat beside her, waiting patiently to interrupt.

"She wants to know what the Relic does."

"Good question. Please? Give us the scoop."

Fleur sighed. "Fine. I'll tell you what I know, which isn't a whole lot. My mother taught me a lullaby when I was a kid to help me remember them all." She shrugged. "It's been a while since I've thought about it, so bear with me."

"*Sixth protected flesh of its own. Hungry for breath, it'll watch you drown,*" Fleur recited. "That's the shell. It's a shard of armor from the Svinkraken clan. Before the chieftain infused it with the realm magick, he cursed it so it couldn't fall into the wrong hands. Most of the chieftains created failsafes, but few are known. I guess that would kinda defeat the purpose. This one is a deadly Relic. It's triggered by blood—even if it's just a scratch. The magick is transferred to the intended victim, and within seconds, they will succumb to death. Drowned in their own breath."

"How does one drown in their own breath?"

Fleur shrugged. "Beats me. And I have no intention of finding out."

That won't work, though—will it? Not on creatures without flesh. Like the Grima?

"I don't think so. Blood is required."

Then that's not the Relic. Lenora's light faded slightly. *That can't help the Guardians push back the Grima.*

"I doubt it."

"What?" Theda asked.

Fleur looked from Lenora's crestfallen expression to Theda. "It's not the Relic Lenora needed."

"So, we're back to square one." Theda nodded. "Don't worry, Lenora. We'll figure it out."

"Enough Dugal Griffin, huh?" Fleur didn't want to talk about Dugal Griffin anymore, not until she could work out the jumbled knots in her head.

Right. You're right. Who's next.

"Suspect number two—Poppy Albright" Fleur pulled her computer onto her lap. "Ready to cyberstalk your stalker?"

Hell, yeah.

Theda chuckled as she grabbed her computer. "So, cathartic."

Silence descended as they bent over their task. Out of the corner of her eye, Lenora flickered, her face hovering over Fleur's shoulder, drinking in the pictures on the screen. Lenora pointed to an image of herself in a crowd of people, Poppy's wide grin just inches behind her. *She's everywhere. I don't understand.*

Fleur scrolled through Lenora's Instagram account. "Look at this." She turned the screen toward Theda. "Poppy. Again."

Theda shivered and looked at the screen in front of her. "The woman is obsessed. Look, here ..." She scrolled up to a picture on Poppy's Instagram page. "She's created a boomerang—It looks like she and Lenora are drinking together—it's the same party, but look, in Lenora's picture, she's at least two seats down at the bar."

"Poppy is in almost every picture—a random floating head. Not *with* Lenora."

"Unless you look at Poppy's page. She's doctored these pictures." Theda expelled a breath. "She was using Lenora to sell her business. Do you think she knew?"

No. Lenora floated away, pausing beside the window, her light brightening the dark corner. Her aura was red with rage. *No way I knew.*

"Unless you did, and you confronted her about it, then BAM.

You're dead." Fleur knew it was useless to calm her. The evidence was pretty damning. How did the police miss this?

She was stalking me. Lenora's light was buzzing with tension. She cursed, shaking one of the small ceramic sundew pots with her anger.

Theda looked up, startled. Her gaze darting from the window to Fleur.

"Lenora's a little upset," Fleur explained.

Theda arched a dark brow. "She can move things?"

"Sometimes. Extreme emotion manifests differently with each spirit." Fleur shrugged, not willing to elaborate more. "She's pretty pissed."

"Well, she was using Lenora's status to help her own. I'd be pissed too, but you're missing a big point. If Poppy killed her, she'd kill her business."

"What if it was more than a business thing? I caught her, Theda —spying on us in the Khade House. Just like Sato said, a face in the window."

"So, she's nosey."

Lenora released a bitter laugh and shook her head.

"She went through Lenora's trash. Maybe to find objects to prove her association, or maybe because she has some crazy ritual sacrifice planned, huh? It's possible." Fleur scrolled through Poppy's Instagram. "I mean, look at this. It's not all business oriented. She's wearing the same outfits, even her nail polish is the same. It's like she wanted to be Lenora."

She's twenty years too old. Gross.

"It still doesn't mean she killed her," Theda insisted.

Fleur sighed. "Really, Theda? You're taking her side?"

"Someone has to! You both have her convicted of a crime you have no proof of. One of us has to be reasonable."

Fleur frowned. Was she being too harsh? Sure, Poppy had dreams of grandeur, but what if those dreams soured? What if she approached Lenora in friendship and was refused?

"Maybe Javier found something more," Fleur reminded, reaching for her phone. "I'll call him."

"No. Don't harass him." Theda set her computer down and stood, moving into the kitchen to open a bottle of wine. "There's time enough later."

"Maybe I'll just go have a little chat with her tomorrow. See if she needs a new best friend." Fleur smirked.

"Fleur." Theda took a sip of wine. "Do you want to do this now?"

Fleur hesitated as a shudder raced over her. "The likelihood of Poppy being anything like Griffin is low. I'll just pop in for a friendly chat."

Lenora brightened and drifted into the room. *Do you think it'll work?*

Fleur grinned. "Of course. We have something in common."

What?

"You."

Lenora smiled.

Theda groaned.

TWENTY-FOUR

LENORA

Fleur's car was ridiculous. I hovered over the cracked red leather passenger seat—if it could be called that. It was more like a bench, a very tiny bench, barely large enough to fit Fleur, let alone a passenger. I narrowed my light, flickering as she chugged around a corner and up the small hill toward my home.

It was odd thinking of that too-large, echoing house as my home. What was I like before? Did I make the house my own? Was I happy there? I wanted to believe I was, but part of me knew the life in that house had died with my family.

I wished I could remember them. I wish I knew what my mother smelled like and if her hands were warm and soft. What did my father's hugs feel like? Did he smell like pine or peppermint? I stared out the window at the sloped roof looming in front of us. I tried to imagine my brother's laugh—shouldn't I at least be able to remember that?

My light colored, and I closed my eyes, calming my aura from red to blue. I imagined the flow of air swirling into my chest cavity—a phantom presence in my hollow chest.

What's so special about this car, anyway? Wouldn't something more ... dependable be, ah, safer?

Fleur laughed. "Nothing is safe. The Subie has been good to me. We're, like, best buds."

I've never heard of a Subaru 360 until now.

"Most haven't. It's Japanese, one of the first imports, and, get this"—Fleur grinned—"classified as one of the worst cars to own in 1968. Only a handful were imported, making her a collector."

One of the worst cars to own? And you bought it? I shook my head.

"Seemed like a good fit. We were both a mess. Maybe she was my therapy, huh? I just had this huge falling out with my dad. I was on my own, broke, and bombarded by Atua with no real knowledge of how to protect myself. So, I learned how to restore a car."

Her voice quivered. Fleur rarely spoke of her father. I knew, as a child, she worshiped him, then felt betrayed by him. Everything I knew of Fleur's life revolved around her childhood before they came to this realm.

Fleur pressed the brake, and the Subie rolled to a stop along the curb in front of Poppy's rambler. "You ready?"

I brightened with excitement. *Yes.*

While Fleur was chatting Poppy up, I would investigate. Being made of light meant no door or wall could hold me. Funny how some of the ghost stereotypes are true.

Fleur unfolded herself from the car and straightened her leather jacket. Black, like most of her wardrobe, over a dark maroon turtleneck and a pair of dark gray trousers rolled to the cuff of her combat boots. She wore her gray hair piled high on her head in a messy tangle, fringe framing her round face. She tugged at her messenger bag, draping it over her shoulder, and jerked her head toward the entrance.

Showtime.

Poppy answered the door on the first chime, swinging it wide enough to reveal a bevy of candles lit on the hall table behind her. Her smile faded as her gaze swept over Fleur. "Hello, again." She fluttered her lashes as if trying to regain her composure.

Fleur took a step closer, a smile settling under the pale apples of her cheeks. "Can we talk?"

"Oh." Poppy shifted in the doorframe, her hand still clutching the knob. I wondered if she wanted to slam it closed. "I have a client ..."

"It won't take long," Fleur insisted. "I just thought it would be nice to reminisce—I miss Lenora too."

Poppy's face softened, her aura calming from red to soft yellow, and she glanced at the watch on her wrist before nodding. "Of course, we all need to heal from this terrible tragedy." She stepped back, sweeping her arm wide. "Please, come in."

I followed Fleur through the stark white entry, the only color coming from the amber glow of the candles on the long table. Sterile, despite the warmth. She led us past an open kitchen. The white quartz counters gleamed under the bright button bulbs cut into the ceiling. A skylight slanted gray light over the kitchen island, contrasting the pearlescent walls. A glass kettle boiled on the counter beside a pair of cream-colored pottery mugs and a sachet of loose-leaf tea. Its whistle leaked through as we passed. Poppy smiled weakly and gestured to the living space as she pulled it off the burner but didn't offer any.

I drifted around the room, taking in the tall ceilings and gas fireplace flanked by bookcases void of books. The room, like the rest of the house, was painted white. Only the live edge pine shelving offered any warmth. The room was minimal. A round, brown leather ottoman sat in the center, surrounded by a plush ivory sofa and two wood-framed chairs, their cushions patterned in varying white and cream stripes. A ribbon of smoke drifted over a small bushel of herbs in a black metal bowl on the round copper table between the chairs. I wandered over to it, wondering at its purpose. The smoke curled around my light as it rose toward the vaulted ceiling.

Fleur watched me, her eyes darting from my light to the smoke. "Smudge stick?"

"Yes, to purify." Poppy straightened a stack of magazines—all yoga and health oriented, on the side table.

Fleur leaned over, sniffing the air, and smiled. "Pine needles?"

"Of course. There's yerba santa, juniper, and ah"—she sniffed— "sweet grass, too. It's a healing bundle." Poppy gestured to the spotless room. "I hope you don't mind the mess,"

"Not at all. It's very ... white."

Poppy nodded. "Creating an unpolluted space is very important to my work."

"So, how does this work?"

Poppy sighed and draped herself over the arm of the sofa. Fleur sat in the chair opposite and crossed her legs, folding her arms over her chest.

"Well, most of my clients are experiencing, or have experienced tragedy, whether it's internal or something more tangible. My goal is to help them calm the waters, so to speak." She narrowed her gaze. "How can I help you, Fleur?"

Fleur cleared her throat and leaned back. "I'm struggling with Lenora's death ... she was just so ... vibrant and kind." Fleur's eyes watered, and she snuffled. "I-I just—miss her."

I giggled. She was a horrible actor.

Poppy straightened and reached out her hands, palms up. "Let's meditate together."

Fleur unfolded her arms, cringing as she grasped Poppy's hands. I glanced at Poppy. She didn't seem to notice anything amiss as she stood, leading Fleur to the open area beside the fireplace—the ploy worked.

They sat cross-legged opposite each other, hands still clasped, on the floor, pillows propped up against the hearth in a crescent. Poppy closed her eyes and squeezed Fleur's hand. "Let's breathe together. Inhale ... exhale ..."

Fleur released a deep breath. Opening one eye, she nodded to me.

That was my cue.

I drifted down the hallway to the left, over the bamboo floors, past the white walls decorated with wooden sconces between scattered macramé wall hangings. Did Poppy craft them herself? Knots wound around thin branches of wood, their tresses hung in thick knots, some more complicated than others.

The first two rooms I found were vacant and decorated with plant life and wrought iron candlesticks—guest rooms, I guessed, my light drifting over the cream-colored comforters and scattering of pillows. Next was a guest bath, judging from the carefully placed towels and bathing accessories.

I frowned, drifting toward the last door at the end of the hall. This must be her room. I wondered how Fleur was faring and paused, listening for the cadence of conversation, but only the faint strains of digitized rainfall met my ears.

The door was locked, not that it could stop me, but I wondered why she would bother locking it if she lived alone. Maybe she worried about her clients nosing around on the way to the bathroom?

I drifted through the door. A heavy hum filled my head as I passed through, shifting around the weighted matter as the molecules buzzed and swarmed around me. I untangled my light from the whirl of atoms making up the wood door. Relief washed over me as I brightened the dark interior. Peering into the darkness, my vision adjusted as my light darted over the clutter like a flashlight only I could see.

My hand pressed against the phantom of my heart, and I stared wide-eyed at the room before me.

Pillows of all sizes, colored in warm earth tones, scattered over the round geometric print rug. Two windows covered in black curtains divided the wall to my left, leaking light onto the shag carpeting. Clothing lay in clumps on the floor, mingling with pillows and piles of papers. I drifted further, my light illuminating the scattered remains of Poppy's hidden life. An overturned soda can leaked sticky cola onto a stack of mail. Letter crumpled as if by an angry fist. I peered closer. *Lenora Khade*, the address read.

My light flickered, my gaze darting past the mail like a fresh burn on nonexistent skin. I wanted to write it off as a coincidence. But I knew, after skimming her social media and Sato's story about the stolen mail, that it was intentional.

I wavered, searching for something to make sense of it. Had I done something to her?

I stopped. My form frozen.

Paintings—*my* paintings, surrounded a quilted bed. Five large canvases cluttered the walls—art I had auctioned at various charity events, according to the post beneath the Instagram picture. Had Poppy bought them all? But why? Why would she keep them hidden away? I drifted closer to the smudged acrylic. My light flickered, coloring red with fury. I lifted my hand, my fingers falling into the painted tree and its solitary swing. I closed my eyes, wishing I could remember anything about the painting.

A scrap of paper poked out from behind the canvas. I focused my energy on it, my fury strengthening until I could nudge the painting aside.

Beneath the canvas were dozens of pictures of ... me. Me walking up the street; me at an event, a cocktail party, a concert; me drinking coffee; me checking the mail—my eyes darted from one photograph to another, skimming the printed articles attached to each one. She knew my schedule. How was that possible?

I drifted back, my light darkened to garnet. My form desperate for breath. The room glowed as I drifted around, my anger pulling canvases from the walls. More pictures, more notes—a grocery list smudged with dirt—a magazine with a coffee stain on its cover, used paintbrushes.

My trash. She collected my trash for her sick little collage.

I needed to tell someone, but I had no breath, no voice. I was nothing but light and feeling. I cursed. Then again, louder. The room flickering as my red light throbbed.

Then I saw it.

She labeled it, The End. I scoffed at her lack of originality and drifted closer. A picture of me and Sato embracing in front of the gate to Khade House. I looked at the frayed and faded lace hidden within my light—the same blouse I wore in the picture. My hair fell in curls down my back, hair that held no texture anymore, and a body that hours later would be empty of life.

I screamed.

CHAPTER
TWENTY-FIVE

FLEUR

Lenora was making a racket. Fleur opened one eye and squinted at Poppy. How long had they been sitting there? Days? Hours? Fleur stifled a yawn and tried to keep her breathing even. How this was supposed to help anyone was beyond her. She tilted her head and listened. Rainfall sounded from a hidden speaker, mingling with the distant sound of something crashing.

Then Lenora screamed.

The sound exploded in Fleur's mind, shaking her. She released Poppy's hands and untangled her legs. Something was wrong.

Poppy opened her eyes and exhaled a long breath. "Just breathe, Fleur. We're making wonderful progress."

Progress toward what? All she had was a cramp in her thigh. "Can I use your bathroom?"

Poppy leaned back and nodded to the hallway. "Second door on the right."

Fleur struggled to her feet, resisting the urge to slap feeling back into her legs. Each step was like walking on knives. She hobbled toward the hallway, glancing back at Poppy as she went.

Poppy hadn't moved. Her legs were still curled under her, her head raised, back aligned, but her hands had closed into fists on her thighs. Fleur looked back to the hallway, shaking feeling back into her legs as she moved.

Her gaze on the throbbing red door at the end.

Locked. Fleur pulled two bobby pins from her hair, straightening them as she crouched in front of the door. Fleur slid them over the drivers, lifting each pin—first pin ... second ... until the telltale clicks and turn loosened the knob. She released a breath and stood, opening the door.

Paintings and photographs fluttered around the room in a maelstrom of fury. Fleur inched closer to the whirlwind. Red light flooded the room, pulsing from the heart of the storm. Lenora.

She didn't have time to wonder how Lenora was doing this. She had to calm her. Fleur reached out, her fingers glowing red as they passed through the gale. A photo fluttered, slapping against her hand like a card in a bike's spokes. She grasped it, turning it over in her hand.

Lenora and Sato. Embracing. The date on the back read November 18.

Fleur stepped back and examined the canvases, now torn and frayed, around the room. They looked familiar. She crouched down and lifted one ripped corner. It was Lenora's painting of her brother from the last charity she posted. Fleur released it, and the canvas crashed back into the ruins of Poppy's bedroom.

"Lenora," Fleur whispered. "Lenora, please? Can you hear me?"

She stole my life.

"I know." Fleur wished she knew what to say or how to offer comfort. There was no comfort in this. It was a violation. "We'll tell Javier—he'll arrest her. She'll get what she deserves."

Why? Fleur? Why would she do this? Her voice was strained.

"I don't know, Len. But, please ... we need to calm down, OK?

We'll sort this out." Fleur kept her voice low, mimicking the softness Theda had so often used with her.

The wind stopped, and the room darkened.

"Lenora?"

I'm here.

"You, OK?"

No.

Fleur nodded.

Promise me, she'll be punished.

"Javier will see to it." Fleur prayed she was right.

Lenora illuminated beside Fleur. Her face was flushed, and her dark eyes wide.

Fleur nodded again. "I promise."

"What have you done?" Poppy screeched from the doorway.

Fleur turned, her hands on her hips. "I could ask you the same question."

Poppy recoiled, her mouth twisting into a sneer. "How dare you? You broke into my house and destroyed my prize paintings! How dare you use my love for Lenora for your own nefarious purposes!" Spittle sprayed with each word.

Fleur took a step back. Whatever she had been expecting, this vehement declaration of love was not it. "Love is respecting boundaries. This ... Hell, no. You're a stalker."

"What do you know? My love was pure—we had something, I could feel it, but Lenora never even looked at me! She ignored me, forced my hand!"

"Is that why you killed her?" The words were out before Fleur could stop them. She looked Poppy in the eye. "Lenora didn't love you back, so you killed her?"

"My world died that day!" Poppy crouched, drawing one of the crushed paintings into the cradle of her arms.

"No. Lenora did. And why? Because if you couldn't have her, no one could?"

Poppy glared, gathering a piece of broken collage into her arms.

"I thought you wanted her to represent your mindfulness gig—"

"I did! She refused. Said she wasn't in the habit of selling her celebrity—but I saw her at those charity auctions! She had no problem selling herself to *them*!"

"And that made you furious, right?"

"Of course! She was mine first!"

"Was she?"

"I watched her for years. I saw her pain and wanted to heal her!"

"The 'I saw it first' defense won't work here." Fleur softened her tone. "Why poison? You must have been feeding it to her for months —how'd you do it?"

Poppy stilled, then stood slowly, clutching the debris. "You think I'm a killer? Me? You're a fool. Maybe you should look into the boyfriend or the old man—"

"What old man?" Fleur met Poppy's gaze.

"You dare accuse me? Ha! Find the old man. He's your killer. I guarantee it."

Fleur released a breath and crossed her arms over her chest. "Tell me about the old man, Poppy."

"Why should I?" Poppy straightened, hugging the wrecked painting closer.

"You want me to call the police?"

Poppy pulled her phone from her pocket. "Good idea." She tapped the screen of her phone.

"911, what's your emergency?" the voice on the other end crackled.

Fleur groaned. "It won't work, Poppy."

Poppy ignored her. "I've caught a burglar in my bedroom."

"Are you in danger?"

"Not yet."

Fleur shook her head. "I'm not a burglar!" she exclaimed.

"Please," Poppy cried, tears spilling from her eyes. "I'm scared."

The woman was a terrific actor.

"Police are on their way. Are you in a safe location?"

Poppy backed out of the room. "Please hurry!"

Fleur threw her hands in the air. "This is ridiculous. I'm not a burglar."

"Please!" Poppy wept into the phone. "She's screaming at me!"

"Calm down, ma'am. The police are almost there. Can you get to the door?"

Sirens. Fleur rushed to the window and brushed the drapes aside. Shit. Cops. How'd they get here so fast? "Dammit, Poppy!" She rushed Poppy, but she was too late. With a cruel grin, Poppy slammed the door, the lock clicking in place.

Fleur raced to the window. She had to get away.

Lenora stood staring at the closed door. *She was obsessed with me.*

"Yeah, I got that. We've got to get outta here." She tugged at the window latch, dragging her fingers over the bolt. Why would she seal her windows? What if there was a fire? Fleur pulled the latch again.

Voices in the hall. Shoes creeping along the hardwood. Shit. She bet they had guns drawn. Fleur pulled the curtains back and pounded on the window again.

Such a sad woman. Lenora shook her head and drifted around the room. *I wonder if I knew.*

Fleur threw up her hands. "You didn't. You didn't give her the time of day, Lenora—that was the problem. She just wanted to be seen."

The footsteps outside the door.

But why me?

The door swung open, and two officers flew in, a third sauntering behind.

Fleur cursed. Colorfully.

"I should have known." Javier shook his head and pulled out a set of handcuffs. "Hiya, Harkyn."

CHAPTER
TWENTY-SIX

FLEUR

Theda was going to be furious.

Fleur shifted on the cramped plastic chair next to Javier's desk, her hands cuffed to the corner. He left her there, shaking his head as he moved to the office at the end of the bullpen. His captain, Fleur guessed. She hoped he was getting a good scolding for arresting her, like in the movies. Fleur bit back a grin and imagined Javier cowering under the weight of his captain's anger.

A door slammed. Fleur twisted in her chair, hoping to see a chastised Javier slinking back to her. Maybe everything would work out just fine.

Instead, he grinned. Damn. Fleur frowned. Maybe not.

"Well, Fleur," Javier began as he lowered himself into his chair and leaned back, "wanna tell me about it?"

He adjusted his glasses, smudging the rims with his fingers. Fleur leaned back in her chair and studied him. His gray T-shirt was frayed underneath the worn collar of his faded green button-up.

Javier preferred his clothing to be nondescript, like his brown loafers and the unflattering cut of his jeans. His hair curled carelessly over his forehead, darkening the corners of his eyes.

He raised a brow, tapping the tip of his pen against his desk. Waiting.

She wondered how many of her words would land her in a jail cell versus her bed.

Fleur shrugged. "Poppy did it."

"Oh, yeah?"

"Yeah. She was stalking Lenora. You saw the art and photographs. Hell, one look at her socials would tell you everything. The woman is obsessed." But she didn't have a Relic. The thought popped up, unwanted, and Fleur pressed her lips together.

"Doesn't mean she's a killer."

Fleur shook her head. "What? Of course, she is! You saw—"

"I saw a dangerous obsession, yes, but Poppy didn't kill Lenora."

"How do you know?" Fleur persisted, her body tensing.

Lenora materialized beside her, her light waning after the shock and anger she experienced at Poppy's house. *Let him talk.*

Fleur turned to her. "Where have you been?"

I needed a ... moment. Lenora drifted over to Javier. Her expression resigned. *He's not lying. Poppy didn't do it.*

Javier's gaze darted around her, his shoulders stiffening. "Lenora?"

"How do you know Poppy didn't do it?" Fleur asked again, returning her gaze to Javier.

"Her alibi checked out." Javier leaned forward, resting his elbow on the desk. "At the time of death, Poppy was on the phone with the cable company."

"That could be fake."

"C'mon, Fleur. We know how to check an alibi. The company confirmed it."

"How do they know it was Poppy and not someone else?"

"She got a package, had to sign for it. The delivery driver confirmed it was her."

Fleur huffed and leaned back in her chair. "But she was stalking her."

Javier blew out a breath. "Yes, and if Lenora was still alive, we could charge her with harassment."

"So, she gets nothing? What if she finds someone else to stalk? She's not OK. She needs help."

"We can recommend counseling, but that's all. Like I said, without a complaint from Lenora, our hands are tied."

"But you saw the pictures!"

"It isn't a crime to hide pictures in your room, Fleur. It's only a misdemeanor if Lenora felt threatened enough to report it—which she didn't."

"But Lenora was terrified—she went into hiding because of it."

"Then she should have reported it."

Lenora colored red, then dimmed. *He's right. I did nothing about it.*

"She gets to go free?" Fleur wanted to punch something.

"She gets a warning, and, hopefully, she seeks therapy."

Fleur grunted. It wasn't fair. Poppy made Lenora feel unsafe in her own home, but because Lenora didn't report it, nothing could be done. It was worse than unfair—it was bullshit. "What about spying on a police investigation?"

Javier scratched his beard and shook his head. "We can't prove that was her."

"Did you ask her?"

"She denied it."

"Of course she did." Fleur huffed. "So, what do we do now?"

Javier's eyes softened. "Go home. Have a glass of wine. If I need insight into the case, I'll ask."

None of those sounded like workable options. "You have a lead?"

"We're working on it?"

"Sato?"

Fleur ... Lenora warned.

"No."

"No? What? He's the boyfriend, and she broke up with him right before it happened. The poison was ingested gradually—who better than a live-in boyfriend?"

"Sato's alibi also checked out. He was at his cousin's—she vouched for him."

"But you said it was gradual. He could have poisoned her earlier—"

Fleur. No. It wasn't Sato.

"Stop, Fleur." Javier shook his head and pulled out the key to her handcuffs. "Sato was cleared, he may have had a motive, albeit weak, but he didn't have the means."

"What does that mean?"

"Sato knows nothing about poisons, how to administer them, and has no access to them."

"He could have learned all that. C'mon, Javier. He's lying to you, and you know it."

Javier paused, considering her. "I won't argue that he's lying about something, but killing Lenora, isn't it."

Fleur groaned. That's two strikes, damn. "What about Griffin? He's as creepy as they come and admitted to having a distant relationship with Lenora. He stood to inherit, didn't he? That was one condition of his guardianship."

"Griffin also has an alibi."

"But what if he hired someone to do it for him?"

"He didn't."

"They could be on his payroll—the payments would be untraceable then, right?"

"You watch too many cop shows, Harkyn."

"What about the housekeeper?" Fleur swallowed back the sour taste of desperation.

Javier narrowed his eyes. "This isn't a game of Clue. You can't just keep guessing until you get lucky."

"I don't know how you play Clue, but I have more strategy than that."

Javier looked doubtful.

"Well? Did you check with the housekeeper?" Fleur persisted.

"We did."

"And?"

"And nothing, Fleur. If you need to know, I'll tell you." Javier unlocked her cuffs and nodded to someone behind her. "Theda's waiting. Leave it alone, OK?"

"Leave it alone? You brought me into this—"

"And I shouldn't have." Javier shook his head and stood. "You're free to go."

"Wait! Poppy mentioned an old man ... could be a red herring, but—"

"It's not."

"What?" Fleur's head came up, her gaze meeting Javier's. "How do you know?"

Javier took a breath and pulled a photo from the box of debris beside his desk. "Poppy had a picture."

"Of course she did," Fleur scoffed.

"It was taken four years ago, angled from behind Poppy's hedges, if I'm not mistaken." He held the picture up, glancing at it.

"So? Do I get to see it?"

Javier's gaze met hers over the photograph. "Promise not to freak out?"

What the hell was he talking about? Fleur huffed. "Gods, Javier. I can look at a photograph without freaking out, you know."

Fleur glared at him as she grabbed the picture from his hand.

He was right—the angle was from behind the hedge. Fleur peered closer. Lenora stood on the sidewalk in front of her gate, her hair shorter, curlier—she smiled up at a man, her hand extended as if to shake.

It started in her stomach, then rose like bubbles into her throat.

Fleur gasped and shook her head, her eyes glued to the man in the picture.

The elbows of his navy cardigan were patched with faded leather. The soup stain on the left breast was at least a decade old, and it smelled of sage. It was his thinking sweater, the only piece of wardrobe Viola didn't replace. Fleur would know that sweater anywhere.

She looked from the photo to Javier. "I don't understand ...," her voice trembled.

"I don't either." Javier shook his head. "But, somehow—Lenora knew your father."

THEDA DROVE IN SILENCE. Fleur tugged at her seat belt and pushed the button for the seat warmer. Theda's Jeep was luxurious compared with the Subaru—no road noise, no squeaking brake pads, and warmth. She glanced out the window. A streetlight glinted off the black sedan behind them. Fleur sighed, the rain's patter heavy in the silence.

Lenora knew her father.

Fleur's heart pounded in her ears. It felt like a missing piece, like a solid lead—like her worst nightmare.

What was she supposed to do with this information? Lenora couldn't help, and her father ... he made his choices, which left who? Viola. Fleur snorted. No way Viola knows anything about this. But she'd have to try, Fleur realized. Viola might be the only one who knew why Arik was with Lenora that day. Gods help them all.

She snuck a look at Theda, her hands clutched the wheel, her eyes straight ahead. "Look, I'm sorry—"

Theda didn't look at her. "Don't."

Fleur bit her bottom lip and turned to the window. She didn't know whether Theda was pissed about her getting arrested again or that she was talking to Javier, but either way, she needed to make it right. "Theda—"

"Stop, Fleur. I don't want to hear it."

"I did nothing! I swear. Lenora found Poppy's creepy little shrine and went crazy. All I did was walk in on it and try to calm her."

"You accused an innocent woman of murder."

Fleur smirked. "I wouldn't say she was innocent."

"That's not for you to judge. Don't you get it? You're not the police. You have no experience with this—you can't just accuse people when you feel like it."

"You didn't see—"

"You shouldn't have gone. I don't know what you were thinking. After Griffin, I never should have gone along with this."

"You're not my keeper, Theda. Lenora needs help. The police are no closer to figuring this out than we are. I have to do something."

"Do you? Do you *really*? Listen to yourself, Fleur. You don't know this ghost. You don't owe her anything."

But she did. Fleur huffed and looked at her hands clasped in her lap. She owed it to Lenora to finish this, to get her memories back. It might be a fluke, but somehow her father was involved. Fleur needed to find out what he was doing. And if that meant solving Lenora's murder, then that's what she was going to do.

"I warned you this would happen," Fleur reminded her. "But you told me to do it. 'It'll be exciting,' you said."

"I was wrong."

Theda parked in front of their apartment and turned off the engine. She didn't move. She slipped her hands off the wheel and looked up at the streetlamp. Fleur waited, her body tensing with every breath Theda took.

Fleur resisted the urge to squirm and turned her gaze to the rain-soaked window. A black sedan pulled up to the curb behind them—Fleur squinted into the mirror. Weird. It was the same car she saw as they were leaving the police station.

"OK," Theda whispered to herself, then turned to Fleur. Her

unwavering brown eyes studied her, her hand reached out, seeking Fleur's in the dark car. Her thumb moved back and forth over Fleur's knuckle, pausing with each new thought. This was Theda's method. Silence, weighing her options until the tangles were all worked out.

"Tell me your plan," Theda said, finally.

Fleur's eyes widened. "Really?"

"Don't make me regret this." Theda sighed.

"Why?"

"Because you won't stop, will you? It doesn't matter how angry I get. You'll see this through. I can either fight you or help."

"Are you sure?" Fleur could barely hear her own words over the relief pouring through her veins. She leaned back against the seat. Theda wasn't giving up on her.

"Go on, tell me." Theda offered a small smile.

Fleur's heart swelled.

"Poppy didn't do it, at least that's what Javier said, and I think he's right. She loved Lenora. I don't think she had it in her to kill her." Fleur released a breath and shifted to face Theda. "I prodded Javier about Sato—even though Lenora's convinced of his innocence. But he's got a solid alibi unless his cousin is lying for him, but we'll leave that for now."

Fleur didn't mention Arik. She couldn't find the words.

"So that leaves ... Griffin?" Theda frowned.

"He had the most to gain, financially."

"PR like that is bad for business. He wouldn't risk it unless he was sure he wouldn't get caught."

"I'm not convinced that he's innocent. The man reeks of guilt and sandalwood. It's gross, but we have no proof aside from my vision and the Relic in his office. Still, he could have hired a hit or whatever." Worry nagged at her, but she pushed it aside.

"Hired a hit? Griffin is creepy and has possible knowledge of the realms, but that doesn't make him a killer."

"Right. So that leaves the housekeeper."

"What did Javier say about her?"

"Nothing. He wants me to leave it alone."

Theda snorted. "I thought he knew you better than that."

"So, I thought I'd give her a visit, see what's up." Fleur grinned.

"*We'll* visit." Theda nodded at her.

Fleur's breath caught in her throat, and she nodded. "You want to come?"

"I'm part of this too, OK?"

"OK," Fleur repeated, squeezing Theda's hand.

TWENTY-SEVEN

FLEUR

She waited until after work the next afternoon to call on Opal Barlow. After Lindy's guilt trip on the phone yesterday, she didn't dare take another day off. Fleur scowled at the GPS on her phone as the arrival time extended from fifteen minutes to thirty on the traffic-heavy commute.

Gods. She hoped this wasn't another dead end. Poppy was a bust. The photograph of her father and Lenora, although curious, couldn't have anything to do with her death. It was taken four years ago. Poppy was trying to deflect. Fleur hated that it worked. Dammit. How did Lenora know Arik? And why the hell was he at her house?

Javier let her keep the picture, and Fleur spent most of the night studying it under the dim light of her phone. Arik looked relaxed, smiling even. It wasn't the first time they had met—Arik was never that open with strangers. Viola was no help either. The call consisted more of Viola gushing about Lenora's tragedy than any useful information. She didn't tell her about the picture. The last thing Fleur needed was her stepmother involved, and knowing Viola, she'd get involved.

Maybe Opal knew why Lenora was meeting Arik outside her house three months before his death.

Flipping on her blinker, Fleur glanced at the side mirror. A black sedan two cars down followed suit. "Weird."

"What?" Theda asked without looking up.

"A black car—that's twice."

Theda straightened and twisted in the passenger seat. "Twice what?"

Fleur shook her head and inched into the left lane. The light ahead turned red, and Fleur pressed the brake, her windshield wipers working double time in the sudden downpour. "Probably nothing. Weird."

"Because a black car is behind you?"

"Last night too."

"Do you know how many black cars are in Seattle?"

"Yeah, yeah, yeah. Told you—Griffin gave me the creeps. Now, I'm paranoid."

Theda laughed and squeezed her hand. "Don't worry, I'll protect you."

"Gee, thanks." Fleur grinned, nodding to the book on Theda's lap. "Figure it out yet?"

"Nope." Theda held up Lenora's copy of *Persuasion* and flipped through it. "She's highlighted specific passages, but look, these numbers in the margin, here?" She pointed to a group of numbers. "It makes little sense. I've tried rearranging the letters of the first word in the sentence under where they fall in the alphabet, but all it gives me is nonsense—it has to be a code, but I just don't know what." Theda huffed and closed the book.

After her stint at the police station, Fleur realized she needed to regroup. She pulled the book and USB out of her bag and asked if Lenora recognized them, but as suspected, Lenora's light dimmed. Fleur didn't think she would, but she had to try. Theda was relentless, though. She spent the evening flipping through the worn yellow pages of the ancient paperback.

"Maybe Opal knows something?" Fleur added it to the list of questions she had for the former housekeeper. She pressed the gas and turned down the quiet, tree-lined street leading to Opal Barlow's residence.

Theda sighed and tucked the book back into her purse.

The house was a two-story Tudor bungalow with a pitched roof and overlapping gables. The glass roof of a sloped greenhouse rose from the back garden, peeking through the fence encircling the small corner property. Opal Barlow didn't appear to be hurting from her dismissal.

They parked on the street. Fleur pulled her hood up against the rain that had slowed to a drizzle and moved to the narrow walkway lined with rounded cedar shrubs. She paused, glancing back down the street, but it was empty.

Get it together, Fleur scolded herself as she climbed the stairs to the porch.

Lenora perched on the shoulder of Theda's olive raincoat, using the edge of its hood to protect herself from the splatter of rain.

The door opened before Fleur could raise her hand to knock.

"Yes?" The man wore a red T-shirt with a faded black skull. The words Not Today were printed across the front beneath an oatmeal cardigan. He looked to be in his late forties if the streaks of gray peppering his brown beard and sideburns were any indication. He eyed them, his hand still gripping the door.

"We're looking for Opal Barlow." Fleur smiled, hoping to put the man at ease.

"Why?" he asked.

"We're friends of Lenora Khade," Theda said, offering a sad smile, "and we hoped to offer our condolences."

He grunted, tightening his grip on the door. "Lenora's friends didn't give a hoot about Opal when she was alive. Why should you now?"

A light turned on in the hall behind him, followed by the soft fall of footsteps.

"Who is it, Henry?"

"No one." Henry's gaze didn't leave Fleur's as he spoke. "They were just leaving."

"Opal?" Fleur asked, stepping closer to the door. "We're friends of Lenora's."

A woman with a halo of blonde hair curling around her face moved into view. Her bright blue eyes narrowed on them a moment before her expression relaxed. "They're not reporters, Henry."

"They're not friends either."

"Oh, stop." Opal sighed and rested her hand on Henry's shoulder. She looked between Fleur and Theda, her gaze resting on Lenora's butterfly. Her eyes clouded with tears. She sniffed, wiping them with the back of her hand. "Let them in."

"But—"

"Not everyone is the enemy." Opal pulled gently at Henry's shoulder and looked at Theda. "You have a swallowtail tiger moth on your shoulder."

Theda smiled. "I know."

"They were Lenora's favorite."

Henry frowned, opening the door wide.

Opal ushered them into the small living room, gesturing to the loveseat in the center. Henry grumbled something about packages as he retreated down a short hallway. The sound of a door opening, followed by the slam of a screen, echoed in the hallway as Henry went outside.

Fleur took a seat on the sofa, Theda beside her. Lenora fluttered around the room, hovering over Opal before settling on the arm of her chair.

Opal rested her hand beside Lenora, her fingers almost touching the moth's delicate wings. She sighed, her eyes closing as if she could feel Lenora's presence.

"So," Opal began, opening her eyes and fixing them with a hard stare, "you're not friends. Lenora's friends never found out my name, let alone visited. Who are you?"

Theda cleared her throat and looked at Fleur.

So, it was to be the truth. Fleur leaned back and crossed her legs in front of her, nudging the coffee table with her boot. Fine. She'd humor Theda—not that Opal would believe them.

"I'm Fleur Harkyn, and this is my partner, Theda Okan. I'm a medium and seer. Meaning, I can see and speak with ghosts." Fleur took a deep breath, her eyes on Opal, waiting for any kind of reaction. When none came, she continued. "Lenora found me at the conservatory after her death and asked for help ...," she trailed off. Waiting.

The sound of packing tape stretching and ripping from the back garden grew louder as the room quieted. Opal drummed her fingers on the wooden arm of the chair, but Lenora held fast. The housekeeper looked to the moth, then to Theda, searching for affirmation before her gaze landed on Fleur once again.

"Lenora found you?" Opal said, half to herself. "You're looking into her death?"

"Yes, we are."

"Are you detectives?"

Fleur coughed. "Not technically."

"Private investigators?"

Fleur took a breath. "You could call us that, I guess, but I like to think of us as helpers."

Opal considered them. "Do you do this often?"

"Not really. When I was a kid, I messed around with last requests, but this is my first murder ..."

"Murder? You're investigating Lenora's death because her spirit asked you to?"

"That sums it up."

A laugh hiccupped from Opal's throat, followed by another. She covered her mouth as if holding in her mirth, her shoulders shaking.

Theda turned her worried gaze to Fleur, expecting something

other than laughter from Opal. Fleur shrugged, waiting for Opal to compose herself.

"I'm sorry," Opal gasped. "Oh, this *is* good." She smiled. "I needed that—it's been days since I've cracked a smile. A psychic detective who's never detected and her ..." She turned to Theda. "Are you her sidekick?"

Theda narrowed her eyes. "I assure you, we are serious." She nodded to the moth on the arm of the chair. "You said tiger moths were Lenora's favorite? I suppose that's why she returned as one."

As if on cue, Lenora rose and fluttered to Fleur's shoulder, startling Opal with her movement. The former housekeeper quieted, her fingers curling into a fist.

"You're joking, right? I mean, I've heard some crazy stories, but this—" She broke off, then turned to Fleur. "If you've talked with Lenora, then you should know something about her? Right? That's how this works, isn't it?"

She should have known Opal would pick up on that. Of course, it's the most common way to find the truth in this scenario, but Fleur had no truth to offer. Lenora's erased memories were fast becoming a thorn in her side.

"Yes." Theda nodded. "That's how it works."

Opal fixed her gaze on the butterfly. "What kind of tea did I make for her and her brother when they were small? Hmm? If you can tell me that, I'll consider answering your questions."

The moth brightened as Lenora shifted into her spiritual form, her light tinged pink as she hovered beside Fleur.

I don't remember, Fleur. I just ...

Fleur closed her eyes, focusing her thoughts on an image of Lenora and Edgar as children—an old photograph in Lenora's room. She wished she had paused over it, taken in more than a precursory glance. The air shifted, sweetening with the aroma of honey and clove—Opal had just brewed a pot of chamomile. It clung to her. Fleur inhaled, merging the lingering aromas with what she saw of the photograph. She saw Lenora, her rich brown hair braided, she wore pajamas—like her brother—ballet dancers and dinosaurs. The room cooled, a light breeze fluttered. Breath on heat, cooling the liquid. Mugs in their hands. Legs tucked under quilts. "Edgar had trouble sleeping," Fleur murmured, tilting her head as she gave the image its freedom.

Lenora hated the brew. Fleur could feel her revulsion—no, not the brew. Milk. Lenora hated milk. Why? Her stomach. It hurt her stomach, but she drank it anyway ... for Edgar. He mimicked her, sipping the warm milk in unison. Not just milk—ginger, valerian root, turmeric, and ... What was it? It smelled like summer and heat.

"Not tea. Golden Milk," Fleur blurted, her eyes on Lenora. "You hated it but drank it for your brother."

Lenora's light brightened with her smile. *Milk? I didn't like milk?*

"No, it hurt your stomach, but you never told Opal." Fleur's gaze drifted from Lenora to Opal, sitting wide-eyed, mouth agape.

I did it for my brother. Lenora repeated, a smile spreading over her face. *Did you see us just then?*

Fleur nodded.

Were we happy?

"Yes." Fleur watched Lenora's light soften, then turned back to Opal. "Lenora was lactose intolerant but never told you. She didn't want you to think she hated it. She knew how much care you took in crafting it."

"Did she just tell you all that?" Opal whispered.

"No." Fleur sighed. "Lenora remembers nothing. I divined the milk using a photo I found in Lenora's attic. And your scent. Scent is a powerful help, you know."

"My scent?"

"Soil and clove. You take honey in your tea, right? It coats your breath. And you've been digging? There's soil under your fingernails."

Theda rested her hand on Fleur's thigh and squeezed.

"But—that's amazing." Opal shook her head. "How do you do that?"

Fleur waved her hand, dismissing Opal's question. "I was born like this."

As a child, Fleur's mother taught her how to divine the air, separating scents and their lingering memories—a gift she rarely used now. If she allowed the memory to take hold, Fleur's seer's eye could enter another's experiences. But that needed magick and focus, something Fleur never quite mastered. Once they arrived in this realm, the stench of progress coated everything. Smog and exhaust fumes, dust and decay all fought for dominance over the bright fragrances of flora and rain. Fleur exhaled, allowing the headiness of the memory to fade.

Opal's gaze darted around the room. "Where—"

"She shifted back to a spirit," Fleur said. "Lenora can't communicate as a moth. It is a disguise for defense only."

"Defense?"

"Did you think we would be safe in death?" Fleur asked.

Opal shook her head. "I never thought about it at all."

No one does. Most take safety in death for granted. One would rather hear about the serenity, the calm—the golden twilight glinting off the gates of heaven. A common enough trope—but to tell of a death without heaven or hell, with repercussions and choices weighted as heavily as life, would break the fragile bond most have with their end. We will all die, but death is just a continuation. Arik warned her that most refuse to believe in the Great Tree. It gave us breath, the very oxygen we need to survive, and we return to it once our bodies revert to husks. The Soulkeepers' choice, given to every fresh Atua, dictates our continuation. Some, like Arik, choose to continue into the Great Tree and the new world that awaits, while others linger here, unfinished.

And others, like Lenora, are tasked with something greater. The realization dawned, and Fleur's gaze snapped to the spirit. Of course, it all made sense. That's why she could manage the other Atua—why no gnats hovered around her. That's why the Soulkeepers replaced her memories. Lenora must have discovered something useful to the

Soulkeepers. Gods. Did she, like Griffin, know about the Relics? The idea was too impossible to consider. Questions burned like hot coffee on her tongue.

Fleur swallowed and turned back to Opal. It would have to wait, and Fleur hated waiting. "So? Will you answer our questions?" she asked, mustering as much patience as she could.

Opal nodded. "I'll try."

Fleur pulled the photograph from her pocket. "Do you know this man?" She hadn't intended to lead with that, but the photo was in her hand before she could stop herself.

Beside her, Theda gasped. "Where did you get that?"

Fleur ignored her, keeping her gaze on Opal.

Opal reached out. "Do you mind?" She took the photo. Her eyes darted over the picture, widening slightly in recognition before she shook her head. "I'm sorry. I don't. It's an old photo, isn't it? Lenora's hair is short—she grew it long the last few years. Who is he?"

Her aura changed, Fleur—her edges tinged with brass. She knew him too. Lenora shimmered and inched closer to the photo.

Fleur stared at her, Lenora's words ringing in her ears. "Four years ago, to be exact. He was a bookseller, a collector." She narrowed her gaze, goose bumps spreading over her arms. "Do you know why Lenora might have met with him? Did she collect books? Did she hire him for something?"

Opal shook her head again. "I can't imagine why she would. She liked books, but to read, not collect …," she trailed off, her head tilting as if shaking a memory free. "But there was one … Len found it somewhere. She never gave me the details. Said it was a history book. I think this was around that time."

"Do you have this book?"

Opal shook her head. "I never saw it, but she led me on a merry chase looking for a Relic she read about—"

"Relic? Is that the word she used?" Fleur interrupted. Curiosity trembled her hand as she took the photograph back. Opal put on a good act, but not good enough.

Opal blinked as if realizing her error. "I think so. I remember thinking it was a weird way of describing it."

"What was it?"

"Some wind spinner we found in an antique shop in Pioneer Square." Opal shrugged. "It was pretty, too small to do much ... but it made Lenora happy."

"Do you have the name of the antique shop?"

"Lord, no. That was years ago."

Fleur tried not to huff in frustration. Opal was hiding something. Whatever that book was, it was important. That must have been why she called Arik. But why Arik? Her father wasn't an expert, not even close. He was a bookseller, nothing else—at least, in this realm.

But ... Opal called it a Relic. Fleur turned to the spirit hovering over the coffee table. "Does this sound familiar?"

Lenora shook her head, her light dimming. *No. I'm sorry, Fleur ... I'm trying, I swear, but all I hear is you humming—the lullaby, I think?* Frustration tinged the edges of her light pink. *And a woman's hand.* Lenora closed her eyes, her body wavering as if she were pushing a brick wall.

"What did she say?" Opal asked, her eyes wide.

"She doesn't remember." Fleur took a breath. It was fine. They'd figure this out. Patience, she reminded herself.

"You said Lenora liked to read. Do you recognize this?" Theda fished *Persuasion* from her purse and held it out to Opal.

Opal touched the cover and nodded. "Lenora's favorite. She preferred gothic novels, like *Rebecca* and *The Mysteries of Udolpho.*" Opal's eyes misted. "She loved the classics—she would quote Shirley Jackson, but she had a soft spot for Austen, particularly this book."

Theda smiled and opened the book. "Any idea what these mean?" She pointed to the highlighted numbers in the margins.

"481996 is Lenora's birthday." Opal's brow creased as she took the book from Theda. "And this one?" She pointed to another page. "10231999—that's Edgar's birthday."

The numbers were dates. Damn. Why hadn't she thought of that? "Are they all birthdays?"

"No." Opal closed the book and handed it back to Theda. "A few are just dates, but June sixth was her parents' anniversary, and December nineteenth was the day her parents and brother died."

"What do you think it means?"

Opal shrugged. "Lenora was always secretive."

"What can you tell us about her?" Fleur asked, leaning back.

"Lenora was a soft soul—caring almost to a fault, but she hid it behind that wit of hers." Opal paused, ignoring the slam of the back door as Henry came back inside. "She was sharp, not like her brother, though. What Edgar lacked in empathy, Lenora made up threefold."

"What do you mean?" Fleur asked, her gaze flickering to Lenora. The Atua glimmered as if warmed by Opal's words.

"Just that. Edgar might have gotten his father's brains, but Lenora got his heart."

"Was Edgar gifted?" Theda wondered.

"You could say that. Rodney called him a prodigy. There wasn't a mathematical problem he couldn't solve in less than a second. His brain worked like that, all probabilities and algorithms. He saw everything as an equation to solve. It infuriated Annibel. She didn't understand him, and she hated herself for it—started drinking. You know how it goes, a sip here, a glass there. When Edgar placed out at university level by ten, Annibel threw her hands in the air. She was proud of both her children, but she only had a fondness for Lenora. Rodney took Edgar under his wing, had him working for the company before the boy was twelve. Annibel hated it. She wanted her kids to have a regular upbringing, you know—friends, birthday parties, sleepovers." She sniffed. "Not that Edgar ever had the chance."

"And Lenora?"

"She was bright enough, but nothing compared to her brother. But they were two peas in a pod—did everything together. Lenora had a talent for art, so Annibel and I nurtured it." Opal smiled, her gaze drifting to the painting over the mantle. "She painted that."

It was a watercolor of an iris. Fleur gazed up at it, appreciating the blend of violet and indigo, the brightness of yellow. She turned to Lenora, watching the spirit drift to the fireplace, her hand outstretched as if she could find something of herself in the medley of color.

Did I like irises?

"Why irises?" Fleur asked.

"They mean wisdom." Opal's eyes clouded. "And hope, courage —I told Lenora they suited her."

Theda nodded to the window behind Opal's chair. Her arms folded over her chest, her index finger tapping the fabric of her rain-coat. "Your greenhouse is impressive."

Opal wiped her eyes and turned, a smile curling the corners of her mouth. "It's our little venture. Barlow's Blooms—we opened two years ago on Etsy." Her smile dimmed. "The name was Lenora's idea."

"How's business?" Fleur wondered.

"It's getting there. Not good enough for Henry to quit his day job, but it's nice being able to put my degree to good use."

"Your degree?"

"I'm certified through the University of Washington's Center for Urban Horticulture. I paid my way as a childcare worker for the Khades."

"But you worked for them for nineteen years. Why did you stay?"

"The kids. Then, after the crash, I couldn't leave Lenora. Not with Dugal Griffin waiting to get his hands on her money. So, I became her housekeeper."

"Why do you say that? Did Griffin need money?" Fleur arched a brow.

"He lost everything back in 2001. Started working for Rodney afterward. They were competitors once but made their peace. Rodney and Griffin were close after that. But I never trusted him."

"Why not?" Theda asked, ignoring Fleur's frown.

"The man used companies like toilet paper. Rodney didn't seem to care as long as they profited. Griffin would buy the company and strip it down, blending whatever technologies he could into Khade Securities, then sell whatever was left at an inflated price. Never saw most of that money, though. Griffin had his share of offshore businesses."

"He was swindling Khade?"

"If you ask me, yes. But Rodney trusted him." Opal shrugged. "Must have known something I didn't, not that I know how to run a securities company."

The memory of Griffin's hard blue eyes flared in Fleur, but she swallowed it back.

"You know Lenora was poisoned?"

Opal hung her head and nodded. "That's what the detective said." She took a deep breath.

Her aura changed again. Lenora fluttered around Opal, her eyes wide. *She's hiding something. Metallic edges mean deceit.*

Fleur studied her. Opal's eyes darted around the room, lingering on the iris painting, then flickering between her and Theda. The question made her uncomfortable, she thought, noting the way Opal pulled at the threads on her sleeve. "You know something?"

Opal shook her head. "No, no. It's just ... I can't imagine anyone —it just doesn't seem real. I just saw her that Saturday ..."

"I thought she dismissed you?" Fleur tried to lighten her tone. Opal was hiding something. She could feel it.

"She didn't dismiss me. I left. It was time. Lenora was coming into her own, and Henry wanted to get the ball rolling on the greenhouse. Three years ago, I proposed to leave, but Lenora was having none of it. Last year, once Barlow's Blooms became more established, she agreed—but that didn't mean I stopped caring. Lenora came over regularly. We'd discuss the garden, her art, Sato, the usual stuff."

"Did she tell you about the stalker?"

Opal nodded. "I begged her to go to the police, but she refused. Said it was pointless, that it would only encourage them."

"Did you agree?"

"No, but Lenora never listened. She knew her own mind, and once she settled on something, nothing could budge her."

Theda nodded. "Sounds like someone else in this room."

Fleur grimaced. "Nothing wrong with determination."

"Lenora was stubborn." A smile fluttered around Opal's mouth. "And she knew it."

"Do you have any idea who did this?" Fleur asked.

Opal sniffed, her eyes welling. "I don't, I really don't. Lenora didn't have enemies. She was such a gentle soul. After her parents died, she struggled. That's when I—we stepped in. Henry and I moved in after her parents died. It's always been the three of us. She was like a daughter to me."

Theda made a sound, something akin to a cry, and reached for Opal's hand.

Tell her I'm OK, Fleur. Lenora hovered over Opal, her hands extended as if to comfort. *Tell her she saved me. I can't remember her, true, but I know how I feel, and I felt at home the moment I saw Opal.*

Fleur leaned forward. "Lenora says you saved her and that she was OK because of you."

Opal pressed her hand to her heart and swallowed a sob.

Theda turned to her, blinking back tears, and Fleur knew she was thinking of her aunt—of all Alma did to rescue her from her stepfather. Theda saw a kindred spirit in Opal, and Fleur worried about what she would say when she told her Opal was lying.

TWENTY-EIGHT

LENORA

I f I wasn't killed because of who I was, then it had to be what I knew.

But what *did* I know? What if it was something I didn't know I knew until it was too late? Or ... what if I knew what I knew but didn't know someone else knew, and that's who killed me?

You've almost got it, lass. Oliver's brogue bubbled in my head a moment before he appeared beside me. *It's tricky, you've got yourself into a right mess, but you're close. I can sense it.*

"Who is this?" Fleur studied the older spirit with a frown, her gaze sweeping over the thick beard covering his chin and the wisps of plaid hovering within his light.

With a flourish, Oliver sunk into a deep bow, his arms swept out, his head dipped, an impish grin on his face. *Sir Oliver MacHaddie, at your service.*

What are you doing here? I wondered, my light flickering.

Oliver straightened, his aura warm yellow. *The situation upstairs is progressing, and I—*

"You were sent to babysit?" Fleur practically growled.

More like offering aid if needed. His light was calm, a smile crooked the corner of his mouth. *And, yes, I was told to check in on your progress.*

Fleur huffed and turned toward Theda's desk, pulling a stack of index cards from the drawer. "We've got this covered, thanks."

"What the hell is happening?" Theda's eyes were wide as her gaze darted around the room. "Is there another ghost?"

"Sir Oliver Something-or-Other. He's a spy for the Inbetween."

Now, lass ... Oliver straightened his shoulders. *If I was gonna spy, I'd hardly reveal myself, now, would I?*

"A spy?" Theda paused and shook her head, raising her hand as Fleur opened her mouth to explain. "Nope. Forget it." She turned in the direction Fleur was facing and nodded to an empty corner. "Welcome, Sir Oliver, uh ..." She faltered, unsure how to continue.

Fleur rolled her eyes. "Gods help me."

No use calling on them. They've got enough to oversee. Oliver's light flickered slightly.

I swear Fleur wanted to punch him.

We have it in hand, Oliver. I glided between him and Fleur, ignoring her grunt as she moved to the hall closet and began rummaging.

So, you've found it?

Uh ... no. But we're close. I drifted toward the wind spinner on the side table. *Do you know what this is?*

Oliver studied it, the dark caverns of his eyes moving over the cool metal, pausing on the goddess symbol. *Could be a Relic—but it isn't mentioned in the grimoires I've read. The symbol is curious, must be Relic adjacent? Perhaps a guide?*

"I'm starving. Pizza?" Theda announced, oblivious to our conversation.

"Gods, yes," Fleur moaned, doing her best to ignore us.

I flickered green with envy. I wanted to bite into a steaming hot slice and taste the gooey tang of mozzarella and tomatoes. Instead, I kept my focus on Oliver and the wind spinner. *A guide? Like a map? How do we know it's to the Relic we need?*

"It's not a map," Fleur's voice drifted out from the closet.

How do you know? I asked, frustration tinging my light.

"There are no maps. Think about it—when the sheath imploded, the Relics were flung into the universe, landing here. Why? Because it was safe here. No magick, right? Self-preservation." She poked her head out of the closet. "It's like the first thing Mother taught me."

Aye, she has a point.

Then how did Dugal get one? I countered, unwilling to concede just yet.

Fleur scowled and turned back to the closet. "I don't know … yet."

Oliver drifted over to the closet and peered inside. *What're you doing in there?*

Suddenly, Fleur exclaimed and hauled a dusty old corkboard out of the closet. "I knew this would come in handy." She stood triumphant, grasping the board in both hands.

Theda looked up from her phone and frowned. "I thought you threw that away."

"I never got around to it." Fleur set the board on the low book-case and leaned it against the wall. It filled the narrow space between the window and the entryway.

Oliver grinned. *You've got yourself a right proper war table now.*

I smiled. *More like a war board.*

"All right. Pizza is on its way—mushroom, artichoke hearts, and extra cheese," Theda announced, pocketing her phone.

"Perfect." Fleur plopped down onto the sofa across from the war board. She pulled her gray hair into a braid, securing it with the band she kept around her wrist, and stared at the weathered wooden frame. She wore what I now consider her uniform: faded black jeans, combat boots, T-shirts with obscure slogans like the navy and orange floral print declaring Someday We'll All Be Dead stretched across her curvy figure, and of course, her cardigans. Fleur seemed to own a limitless number of sweaters, from cropped cardigans to fluffy turtlenecks.

Oliver drifted over to rest on the arm of the sofa, mindful of the dewy, carnivorous plants guarding the windowsill. He sat straight and quiet, his focus on Fleur.

"So, where do we start?" Theda slid past me and perched on the arm of the chair beside the board, index cards in hand. "Maybe with that photograph you neglected to tell me about?"

"Gods, Theda. I was going to tell you. I just ... needed to figure it out myself." Fleur frowned, fisting her hands in her lap.

Theda leaned forward and grasped Fleur's hand. "I know, but maybe next time we can figure it out together?"

"It kinda freaked me out—seeing a photo of my father in Poppy's sick little collage. But it was taken four years ago. It can't be part of this."

Oliver grunted.

Opal said I was looking for a Relic, remember? I began.

"But, maybe that's why she came to you?" Theda pointed out. Unknowingly interrupting me. "You said your mother was looking for them."

I brightened, turning to Fleur. Was that why the Guardians chose me to companion Fleur? Why they erased my memories? But wouldn't I be more help if I knew what I had known? My light wavered with a flutter of memory. Wind. Something to do with wind? I frowned.

Oliver stared at me, nodding slowly. *Chase it, lass.*

But how?

"Maybe ..." Fleur stood, bringing my attention back to her, and picked up the mandala spinner the police found in my pocket. "This isn't a Relic, and it's not a map to one. There's no magick in it—no heat."

"But it has the symbol?"

"I don't understand it." Fleur looked at me. "Anything?"

I closed my eyes, my light rippling around me. I focused on the girl in the photograph, the short russet curls framing her face, and her warm smile. She felt other, strange, like an alien, but she was me. I pulled at her arms, turning her around and around my mind, prying into the intimate details of her skin, but I only heard the same melody as before—the same memory. Fleur's memory.

I hummed the tune and opened my eyes.

Fleur stared at me, her body tense. "Where did you hear that?"

From you. Every time I try to remember, I hear that. It's the lullaby your mother taught you, right? About the Relics? The rhythm is the same as the couplet you shared.

Keep at it, Lenora. Oliver prodded. *The Soulkeepers can only do so much—your memories and Fleur's might not be so vastly different? Hmm?*

I turned my startled eyes on him. *What do you mean?*

You both know of the Relics. That much is clear. Maybe there are other things connecting you too. Follow the threads.

Fleur closed her eyes and released a long breath. She turned from me, rubbing her temples, and focused on the war board. "I need to think. OK? OK. What do we know?"

Theda hesitated. She opened her mouth, then closed it and looked down at the index cards in her hand. "It might be something, Fleur. That book Opal mentioned, whatever it is, and the wind spinner might be what we need to figure this out."

"Whatever Lenora was doing with all that—with my father— was years ago. We need to focus on now." Fleur shook her head.

She was wrong. I knew that with the same certainty that I knew anything about her. Fleur was scared. But why? I hovered over the mandala wind spinner. *Then why was this in my pocket when I died?*

Fleur blinked. "Lucky charm?"

"C'mon, Fleur," Theda scoffed, guessing my question. "It's not exactly a rabbit's foot. It has the symbol. It's all connected. But how?"

I pulsed, waiting.

"It's not possible." Fleur looked between us, her gaze landing on the spinner. "No one in this realm knows about the other nine. The goddesses made sure of that. If something had leaked out—and that's a *huge* IF—it could start a war. Or worse. Do you understand that? Think about this realm, about the greed, the imperialism, the fear, now add magick to it. It's a nasty combination and one that just *can't* happen."

Oliver nodded in agreement.

"Dugal had a Relic, and you said yourself he knew what it was. Hell, Fleur—he knew who you were. How? We can't just ignore it." Theda printed my name on an index card and tacked it to the board. She scribbled the names of my family and the date of their car crash and tacked them to the left of mine, then Griffin, Sato, Opal, and Arik to the right. Below my name, she pinned the photo and me and Arik.

"Theda ..." Fleur's voice was strained.

She's on to something, that one. Fleur might want to listen to her partner more. Oliver mumbled, leaning closer to my ear.

Fleur shot him a glare. "I heard that."

Oliver raised his hands as if in surrender and turned back to Theda.

"It's connected, Fleur. We just have to figure out how," Theda continued.

The buzzer went off.

"Come on up." Theda buzzed in the pizza delivery.

Fleur dropped her head in her hands and groaned. "Fine. You're right. I know you're right, but ... Gods, I don't even know where to start. The Relic Dugal has isn't the one Lenora needs. That means there's another one out there connected to all this." Fleur sucked in a breath. "I've spent my adult life ignoring this. Pretending my mother's promise wasn't now mine. And now it's slapping me in the face, and I just ... can't. OK? I don't know what to do."

Theda sat beside her and draped an arm over her shoulder. "Maybe it's time to let go? I know fate isn't exactly your favorite topic, but this ... I don't know. Feels like fate."

Oliver chuckled. *This one ... she's a keeper, lass.*

Fleur glared, opening her mouth, then closed it. I could sense the narratives warring inside her. The impossible truth, or her version of it? She narrowed her eyes and huffed, then looked up at me. "What do you think?"

I glanced at the few clues—our only link to my life. Fleur wanted me to agree with her—to let it go. Her aura tinged pink with frustration. I looked from the corkboard to the wind spinner, then back to her. Opal said I was stubborn, and she may be right, but I was also patient. *The only thing we know is that my death is connected to a Relic. Figuring out one will lead to the other, right?*

Fleur nodded. "Yeah. Find the killer, find the Relic. Gods." She shuddered. "Back to the drawing board."

Oliver rose, his light rippling in the invisible wind and brightened. *I've seen enough.*

What? That's it?

Fleur looked up at him. "Finally."

I was told to observe. And I have. Follow your threads, and listen ... He nodded to Theda, *to this one. She's wiser than she knows.* Oliver smiled at me, and a moment later, he was gone.

Theda shivered and rubbed her hands over her arms. "Something happened?"

"Oliver left." Fleur exhaled.

"Oh? Why?"

Fleur shrugged. "Who knows? He's a spirit, probably had to go report our progress to some fancy Guardian." She turned back to the board. "So, what do we have. Evidence-wise?"

Theda folded her arms over her chest and nodded at the board. "We need to figure out the code in *Persuasion*."

Fleur exhaled, resting her chin on her palm. "And open the USB drive."

Sato could do it.

Fleur tilted her head. "Maybe?"

"Maybe what?" Theda asked, pulling cash from her wallet for the pizza.

"Maybe Sato is a bigger part than we thought."

"How?" Theda asked. "He seems pretty harmless."

"He has a record."

"He's a juvenile hacker. Nothing serious. Most kids nowadays mess around like that."

He knows something he's not telling—just like Opal. The USB drive is protected by a virus we can't fix—not even the cops could figure it out. That was Sato.

Fleur looked at me. Her gaze steady. "What makes you say that?"

Why *had* I said it? Sato and I were together for four years, and from what he said, we had a pretty strong connection—a connection he still worried over. He said I sent him away, but what if I didn't? What if I needed him, and he's protecting me—even now?

Sato is important. Trust me.

Fleur studied me. "You sense something, don't you?"

I flickered. I didn't know what I sensed, but the feeling was absolute.

A knock at the door spared me from answering.

Theda stood, pulling the money out of her pocket as she opened the door and gasped.

Fleur's gaze darted to the entryway, and she cursed.

"Hello, ladies." Javier grinned, holding the pizza box like a peace offering.

CHAPTER
TWENTY-NINE

FLEUR

J avier grinned like an idiot.

Fleur scowled and folded her arms over her chest. "What are you doing here?"

"Where's the pizza guy?" Theda held up her money.

Javier handed Theda the pizza and moved into the room. "Don't worry. I tipped him well enough to let me deliver it."

"And he let you?"

"I may have flashed my badge and waved a twenty at him. He's happy enough."

"Gross, Javier. You probably scared the poor guy." Fleur narrowed her eyes. "And now the building thinks we're criminals."

"Don't be so paranoid. I doubt anyone saw."

Theda rolled her eyes. "Oh, trust me, everyone saw."

Fleur huffed, turning to Lenora as Theda set the pizza on the kitchen table and began dishing it out. Javier sat in the chair opposite Fleur, his gaze landing on the war board. He whistled. "I thought I told you to leave it alone, Fleur."

Fleur glared, ignoring the accusation in his tone. "Why are you here, Javier?"

Lenora flickered and drifted over to him, her light brightening. *He's checking up on you. He didn't believe you'd stop.*

"How do you know?" Gods. Doesn't anyone trust her to figure this out? First, the Atua, now this.

Look at him. Lenora smiled and fluttered over him. *His aura is yellow.*

Javier glanced at her. "Can I assume you're not talking to me?"

"Yes, and no." Fleur pinched her lips together. Seeing him sitting there in the chairs she and Theda had bought together pressed a weight on her chest.

Theda handed her a plate, then offered one to Javier. Fleur's eyes widened as he accepted it and bit down on the mushroom-packed slice. She set the plate in her lap and fisted her hands, frowning at Javier.

"Don't be like that, Fleur," Theda reprimanded. "It's rude to eat in front of him."

"I don't care. We didn't invite him. He shouldn't get a slice."

Javier took another bite and chewed slowly, his eyes never leaving Fleur's.

Lenora flickered and drifted to the window, illuminating the sundews scattered along the sill, their stems curling in her light.

"No gnats? Isn't your ghost friend here?" Javier's gaze shifted from Fleur to the window.

Fleur looked at Lenora. "She's here."

"Did you douse her in insect repellant?" Javier snickered at his own joke.

"Don't be ridiculous."

Theda sat beside Fleur, her pizza in hand. She took a bite, ignoring the glares shooting past her. "Maybe it's because she can shift into a butterfly?" Theda murmured between bites.

Javier looked around the room. "There were always gnats. They drove me crazy. It's too bad you didn't find this one sooner."

Lenora floated over to him her, light flickering lavender. A gnat landed on Javier's pizza.

Fleur smirked.

Javier groaned and waved his hand over his slice, his gaze darting around. "Not funny."

Lenora grinned and drifted away from him.

"So," Javier began settling back into the chair, "what did Barlow have to say?"

"Who said we talked to her?" Fleur asked, determined to match his casual behavior.

"Come on, Fleur." Javier took a bite of pizza. "I'm not an idiot," he said around a mouthful of cheese.

"You talked to her too. Maybe you should go first?" Theda reasoned, arching a brow.

Javier looked between them and set his plate on his lap. He swallowed. "Nothing. She only admitted to seeing Lenora the Saturday before but wouldn't elaborate."

Fleur stared at him, her pizza forgotten, a curse blooming on her lips. He set her up. "Dammit, Javier! You wanted me to visit Opal, didn't you? That's why you were so vague about it." She glared, wishing Theda had never opened the door. "You used us."

Javier shrugged. "So?"

Theda groaned and settled on the sofa, taking a bite of her pizza.

Of all the sneaky ... Fleur pinned him with a glare and clamped her mouth shut.

"C'mon, Fleur. I couldn't condone your actions after what happened with Poppy, you know that. My captain was pissed. But I knew you wouldn't stop investigating—especially not after finding that." He nodded to the picture of Arik and Lenora tacked to the board.

She knew she was overreacting, but she didn't care. Fleur was tired. She already had two strikes under her belt and a bevy of facts leading to her own history—not Lenora's. They were missing something. Why did everything lead back to a Relic? Sure, Griffin has one, but its magick was weak, and Lenora was poisoned—no cuts or bruises on her. A blood Relic like the shell armor shard would leave its mark. Griffin's Relic was a different matter, one she would resolve as soon as this maddening case ended. Fleur frowned, her gaze flickering from the photo to Lenora. She was in over her head—she needed guidance or a little truth.

"She confirmed she saw Lenora the Saturday before her death," Theda offered, ignoring Fleur's growl. "Told us about her time with the Khades. She and Lenora were awfully close."

"Is that it?" Javier took another bite of pizza.

Tell them. Lenora drifted closer to her, her light wavering. *Opal was hiding something. Her aura was metallic and wavered from blue to green. She has a lot of guilt about something—guilt and loyalty.*

"She didn't tell us everything," Fleur muttered.

"What more could she have said?" Theda asked. "Lenora was like a daughter to her."

Fleur turned to Theda. "That's why she was lying." Her voice was gentle. "She lied when we showed her the picture, Theda, and when we mentioned the poison—"

"Don't you dare, Fleur." Theda frowned, her eyes narrowing. "Opal didn't do it."

Javier raised a brow but remained silent.

"I'm not saying she did. I'm just saying she knows more than she told us." Fleur turned to Javier. "When we asked her about the poisoning, she fidgeted. She looked at everything but us. Her answers were vague and—"

Tell them about her aura.

"She was guilty of something, and she knew I saw it. That's why she got all weepy at the end. Sure, she loved Lenora, but she was involved somehow, trust me."

Javier set his pizza aside and leaned forward, his gaze meeting Fleur's. "Are you sure?"

Fleur nodded, the weight of Theda's gaze pressing against her heart. "Yes."

CHAPTER
THIRTY

LENORA

Fleur and Theda needed space. Javier sensed it. He pushed to his feet and donned his coat, murmuring about looking into Opal further.

I fluttered around them—the tension was palpable. I wanted to help but knew my presence would only make it worse. Theda believed Opal and Fleur's skepticism was like a wedge between them.

They needed to talk, to find the warmth in their relationship again.

I would just be in the way.

My light faded, replaced with the torrent of wind pushing me back to the Lobby, back to the purposeless souls with more memory —more everything—than me. I didn't want to go. I didn't want to see Ellory's indigo light welcoming and scolding.

The tree's heavy bough curled around me, tugging my slight form closer to the gateway.

The Guardian was waiting for me. *They will be fine.* Ellory's words bloomed in my mind as I drifted past her.

How did she know? I wondered, trying to calm my anxiety. *I don't want to be the ghost that breaks them.*

You are the first spirit in their partnership. Theda must learn, and Fleur must be patient. Ellory's light curled like smoke around us, its edges coloring pink. *Fleur can be stubborn, but she will find her way— she always does.*

Do you know Fleur? The understanding in her voice was jarring. I studied her. Ellory always spoke of Fleur in familiar terms. Until now, I had just assumed that was her way, but something nagged at me. *Did you know I met her father? Is that why I have her memories?*

Why is not important, Lenora. Be secure, knowing that you are where you are most useful. The rest will come in time.

Ellory flickered, her aura deepening indigo. Above us, the branches shook, their leaves, once the bright green of spring, darkened, a few turning dark rust—fluttered around us. I craned my neck as if I could see beyond the canopy to the realm above. Instead of the bright blue summer sky, the space was murky, clouded like the Seattle winter on the other side of the gate. *The Shadelings are getting closer?*

We do our best to hold them off, but they're relentless. I fear ... Ellory turned from me, her gaze not on the threatening presence above the branches but rather on the polished hardwood floor below us. *You found a Relic.* It was not a question.

Not the right one. I drifted closer. *Maybe if I knew what I was looking for?*

You will know it, just as you knew it once before, but for different reasons.

I knew it! I wanted to shout, but instead, my light flickered manically. *I did find a Relic before I died. Is that what killed me? Was it a blood Relic like the shard in Dugal's study? Wait.* I paused, a thought occurring suddenly. *Was it the shard?*

Ellory shook her head. *You were poisoned, Lenora. You know that.*

There was no Relic. Her light brightened and faded quickly. *But yes, you knew of one once.*

Which one?

Keep looking, but hurry—

Just tell me, Ellory. Please?

I cannot. You are getting closer.

Is that why you sent Oliver to check on us?

Perhaps. Perhaps Oliver went on his own. Patience was never his strong suit.

I groaned, remembering his words the day we met. He wanted to be useful, so the Guardians kept him around. Nosey spirit. I shook my head and turned back to the matter at hand. *Does Fleur know which Relic we need?*

She ... does ... but she doesn't realize it yet.

But you know why, don't you? Just like you know Fleur and me. We're connected, aren't we? I persisted, unwilling to give up the thread. Wishing she would tell me something useful.

Ellory turned, drifting further into the Lobby. I followed, not caring if she wanted me to. Guardians never spoke of their past. Some say the Soulkeepers erased their memories like they did mine, but instead of replacing them, they were adrift with only their purpose to guide them.

The Guardian paused, her light dimming, and looked back at me. I hesitated, curiosity illuminating my light.

I know many, Lenora. Fleur is but one. Her light darkened, erasing her momentary irritation.

Please, Ellory. Talk to me. Urgency ebbed around me. I needed to know.

I know what is needed. Like you.

Ellory was lying. Her vagueness a cover-up for what, I didn't know ... yet. Is that why she mentored me? Because of my connection to Fleur? My light pulsed. Did Ellory know Fleur in life? Was she part of this? Is that it?

I know what is needed, she repeated, her light still.

I stared, chastened by her tone.

Use your time here wisely. There are many gates open to you.

What do you mean? I twisted, eyeing the tree's core and the portals carved into it.

Ellory's gaze met mine. Her face beamed bright white, illuminating the delicate slant of her eyes. Her form was calm once again. My light wavered under her scrutiny—the need to question her fading with each second.

You are not incapable, Lenora. You're getting closer. Go. Seek what you need. Fleur will be waiting.

Her words echoed around me, propelled by something more than wisdom. *You mean I can leave Fleur?* I wondered, excitement rippling my light.

When needed, and only to aid.

Ellory stared at me, and I wondered what color her eyes were in life. I imagined them warm hazel, curling above a soft smile—full-lipped, softening the harsh angles of her face. The certainty of that image surprised me. I turned away, unable to look at the cold, mouthless light she had become. The Soulkeepers took more than her memories when they cultivated her; they took her bloom.

Go, Lenora. She nodded.

I drifted toward the gate beside us, its light orange instead of Fleur's purple. I didn't look back as I crossed.

Wind tore at me, propelling me forward, and I wished I could feel its slap against my flesh. It stopped abruptly, and silence descended. I crossed into a room bathed in shadows, hesitating as the clouds shifted and the moon's ethereal glow filtered through the windows lining the back wall of Opal Barlow's living room.

THIRTY-ONE

FLEUR

"Opal didn't do it, Fleur." Theda crossed her arms over her chest.

They sat alone in the living room. The amber glow from the table lamp illuminated the curves of Theda's face. She wore her curly black hair in a knot at her nape, baby hairs scattered and twisted, framing her face—softening her hard glare. Fleur sucked in a breath and resisted the urge to reach out, to feel her smooth skin. She wanted to pull Theda close and tell her she was right, to stop the ravine from deepening between them.

Instead, she sat still, her fingers pulling at the hem of her sweater.

Fleur couldn't give her what she wanted. Opal hadn't given them the whole truth, and she couldn't just ignore it.

"I'm not saying she did, but she lied. That's something to look into," Fleur said, daring to rest her hand on Theda's arm.

"How do you know she lied? Is that a new talent? Are you a lie detector now?" Theda struggled to keep her voice level.

"Lenora read her aura."

"The ghost read her aura?" Theda blanched.

"Yes. Look—"

"No. No. No." Theda shook her head. "I'm tired. You and the ghost can continue, but I'm out."

"Theda ..."

"What? What do you want from me? You just keep accusing everyone—that's not how it's done, Fleur. Opal is innocent. She loved Lenora—cared for her like a daughter. Why would she kill her?"

Fleur bit her lip. Theda identified with the connection Opal had with Lenora. A surrogate mother. A friend. Theda understood those emotions keenly and would advocate for Opal to her dying breath if she could.

Just as she did with her aunt after her mother died.

"I'm just saying there might be more to the story."

"Then let the police manage it. Javier didn't think she did it, not until you convinced him." Theda pulled her arm away and scooted to the edge of the sofa.

"Javier sent me to question her, Theda. He wanted my input. Someone's life is on the line. I couldn't just ignore Opal's half-truths."

Theda shook her head and stood. "You're right. Someone's life is on the line, but not Lenora's. She's dead, Fleur. If you continue with this, the only life on the line is Opal's." She tilted her head toward Fleur and pressed her lips together.

"This isn't the same—"

"No. You don't get to tell me that. It is the same. Opal did nothing but love and care for Lenora—she saved her after her family died. I know Opal isn't Alma, but damn it, Fleur, Opal isn't your father either. Don't punish her for your baggage."

Fleur closed her mouth and leaned back, her heart pounding in her ears. That was a low blow, one Fleur never expected Theda to take. She stared at Theda, unsure how to continue. Her father abandoned her, maybe not physically, but the hurt was the same. And unlike Theda and Lenora, Fleur had nowhere to turn. Seeing him in that photo was like a slap, jarring her awake, but it didn't change the fact that Opal lied—not just about knowing Arik. She shook her head, a bitter laugh escaping as she turned from Theda's furious glare.

"Maybe you're right," Fleur began, choosing her words carefully. "But the only way I'll know is if I ask more questions ... if the *police* dig a little deeper."

Theda wasn't backing down. "Bullshit."

"What do you want from me, Theda?" Fleur asked, swallowing back the tears building in her throat. "I told you how this would go. I was honest, and you've done nothing but fight me."

Theda toyed with her bracelet, twisting the slender gold rope around her finger. Her face softened, but her body was still taut. Fleur wished she would sit back down and discuss this at the same level. She tilted her head up, her gaze meeting Theda's.

"I don't know what I want." Theda's lip trembled. "I feel ... I don't know, like, we're not just us anymore—like someone has pulled the seam tying us together, and I'm the only one trying to mend it."

Fleur's heart clenched, dropping into her stomach. Her gift had brought nothing but loneliness—hurting everyone around her. She wouldn't let that happen again. Fleur offered her a sad smile and patted the sofa beside her. Theda closed her eyes, releasing the tension in her shoulders as she sat down.

"We're still us, Theda. I'm not going anywhere, I'm yours, and you're mine, OK? Do you want me to stop? I'll stop—for us."

Theda sniffed and leaned into Fleur. "Would you?"

Her heart dropped further, and Fleur nodded. Regret webbed around her—regret that she was letting Lenora down, regret that she had put her hope in Theda and was still shut down. It's not Theda's fault she couldn't understand—it was Fleur's for laying the burden of understanding on her delicate shoulders. "I'll talk to Lenora when she gets back."

Theda draped her arm around Fleur's shoulders. She leaned closer, tucking her head into the crook of Fleur's neck. "Thank you."

Fleur swallowed and tightened her arms around her. Had she expected too much from Theda? Tears filled her eyes, and Fleur blinked, afraid they would fall—afraid of tucking all the parts of herself she had given freely back into their dark corners. She wasn't the only one with dark corners—Theda kept hers well hidden, but Fleur knew they were there.

Fleur only knew half of the story, but she understood Theda's unspoken words. She felt Theda's heart race beneath her hand and heard her whispered fears. Heka Okan died of a drug overdose when Theda was thirteen, leaving her in the hands of her stepfather. Rick was her mother's dealer. He doled out whatever barbiturates he could get his hands on to whoever could pay. He cared little for Theda but enjoyed the money he garnished from the state to care for her. Theda didn't speak of her fear or the man responsible. Her anguish was her own—she survived and never looked back.

Fleur pressed a kiss into Theda's forehead, cursing herself. She was so involved with the mystery she didn't consider how it would affect Theda.

Theda exhaled and tightened her arms around Fleur.

She would end it, Fleur told herself, and then they would figure out how to rethread the seams she had so callously torn.

THIRTY-TWO

LENORA

Moonlight cascaded over the loveseat that, only a few hours earlier, Fleur and Theda had sat on. It was strange, listening to someone relay my life in such vague terms, but Opal's words were all I knew of myself, and I lapped them up like a hungry puppy.

Then her aura changed, muddied—revealing her deception. I agreed with Theda, Opal couldn't have done it, but my instinct centered on that change, and I knew she was omitting something—something important—something I needed to know.

I drifted around the room. It looked innocent—almost bare of memories. Framed photographs sat on the side table—Opal and Henry, selfies taken in the greenhouse, in front of the sign for Barlow's Blooms. Opening day? A pothos trailed its limbs over a bookshelf, covering the ledge with its variegated leaves. I skimmed the books behind—Edgar Allan Poe, Charlotte Bronte, Anne Radcliffe, Shirley Jackson, Daphne du Maurier—classics, the same books she told us earlier I had loved.

I turned, fluttering down the hallway past the dining room. The table and four chairs all but filled the small space. Walls covered in watercolors rather than family photos.

A loud snore burst through the silence, followed by a stream of mutters. Henry, I guessed as I drifted up the stairs. Three rooms branched off the narrow landing. I entered the one closest. It was an office. Two desks sat head to head at the center. Bookshelves covered the wall opposite a stretch of windows. I hovered over the desks. It was easy to see which was Henry's—he had multiple computers set up and an ergonomic keyboard. Beside the second computer screen sat a well-worn tennis ball imprinted with the lines of his fingers—a stress ball of sorts, I assumed, and looked to the other desk.

A single closed laptop sat on a stack of hard-covered books—textbooks on botany, urban horticulture, and soil science. A note-book lay open to a page of scrawled notes bullet pointing to different climate changes and how to adapt in various cases. Opal's hand-writing slanted dramatically, making her cursive difficult to read. I drifted back, eyeing the books lining the built-in behind her desk until my gaze landed on the center shelf.

Understanding Modern Poisons, the title read. Beside it, the *Apothecary's Guide to Poison* and *Herbs that Kill.*

I clutched at the phantom beat of my heart.

Opal studied and knew how to administer poison.

Dear God ... was that what she omitted? Her knowledge of the drug that killed me?

I backed out of the room and down the stairs, my light blurring in the hazy moonlight. There was something more. Knowledge was one thing, but was it enough to lie? I suppose it would make sense to omit, considering I was poisoned, but if she was innocent, wouldn't it have been better to come clean? That she kept her knowledge a secret was enough to draw suspicion.

The room seemed darker than before, shadows thickened the corners, but I paid them no mind as I moved closer to the fireplace.

Moonlight beamed through the window, highlighting the painting above the mantle. The iris I painted in life.

Irises meant courage and hope—Opal thought they suited me.

Courage. My light flickered, paling in the moon's bright glow.

Shadows curled around me as I drew closer to the painting, bathed in moonlight. Everything faded—everything but the painting.

I leaned in, my light filtering through the frenzy of atoms—I don't know what I thought I'd find. Something more than the bold brushstrokes and splatter of color—something deeper.

A safe. Behind the painting.

I sunk deeper. The buzz of molecules filled my head, pushing and pulling at my essence as if I was something tangible.

The safe was empty except for a small bottle. Square amber glass with a narrow neck opening—and old apothecary vial. Unlabeled. I moved closer, wishing I could touch it, smell it ... when a small sticker on the back caught my eye.

0.5 ml to end.

To end what? My life?

I pulled back. My light dimming. Was this the poison that killed me? Then ... that would mean Opal—I blanched, shaking my head. No. Opal couldn't have done it. She loved me. She said she loved me.

I needed to get to Fleur. She would know what to do. She could talk to Opal. My head spun as I turned from the painting, its light now vanished.

I blinked, barely making out the room. Where was the moonlight? Behind a cloud? Fear crept into me, darkening my aura. Something was wrong.

Shadows swarmed closer, dripping like ink onto the hardwood floor.

Grima. They wove in a clustered tangle. Pitch-black bodies pressed forward as their smoke drifted around me. My light darkened, dragging against the hardwood—heavy with failure. Opal. Sato. My parents—Edgar. I was alone, even in death. Needles pierced and prodded like surgeons digging through my glow to the fleshy soul within. I slapped at them, struggling against the hollowness. Wave after wave of hopelessness crashed into me, pulling my brittle pieces.

I needed light. Scanning the room, I rushed to the window, praying there was enough glow to hold them at bay.

My vision grew murky, the edges blurring, and I retreated— tumbling through the window and out of the house, the hum of atoms shaking me from the sorrow. I escaped into the warmth of the greenhouse, my light struggling to hold my essence. I inched closer to the grow lamps, desperate to absorb their glow. Courage. I flickered, strengthening my core.

I hovered over potted herbs and grasses. Shadows darkened the windows, slithering over the cool frames. Closing my eyes, I pulled my light inward like a ball of fire. I focused on the glimmer, envisioning a chrysalis and my birth.

Wings fluttered, kicking up the air and ruffling the leaves of the plants below me. It worked! I lifted my wings and landed on the stem of a purple bellflower, my gaze on the shadows, their bodies twisting against the glass.

I stretched out my wings, lifting myself up into the heart-shaped leaves, then down onto the edge of a white flower. Moonlight once again streamed through the windows.

The Shadelings were gone.

I turned in a circle from my perch, my light wavering with relief, when I saw it.

A cardboard sign sticking out of the soil, naming the herb above me.

Belladonna.

THIRTY-THREE

FLEUR

leur!

It was too early for this. Fleur groaned and curled closer to Theda, pulling the comforter over her shoulders.

Fleur! Wake up! I found it. The poison that killed me.

One eye popped open, then the other. Lenora hovered beside her bed, her light beaming like waves of moonlight over the room. Fleur lifted her head and blinked at her.

I thought that'd get you up. Lenora smiled and drifted to the door. *C'mon.*

This had better be good. Fleur removed her arm from Theda's waist, stilling as she moaned and turned on her side, a light snore bubbling forth. Fleur rolled off the side of the bed, tugging her over-sized T-shirt down as she straightened and slipped her feet into the knit slippers Alma made last year for Christmas. Her heart pounded as she tiptoed down the short hall into the living room. She would tell Lenora she was done—her stomach flipped with the mere thought. Fleur pressed her hand to her abdomen and took a deep breath. She didn't want to quit, but she didn't want to lose Theda either ... She didn't know what to do, and she hated it.

"What's going on? What did you find?" Fleur whispered as she shuffled into the kitchen and poured day-old coffee into the mug on the counter. She should clean it first, Theda would hate that she didn't, but Theda wasn't here.

I investigated Opal's house.

"What!" Fleur's voice rose, and she glanced to the hallway, listening for movement from beyond the bedroom door.

You're not the only one who can be productive, you know.

"But I thought you had to stay with me when in this realm?" Fleur narrowed her eyes and took a sip of the cold coffee.

So did I, but Ellory—

"Ellory?" Blood drained from Fleur's face. It could be a common name, she told herself, ignoring the memories that sparked and clawed at her skin.

She's a Guardian. Lenora peered at her, her light drawing her closer. *I think she knows you.*

Fleur clutched the mug and took a sip. The bitter coffee coated her throat. Breathe, Fleur scolded herself. She wouldn't—couldn't—think of this now. She turned to Lenora, pushing her past behind her.

But memories are not as easily dismissed. The sound of laughter rang in her ears like a delicate tinkling of bells. Her mother laughing—her parents happy within the walls of the Harkyn manse. Her family home, alive with benevolent spirits. A family of mediums living in harmony with the dead—they were all gone now. Dead, but for her uncle, alone in the now crumbling manse.

Fleur? What's wrong? Lenora's voice was distant and laced with worry.

Fleur inhaled the scent of strawberries and summer dew, the tingling warmth of the sun off the eastern sea. Warmth carried over the cliffs on a balmy wind, a gift from the goddesses to ease the spirits.

Gods, no. Fleur blinked. Lenora's light faded as the vision slammed into her.

She was a child. Her body, soft and malleable as she climbed the cliff and crags of her home. Bathed in delicious freedom, Fleur stretched her arms high above her head and faced the setting sun as if daring it to descend. Fireflies flickered and wove through the moss-covered rocks, mingling with scattered spirits, their lights twinkling like thousands of dying stars. Her father called for her, his voice echoing through the spirits until it reached her. A summons to her mother's side.

Her mother smelled of cinnamon. Fleur sat at her bedside, clutching her hand. Her skin was smooth, like parchment, and just as brittle. Fleur grasped at her fingers, fighting a helplessness she couldn't understand.

Death wasn't an end to a family of mediums, but Ellory Harkyn wasn't given the Soulkeepers' choice. Instead, she was taken to the Inbetween, leaving her daughter alone to struggle with her developing magick.

Cinnamon laced with the putrid air of decay.

Fleur stifled a cry, swallowing back the bile in her throat. Her hold on the mug tightening until her knuckles whitened.

Did you just have a vision? Lenora asked, drifting closer, her eyes wide with curiosity.

"Yeah, kind of." Fleur shook her head, determined to push her memories back into the locked box in the pit of her stomach.

Lenora considered her, her gaze sweeping over Fleur. *It was Ellory, wasn't it?*

Fleur shrugged. "Doesn't matter. Tell me what you found at Opal's."

Lenora looked skeptical, and Fleur worried she may pepper her with more questions about her vision. *Ellory told me I could move freely, but only to aid you. She said to seek what I need, so I went through the gate and found myself in Opal's house.*

She didn't like hearing her mother's name. Fleur pressed her lips together and tried to focus. How was any of this possible? Lenora could shape-shift, lost her memories, and didn't attract gnats. And now she was free to roam? "What kind of spirit are you?"

Lenora looked down at her hands hidden within the folds of light. *I don't know. I'm still learning what I am. Ellory said my death was unfinished and that they chose me for more, like her.*

"*Stop* saying her name." Fleur bit out the words like poison on her tongue. "Sorry. I'm a little tense. Just call her the Guardian, OK?"

Lenora flickered, her light tinged gray. *Sure. Sorry.*

"Opal's house?" Fleur prompted.

There's a safe behind the iris painting over her fireplace. It holds a vial of … well, I don't know what, but it looks ominous. Also, she is studying poison. She had books about different poisonous herbs all over her office, and … Lenora paused, her light coloring red. *She's growing belladonna in her greenhouse.*

"Holy shit." Fleur didn't know what to say. This was huge. Opal wasn't just omitting something; she was hiding the murder weapon. Fleur straightened and set down the mug. "We have to tell Javier—" She broke off, her promise to Theda echoing in her ears.

This would crush Theda. Fleur's heart splintered, and she hung her head. She couldn't just ignore something like this. Theda was right. She held Opal's life in her hands, just as Opal had with Lenora. Difference was, Fleur wasn't casting judgment, wasn't playing God with someone's life. She had evidence—damning evidence and turning it in to the police was the responsible thing to do.

Fleur? Lenora fluttered closer, as if she could sense her heart cracking.

Fleur lifted her head and frowned. "I have to tell Javier," she repeated, her words giving her courage.

Lenora nodded, her glow returning to white.

"Are you OK?" Fleur studied the spirit. This wasn't just about Theda. This woman—a woman who had protected Lenora as a child, who comforted her, a woman like a mother to her—possibly killed her.

No. I didn't want to find this. I didn't think Opal was capable of this, but ... She wavered. *I don't know how to feel. I don't know Opal or what our relationship was like, only the stories she told us, and they could have been lies.* Her words grew more staccato as she spoke. She looked at Fleur, her luminescence fading. *I'm tired of only having a secondhand account of my life.*

"Fleur? Did you start the coffee?" Theda's voice drifted down the hall.

Fleur bit her lip and rolled her shoulders. This was it. The moment she first knowingly lied to Theda. She moved down the hall and slipped back into their bedroom. Theda sat up. Her nightgown slipped, revealing the gentle curve of her shoulder. Fleur closed the distance between them and kissed her, praying Theda never discovered what she was about to do.

"Mmm, good morning to you, too." Theda smiled, kissing her back.

"I have a few errands to run." Fleur stepped away, grabbing her jeans from the floor. She pulled them on, tucking her nightshirt into them. "Viola has a list—it wouldn't be Thanksgiving without Viola's list." She hated how easily the lie rolled off her tongue.

Theda laughed. "She's getting an early start, huh?" She slid to the edge of the bed and reached for her robe. "I guess I should too. The yams won't make themselves."

Fleur stuffed her phone in her pocket before grabbing the fuzzy black sweater from the hook by the door and putting it on. "I won't be long. Don't toast the marshmallows without me."

Theda pressed a kiss to her forehead and moved to the bathroom. "Never."

She waited until the door closed before moving back into the front room. Lenora waited, her light throbbing with anticipation. *You didn't tell her.*

Fleur shook her head, moved to the front door, and grabbed her leather jacket from the closet. "C'mon."

THIRTY-FOUR

FLEUR

The Subaru idled at the red light. It was still dark out, making it before seven—too early to be wandering the streets on Thanksgiving morning. But she wasn't wandering. She was on a mission. Fleur flexed her fingers on the wheel and tried to focus on the empty road ahead of her. Her body tingled with nerves.

She didn't know which thought was more disturbing—that Lenora's Guardian had her mother's name or that she was about to betray Theda's trust. If, by some strange thread of fate, Ellory was her mother, and she was the Guardian responsible for Lenora seeking her out ... Fleur gritted her teeth—if that was true, then she couldn't turn her back on the case. Stop it, Fleur, she scolded. Her mother was dead, gone to the goddess feast in the Great Tree, her father told her himself.

Fleur frowned. Arik would have told her anything to ease her pain that day. Tears welled in her eyes, blurring the red light. She blinked, hating how easily she wept lately.

But ... if Ellory was her mother's spirit, then to honor her, she must betray Theda.

It was too much. This entire case grew bigger and more intrusive every moment. First, Griffin has a Relic, then the photo of Arik with Lenora, and now ... now her mother was Lenora's spirit mentor?

The light turned green, and Fleur shifted, ignoring the chug and whine of the Subie's clutch. She turned into the East Precinct's parking lot, pulling into one of many empty spots.

Fleur clenched her fist, trying to stop her hand from trembling, then pulled the tarot deck from her pocket. The heft and flutter of the cards comforted her. Cutting the deck on her lap, Fleur shuffled them back together until her pulse calmed. She pulled the top card and took a breath.

Two of Wands. Inverted. Fleur groaned.

Even the cards told her she was a coward. Indecision, fear—choose a direction. Start your journey. Don't be afraid.

Aren't we going in? Lenora unfurled her light onto the red leather.

"I don't know yet."

What's wrong, Fleur?

"What makes you think something's wrong?"

Lenora shook her head. *I can read your aura, remember? You've been upset since I woke you. Is it because of your vision? Or Opal?*

Shit. Fleur groaned and pocketed her cards. "Truth?"

Please.

"Theda asked me to stop helping you last night."

Lenora was silent. Her light was colorless in the dim streetlamp.

"And I was going to. I'm sorry, Len, but I can't lose Theda ... I just can't."

Then why are we here? Lenora asked, turning to meet her eye.

Fleur released a shaky breath and stared out at the parking lot. "Tell me about Ellory." Damn it. She didn't want to ask that. Fleur sniffed. She didn't want to know, but she needed to.

She's a Guardian, has the ear of the Soulkeepers, and keeps the rest of us in line. Some think of them as our jailers, but Ellory isn't like that—

she's kind, I think she wants to help. She's different. I can sense it. Lenora paused and focused on Fleur. *She had hazel eyes in life, wide upturned eyes, didn't she? And dark gray hair, long—almost to her waist. Her voice is husky and soft ...*, she trailed off.

Fleur wiped at her eyes, wishing the tears would stop, and covered her face with her hands, choking on sobs straining against her throat. Her mother's voice, humming the lullaby as she put her to sleep, echoed in the back of her mind. She focused on the melody, the cadence of her mother pulling the blankets over her and pressing a kiss to her forehead.

She's trapped by the Soulkeepers, Fleur. They erased her memories like they did with me when they made her a Guardian, but she remembers you —I know it. Somehow, she knows you. Lenora's voice tore at Fleur's heart.

Ellory didn't make it to the Glorious Feast like Arik. They did not give her the choice. Fleur sniffed, gathering herself as she wiped her face on the sleeve of her coat. Her mother wasn't gone.

And she sent her Lenora.

This case wasn't *just* about Lenora or some damn Relic to stop the Grima assault. Fleur wanted to scream. No, this whole damn thing was about her, too. The impossibility of Theda's request surged within her. Even if she stopped ... the facts would still be there, waiting. The urge to run back to Theda and pull the blankets over her head overwhelmed her.

Fleur released a strangled laugh and shook her head. "Shit. Do you see now? What am I supposed to do?"

Lenora dimmed and wavered, her voice low. *You're going to tell Javier.*

"If I do that, I'll betray Theda."

It doesn't have to be one or the other. Talk to Theda. I'm sure she'll understand.

"No." Fleur sniffed. "She won't." She could turn around, go home —pretend none of this ever happened, just like she'd done her whole life.

But she knew it wouldn't work. Her threads were woven— Hemsut, the Goddess of Fate, ensnared her. Just as she had her mother all those years ago.

Lenora offered a smile. *I'm sorry, Fleur.*

"Me too."

Fleur zipped up her jacket and stuffed her phone in her pocket. "OK. Let's do this." She opened the car door.

Javier sat hunched over his computer screen, eating a burrito. Sauce dripped over the wrapper and down his hand onto the file open on his desk. Fleur didn't need to look at the logo stuck to the foil wrapper to know it was a Mojado burrito from El Camion. She paused at the bullpen's entrance, her gaze fixed on the tilt of his chin.

They met at a bar on University Avenue. She was finishing up her master's degree, and Javier was at the academy, following in his brother's footsteps—his brother, who was killed six months before. Fleur often wondered if Javier would have entered the police academy if Diego had lived. There was a restlessness in him that matched her own—tragedy shaped and molded him—a kindred soul to wander the earth with.

But he wasn't—the moment her truth was revealed, he ran.

And maybe she did, too ... a little.

Damn it, Fleur shook herself. She was a mess.

Fleur sniffed and wiped her nose with the back of her coat. Lenora beamed beside her as they wove around the scattered desks, most unattended.

Javier looked up. Noticing the sauce, he leaned back and cursed, setting the burrito carefully onto a napkin. Fleur smiled as he struggled to wipe the spill from the legal documents in front of him.

He continued to pat the stain with the damp paper towel as she sat down in the chair beside his desk, his eyes on his task. "Shouldn't you be pestering some cashier for cranberry sauce, or did Viola cut you free today?"

"There's still time."

He glanced up at her and frowned. "You look like shit. Everything OK?"

Fleur knew he saw the tension between her and Theda last night —he left as quickly as he could. She furrowed her brow and sighed, her gaze dropping to her hands. "Yeah, fine. Don't worry about me."

Javier shrugged and tossed the paper towel in the trash. "Suit yourself." He stared at her, his face softening. "I do worry, you know."

I told you he cared. Lenora looked smug.

Fleur scoffed and leaned back in the chair.

"I can't just dismiss a person from my mind because we're no longer together." He shrugged again and shook his head. "So"—he straightened in his chair—"why are you here at six forty-five on Thanksgiving morning?"

"Opal."

"What about her?"

"Did you look into her?"

"I'm in the process—why?"

"Did you find what she studied at university?"

Javier glanced at his computer screen. "Urban horticulture, botany ..."

Fleur sighed. This was like pulling teeth. "C'mon. Think. How was Lenora killed?"

"I'm not an idiot, Fleur. I see where you're going. So what? Did you find something?"

"No, not me ..."

Javier groaned. "You had the ghost investigate, didn't you?"

Lenora brightened beside her. *He doesn't have to be rude about it.*

"Just look in her greenhouse, OK?"

And behind the painting.

"And check behind the painting in her living room." Fleur nodded once and stood.

"Why so cryptic?" Javier asked, picking up his burrito.

Fleur shrugged again and nodded to his burrito. "Is that your Thanksgiving dinner?"

"More like breakfast. Don't worry about me, Harkyn." His mouth curved. "And thanks for the tip."

CHAPTER
THIRTY-FIVE

FLEUR

I t happened so fast. One minute, they were toasting Thanksgiving. The next, Theda was sliding on her coat, her face flushed with anger. Alma and Viola stunned, turkey steaming from the center of the table and tears streaming down Fleur's face.

They arrested Opal that afternoon.

Fleur wished she had the foresight to ask Viola not to mention the Khade murder, but she didn't, and Viola did ... and Theda knew what had happened before Fleur could say a word to defend herself.

Lenora flickered and dimmed, hovering beside the table.

Theda pulled open the door. "I should have known the ghost would win." The words dripped like poison as she slammed the door behind her.

"Fleur?" Alma's voice was soft, hesitant. "Honey, what's going on?"

Fleur turned to Theda's aunt, the woman Theda loved most in the world, and to her horror, a sob clogged her throat. She coughed, lifting her napkin to her face, and took a deep breath. Then another …

"Fleurie? What did I say?" Viola's wide eyes looked from Fleur to the door, and back again, her fingers clutched around her wineglass. "Did she know the Khade girl?"

Fleur shook her head.

She knew Theda would be upset if they arrested Opal, but she didn't expect the instant anger. She didn't expect Theda to storm out without saying a word. The hurt that flashed in her eyes stole Fleur's breath. She had betrayed Theda. She knew that the moment she spoke to Javier but didn't truly understand until the door slammed.

Alma stood and set her napkin on her plate. She wore her black hair braided and coiled, highlighting the slender curve of her neck. Alma was a graceful woman, small and birdlike but fierce like a raptor. Her piercing gaze landed on Fleur. "I'll go check on her."

All Fleur could do was nod.

Lenora brightened beside her chair. *Are you OK, Fleur?*

She sighed. No. She wasn't OK. Fleur looked to Viola. "Sorry to ruin your dinner, Vi."

Viola huffed and leaned back in her chair. "Hardly." She narrowed her eyes. "What's going on with you two?"

"Just a minor disagreement …"

"Cut the shit, Fleur." Viola's voice stung like a whip. "That was more than a minor disagreement."

Tell her, Fleur. It isn't fair to leave her in the dark.

The words rolled onto Fleur's tongue, but she bit them back. It wasn't the time. She looked at Lenora. The spirit hovered, idling beside Viola, her gaze expectant, and closed her eyes. She didn't want to tell Viola. Saying the words made her actions more real.

"I've never seen Theda so angry." Viola shook her head, her brows knit together in thought.

"Vi—"

"This is about the Khade case, isn't it? I know you're helping

Javier—research, you said, right? Theda didn't like that, did she?" Viola's gaze held steady.

"Something like that," Fleur mumbled, looking at her napkin.

The door opened, and Alma strolled back to the table. "I'm taking Theda home." She turned to Viola. "Sorry about this, Viola—I'll call you later."

Viola stood and hurried to Alma. They embraced Alma's gaze on Fleur as she tightened her arms around Viola.

"No worries, Alma. I hope everything is alright." Viola smiled as she walked her to the door.

Alma pulled on her puffer coat and draped Theda's scarf—the one Fleur gave her last Christmas, over her arm. Fleur wanted to race out the door, to pull Theda into her arms and beg her to listen—to explain why she did what she did, but her body froze to the chair.

Shaking her head, Alma opened the door and looked back at Fleur, her eyes softening. "Give her time, OK?"

Tears welled in Fleur's eyes, and she nodded at Alma. Was that it? Theda left ... left her—

"Fleur." Viola's voice was stern as she sat back down.

"Not now, Viola, OK?" Fleur pushed back from the table, blinking back the rush of tears that threatened to fall. She looked around for Lenora, but the spirit had vanished. She was a fool to think Theda wouldn't find out. What had she done? The weight of her decision tightened in her chest.

"Yes. Now." Viola sat back in her chair and stared at Fleur. "I won't say I'm not pleased that you and Javier have started talking again, but did you even consider Theda's feelings?"

Fleur groaned and turned away. She'd done nothing but consider Theda's feelings through this whole damn mess. She stood, tossing her napkin onto the table beside her still-full plate of turkey, green bean casserole, and yams—Theda's yams—and moved into the living room.

Viola had set the television to a crackling fire. It hissed and burned, enveloping the small room with imaginary warmth. Her gaze drifted over the fire to the bookshelves flanking the TV, filled with leather-bound volumes, aged and worn classics Arik had collected from various antique shops and flea markets. Photographs scattered over the shelves. Viola and Arik, Fleur and Arik, the three of them in front of Haystack Rock, on their annual family vacation to the Oregon Coast. There were no photographs of her and Viola. Nothing newer than five years ago—Viola had tried. She would pull out her phone and wrap her arm around Fleur, hoping that this time she would get a picture of the two of them to add to the collection, but Fleur always pulled away. Maybe that's what she did ... pull away. She did it from Arik, then Javier ... and now Theda.

Fleur bit back a sob and collapsed onto the velvet sofa across from the television. She wished the soft creamy fabric would suck her in, hide her from the choices she made, from the disappointment she was.

She forgot everything, but not you. Lenora's words echoed in her ears.

Her mother. The first to abandon her was also the one Fleur was most desperate to see. She spent her lifetime pushing all memories of her into the darkest, most cherished part of her heart. She wanted to keep them safe, but they withered, blocking her from the tenderest part of herself. Now they were free, free to beckon, and they ached like a bruise unable to heal.

Fleur didn't want to remember the life she had before. Nothing came of it but death and exile.

Viola sat down beside her, the sweetness of her perfume lingering with the scent of freshly baked pumpkin pie. Fleur crinkled her nose and leaned back. "I ruined everything."

"I doubt it's that bad."

Fleur snorted and turned to Viola. "She asked me to stop working on the case, and I told her I would, but then I discovered something ... something that I had a responsibility to tell Javier about ...," she trailed off, exhaling.

Viola reached out and folded Fleur's hand in hers. Her soft blue eyes studied her, weighing her words. "Did it have to do with the woman they arrested this morning?"

Fleur nodded. "But I didn't tell him. I just hinted that he should look at her greenhouse. I didn't think it would matter. If the police figured it out, then I wouldn't need to tell them. It was stupid."

"And you didn't talk to Theda about it?"

"I didn't want to worry her."

Viola pinned her with a stare. "Fleur, we both know that's not true."

Another sob bubbled up in her throat. Fleur swallowed and looked at the fire crackling on the TV screen.

"Then I opened my big mouth. See, gossip only makes problems," Viola muttered, tightening her hold on Fleur's hand, forcing her to look at her. "But if you had been honest, it wouldn't have been an issue."

Fleur grunted and rolled her eyes. "Thanks for the pep talk." She tried to pull her hand away, but Viola held fast.

"I'm not finished." Viola tugged on her hand, pressing it between both of hers. "Honesty will only serve a relationship so far—be honest about your feelings, about who you are, and you've done that, haven't you?"

"Yeah ... I thought she understood—"

"Understanding another person is harder than you think. You can't just tell them your truth and assume they understand it. Theda can't relate to who you are. She doesn't know what it's like to see what you've seen. Just as you can't relate to her experiences, but you both try, and that's what counts."

Fleur raised a brow, a flush creeping up her neck. Had she assumed Theda would understand? She was so determined not to make the same mistakes; she made new ones.

"I know your father wasn't honest with me," Viola murmured, turning to the fire. "But I knew who he was, even though he tried to hide it from me. I knew, but I'll never understand. Just like I'll never understand you."

Fleur sucked in a breath and stared at her. She knew? Her body tensed, and she sat up. "What did you know?" she asked carefully.

"Arik was horrible at secrets." Viola shook her head. "I always caught him talking to himself. At first, I thought he was just like everyone else. Hell, I talk to myself too, but never so animatedly. He wasn't talking to himself. He was having a conversation. I thought maybe it was from the trauma of your mother's death, but as time went on, I realized he could see a world I couldn't." She narrowed her gaze on Fleur. "Just like you."

Fleur didn't know what to say. Her body warmed, sweat beaded over her brow. Viola knew. Knew this whole time and said nothing. Fleur wanted to run from the room but held still, waiting for the judgment she knew would come.

Viola smiled sadly and leaned closer. "I waited for him to tell me. I thought it would be easier than confronting him. I didn't want him to deny it or tell me I was seeing things. I knew I wasn't, but I also knew how scared Arik's secret made him and how much he worried about you." She shrugged. "So, I went along with it. Pretended I didn't know that my husband and step-daughter could see ghosts."

"Vi—"

"I thought once Arik passed, maybe you'd say something, but your father instilled the same fear in you. When you and Javier broke up, I thought ... maybe?" She sighed. "I'm tired of waiting, Fleur."

"You know I can see ghosts." The words were alien on her tongue. "And you aren't scared?"

"Why would I be?" Viola tilted her head. "Did Theda know?"

"I told her from the beginning."

"Good." Viola exhaled as if everything had hinged on that question.

Tears welled up in Fleur's eyes, falling before she could wipe them away. She sniffed and pulled her hand back, surprised when Viola let her go. Viola knew and still cared about her ... the thought exploded like millions of stars in her chest, and her body relaxed. "You knew ..."

"I don't know all the details. Like the séance ..." She frowned. "I thought you'd get a kick out of all the fake mumbo jumbo, but there were actual spirits there, weren't there?" She paused and watched Fleur nod. "Damn. I should have known." She shook her head.

Fleur reached out and touched Viola's arm. "It's OK. I can handle myself."

"But something happened, didn't it?" Viola's blue eyes searched hers.

Fleur nodded. "A spirit found me."

"The one that possessed Madam Olga?"

"Yeah. I've been helping her."

Viola's eyes widened as realization dawned. "Lenora Khade!" Her hand pressed against her chest, and she glanced back to the table. "Theda knew?"

"Theda knows everything." Fleur closed her eyes. "Well, almost everything."

Viola inched closer. "What happened?"

"Lenora found belladonna growing in Opal's greenhouse, but Theda is convinced Opal's innocent." Fleur cringed. "I get it. I know Theda sees the same doting mother figure in Opal that she had in Alma. She took it personally, and I understand why, but when Lenora told me what she found, I couldn't just do nothing." Fleur couldn't bring herself to mention Ellory.

Viola tilted her head, a frown tickling the side of her mouth. Flour could almost hear her wheels turning. "I don't think that's it."

"What?"

"Theda's anger."

"What do you mean?"

Viola sighed and folded her arms over her chest. "I mean, sure, she's pissed that you were still working the case when she asked you to stop. But ... think about the reason she asked in the first place, huh?"

"Because of Opal. I told you." Fleur shook her head, not wanting to rehash it over and over again.

"No ..." Viola shook her head. "And maybe I'm projecting a little, but as the non-ghost-seeing member of a relationship, I'd say she's jealous."

Dammit. Fleur groaned, wishing the ache in her heart would fade. "The thing is ... she wanted me to take the case. Practically begged me, said it would be fun, but then was upset when everything I warned her about happened."

"Maybe she didn't understand what that meant for you, just like you didn't understand what that meant for her." Viola sighed.

Fleur pressed her eyes closed. Damn. Was Viola right? Was her defense of Opal more than what Fleur thought? Gods ... "Ah, no. I should have seen it. Dammit. I'm the worst."

"Of course not. Stop being dramatic."

"I tried to include her—"

"I'm sure you did. But you also did a lot without including her, am I right?"

Fleur hung her head and groaned. She didn't care if she was being dramatic. The whole thing felt dramatic—crushingly dramatic.

"Lenora Khade," Viola repeated, shaking her head. "Is that why you asked me if Arik knew the Khades?"

Fleur nodded. "We found a photograph of him and Lenora. It was ... surprising."

Viola shook her head and frowned. "He never told me. Why wouldn't he tell me?"

"I don't know. Vi. I can't imagine how they met or what Lenora wanted from him."

"You don't think Arik would reach out?"

"C'mon, Vi," Fleur scoffed. "You knew Dad. No way he sought her out."

Viola looked at her hands folded together in her lap. "Theda didn't know you talked to Javier, did she?" she asked, changing the subject.

Fleur shook her head, leaned closer to Viola. "Oh, Vi, I don't know what to do."

"I know." Viola wrapped her arm around Fleur's shoulder and squeezed. "We'll figure it out. I promise."

THE DREAM WAS OLD, but Fleur recognized its weightlessness. She was home.

The sunset was brighter, more orange—clouds curled and twisted around the sky as if fired from a Fey's bow. Fleur stood on the edge of the cliff, her toes gripping the edge as she tried to get as close to the sky as she could. Of all the Disir, the Fey were her favorite—warrior creatures—the Air Disir crafted the heavens, just as the Earth Sprites did the soil beneath her feet and the Water Nymphs in the ocean below her.

She could jump. One leap and she would fly, just like the Fey. Fleur hugged herself and lifted her head, the wind pressing against her skin.

"Fleur!"

The call twisted around the breeze, blossoming in her ear. Fleur turned, the wind pushing her back onto the mossy ground, back into the safety of the cliff. She stumbled, her arms rising to steady herself.

Beside her, a spirit fluttered, its light rippling in the wind like a banner. Fleur thought she knew all the Atua that dwelled on the Umbra Clyffes, but this one was new, more potent, and brighter than the rest.

"Did my father send you?" Fleur asked, brushing her hair out of her eyes. Fear cramped her stomach. "I'm not ready yet." The Legacy Council, comprised of the seven chieftains from each prominent family, wouldn't understand her vision—they would condemn her. Fleur heard enough whispered comments between her father and uncle to know that.

No one sent me. The spirit turned her face to the sun as if gathering strength from the rays.

"I don't recognize you." Fleur took a small step closer, wondering if the Atua had died recently.

I've changed. Like a moth, fresh from its chrysalis.

"What were you before?"

The spirit turned to her and smiled. *A caterpillar.*

Fleur giggled.

Go now, dearest. Your father is waiting.

The spirit moved closer, her features unfurling like a newly birthed petal. Her light flashed, and for a moment, Fleur could see beyond her luminescence to the woman she once was. She gasped, tears filling eyes that beheld the remains of a cherished memory.

Ellory's hazel eyes crinkled as she leaned forward and held out her hand. Less than flesh, but more than light. *I haven't left you, Fleur.*

Fleur reached out, her finger curling around the remains of a silky gray curl. She remembered its softness, and her heart swelled. "I thought you'd gone ..."

Not yet.

Fleur frowned and dropped her hand. "But you will."

"Fleur!"

Another call, deeper, more urgent. Her father.

It was time.

Fleur looked up at her mother, her light once again casting her features in shadow. "Don't leave me, Mutta. I'm scared."

Ellory dimmed. A knowing smile washed over her face. *You are brave, Fleur.*

"I'm not." Fleur's face crumbled as tears spilled from her eyes. "I'm not, Mutta."

Ellory nodded. *You are.*

"Do you have to go?"

Her mother looked up into the setting sun, her light mingling with the translucent rays. *I'll always find you, dearest.*

The corners of the dream curled as if set aflame. Fleur gasped, calling out until her throat ached. Darkness seeped in, spilling over the fading light.

Fleur moaned, pulling herself into reality as a drowning creature might a sandy shore. No, no, no ... It couldn't be real. That wasn't how the dream went—her mother wasn't there. Was she?

The hall light flicked on, and for a moment, Theda's name echoed in her throat, and her world was still whole.

"Fleurie? Hon? You OK out here?" Viola crept down the hall, wrapping an oversized cardigan over her chest. Her feet were bare. "I thought I heard a cry."

"I'm fine, Vi. It was just a dream." Fleur pressed her face back into the pillow.

Viola paused at the edge of the room. Her shoulder-length brown hair was up in a ponytail, making her look far younger than her fifty-odd years. She glanced at the darkened kitchen, then back to Fleur before shaking her head. "I'll make some tea."

Fleur didn't want tea.

She wanted to speak to her mother again.

The splash of water filling the kettle loosened the remains of Fleur's dream, spilling them into the funnel of forgotten things. She tucked her head further under the blanket, holding tight to the thread of dialogue, to the sound of her mother's voice one last time.

Had it been a dream? Or a memory?

Fleur whimpered as she relived the splintered images. It was no vision—the cadence was too familiar. She remembered her father calling her back to the house, the warmth of the sun on her pale skin. Minutes later, she was before the council, being assessed and exiled. The vision, her first, still bitter on her tongue. But she had been alone in her memory—hadn't she?

"What was your dream about?" Viola asked from the kitchen.

Fleur pulled down the blanket and groaned. It had to have been a dream. She peered over the back of the sofa at Viola moving around the kitchen, a box of chamomile clutched in her hand. "It was nothing."

"Dreams are never nothing. You know that."

"I don't want to talk about it."

"Yeah, but you should. It will help you remember."

Fleur sat up and ran her hands through her tangled hair. "Remember what?"

"Your mother."

Fleur gasped, her gaze snapping to Viola. "What did you say?"

"You were dreaming about your mother, right? I heard you cry out. You said, 'Mutta.'" Viola shrugged and set two mugs on the counter beside the kettle.

"I said that?"

"You used to cry out when you were little. 'Mutta,' you'd shout, waking yourself up, then you'd cry. Arik would always hold you until you fell back to sleep." Viola looked up, meeting Fleur's eye. "You still have the same dream?"

Fleur shook her head. "I've never dreamed about her before."

The kettle whistled, and Viola lifted it off the burner, pouring the steaming water into each mug. "Or maybe you've just never remembered until now." She set the kettle down. "I wonder why?"

Fleur knew why. She knew with a certainty reserved for the most ardent of believers—

Lenora.

CHAPTER
THIRTY-SIX

LENORA

The light leading into the Lobby dimmed from warm amber to dull yellow as I passed through. I shivered, my body remembering the sensation of cold ... of emptiness. Something was wrong.

Spirits gathered together, their auras tinged red with anxiety. Between them, Guardians wove calmly, brightening their light in comfort as a flutter of wrinkled brown leaves and cedar fronds fluttered around them.

Had the Grima gotten closer?

I searched the clusters for any sign of Ellory. My light flickered with impatience. A collective gasp echoed around me as a wave of shadow passed over the canopy, darkening the Lobby's warmth. I cursed. Wishing for the thousandth time I knew anything that could help us.

Fleur knows which Relic will aid us. You must convince her to find it. Ellory hovered behind me, a tinge of pink frustration fading from her aura. She nodded to the canopy, its branches sparse and vulnerable.

238

Most Guardians have joined forces with the Soulkeepers to ward them off from above, but they can only last so long. We need that Relic.

Then tell me what it is and how to find it. Please, Ellory. I can get it, but I need to know what it is.

I can't. It isn't our way. This is your journey. I cannot carry it for you.

Dammit. Even now? Even as the Shadelings grow closer? Ellory! Just tell me!

The Guardian shook her head and turned away. I followed, studying her. The likeness was there now that I knew to look for it. How could I have missed the slant of her nose and the same round eyes? Fleur had the same curve of her cheekbone, but her face was rounder, softer than Ellory's.

I looked pointedly at the Guardian spirit. *You should have told me who Fleur was.*

I conceal nothing. Secrets are forbidden.

So that's how it was. Ellory's will was still her own, but at what cost? Should the Soulkeepers discover her strength, they would steal it from her.

You are close. You must hurry. Ellory's gaze flickered from me to the higher branches. The air was still, like a city street in the wee hours of a winter morning. *They grow more daring.*

Hurry? Why? Why me? If you know where the Relic is, why can't you get it?

It is not my fate to do so. It is yours.

But that's ridiculous! You're putting all this on me when you could easily get it yourself? Why Ellory?

You must finish what you've started. Ellory's tone hardened, her aura flaring red. *Don't you think I would end this if I could? The terror—* she broke off, raising her chin. *It's your path, Lenora. Not mine.*

I could taste the venom in her words. My light flickered, wondering if I had pushed her too far with my questions. All this talk of fate was biting at me. I wanted to ask more but knew, like everything else, Ellory would withhold.

The time will come for you to ask, but not yet. Ellory's light was calm, fading from red back to indigo. She met my gaze, her composure in place once again. *You and Fleur have a common enemy.*

Opal? But how?

Not Opal. Talk to Fleur.

I wanted to grit my teeth, but instead, my light flickered with frustration. Fleur wanted out. *She doesn't want to talk to me.*

She will. Ellory's light calmed. *This is unfinished. Opal was just the first step. Accusing her will lead you to the truth.*

I didn't want to know what she meant. I was too afraid of the answer.

If Opal wasn't my killer, then Fleur had sacrificed everything for nothing ... and I led her to it. Ellory wanted me to investigate Opal. She opened the gate for me. Color drained from my light. I found the poison but no evidence that Opal had used it on me. Maybe the police found something—they would have had to, to arrest her, wouldn't they?

There is no fault here, Lenora. You have merely mistaken the middle of the story for the end. Keep searching. Ellory flickered and gestured to the gate.

It flared to life as if waiting for her summons.

I hesitated, my words heavy against my light. *How do you know Opal didn't do it?*

Do you really have to ask?

Dammit! Just tell me! Something! Anything! Please?

I have told you what I can. The fate of this realm rests on you and Fleur.

I wanted to scream. Instead, my light flickered, and I turned from her, my light drawn to the lavender gate ahead.

You will succeed, Lenora. You have to.

THIRTY-SEVEN

FLEUR

"Fleur! Honey, wake up." The sofa dipped as Viola sat beside her.

Fleur groaned and pulled the blanket over her head. The bitter aroma of coffee tickled her nose, mingling with the sizzle and pop of bacon frying. She didn't want to get up yet. She didn't want to face a world without Theda, a world mired by the weight of her actions.

Last night felt like a dream, a dream within a dream. First, Theda stormed out, then Viola's revelation, all followed by ... her mother. Damn. It was too much. Way too much to deal with right now. Viola said she dreamed about her mother when she was little ... Gods. What else did Hemsut have in store for her?

Sitting in the dimly lit living room sipping tea in the wee hours of the morning with Viola had been nice. Tears sprung into Fleur's eyes, and she wiped them on the blanket. Viola didn't question her need for silence. She simply handed Fleur a mug of tea and sat quietly in the armchair across from her. Silence from Viola was rare. Fleur sniffed. Maybe she had judged Viola too harshly all these years.

Viola nudged the blanket. "Fleurie? There's no time for moping." Viola peeled the blanket from Fleur's face and held up the newspaper. "Look."

Khade Housekeeper Released, Charges Dropped.

The font was large and blaring, trumpeting her mistake.

Fleur moaned, a string of curses crowding the surrounding air.

Opal Barlow was innocent.

"It says the vial they evaluated was an antidote, um, for ... Atropa belladonna," Viola read aloud. "She was studying the effects and how to extract something called atropine—oh, I've heard of that. How interesting—" She cut off, looking Fleur in the eye. "She didn't do it, Fleur."

Fleur's stomach dropped. She was wrong. Again. Only this time, it had cost her everything. She pushed the newspaper away and fell back against the pillow. That's it—she was done playing detective. Fleur didn't care that her dead mother's spirit wanted her to continue. This case was as much about her as Lenora and Fleur were done. She didn't want to know anymore. All she did was make a mess out of everything.

"That's great, Vi," Fleur muttered, turning toward the back of the sofa. "Just great."

Viola nudged her with the newspaper. "You should go talk to Theda. Tell her you're sorry. Tell her you were wrong."

Fleur snorted. "She knows, Vi. That headline is only going to piss her off more."

"So?"

"So, I screwed up. Big time. It's gonna take more than groveling to get her back."

"You don't know that."

Fleur grunted.

"Send her flowers," Viola suggested, moving back into the kitchen. "A dozen roses every day, like they do in the movies."

"Life isn't like the movies."

Tongs scratched against the frying pan as Viola removed the bacon, draining it on a paper towel while she poured eggs into the pan. "Stop it, Fleur. This isn't the end of you two. After all, you both have been to each other? No way. It's just a setback."

Fleur opened her mouth, dozens of arguments clogging her throat, when her phone buzzed.

"Well? Who is it?" Viola asked as she stirred the scrambled eggs.

Gods. Viola was getting bossier with each moment.

Fleur groaned loudly and pushed herself into a sitting position, tucking the blanket around her legs. She wasn't ready to leave the sofa just yet. Her phone buzzed again. Fleur eyed it, her heart thudding in her ears. It could be Theda. Gods. Please make it Theda.

Javier's text flashed on the screen. *Saw the paper? Good try.*

Fleur closed her eyes and inhaled, envisioning her lungs expand and contract. Calm. She would not respond in anger. She would not cringe in embarrassment. She would stand by her theory. It was an excellent theory. How was she to know of Opal's venture into toxicology?

You and Theda, OK? Another text from Javier brightened her screen.

Her hand shook with the urge to throw the phone across the room.

"Fleur?" Viola scooped eggs onto a plate and set it on the counter. "You need to eat."

She exhaled and turned off her phone. "I'm coming."

Viola smiled and pushed the plate closer to the edge of the counter. "Was that Theda? I told you she'd come around."

"It wasn't her," Fleur grumbled as she stood, wrapping the blanket around her shoulders.

Viola raised a brow and poured coffee into an owl-shaped mug.

The mug Fleur made in pottery class her junior year in high school—the mug her father used every morning until his death. Fleur paused, her feet suddenly unable to move. How long had it been since she saw it? Clasped in Arik's hand, shivering as a cough spasmed through him. She had visited at Viola's urging. The doctors didn't think he had much time. Fleur didn't want to visit. She didn't want to see her once-imposing father diminish, but she did. Fleur arrived in a flurry of anger days after her relationship with Javier ended. She was full of accusations and bitterness. Arik just sat there, grasping the pottery owl, sipping peppermint tea. She wanted him to argue, to see some of his old spark—anything but the frail man he had become.

That was the last time she saw him and the damn mug.

And now it sat in front of her, coffee steaming from its brim, milk, and sugar in small containers beside it. Daring her to drink.

"No?" Viola shook her head. "The two of you are too stubborn for your own good."

"I told you. She won't call." Fleur picked up her fork and prodded her eggs, ignoring the mug.

"Well?" Viola took a bite of bacon. "What are we going to do about it?"

"We?" Fleur nearly choked.

Viola nodded and opened her mouth, only to close it again and glance around the room. "Are we alone?"

Fleur rolled her eyes. "Yeah."

Viola's shoulders drooped, and she nodded. "Good. Now then, first things first ... are you finished with this murder nonsense?"

"It's not nonsense."

"Fleur, you're no detective, and while I enjoyed seeing you and Javier talking again, I think you should leave the detecting to him."

"I was helping. Lenora and I were working together ..." Fleur sighed, suddenly wishing she could vanish like Lenora did earlier.

"Lenora Khade ... it still blows my mind that she's the ghost that found you."

"Right? Would you have turned her down?"

Viola frowned and scooped up a forkful of eggs. "That's not the point."

Fleur huffed. "That's exactly the point. The case is crazy, and for a minute, I thought I had a chance, a real chance at helping her—" *Helping us.* The words popped into her head, and Fleur paused, her failure piercing her heart.

And you will. Fleur. It isn't over yet.

Lenora hovered beside her, bright white with optimism.

Fleur shook her head. "No way, Len. I've screwed up enough. Opal's innocent. Theda's gone. I'm a laughingstock, not a detective."

Viola gasped. "She's back?"

She knows? Lenora colored yellow and drifted to Viola. *How does she know?*

Fleur smiled at Viola before turning to Lenora. "She's always known."

Sneaky. I like it.

"What did she say?" Viola asked, her eyes wide. "Is she asking about me?"

Fleur glanced between her stepmother and her ghost. "Lenora says hi."

Viola shivered, a grin spreading across her face.

Lenora giggled.

Fleur turned to Viola, brow raised. "You're not scared?"

"Why would I be? She's not violent, is she? Like in the movies?" Viola shook her head, her gaze searching the room. "What does she look like?"

Tell her I'm covered in blood with bits of flesh falling off. Lenora was obviously enjoying this.

Fleur grimaced and shot a glare at the spirit. "She's made of light. Spirits are just essence without a husk. Transparent, like the sheer curtains you have over there"—Fleur nodded to the windows in the living room—"but bright and seamless."

Boring. Lenora frowned playfully.

"I always imagined ghosts looked like they did in life, but maybe a little shabbier, like Jacob Marley." Viola lifted her mug of coffee— Fleur noted she too drank from one of Fleur's pottery rejects, this one simpler and rounded with a heart-shaped handle—and took a sip.

Fleur blew out a breath, pushing down her irritation. They had bigger things to worry about than Lenora's lack of mass. "She's shaped like a person, well ... half of a person—no legs, I guess?" Fleur considered Lenora. "She's abstract, but I can see the outline of the clothes she wore in life."

You can? Lenora twirled slowly.

Fleur nodded. "And I can see her face. Her words just kinda echo in my head, like thoughts."

"Well, that's not at all what I expected. It's softer, more delicate, somehow ..." Viola trailed off, staring at the emptiness over Fleur's shoulder.

"She's over here." Fleur nodded to the edge of the counter where Lenora hovered.

"Oh. Of course." Viola cleared her throat and looked at Lenora. "Nice to meet you, Lenora."

Tell her likewise ... oh! And that she has a lovely home.

Gods. Fleur was not in the mood for this. "Now, if we can get back to the matter at hand ..."

Opal?

Fleur glared at her. "Theda."

Oh. Lenora colored green, then white as she drifted closer. *So that's it? You're done?*

"Of course, I'm done, Len. I've made a colossal mess out of all this, and for what? We're no closer to finding your killer, and Theda isn't talking to me. I'm out." Fleur gritted her teeth and looked at the ceiling.

But what about Ellory? She—

"She's dead. She doesn't get to have a say in my life anymore. I was wrong to go to Javier. I let myself get carried away by a fantasy. My mother is dead, gone—she left me alone when I needed her most. Left me to figure out my gifts, and I failed. I was the one who spoke up and got us exiled. My father tried to caution me, but I didn't listen. I never listen. I failed then, just like I failed now." Tears swam in her vision. Fleur blinked rapidly, praying they would hold.

"What's this?" Viola asked, her gaze on Fleur. "Your mother?"

Fleur shook her head and backed away from the counter, her breakfast forgotten. The urge to run washed over her. "No. I won't rehash this again. I'm done." She moved to the sofa and pulled her sweater off the arm, tugging it over her T-shirt and leggings. "I should leave." She pulled her messenger bag over her shoulder and grabbed her jacket off the floor.

"Fleur—"

"No, Viola, just … stop. I need my bed and my things"—she paused—"*our* things … I need to make this right with Theda, OK?" She moved to the front door and grasped the knob before she looked back. "I'll call you, Vi. I promise. Lenora … I'm sorry."

She didn't slam the door. She wanted to—her fist tightened on it as she jerked it closed. Instead, she took a deep breath, counted to three, and closed it with a snap.

Fleur yanked open the Subaru's driver-side door and climbed inside. The car was cold and damp, the red leather seats foreign to her. Twelve hours ago, she and Theda sat shoulder to shoulder, giggling about … Fleur cursed. It didn't matter now. She screwed up everything, just like she did with Javier, with her father …

She turned the key, and the Subie flared to life. A stream of white exhaust plumed the air behind her. The car idled, chugging quietly in the background as it worked furiously to thaw the windows. Fleur stuffed her hands in her jacket pockets and shivered. The tarot deck pressed against her knuckles, and for once, the reminder of fate couldn't calm her anger.

She didn't know what to think, what to do … every action felt pointless and cruel. Fleur lowered her head and exhaled. Everything was a mess. *She* made everything a mess. Her history—her baggage was heavy and convoluted. It was wrong of her to bring Theda into this. It was wrong of her to make promises she couldn't keep. Her head ached with frustration. She was no detective, and it was unfair of her to even try. Theda was better off without her. Just like Javier—and Lenora would be. Fleur swallowed down the bile clogging her throat—the thought scraped her tender flesh. That was her truth, wasn't it? Not the spirits, not the visions, not even her home realm. Fleur's truth was her loneliness. No matter how much she fought it ...

She was always alone.

THIRTY-EIGHT

FLEUR

Alma answered the door at the first knock.

Fleur smiled weakly and stuffed her hands in her pockets. "Is she here?"

Alma nodded and stepped onto the front stoop, shutting the door behind her. "She doesn't want to see you."

Fleur exhaled and nodded, looking down at her combat boots. She knew this was a strong possibility. She weighed the pros and cons of this move while her car idled, parked in front of the aged row of townhouses lining the narrow side street.

"OK. Yeah, I figured." Fleur bit her lip and shook her head, damning the ounce of hope that had pushed her to the door. "I had to try, right?"

Alma took a step closer and reached out, squeezing Fleur's arm. "Give her time, OK? She loves you, remember that. But, Fleur"—Alma paused, waiting until Fleur looked up—"she feels betrayed. That's not something you can just get over."

Fleur hung her head. Guilt, like a blade, tore her flesh and hollowed her stomach. "I don't blame her for not seeing me. I don't even want to see me." Fleur met Alma's gaze. "But I'm done. I was wrong. Tell her that, will you? Tell her I love her, and she was right. She's always right—I should have listened, I should have ..."

"Stop." Alma leaned forward and pulled Fleur into a hug. The scent of vanilla clung to her, layered with the sweet tang of pancake batter. Fleur's stomach growled. Alma smiled as she pulled away. "Theda knows you're sorry. But she has demons of her own to work on. This isn't about right or wrong."

Fleur inhaled sharply and nodded as she took a step back. "Yeah. I know." She looked up at the cloudy sky. The urge to push past Alma, storm into the house, apologies dripping from her lips overwhelmed Fleur and she shook her head. No. Theda didn't need her making this harder, and Fleur would respect that, or try to. She looked back at Alma. "Just ... tell her I love her, OK?"

Alma smiled gently and nodded. "I will."

Fleur pressed her lips together to stop them from quivering. She would not cry. Not now, not yet. Nothing was final. Theda needed time. That was fair. Fleur would give her all the time she needed. She turned from Alma and moved toward the Subaru's dirty white silhouette. She looked back and watched Alma step into the house. Fleur lifted her hand to wave, then stopped as Alma closed the door behind her.

The drive home took forever. Fleur gritted her teeth when an red sedan pulled out in front of her, splashing her windshield with grimy water. Her hands trembled on the wheel, her heart pounded. The car's rumble faded to silence as her mind pulled and twisted each thread of thought. Theda, Lenora ... her mother. Damn. Why was her mother involved? Why, after all this time, did she send Lenora to her, and why, for the love of the Gods, did she want her to solve a murder she was ill-equipped to handle? Damn. Damn. Damn.

The answer blossomed behind her eyes. The Relics.

Fleur scoffed. Of course. That's what it's always about, isn't it? How Lenora was tied to it didn't really matter overall, Ellory sent her for one reason. The Inbetween was threatened, and Fleur, whether she wanted to or not, was the key to helping them. Lenora was just a pawn.

Or was she? Dugal had a Relic, and Lenora was connected to him. Ellory told her from the beginning that they needed a specific Relic to defend themselves—

Well, to hell with that. She was done. Fleur pressed the brake and shifted, slowing the car as she slid into the parking spot outside their apartment. She did what was asked. She found a solid lead. It wasn't her fault if the suspect was innocent. How was she to know Opal studied poisonous plants? Who does that? And why would she have an antidote in a safe? Why didn't she just tell them about it when they asked? And as for the Relic? Hell, the Soulkeepers were more than capable. Let them manage this. She was out. Finished. Screw them all. Fleur shook her head and shifted the Subie into park. It chugged and sputtered in the rain, waiting for her to turn the key, open the door and move forward.

But there was no moving forward from this. Fleur leaned back, releasing the wheel. Rain splattered the windshield. She watched raindrops race, blurring the landscape. Maybe Viola was right. Accepting someone's truth differed from understanding it. Maybe she assumed too much and offered too little in return? How could Theda possibly understand what her world was like? She was magickless, mundane ... Fleur blew out a breath. She had expected too much of her—she had expected too much of both of them.

She reached for the door handle, her fingers gripped the metal latch, but didn't move. Don't be a coward. Go. Get out of the car. Her eyes welled and Fleur cursed. She didn't want to enter the empty apartment. She didn't want to see the corkboard covered with pointless evidence propped against the wall or smell the sweet remains of Theda's yam casserole lingering in the air.

A tear spilled down her cheek. Fleur sniffed and brushed it away with the back of her hand.

Shit. She hated this.

CHAPTER
THIRTY-NINE

LENORA

I watched Fleur sleep. I lengthened my wings and grasped the edge of her headboard, my hind wing brushing against the metal. She went to Alma's house, and from the tears in her eyes when she entered the apartment, I assumed it didn't go well. I stayed out of her way as she removed her coat, tossing it and her messenger bag onto the sofa. She didn't look at me. She had to have known I was there, but she didn't acknowledge me. I wanted to say something, to offer solace, but nothing I could say would calm her. She blamed me; I was sure of it.

So, I waited. Watched her sleep and tried to contact Ellory.

I needed answers, and so did Fleur. And both of us needed that Relic.

She doesn't blame you, Lenora. Ellory's voice blossomed in my mind, startling me. The air shifted as she appeared beside me, her light dimmer than usual.

I would.

She blames me. Ellory spoke quietly, as if the revelation shocked her.

Talk to me, Ellory. I need to know more.

You have her memories, Lenora. You can see.

I wanted to groan. *Not you. I saw her father, her home, but never saw you.*

An omission by the Soulkeepers, no doubt. The resignation in her tone did nothing to dispel my shock at hearing her reference them. The Soulkeepers were not to be spoken of. We knew of them instinctively, like an ever-present thought nagging at our core, but never voiced.

Why?

Silence. Ellory's eyes were on her daughter, her light throbbed and quickened before calming once more.

In life, I was a seer, like Fleur, Ellory began. *A powerful medium from a legacy of mediums, but my power came at a cost. I knew this and tried to educate my daughter before I was taken. But she was so young, so stubborn and idealistic ...*

What cost? I don't understand.

Ellory paused, as if unsure how much to reveal. I wanted to prod her but knew how dangerous it was for her and how cautious she must be.

If the Soulkeepers were to discover she kept any memories ... well, I didn't know what they would do, but it wouldn't be good.

I had certain abilities that were sought after—

Fleur's phone vibrated on her nightstand, and Ellory fell silent. She watched her daughter curl her legs, and hug the blanket to her. Fleur's breathing was deep and nasal, her mouth cracked. She snored. Her breath ruffled the edge of the sheet.

Trust Fleur, Lenora. Ellory reached out, her hand hovering over the pale flesh of Fleur's cheek. Her light flickered, a second later she was gone.

I couldn't move. Doing so would disturb the memory of Ellory's actions, the kindness, the ... love. My heart ached, and I wanted to shake Fleur, to wake her up, not just from her self-imposed pity party, to make her see—

But who was I to make anyone listen? I couldn't even remember the color of my eyes.

I turned to face the apothecary cabinet hanging on the wall. I noticed it before, in passing. It looked like a regular old cabinet, two doors with faded nickel hinges above a trio of small drawers. The wood was old, splintered in the corners and darker in spots. I didn't give it a second glance until now. Now it glowed.

What was this? A piece of her life in Evirdahl? It must be if it contained what appeared to be magick, at least to my amateur eye. The cabinet brightened, almost as if it were its own sun. I raised my hand to block the rays, but hesitated.

I fluttered closer, hovering near the starburst-shaped knob. Until now, I had done my best to stay out of Fleur's memories, taking only what I needed to help her. But the cabinet's familiarity drew me in like the promise of Turkish delight on a winter night.

My aura brightened. I reached up, my fingers suspended over the pointed star latch. Whatever Fleur put in there was sealed for a reason. I wanted to touch it. To allow my light to mingle with the warmth of molecules and magick.

I closed my eyes and leaned closer.

Heat. Scorching heat seared the surrounding air. I struggled against it, brightening until I matched the glow coming from the cabinet. Fighting was useless. It tugging at my consciousness. A young girl with gray curly hair and wide brown eyes clutched a woman's hand. Tears streamed down her face, pooling under her chin. I couldn't look away.

This was Ellory's death. This was the memory I couldn't see.

Part of me wanted to turn away, as I had with most of Fleur's memories, but a larger part demanded I watched, pulling me closer until the tears falling from Fleur's eyes were my own.

"Do you remember what I taught you?" Ellory's voice was thick and hoarse. She coughed, her lungs spasming within their delicate cage. She held a cloth to her mouth, its fibers stained dark red with blood.

Fleur sucked in a sob and turned her tear-stained face to her mother. She tightened her hold on Ellory's hand, willing her strength to her mother. "I remember everything, Mutta."

"The Relics, Fleur. Do you remember the spell to hold them?"

Fleur nodded. "Fadir will help—"

"No, Fleur. Your father cannot help you with this. It is your gift, to sense the goddess magick, just as it was mine. Hemsut knew, despite everything—she knew." Ellory closed her eyes and released a long breath. "Only you can carry out the goddesses' request now."

"But I don't know where to start." Fleur shook her head and exhaled. "How will I find them? How do I know what they are?"

"The universe will deliver them to you, look for signs, for the pockets of unusual in normalcy. You will know."

"But that could take forever," Fleur lamented, staring at her mother's hand clutched within her own. "What if I mess up?"

"Then you try again, my girl." Ellory smiled sadly and squeezed Fleur's hand. "Hemsut has willed it—this is our destiny. You will succeed."

"What if I don't want to succeed? Why can't I just keep you instead? I want to keep you, Mutta." Another sob rippled Fleur's frail shoulders.

"I'll always be here—" Ellory coughed, her body doubling over with anguish. Blood dripped onto the cloth, smearing her lips. "Sing it, Fleur. Sing the lullaby to me."

Fleur shook her head. "No, Mutta."

"Please ... Fleur."

Fleur looked up and met her mother's eyes. Ellory nodded softly and pulled her daughter's clasped hands to her heart.

The tune was raw, but Fleur hummed it quietly, emphasizing each couplet.

"The words, dearest ..."

"*The first, once whole, was torn asunder. Its halves will bring a potent thunder. The second, lost in time unknown, may be found with seedling sown. The third once sung a delicate tune. Left to bone, it shimmers in ruin. The fourth bloodied the end of a bow. A scratch will leave you deep in shadow ...*" Fleur trailed off, humming the melody as she searched for the rest.

"*The fifth is unseen, but not unheard. Incased in wood, it leaves you fractured ...*," Ellory sang softly.

"*The sixth protected flesh of its own. Hungry for breath, it'll watch you drown ...*" Fleur crinkled her brow, cleared her throat, and continued. "*The seventh embraced an amber grave. With heart made whole, a life it can save. The eighth and ninth once held three hands. Untamed travel, stilled by caught sand.*" She paused. The last verse just out of reach. "*The tenth ...*"

"Go on."

"*The tenth ... now bleak, once flourished with life. Its darkness preys on all creatures' strife,*" she whispered, her eyes wide.

Ellory leaned down and planted a kiss on her daughter's brow. "Never forget that, Fleur. Promise me."

"I won't forget." Fleur nodded to her mother, humming the simple melody under her breath.

My light dimmed as the memory faded. Ellory said Fleur had to carry out the goddess's request now—meaning she was passing on her quest to her daughter? I hummed the melody, its importance surged within me. Ellory showed me this for a reason.

"Stop humming that," Fleur growled, sitting up in bed.

I turned from the cabinet, my light brightening with surprise. *Humming what?*

"You know what."

Why?

"Because it's not yours."

The Relics are a part of this.

Fleur glared and dropped back against the pillows. "I don't care. I'm out, remember?"

You know the Relics better than anyone. Your mother sent me to you, for God's sake. Don't you care, even a little that the Inbetween is in danger?

"No." Fleur turned her head into the pillow.

Stop behaving like a baby. I'm sorry things didn't go the way we planned, but I'm not giving up. I can't. I'm involved somehow, and I need to know.

"I'm not stopping you."

I rolled my eyes and moved closer to the bed. Fleur was being ridiculous. I stared at her, my light wavering as the lullaby's words washed over me.

The first, once whole, was torn asunder. Its halves will bring a potent thunder. I recited, inching closer to her. *Thunder? Like a storm? Whatever it is, it's broken, right? And you need to find both pieces for it to work? Am I close?*

"Shut up."

Not until you talk to me.

Fleur groaned. "Is this my punishment?" She looked at the ceiling, speaking to an unseen force. "Is this because I lied to Theda? I'm forced to relive painful memories at the whim of a ghost?"

She can't hear you, I muttered, unable to keep the sarcasm from my tone.

Fleur turned away from me and pulled the blanket over her head.

My light flickered red with frustration. I swallowed back my words, knowing I wasn't getting anywhere, and moved into the living room. I wanted to scream. How dare she just brush me aside when all I'm doing is continuing what we started? I wasn't asking her to do anything but answer a few questions. How was I supposed to figure out how my death linked to the Relics if she wouldn't tell me anything?

I hovered in front of the war board, my gaze drifting over the index cards Theda placed there. In front of it lay my belongings—the few things I had on me at my death. I studied the USB drive, dipping my finger into it in the dim hope that I could glean something from the matter before turning to the book. *Persuasion* by Jane Austen—

Opal said it was one of my favorites, which might explain the comments within, but why the dates? Didn't Opal point out that the numbers scrawled were dates of significance? They had to mean something, didn't they? I wished I could open the book, but even in my headiest emotions, I didn't think I could do more than push the book from the table.

My gaze fell on the wind spinner. Oliver suggested it was a map, but Fleur said it wasn't. It's significant. It had to be. It might not be a Relic, but it was tied to one, I just knew it. I leaned toward it, my light illuminating the dips and crags of the iron mandala. There, in the center, the goddess sigil—the crescent moon, eye and sun.

The lullaby hummed in my head. From snippets of conversation, I gleaned the symbol's importance, but why? What did it mean, and why did I have it on me when I died?

The fourth bloodied the end of a bow. A scratch will leave you deep in shadow. The fifth is unseen, but not unheard. Incased in wood, it leaves you fractured ...

"Seriously?" Fleur stood in the hallway, staring at me. "You won't give up, will you?"

No. I stood my ground.

Fleur opened her mouth, about to shut me down when the buzzer sounded.

Neither of us moved.

CHAPTER

FORTY

FLEUR

I t was a standoff.

No way Fleur was going to move first.

The buzzer sounded again.

Lenora flickered, her light brightening the corkboard. The remains of her life strung across it like a crime scene.

Another buzz.

Fleur's heart sped up as she tore her gaze from Lenora and looked at the intercom on the wall. It wasn't Theda. She had a key, but Fleur hoped all the same.

Aren't you going to answer that?

"I'm not really in the mood for company." She gave Lenora a pointed look.

But what if it's Theda? The question hovered between them.

"It's not her."

I didn't say it was.

"Good."

OK. Then answer it.

Fleur gritted her teeth.

Lenora shrugged. *It's not like I can answer it.*

Damn. She was right.

Another buzz, this time longer, as if the interloper leaned on the button.

"Fine," Fleur almost shouted as she moved toward the intercom. She pressed the button. "What?"

"Jeez. What's wrong with you?" The voice was gritty but recognizable. Sato.

"What do you want?"

"Let me up."

"No. I'm off the case. Go away."

"Open the door, Harkyn." Javier this time. Shit. Were they together?

"Go away, Javier."

"Not until you let us up."

"That makes no sense."

"Let us up, we'll talk, then we'll go away. It's the only deal on the table."

Fleur huffed and turned to Lenora. The damn ghost was grinning.

"I hate you," Fleur groaned as she pressed the buzzer and opened the gate.

"Yeah, you, too." Javier laughed. Fleur heard the gate open and their footsteps as they shuffled through before she let go of the button.

She took a deep breath, focusing on the expanding of her lungs. She closed her eyes and straightened her spine. It was no use. Tension rose like a tidal wave, tightening her muscles until her body trembled with frustration. Why couldn't they all just leave her alone?

Why was Sato with Javier? The thought nagged, unwinding the small threads of calm she struggled to maintain. And why the hell was Javier here? What time was it? Didn't he have some crime to solve? Crime that didn't involve her?

Three strikes, and she was out. She presented them with three leads. She had more than done her job, and she was wrong every time. Why couldn't they all see that and let her get back to the business of mending her relationship?

Fleur blew out a breath and opened her eyes. Lenora wavered near the corkboard, staring at the metal mandala. Fleur shook her head, wishing she could ignore the spirit.

But she couldn't. Not now. Not with the words of her mother's lullaby dripping from her lips.

Dammit. She should have kept up her mother's search, just like she promised. But ... didn't anyone realize how deep the cut of her mother's death went? She wanted to help, but instead they feared her—exiled her. Even her own father denied her the chance to be who she was. Of course she didn't want to have anything to do with them. She'd made her choice abundantly clear.

At least tell me why it has the goddess symbol if it's not a Relic? I don't know all the rules. Lenora asked, pointing to the mandala's center.

Fleur didn't want to answer her. She didn't want to let her in, because to share it would mean she had to open herself up to it—all of it, and Fleur liked the isolated pieces to stay just as they were.

But the Soulkeepers opened it for her when they gave Lenora her memories, as did her own mother's spirit—Fleur swallowed back a sob and wiped her eyes.

"I don't know." The words burned in her throat. She had only seen one other Relic in her life, aside from Dugal's shell shard—the opalized skull her mother found when she was small. Fleur's gaze flew to her bedroom and the cabinet on the wall there. Her mother's cabinet, enchanted with the protections to keep the Relics safe. Empty, but for the bird skull. A shudder crept up Fleur's spine. She shook her head and turned away from Lenora and the mandala.

Javier knocked, snapping the tension.

"You have five minutes," Fleur said as she opened the door and moved back into the room, leaving Sato to shut the door behind him.

Javier stuffed his hands into his pockets and looked around before turning his gaze on Fleur. "No Theda?"

"No."

He nodded and took a seat in the armchair.

Sato collapsed onto the sofa and began pulling off his jacket. "Is Lenora here?"

Fleur frowned. "I can't get rid of her."

Stop taking your anger out on me. Do you think I have a choice here?

Fleur didn't need to look at Lenora to know she was red with frustration.

"Good." Javier leaned forward, resting his forearms on his knees. "I've got a few questions."

"Me too," Sato announced, sitting up straighter and glancing at the kitchen. "You got any food?"

Fleur glared. "No." She looked back at Javier. "Four minutes, now."

"OK, OK …" Sato rolled his eyes and leaned back.

"You heard about Opal, right?" Javier asked.

Fleur nodded. "Strike three."

"It was a solid lead. Don't beat yourself up over it," Javier remarked, fixing Fleur with a hard stare. "Sato came in after we arrested her, confessed to killing Lenora, tried to get Opal off the hook. He told us to evaluate the vial, which we were already doing. Anyway, long story short—we need the USB drive. Sato says every-thing we need is on it."

Fleur shrugged, ignoring the thud of her heart as it raced. She didn't care. She gestured to the drive, sitting on the bookshelf. She didn't care, she chanted to herself. "Take it."

Why? What's on it? Lenora brightened and moved closer to Javier.

Javier raised a dark brow. "No argument?"

Fleur gritted her teeth. She didn't care. "Nope. I told you. I'm out."

Sato cleared his throat. "What about Len? You're just going to abandon her?"

Fleur shrugged and crossed her arms over her chest.

Ask them ... please. Ask them what's on the drive.

She pressed her lips together and shook her head.

Dammit, Fleur. This isn't just about you.

Anger welled in her chest, but Fleur didn't budge. She closed her eyes, shaking her head more vehemently. Didn't Lenora understand she couldn't do this? It had taken her years to progress from her mother's death—years! And now the damn Atua wants her to just explain everything as if it wouldn't destroy her? If she opened that door, she wasn't sure she could close it again. Guilt rumbled in her stomach.

Please?

Fleur turned away from the spirit, lifting her gaze to the ceiling.

Sato's eyes widened, and he looked between Fleur and Javier before inching to the edge of the sofa. "Is she OK?" he whispered.

"Give her a minute," Javier whispered back. "I think they're fighting."

"Oh, OK, cool." Sato nodded and sat back, his gaze on Fleur.

Gods. Fleur huffed and moved into the kitchen. She needed to do something. Fleur picked up the teapot and set it under the faucet, allowing the splash of water on the metal pot to calm her.

Please, Fleur. Lenora followed her, her light once again white and steady. *Please, help me. I don't know how to do this alone.*

She was going to give in. Fleur turned away from the Atua. The spirit was right, and Fleur hated it. She wanted to ignore it, to turn off the light and pull the blanket over her head and pretend it didn't exist, but ... She sighed and set the kettle on the burner. She turned the knob, watching as the coil glowed red.

She was going to give in. The damage to her relationship with Theda was done. Even if she stopped now, Theda wouldn't believe her. A leopard can't change her spots, Alma would say. But she would fix this. She would get Theda back, she would put this all behind her and they would start fresh.

Fleur pulled a mug from the cupboard, her fingers tightening on the handle.

She was going to give in.

Damn. This was bigger than just Lenora's death now. It was about Fleur's truth, her history ... her mother. It was about the millions of scattered pieces swept under the rug.

Fleur looked down and groaned. She was going to give in.

Lenora hovered at the archway into the kitchen. Her expression was earnest. *Fleur?*

Fleur looked past her to Javier and Sato seated awkwardly in her living room. She wanted to kick them out, to unwind their casual behavior. She took a breath, then another.

Lenora flickered beside her.

Waiting.

"Well?" Fleur blew out a breath, clutching the empty mug in her hand. "What's on the damn drive?"

FORTY-ONE

LENORA

S ato took a deep breath and looked around the room. "I don't know," he said, his body tensing. "That's the thing. Lenora didn't tell me. She just wanted me to corrupt it so that only I could open it. She said I couldn't trust anyone but her and Opal. That she had discovered something big." Sato shook his head. "She said it could change everything."

"So, you lied before." Fleur fixed Sato with a hard stare. "When you said you knew nothing. You lied. She didn't kick you out, did she?"

"Yeah, I lied. Sue me." Sato flushed, dropping his gaze to the floor. "I was just doing what Len asked. I exaggerated the stalker angle a bit. I didn't know Poppy had ... issues. Len said to keep quiet unless shit hit the fan. Divert attention, she said, then told me to find the medium with gray hair. Didn't tell me your name, OK?"

"So why didn't you tell me everything when we met?"

"You think I was going to just trust that you were the right person? I had to be sure."

"And now you are? Why?" Fleur crossed her arms over her chest.

"I wasn't—your story about Lenora losing her memory was just too convenient," he apologized. "It sounded like an act. But then you told Javier about Opal, and I realized you couldn't have known any of that unless Lenora told you. She was the only one who knew where the safe was besides Opal."

Javier looked up at Fleur and nodded. "Can she tell us anything? Anything at all? Did any of her memories return?"

I flickered, unwilling to bear the weight of their disappointment.

Fleur shook her head. "She's deeper in my memories than she was before." She looked at me and lifted a brow in question.

I shook my head. *Ask Sato to fix the drive.*

"She said to fix the drive."

Sato smiled sadly. "Once I do that, we'll need her authentication. I helped her set it up. She said anyone close to her would know it, but ..." He cursed. "I know she meant me or Opal, but ... I just don't know."

Fleur raised a brow. "So ... Opal *is* involved?"

Javier nodded. "Opal hasn't confirmed it. She's been tight-lipped since her release—"

"Do you blame her?" Fleur frowned.

"She's just doing what Lenora asked," Sato announced. "She made us both promise to keep quiet, no matter what. I don't know what Opal's role was, just like she doesn't know mine—Len said it was better that way."

My light wavered, dimming. I planned this—I planned ... what? My death? Why would I do that?

"Wait ... Lenora planned something, like a break-in-case-of-emergency kind of thing. So, you think she knew her killer? That she walked into this on purpose?" Fleur sounded shocked. Her gaze flew to me as if I could explain anything.

"Maybe?" Sato rubbed his hand over his face and sighed. "The morning she died, she asked me for the USB drive. Said it would be all over soon. She was meeting Opal at the coffee shop across from the conservatory. I let her go. I didn't know ..."

"But Opal didn't do it," Fleur said, her gaze flickering from me to Sato before landing on Javier. "What did Opal say about the meeting?"

"She said they had coffee, then she had a class and Lenora wanted to wander the gardens before heading home." Javier shook his head. "Yeah, I know she's lying. At least I'm reasonably sure she is." He shrugged in frustration. "But I can't do anything about it. She's been cleared."

"So, there was someone else." Fleur ran her hand through her tangled grey curls. She looked at me, her brown eyes softening. "Lenora, does any of this ring a bell?"

I wished I could tell her yes. My light trembled, and I turned from her. I had to remember something ... anything. There has to be a way. Everything I knew was crumbling all around me and I was helpless to pick up the pieces. I shrunk away from them. Away from their eager eyes and curious minds. I shrunk away from my ineptness, my failure. I needed something more than the bizarre history swirling around Fleur. This was about me too, right? It wasn't fair that I wouldn't get a little of myself back.

It wasn't fair.

Look to yourself, Lenora. Ellory's voice blossomed behind my eyes.

My light flickered and I spun around, vainly seeking the Guardian's guidance. *How? How can I look when all I see is Fleur? All I see are the memories of someone else? How, Ellory? Tell me!*

Fleur's eyes widened, and she took a step back from me. Could she see my wildness? Could she hear the terror in my thoughts?

Close your eyes. Ellory's voice was steady.

They took everything from me. My mind was like a spool of thread loosening. I tried to focus on Ellory's voice, but all I saw was her pale hand clutching Fleur's.

Look past Fleur's memories. Look past everything you think you know.

It's still there, Lenora. Waiting. You are stronger than you think. Press forward. They stole your memories, but not their residue. Focus, Lenora.

Is this how you did it? Is this how you kept yours?

Silence.

I shuddered, my gaze meeting Fleur's eager one. I turned, from her, from the rest, from the expectance. My light flickering as I turned inward.

I was dimly aware of Fleur moving closer to Javier, of her raised arm and the slight shake of her head when Javier opened his mouth. She was warning them ...

The world blurred into spots.

I closed my eyes.

My mind filled with the rushing of water—the ebb and flow of wave after wave as they pulled Fleur's history away, leaving crystalline gimmers in its wake. My fingers dug through the sand until they were raw and sore, my nails jagged, and a solitary granule shimmered in my palm.

"What's wrong, Len? You're prowling like a caged lion."

Sato was addressing me. Tears clogged my throat—tears? How?

I blinked.

Sato sat on an old damask chaise, his legs crossed at the ankles. He lounged, one arm thrown carelessly over the back, the other held his phone. He tossed his head as he talked, sweeping his shaggy black hair over his eyes.

We were in my attic at Khade House. Sheer curtains covered the tall arched window behind him, and a dim ray of overcast light brightened the space.

I inhaled, my gaze darting from the rug-covered hardwood to the crumbling and faded brick fireplace. Edgar's portrait grinned down at me. I painted him smiling. That's how I remembered him, even if others didn't. My mother called him a solemn child, but she didn't see the mischief in his eyes, or help plan the schemes he laid out. Edgar didn't like our mother, couldn't relate to her warmth or her humor. I was the bridge between them, the peacemaker when their arguments became too loud. I was the one who knew him best.

And I remembered.

My body trembled, and I crossed my arms over my chest. A frugal attempt at courage. It didn't matter though—Sato knew me. He could see something was bothering me, just like he knew I was different now. Different from the woman he met four years ago. Knowledge made me different, made me cautious.

"I'm fine. Don't worry so much," I told him as I crouched to search under the bed for my other shoe. "Did you finish with the drive?"

Knowledge no one knew but me.

Sato pulled the slender USB drive out of his pocket and folded it into his fist. "Will you tell me what's going on if I give it to you?"

"Not yet."

He frowned and looked at the drive. "I could hack it, you know."

I shrugged, twisting into a sitting position, and pulled on my boot. "Yeah, but you wouldn't understand it."

"I'm smarter than I look."

I laughed. "I don't doubt that."

"So?"

I stood and moved to him, placing my arms on the back of the chaise on either side of him, and leaned forward until our noses touched. My hair slipped over my shoulder, hiding us behind its curly veil. He tightened his arms around my waist and pulled me even closer. "So, nothing. I'll tell you when the time is right."

He kissed me, or maybe I kissed him. It didn't matter. We moved in one stroke, curling into each other as if we were returning home. He smelled of black coffee and peanut butter toast, and I wanted to inhale every ounce of him.

"You worry me," he murmured, kissing my cheek and tucking a strand of hair behind my ear.

I leaned back. "I know what I'm doing."

He sighed. "Doing about what? Doing with who? Please, Len? Tell me something. Maybe I can help?"

I smiled and swallowed down the lie in my throat. "You are help-ing." I took the USB drive from his hand and held it between us. "Don't worry. Please?"

I couldn't tell him what I learned—or that I confirmed my darkest fears last night as I peered into the warehouse window. I didn't know what words to use, or how much anger I could hide. How do you tell someone your life was a lie without understanding it yourself? Opal would understand. She knew my family. Opal was there at the end, hovering over me when tears clogged my throat but wouldn't fall. She understood when I told her it didn't feel real, that my world had tilted and only I could right it again. She thought I spoke in grief, and I did mostly, but my words stemmed from some-thing bigger than grief, something more tangible—revenge. I couldn't tell her what I found after years and years of searching. I couldn't share the horror of my discovery, the fierceness of my sorrow at being right.

"Does Opal know what you're doing?" Sato prodded.

I shook my head. "No, and please, Sato—don't tell her about the drive."

He huffed and gave me a hard look. "What about Dugal?"

"No."

I clutched the drive in my hand. Everything I discovered was on it. My insurance policy if this all went wrong.

My heart thudded in my ears as I slipped the drive into the pocket of my jeans. I stood, smoothing the wrinkles from my blouse. I picked up my cardigan from the back of the armchair facing the empty fireplace and slid it over my shoulders. "Please, don't make this harder." I turned from him, trying to keep my voice even. "I need you to trust me, OK?"

Sato stared at me, his brown eyes boring holes into my flesh. I wanted to squirm, to tell him everything, to know that even if this all went wrong, someone would know why.

He nodded. "I trust you."

I smiled and pulled on my gray quilted bomber jacket. The right pocket hung lower, heavy with the weight of the wind spinner. Learning there was a way, albeit a small one, to change what was done was nothing compared to finding the tool to carry it out. It took years of hunting and study until I discovered the small metal spinner in an antique shop on Nob Hill. Opal thought I was crazy when she saw it but knew better to question my excitement. That was the beginning. That was the moment I knew the fables and lore I had uncovered were, in fact, truth.

My hand traced the outline of the spinner in my pocket as I turned back to Sato.

He stood close behind me, his face flushed as if he knew this was goodbye.

Lenora ...

I shook my head, pushing her voice back.

Lenora!

Fleur's call was soothing as if she feared what would happen if she shook me awake.

I leaned closer to Sato. His arms wrapped around me, two steel bands offering protection, solace, and love.

"I'll find you," I whispered, fighting the light clawing at the back of my eyes. I wasn't ready to go, but I knew if I didn't leave now, I never would.

The room rumbled and darkened. Sato's arms, once sturdy, fell from me. I tried to reach out, to hold on, but the room was too dark. I blinked, hovering between longing and truth, and realized the only light around me was my own.

"Lenora?" Fleur stood beside me. She looked like she wanted to reach out and steady me. I wanted to scoff. How could she? I was nothing.

I'm OK. I blinked at her, then turned, noting that both Javier and Sato sat frozen in their chairs, their wide eyes trained on Fleur.

Fleur stepped back, rolling her shoulders, and inhaled. "OK, yeah ..."

I looked at Sato. I remembered the warmth of his arms. My light flared and flushed, and I held still, afraid of what I might do—afraid of what my emotions would cause.

I was dead. Whatever I tried that day didn't work.

I wanted to inhale, to remember the salty taste of him. Sorrow crept into me and spread its wings, dousing whatever hope I had left.

"Lenora." Fleur cleared her throat, dragging my gaze back to her. "What lore? You said finding the wind spinner confirmed that the lore was truth ..."

You saw my memory? I couldn't keep the sting from my voice. That memory was all I had, and now Fleur had it, too.

Fleur nodded. "You thought your parents were murdered, didn't you? That's what you were researching." She glanced at Javier, then back at me. "What did you find?"

I nodded to the USB drive on the table. *Open it, and we'll find out.*

CHAPTER
FORTY-TWO

FLEUR

S ato pulled his laptop from his backpack and balanced it on his knees.

It made sense. The scattered parts in the whirlwind of Fleur's mind were itching to join the whole. Soon, she whispered to herself, calming the cyclone.

Fleur narrowed her gaze on Sato as his fingers flew over the keys. She hadn't expected the depth of feeling between them. The rush of emotion that flared like a newly flickering flame lapping at Lenora's aura. Despite her attempts to remain firm, Fleur felt her resolve thaw. Lenora knew love, just as she and Theda had. Fleur rarely glimpsed a spirit's tenderness, and it left her raw and uncertain. They needed to find Lenora's truth.

This was no guessing game, no cozy mystery easily solved.

This was a crafted death, and Fleur suspected Lenora knew what waited for her that day in the conservatory and was ready for it.

All they had to do was unwind it.

And that meant Fleur would have to open up to Lenora.

Dammit.

Javier leaned back in his chair and pushed his glasses up. He looked flustered. Not that Fleur could blame him. This was not a typical investigation, and he was out of his depth. She wondered how hard it was for him to come to her, for him to accept her help and the help of a ghost, when he had despised her and her associations five years before.

Fleur knew he was struggling, knew Lenora's spirit was a constant reminder of his brother's death and the simple request he made of her, one she couldn't grant.

Hindsight is a tricky beast. The Atua found her in the precinct parking lot. That should have been her first clue. She knew he died while in prison—natural death while awaiting a parole hearing—untreated stage four lung cancer. He pleaded with her to help him. He just wanted to make amends for his crimes. Fleur didn't follow the news, and Javier wasn't forthcoming about his brother's death, so she never connected the dots.

Some detective she turned out to be.

When Javier saw his brother's image in the window and heard the spirit's laugh, he didn't think. Fleur watched in horror as he punched his hand through the glass, tears running down his face.

Days later Javier came to her, full of questions, and she told him about her gift. He hung his head, asking her why she would do that to him, and offered forgiveness as a request.

Javier wanted to speak to Diego.

It was the one request Fleur couldn't grant. Diego had passed beyond her scope, choosing to take the path to the Glorious Feast.

"OK, OK, OK," Javier murmured to himself as he watched Sato hack the drive. "What do we know? We know Lenora discovered something about her family's death, right? Something dangerous. We can assume she was planning on confronting someone about it. Someone threatening if she felt she needed an insurance plan." He nodded as he spoke. "We know Opal was involved, but not how, and

—" He broke off and looked at Sato. "What else did she ask of you? Did you ever go with her or see anything strange?"

Sato looked up from the screen. "You mean aside from Poppy the stalker?"

"You think she might be involved?" Fleur asked, a twinge of validation warming her cheeks.

Sato tensed and shook his head. "I don't think so. I saw her yesterday when the cop car dropped her off ... She looked, I dunno ... gray? She was on the phone. I paused on the other side of her shrubs to listen." He paused when Javier opened his mouth to protest. "I just wanted to be sure, OK?"

Javier frowned.

"What was she saying?" Fleur leaned forward.

Sato shrugged. "Not sure exactly, but it sounded like she was making an appointment. Hopefully with a therapist."

Fleur shuddered, recalling the wildness in Poppy's eyes. "She really believed she loved Lenora, didn't she?"

"Unrequited love. Isn't that one of the standard ghost messages?" Javier smirked.

"Oh, shut it, Javier. This wasn't love ... and spirits have feelings too."

"Nah, this is an obsession, but none of that had anything to do with Len's death. Lenora had been working on this for years."

"Opal said she found the wind spinner three years ago in Boston, before all this," Fleur agreed. "So Poppy was just a gross coincidence."

"Yeah." Sato nodded. "Len was suspicious. She spent a lot of time digging into her father's relationships, his business connections. She even researched Dugal ...," Sato trailed off, his brow furrowing.

"What?" Javier leaned forward.

"There was this book ... some old fantasy book she found in Dugal's house years ago. I don't know what it was, but Dugal was furious when Len took it. Threatened to cut her off if she didn't return it. Not that he could do that. Lenora had already received most of her inheritance." Sato smirked. "Anyway, it fascinated Lenora, said it read like a history, and it explained the weird artifacts Dugal liked to collect—"

"Artifacts?" Fleur interrupted, her shoulders tensing. "Is that the word she used?"

Sato shrugged. "Nah, Len always called them Relics."

Fleur closed her eyes. Dammit. This must be the book Opal referenced. She wanted to deny it. No books from her realm ever made it here. It was against goddess law to carry knowledge to Mundad. But if one was smuggled over—that would explain how Griffin knew the shell was a Relic. And make him more dangerous.

I knew about the Relics, didn't I? I knew about your home and the realms. Lenora, who had been silent this whole time, glimmered beside her.

"They didn't look like artifacts to me," Sato continued, "but I only saw one. He keeps it in a glass case in his office. It's just a dirty old seashell, right? Looks like every other shell you'd find on a beach. I asked him about it once, but he just glared and said I wouldn't understand true power if it bit me." He snorted and shook his head again. "The dude is weird."

Fleur held her breath, her heart thudding so loud she was sure everyone could hear. "He said that? True power?"

Sato nodded.

"Fleur?" Javier asked. "You OK?"

Fleur took a deep breath and smiled weakly at him. "Yeah, yeah, yeah ... I'm fine." She looked at Sato. "Any luck on the drive?"

He looked back at the screen. "Almost ..."

Fleur inhaled again, willing her heart to stop pounding. She was not OK, far from it. She searched her mind for any notices about stolen books when she was a child. Something like that would have been broadcast throughout the realms. Nothing. No word or missive. But how could that be? If Dugal had somehow gotten his hands on knowledge from Evirdahl ... and he had a Relic, what's to stop him from finding another? He was obsessed with archeology, right? Fleur stifled a groan. All the facts were there in front of her the whole time. The Relic they needed ... the one the Inbetween needed, was in Dugal's possession. But ... how could that be? He wasn't gifted. Fleur was sure Dugal was nothing but a regular old human. The Relics would do nothing for him. It didn't make any sense.

Breathe, she told herself, just breathe. Speculation will get them nowhere. Focus on the now. On the drive.

The kettle whistled. Javier nearly jumped out of his skin.

Sato snickered.

"Tea?" Fleur asked, surprised when everyone nodded.

This is how I'm connected. Fleur—why Ellory tasked me with finding the Relic. I knew where it was. Lenora flickered, her aura bright white, clearly putting the pieces together.

Her mother ... Fleur turned away from the trio in her living room, moving back to the kitchen, and lifted the kettle from the burner. She flipped off the knob and pulled two more mugs from the cupboard. Gods, this was crazy. Lenora, her mother, her ... they were all connected—Lenora was right.

With shaky hands, Fleur lifted the kettle. Get it together, she scolded herself, as she dropped a bag of Earl Grey, followed by steaming hot water into each mug.

"What was the book called?" Fleur asked, moving into the room and setting both mugs on the coffee table beside her empty one. Maybe it wasn't from Evirdahl? The hope slithered dimly around her words. "The one Lenora took from Dugal?"

"*Book of Veils*, I think," Sato muttered without looking up.

Fleur swallowed back a gasp. She knew of it. It was realm history, transcribed into modern text by her uncle. "You do, ah ... know who wrote it?"

"Some guy with initials instead of a first name, you know, like Tolkien."

"Was it AE Harkyn?"

"Sounds like." Sato narrowed his eyes at her.

Javier's head shot up. "Are you related?"

Fleur cursed and closed her eyes, ignoring the simmer of frustration beneath her skin. Calm, she repeated to herself, be calm. But how was she supposed to be calm when each carefully wound thread in the tapestry of her life was unraveling? She wanted to cover her ears. She wanted to tell them to leave. Instead, she nodded, afraid the action would tug another seam loose. "He's my uncle."

Javier's brow shot up. "Your uncle? I didn't know you had any other family?"

Fleur glared. "Of course, I have more family. They're just not here, OK? My father didn't have the best relationship with his brother. It's been years since we spoke." Four years, to be exact. Axel had crossed the veil for Arik's funeral. He stood stoic and alien in the corner of Viola's small living room, accepting condolences as if he had any right to be there.

Fleur shook her head, pushing back the memory. Not now, not yet. She needed to unwind how the book came to this realm before she allowed herself to dwell on the rest.

"Was he at the funeral? I don't remember him." Javier fixed his gaze on her, unwilling to let it go.

"Not the funeral, no. He was at Viola's after for a time. You would have met him if you had bothered to join us." Fleur shrugged, turning to face Sato, hoping that would end things. "How long has Dugal had the book?"

Sato snorted. "How should I know? A long time, by the looks of it. Lots of notations—Lenora was enthralled."

"Notations? Like what?"

Sato shrugged. "I dunno."

Fleur exhaled through her teeth and rested her chin on her hand. She needed that book. It shouldn't be here, not in this realm or any other.

She glanced at the clock, then back to Sato. It was already well past two in the afternoon. She frowned. Breaking into Dugal Griffin's house would be challenging. Breaking and entering wasn't exactly something she did, but desperate times ... and she doubted

Dugal would hand over the book willingly. She'd need to dust off a few spells her mother taught her all those years ago. Magick, she had let fade, magick she wasn't even sure she could wield properly.

Oh, yeah ... piece of cake. While she was at it, she should just steal the shell in his office too. Fleur groaned, chiding herself for the impossibility of the situation.

"You, OK?" Javier asked again, concern brightening his eyes.

"Yeah, fine." She shrugged and turned to Sato. "Well? Did you get in?"

"Almost. I overrode the first authorization and removed the virus." He looked up and grinned. "That was the simple part, 'cause, you know ... I planted it?"

"Yeah, yeah, good job. What's next?"

"Her password."

"Can't you hack that too?"

Sato shook his head and looked between Fleur and Javier. "Nope."

"You knew her best," Javier remarked. "Think ... What could it be?"

Sato sighed, his gaze roaming the room. "Hey, Len? Any thoughts?"

Lenora flared beside Fleur, her aura coloring yellow at Sato's voice, then dimming to blue. She wavered, ebbing in the still air before disappearing. Fleur leaned back on the sofa and shook her head. "Give her a minute," she said to Sato.

Silence enveloped the room. No one moved. Sato's fingers hovered over the keys as if inspiration would move them into the correct pattern. Javier paused, his mug partway to his mouth, his eyes averted. No one breathed.

Warmth swirled into the room on a calm breeze, ruffling Fleur's hair. She turned. Lenora fluttered near the war board, her gaze on the worn-out copy on *Persuasion*.

"The book—Opal said it was her favorite, right? Maybe it's a clue?" Fleur stood, picked up the book, and flipped through the pages.

"Yeah," Sato breathed, "that could work."

The notes, mostly bits of poetry and numbers, filled the book. Fleur focused on the numbers—dates, if Opal was to be believed. Each date linked to a circled letter. Of course. They just needed to arrange the dates in chronological order.

"OK, I think I see it," Fleur muttered, glancing at Javier. "Grab a pen and an index card. Write these down."

Javier pulled an index card off the shelf.

Gods. Why hadn't she seen this before? It's so simple—she had been obsessed with everything but the few clues right in front of her. Her fingers tightened on the pages as she read the first set of dates.

"091503, then the letter R." She flipped past a couple more pages. "Then, 102399 and A; 061389, E; 031591, D; 021217, exclamation point—"

"Wait—February 12, 2017?" Sato interrupted. "That's the day we met."

Javier paused, reviewing the dates he had written so far. "091503 is the day they bought Khade House."

Fleur shrugged. "She's using dates significant to her … makes sense."

"Keep going." Javier nodded back to the book.

102399 is Edgar's birthday. Lenora whispered. Her light over my shoulder brightened the pages. *And this one … 040896? That's mine.*

Fleur offered Lenora a small smile before reading the numbers aloud and noting the letter G connected to them. "This one is weird. It's at the top of the page instead of in the text, and it's just 121911 followed by the @ symbol, nothing else."

Sato smiled. "I told her not to use all letters." He laughed. "She actually listened."

"040917, L," Fleur continued, "060719, V …" She trailed off as she flipped to the last page. The date listed there was just last week.

"Is that it?" Javier looked up.

"There's one more."

Lenora flickered, moving closer to Sato. *Go on. Say it.*

Fleur cleared her throat. "111921, E. That's the day she died."

Javier recorded the dates, tapping the pen on the edge of the index card. "That confirms she knew something was going to happen to her."

Sato picked up the mug of tea from the table and gulped it down, oblivious to its heat. "I didn't want to believe it, you know? It just didn't seem like something people did. Why would she just walk into that, knowing she might not make it out alive?"

"She must have had a good reason," Javier offered.

"I'll find you. That's the last thing she said to me."

Lenora hovered over him, her fingers reaching as if they could offer comfort. *Tell him I remember him. That I kept my promise.*

Tears crept into Fleur's eyes. She blinked them back and took a breath before turning to Sato. "She said she kept her promise."

Sato coughed, wiping his eyes with the back of his hands. "Yeah, I just wish she kept it before she died." He sniffed and grabbed the card from Javier, studying it as he gathered himself. "OK, then. What do we have?"

"Go by year, beginning with '89," Javier offered.

"E-D-G-A-R ..." He paused, then swore softly.

Of course, she used her brother's name. Fleur's gaze snapped to Lenora before she noticed Sato's expression. "What? What's the rest?"

He offered her the card.

Well, damn. Suddenly, it all fit together.

"EDGAR @L!VE," Fleur read aloud, her shoulders hunching under the weight of the words.

Lenora's brother was alive.

Lenora brightened, blinding Fleur to the words on the card. *I knew—I must have seen him ... That's what I discovered, isn't it? Oh, God. My brother ...*

Goose bumps trailed over Fleur's arms as a chill slid over her spine. That wasn't possible, was it? Edgar Khade died in the hospital hours after the crash that killed his parents. It was documented. She looked up. Her gaze met Javier's startled one. This wasn't just a murder investigation anymore. If Edgar was alive, then it just became a kidnapping case, too.

Sato typed in the password, keys tapped slowly as if he was forcing his fingers to move. "I'm in," he breathed, his eyes wide.

"What does it say?" Javier scooted forward in his chair and peered at the screen.

Sato looked up. "Len was right. I don't understand it." He shook his head and stared at the screen a moment longer before turning it toward Fleur. "She addressed the file to you, Fleur."

FORTY-THREE

FLEUR

F leur took the laptop from him, her heart pounding. She pressed a hand to her breastbone and exhaled, once ... twice ... Lenora knew who she was before they met at the conservatory. She was part of this—somehow.

Her gaze flickered to Javier, and she held her breath. As a detective, it was his responsibility to review every lead, and she had just become his newest suspect.

He frowned, pulling off his glasses. He rubbed his eyes. Fleur could see the strain in creases between his eyes. Javier rested his arms on his knees, his glasses dangling from his fingers between them. "Well? Read it, Fleur."

She looked back at the screen. A single file within the USB folder, her name glowing underneath.

For Fleur Harkyn, it read.

Fleur poised her hand over the mouse pad and moved the cursor to the file. Both Sato and Javier waited, confusion mingled with curiosity etched across their faces.

Beside her, Lenora brightened and leaned closer. *Open it, please.*

She didn't want to open it. She wanted to throw the computer across the room and run away screaming.

The pad of her finger pressed down on the mouse pad, and the document unfurled.

Fleur,

You're probably wondering how I know you, and I guess I don't. I know "of" you. I know where you came from and about the task your mother left for you. Don't be shocked, and please don't delete this ... You see, everything I learned, I learned from your father.

Fleur gasped, her gaze shooting from the screen to the waiting faces across from her and the photo of Arik and Lenora tacked to the war board. Her hands trembled as she lifted them from the keyboard.

"You both have to go," Fleur spoke firmly, her entire body on the verge of eruption.

"What? Why? What did she say?" Sato stood and took a step toward her.

Fleur pulled the computer closer and pointed to the door. "Your five minutes ended ages ago. And this"—she tapped the back of the laptop—"this I have to do alone."

"Need I remind you this is a police investigation?" Javier narrowed his gaze at her. "What you have on that drive is evidence."

"Oh, please, Jav, of course I know that. And you'll have it. Just let me do this on my own. OK?" Fleur growled, her emotions getting the better of her.

"But that's my computer." Sato looked lost for an excuse to stay.

"You'll get it back. Gods." Fleur breathed and gestured to the door again. "Go. Just ... Go."

Javier stood. "I'll be back in a couple of hours. I need that drive, Harkyn."

"Yeah, yeah ...," she trailed off, nodding at the door and watched as they both put on their coats and tumbled toward it.

Sato turned, his mouth open and closed with one last protest. He paused, hand on the doorknob, and glanced around the room. "I'll be back, Len. I promise."

Lenora hovered beside him, her light illuminating the curves of his face like a kiss.

The door closed with a snap.

Fleur released a ragged breath and sank against the cushions.

That was rude. Lenora fluttered toward her, arms crossed over her chest.

"Oh, please, just shut up for a minute," Fleur grumbled, rubbing her hands over her face.

Lenora flickered, draping herself over the opposite end of the sofa. *C'mon then. Don't be a coward. Let's read the rest.*

Fleur opened her eyes and turned toward her. "I literally just read that you—living you—knew my origin and about my mother, and you seriously think I can just brush that aside right now?"

Lenora shrugged.

Fleur moaned again.

Read it aloud this time.

Gods. The damn ghost wouldn't give up.

Fleur pulled herself up and glanced back to the computer in her lap. She wiped the back of her hand over her eyes, erasing the salty residue from her cheeks, and took a deep breath.

Desire and fear warred just under her skin. A light sheen of sweat dampened her brow. Her heart pounded with the need to know more, even as her mind prepared her to run from it all.

Fleur cleared her throat and focused on stilling her trembling hand as she began, her voice stumbling over the words.

This must all seem strange and unwelcome—intrusive even, but please, bear with me, and I will explain everything. I'm sure you know my history, dead parents and all. It was splashed over every news outlet for years. One would have to be off the grid to not know my story.

I'll begin with my parents' death. The news got that part right, at least. What they didn't know, what they could never understand, was that the crash was administered by an unseen hand. It took me years to discover the truth. It began with denial, the first stage of grief, right? But it wasn't denial that they were gone. I saw their bodies.

No, it was the innocence of the crash I denied. That sounds foolish, I know, but when you line up the few facts given, you'll see the crash was deliberate.

First, Dugal invited no one into his home. My father, his business partner of ten years, had only been to his house once, at the beginning of their partnership. Dugal is intensely private. That alone stood out, but when you factor in the time of day—sunset—and the windy road slick with afternoon rain ... those facts alone are worth nothing. But the truck driver who slammed into them head-on had no memory of the crash. None. The police said it was a DUI, but the man's blood alcohol levels were clean. He blacked out, but he had no history of such behavior.

Opal said I was grasping at straws. She thought this was part of my grief process. And maybe it was a little. The trial pointed out that the driver was clean, not just of impaired driving, but the defense produced MRIs and detailed medical reports showing nothing that would have caused the driver to black out. So why, on that winding stretch of road, when the sun reflected on the wet pavement, did he? The jury ruled it an accident, but I kept looking, even when there was nothing to find, even when the world moved on.

I'm sure you're wondering what your father had to do with any of this. And I'm getting there, I promise. Please, don't stop reading.

When I turned twenty-one, my holdings returned to me, releasing Dugal from any further obligation. He invited me to dinner to complete the paperwork and celebrate our parting of ways. Dugal liked to collect oddities. Artifacts that had no value to anyone but him, as he said. To me, it all looked like junk a tourist could find on a mudlarking trip.

When Dugal excused himself to take a phone call, I wandered his library. One book stood out, its leather looked almost raw, and its binding was red yarn. I pulled it from the shelf and flipped through, enjoying the illustrations until I saw the page listing the realms and the Relics associated with them. I can't explain it—the page practically shimmered. My *skin tingled, willing me to take it—warning me that there was more to discover, that my research into my parents' death wasn't over, so I stuffed the* Book of Veils *by AE Harkyn into my bag and prayed Dugal didn't notice.*

But he did, and a week later, his henchmen were banging on my door. He may have retrieved the book, but not before I scanned some pages (attached).

Reading the Book of Veils *was, at first, like immersing myself in a fantasy—it couldn't be real, despite reading as if it was. Its textbook presentation was at odds with the content. I wanted to understand why it was important, what a Relic was, and, if my assumptions were correct, how one could overcome the magick, so I looked up its author.*

But instead of AE Harkyn, I found your father.

I met Arik in his bookshop that summer. Little did I know in a few short months, he would be gone. I am deeply sorry for your loss. After a great deal of convincing, he told me about Evirdahl and the ten realms. He didn't want to. In fact, he had his assistant, Soren, turn me away that first day. Soren was against my involvement the whole time. I don't blame him. I'm human, Mundad-born, and not to be trusted. I don't think he ever warmed to me, but your father did, eventually.

Fleur scoffed. That sounded like Soren. Like them, Soren was a refugee from Evirdahl—escaping during the coup that killed their queen. The coup Fleur had predicted ages before and was exiled for. Soren was part of the Legacy Council and had voted for her exile. Fleur never forgot that, no matter if the queen was his sister. Why Arik took him in, Fleur couldn't fathom.

His brother Axel authored the book, but you know that. How it got here? Arik wasn't sure, but he thought it might have been stolen during the Dark Purge centuries ago when the tribes tried to rid themselves of any possible dark magick.

The last day I visited, near the end of August, I think—Arik told me about your mother's promise to the goddess, the Relics and counter Relics ... Then he told me about you.

After talking with your father, I was more convinced than ever that Dugal had a Relic.

I know this sounds crazy. It's a leap. It's just a book, right? What was it that compelled me when I should have disregarded the whole thing? Arik said this realm was powerful once, but without belief, magick fades. Without practice, it grows stale, and in the face of corruption, it will always be corrupted. But there is hope. Magick never completely fades, it just hibernates until hope blossoms, and maybe my eagerness to believe was the hope the book needed. That's why it was so compelling to me ... and Dugal.

Fleur paused, blinking back tears. Her father had opened up to Lenora in a way he never had with her. Heat simmered under her skin, warming her cheeks. Why would he do that? That conversation should have been hers. Fleur swallowed, a sob clogging her throat. How many times had she begged him to remind her of their home, of the Atua that wandered their land? How many times had he denied her? The past was just that, he would say, and we must be careful here not to attract attention. But Fleur was born to attract attention, and Arik never stopped scolding her for it.

I requested a lunch with Dugal to apologize for taking his book. That's when I saw it. On his cane—the symbol the book claimed marked each Relic, etched on the top, and I knew, from studying my scanned pages, that the only Relic small enough to fit inside his cane was the flute. It became an obsession, one I didn't know how to explain to Sato or Opal. Somehow, I just knew Dugal had the wind Relic, and I suspected he had used it to influence the truck driver the day of my parents' accident. It explained how the driver escaped unscathed as well as his blackout.

Arik had taught Lenora well, Fleur noted begrudgingly.

I started following Dugal. His home is heavily secure, as well as his office. Sato hacked a few of his security cameras, but the ones in his study and library were harder, same with his office. I guess I shouldn't be surprised ... a man like Dugal has every reason to be paranoid.

I also started searching for the wind spinner. No way I was going to let him use that flute on me. According to the book, the wind spinner could be used in two ways: first, on initial contact to prevent the flute's influence, the second ... by an Atua able to infiltrate the victim's subconscious and plant the memory of the mandala to halt the flow of magick produced by the flute.

It took me a year to find the spinner—less time than I expected, but as Opal says, fate finds a way. But it wasn't until six months ago that I suspected he was using the flute to gain an edge with Khade Securities. I didn't know how, but I was sure he was up to something.

Sometimes all the signs are there, but our minds refuse to process them. Dugal was thriving, spending increased money on his pet projects, but according to my annual shareholder report, the company had not lever-aged assets beyond the numbers from the previous year for quite some time. I asked to see the financials but was denied—not even Sato's hacking found anything.

I snuck into his office, pretended we had a meeting when I knew he was out of town. It took two hairpins, but I opened his desk drawer. Files filled with altered figures and bank accounts, offshore, by the look of them. Something else caught my eye: a folder at the bottom of the drawer. Medical reports for a John Doe—X-rays, psych tests, and clinical photos of a young boy. I couldn't believe my eyes. I denied it, shoving the file back into the desk, but a note escaped. A handwritten note. I trembled as I traced my finger over the dips and craps of the familiar penmanship. I knew that writing as well as I did my own.

I don't know how I got out of his office or down the street to my car. My mind was tangled and blurry. The photos, the reports, the handwriting ...

Edgar is alive. Dugal kidnapped him, controlling him with the flute Relic.

Please forgive my rambling. I feel like I have to tell you everything, or I will burst. Edgar is a genius, a mathematical prodigy, my father called him. He began writing algorithms for my father when he was ten. He was only twelve when the accident happened, his mind still malleable to the Relic's suggestions. Dugal knew what he was doing. I suspect he's using the embezzled profits to finance his archeological digs. He's looking for the other Relics. I'd bet my life on it.

I know what I have to do. This isn't about me anymore. This is about Edgar too. I had to free him. After ten years under the flute's influence, the only choice was to plant its counter in Edgar's subconscious and pray it was strong enough.

I began a treatment of Atropa berries, just a few in my morning smoothie, to build up my immunity. I know this is risky. Five months might not be enough time, but it's the only way. Small doses of belladonna should achieve the paralysis needed—a coma. From there, I should be able to reach the spirit world. Unbeknownst to Opal, she has supplied me with the tools to enter and, hopefully, exit smoothly.

Currently, Dugal is in Dubai. This is my chance. His second in command, a man named Winston Bradley, checks on his assets while he's away. I followed Winston from warehouse to office for a week, hoping he'd lead me to Edgar. Last night, I followed Winston to the symphony. Before the end of the first movement, his phone vibrated. I watched from my perch on the balcony as he kissed his wife on the cheek and headed out of the hall.

I tracked him to a warehouse in Georgetown, one I had never seen before. Keeping to the shadows, I climbed a stack of crates under the window and saw my brother staring back at me.

There was no recognition, nothing. I worried he would alert Winston to my presence, but he turned from me as if I were a wayward bird caught in the rafters. My heart ached in a way I didn't know was possible. It was time to act.

Arik once told me I should ask for your help. Your father spoke of your magick with such pride and awe. I never knew jealousy until that moment. My family was dead, my brother kidnapped, and the only thing I wanted was to hear a catch like that in my father's voice one last time. You bewilder Arik, Fleur, and I know I'm the last person you want to hear this from, but he adores you. I hope you mend your rift before it's too late.

I want to do this on my own, but I'm not a fool. When Opal told me about the séance, I prayed you'd be there. I hoped if I failed, my spirit would find you. If you're reading this, then Arik was right. My plan and Opal's antidote failed.

You, Fleur, are my safety net. Save my brother. Please. I don't know how many Relics Dugal has, but we need to get them before he hurts anyone else.

Lenora Khade

FORTY-FOUR

FLEUR

Fleur released a pent-up breath and cursed. Loudly. She turned her gaze from the computer to the ceiling, her eyes following the thin crack in the plaster until it reached the hallway. She cursed again, then once more, drawing out the word with a long sigh.

Her father was proud of her—bewildered by her magick, but proud.

Shit.

And Lenora—living Lenora somehow ended up in the middle of this. She was smarter than Fleur gave her credit for. But not smart enough not to kill herself. Damn. Why hadn't she come to Fleur as her father had suggested? Fleur frowned and looked down. Would she have helped? She swallowed a bitter laugh. Probably not. Her father knew that just as he knew Lenora wouldn't approach her unless she had no choice. Gods. It was such a convoluted mess. Fleur shook her head, her eyes landing on the hopeful gaze of the spirit next to her.

Fleur? Lenora asked, her shimmer pulsing. The damn Atua was throbbing with excitement.

Fleur lifted a brow but didn't speak. She didn't know what to say. For the first time in her life, there were no words brimming on her tongue. No emotions simmering beneath the surface, only shock. Hollow and vacuous, a word thief, a paralyzer, a momentary lapse of reality.

And she had no Theda to calm her. A whimper built in her throat, straining to be free, but Fleur swallowed it down. Closing her eyes, she imagined the warmth of Theda's arms around her, the scent of her cocoa butter lotion ... She could do this, Fleur chanted, squeezing her eyes shut until the inside of her eyelids were spotted with gold.

Her fingers itched for her tarot cards, and she folded them together. She didn't need the deck to tell her what she already knew.

This was why Ellory picked Lenora. Fleur wouldn't be surprised if her mother manipulated Lenora's death to her benefit. Ellory Harkyn had a ruthless streak. Fleur only heard the tale—told on her mother's deathbed.

When Ellory realized Fleur was also a seer, she knew it was only a matter of time before the Goddess Hemsut made herself known. Hemsut would ask the same of Fleur as she did from Ellory. Find and restore the Relics or watch each realm crumble— watch those you love die fighting the swell of darkness pushing forward from Qahil. Ellory couldn't watch her child shoulder such a burden and deflected the goddess, hiding Fleur's magick from them.

When Hemsut discovered Ellory's deceit, her punishment was swift. How dare a mere creature try to change fate? How dare she lie to a goddess? With the swirl of her fingers, Hemsut gathered grains of black dust spilling from Qahil and blew it into Ellory's lungs. Fleur's mother died protecting her from the weight of the world, but with Ellory's death, her promise fell on Fleur's shoulders.

Arik knew, Fleur realized. Her father knew the consequences of Ellory's actions. Sweet goddess, his efforts to cloak them, his frustrations when Fleur's magick grew too bold—it wasn't about just hiding them from Mundad. He was protecting her from the goddess.

She cursed again. Tears dampened her lashes, threatening to spill. Bile clogged as a sob strained against the back of her throat. Breathe, Fleur chanted, willing herself to visualize the swell of her lungs with each breath.

Fleur? Lenora asked again. Her eyes were wide above her frowning mouth. *Are you OK?*

A laugh sputtered forth, thick and sour, before Fleur could stop it. Tears splashed against her cheeks as she wiped at them with the heel of her hand. "No. Lenora, I'm not OK."

Lenora shrank back, her light dimming. *I knew everything—about you, about Evirdahl, the realms, the Relics …* She paused, the awe fading from her voice. *Does every Relic have a counter? It would make sense, wouldn't it? That something that powerful would need an antidote, so to speak. And my brother … He's alive. Kidnapped by Dugal and spellbound. I can't believe it. This was never about me. That's why all our leads were dead ends. This is about Edgar. We have to save him, Fleur. As a spirit, I can plant the spinner in his subconscious, just like I said in the letter. I hope it's not too late.* She bit her lip. *You don't think it's too late, do you?*

Fleur tried a smile but worried it looked more like a grimace. She closed her eyes. Lenora asked her to help, and this time she wouldn't fail her. "I know you have questions. If we're going to do this right and save your brother, you need to understand what you're getting into. So, go ahead. Ask."

Ellory said the Relics were part of a larger protective sheath, that it was their power that kept the sheath whole. It makes sense, I guess, but I'm still a little fuzzy on the realms. I must have known all this once … Lenora's aura dimmed as she trailed off.

Fleur took a breath. "OK, yeah, that's as good a place to start as any." She straightened and crossed her legs beneath her, resting her hands on her knees. "Mundad is part of a system of worlds all layered around each other, with my home at the core."

Like a galaxy?

"Not really, more like sediment—layers of dirt, right? Think about geology. There are roughly ten layers circling the Earth, from the exosphere to the inner core, each one building on the other. Well, it's sorta like that. The outer realm, furthest from the core, is Qahil. It's a dead world—that's where the Shadelings come from—once it was as lush as Evirdahl, but its barriers were breached eons ago, and the Grima invaded, destroying everything."

So where are the Grima from originally? A distant realm?

"No one really knows." Fleur's brow furrowed. "Maybe beyond the ten are ten more? A whole other realm system, still undiscovered. It would make sense."

So ... all these realms, but how do you get from one to the other? I'm guessing you don't use an airplane or spaceship?

"Uh, yeah. They're connected by henge veils—kinda like a portal. Most veils are either sealed or guarded now, and you need a special permit to travel between them."

You said Mundad is magickless, right? Was it always like that?

"Nah, once it was nearest in magick only to Evirdahl. As the second realm, it is similar in creature and creation to the core. The clans of Mundad traded with the tribes of Evirdahl." Fleur shrugged. "The stories say it was a prosperous eon, but few remember that far back."

But why are the Relics here?

Fleur took a deep breath, exhaling. It had been so long since she spoke of this to anyone but Theda. "I don't know. My father guessed it was the magick in the soil here that called to them."

And you have to find them? That's what Hemsut wants you to do, right?

"Yeah. It's my gift—I can feel their magick. Kinda like my third eye." Fleur offered her a small smile. "The goddesses crafted them to be part of a whole. Once all ten of them are together again, the sheath will reform. Of course, that's mostly speculation. No one knows if it's possible to recreate the sheath." Fleur paused, wondering if it was more hope than fact.

So why has it taken you so long to find one?

"I didn't want to. I was angry. Getting exiled will do that, OK?" Fleur blinked back unexpected tears and sniffed. "Besides, it's not as easy as it looks. All I have is the lullaby and a containment spell." Fleur shrugged.

Lenora fluttered closer, sweetening the air with a faint current of ambergris. *Thank you for telling me all that, Fleur.* She paused, her light dimming. *What are you going to tell Javier?*

Fleur turned her startled eyes on her. "What do you mean?"

He wants the drive, remember? It's evidence. He's gonna have a lot of questions after he reads that.

She was right. Fleur groaned.

If it was me ... I'd call Sato. He's pretty handy at eliminating stuff like this. Lenora grinned, her aura blushing.

Fleur released a breath. "Good plan." She smiled slyly at the shimmering Atua. "You remember him?"

Not everything. Mostly I remember how my heart swelled at the sight of him and how he smelled. Bits and pieces have returned, but I could live on those two memories forever.

Fleur nudged her light. "What changed?"

Ellory taught me how to reach back. I think it's how she kept her memories, too.

Ellory taught her. Fleur pressed her hand against her chest as if she could control the thud of her heart. Whatever her mother's role, Fleur doubted Ellory expected the Soulkeepers to take her memory. Lenora was magickless, and no use to them. Fleur considered the spirit before her. Such practices were reserved for magickal creatures. The Soulkeepers were callous. They preyed on the talents of certain souls—souls like Ellory

SATO ARRIVED BACK at the apartment five minutes after Fleur called him.

"What? Were you waiting outside the door?"

Sato shrugged. "So? What of it?"

Fleur arched a brow. "What about Javier?"

"Got called back to the precinct." Sato strolled into the room, eyeing his laptop resting on the coffee table. "So? What'd it say?"

Fleur settled back onto the sofa and waved at the chair across from her. "Sit."

"That bad, huh?" The furrow of his brow belied the lightness in his tone.

Fleur wasn't sure how much she was going to reveal. She figured she would let the conversation flow, only answering questions relevant to Lenora and her brother. "Tell me what you know about magick," she began, knowing that the leading question would help her grasp his handle on the situation.

"Magick?" Sato scoffed, then quieted, his gaze shifting around the room. "Yeah, that makes sense, right? I mean this whole thing— you know Len's ghost and all—plus her secrecy, and, well ... you," he stammered, as if a part of the puzzle had finally righted itself.

Don't freak him out. Lenora brightened beside him.

Fleur wanted to laugh. Of course, he was going to be freaked out. Hell, it freaked her out, and it was her history.

She began with the book, explaining its contents, but leaving out the broader knowledge. Sato didn't need to know about her home— at least not yet. Telling him dangerous magickal items were hidden across the globe was enough to take in. She focused on her connection to the book, her father, and Lenora's discovery and death—self-inflicted. It didn't take long for Sato to understand.

"She was going to rescue Edgar, right? Damn! She should have told me. I could have been there. I could have made sure she drank the antidote." Sato cursed again and fisted his hands. "Why didn't she tell me? I knew how big a deal Edgar was to her. Damn, I ... I knew it." He paused and leaned back in the chair. "She didn't have to die." He looked at Fleur. "If she had listened to your father and found you, would you have helped?"

Fleur looked at her hands.

"So that's how it is, yeah? Shit. Fleur. She had to die to get your help." Sato's voice was low.

"Don't take your anger out on me," Fleur said, her voice steady. "I never knew Lenora in life. My father never told me any of this. What I might have done if things were different doesn't matter now."

Sato leaned forward, his body taut. "You could have saved her."

"Yeah. I could have—if I had known." Fleur glared at him, tempering back her anger at his accusations. "But now, I'm going to focus on saving her brother."

Lenora brightened beside Fleur, her light curling around them.

Sato groaned and dropped his head in his hands. Stillness settled over them. Fleur waited. She knew Sato would jump to conclusions, she just hadn't expected him to land on that one.

"So Dugal has a magickal flute, yeah? Like the Pied Piper? What does it do?" he asked, raising his head, his brown eyes softer.

"It's basically mind control." Fleur hated reducing magick to such common terms. "There's a specific melody that, when played with intention, can harness someone's will. The breath of influence, my father called it."

"But it's just a flute, right? I mean, like was it made from magickal wood or something?"

Fleur gritted her teeth. "You could say that, but the magick is in the suggestion, the flute just harnesses its power."

The fifth is unseen, but not unheard. Incased in wood, it leaves you fractured. It isn't the flute, it's the breath, that's why it can't be seen. But Dugal isn't magick. How did he use it?

Fleur turned from Sato to Lenora and shook her head. "That's the only part that makes little sense. He's magickless. His breath wouldn't be powerful enough for it to work."

But yours would, right?

Fleur nodded.

"What did she say?" Sato asked, his eyes widening as Fleur relayed their conversation. He studied Fleur, clasping his hands together. "So. You're a magickal person—am I understanding this correctly? That's why you can see ghosts and all that?"

Fleur shrugged. "Yeah."

Sato released a long breath and swept his fingers through his hair. "OK. Just wanted to be sure."

"Are you cool with that?" Fleur eyed him. "This isn't common knowledge, OK? If you breathe a word of this, I *will* turn you into a hamster."

Sato shuddered. "Can you do that?"

Fleur only smiled.

"Shit. OK, yeah. My lips are sealed." Sato crossed his heart with his index finger.

"OK. If that's finished?" Fleur picked up the wind spinner, studying the etched symbol on its heart.

Relics had counters. A fact that wasn't part of her mother's lessons—at least, not before her death. Fleur wondered if things had been different, if her mother had finished her training, would she have been more apt at hunting the Relics? Did Hemsut know that by exacting her punishment so swiftly, she had denied herself part of what she wanted in the first place? The bittersweet justice of it, curled the corners of Fleur's mouth as she looked between the spirit and its boyfriend.

"We need three strategies, one for freeing Edgar, one to get the Relics—and another to keep Javier from arresting us."

FORTY-FIVE

LENORA

E verything made sense. Every piece we fumbled over, every question we lacked an answer to—all of it fell into place like the edging on a jigsaw puzzle. Now all we had to do was craft the whole.

I lost count of how many times Fleur read my letter, taking notes, then crossing them out, leaving a trail of crumbled notebook pages over the coffee table. She mumbled under her breath as she scanned the pages of the *Book of Veils* attached to the letter. I inched closer, hoping to learn more about the book that had so fascinated me, but her words were strange, another language and they stirred something in me—memories of Fleur's youth, and the lessons her mother taught her. The pages were incomplete and scattered. I must have scanned only what my untrained eye thought was relevant. I watched over her shoulder, despite the shrill of words pulsing beneath my light.

The Atropa berries should have given me an ounce of immunity at least, and the antidote to counteract the poison should have given me three minutes in a deathlike coma before pulling me back. Three minutes—was that enough? I died. I felt my muscles atrophy. The poison worked quickly, dimming my mind to a piercing ache. I appeared in the silent unknown, knowing that I had a job to do. But I failed.

"Griffin always has his cane on him." Sato shook his head. "The only way to steal it is to pry it from him."

Fleur glared at him, rubbing her temples. "Don't be so negative. He sleeps, doesn't he?"

"More than we do, probably," Sato muttered, stifling a yawn.

"That's where Edgar comes in." Fleur nodded. "Think about it. Who better than him to wrestle the cane away? We'll need Griffin's schedule. I bet he visits like clockwork. Once we free Edgar, he can help us get the flute."

"You're banking a lot on a kid who's been in a trance for ten years."

They had been arguing for hours. I looked at the glowing numbers on the microwave. It was almost seven. The overcast glow of morning light peeked through the blinds.

I flickered, lowering my light onto the sofa beside Sato. I wanted to curl into the safety of his arms. The memory of his warmth blossomed, and I clutched at my chest, wishing I could feel the thud of my heart.

Wishing I could feel anything. I thrummed, my light spreading like a spider's web in the surrounding space, tightening my core until the flutter of my wings broke the still air. I lifted myself, landing on Sato's shoulder.

He started, about to jostle me free, but caught himself. His fingers hovered over my yellow wings, and I basked in their warmth like a sun.

The buzzer sounded, eliciting a curse from Fleur.

"That better not be Javier." She looked at Sato as she stood. "Have you finished with the drive?"

Sato rolled his eyes. "I'm no amateur. It's easy to remove a few files."

"Remove, and erase all traces, right? Javier can never know what was on that drive."

"Yeah, yeah. I got you. Don't worry so much."

Fleur frowned as she leaned on the buzzer. "Hello?"

"Fleurie?" Viola sounded rushed.

Fleur blew out a breath. "Vi? What are you doing here?"

"Buzz me in. I have bagels."

My wings fluttered, and I lifted from Sato's shoulder at the sound of Viola's voice. My core ached as the memory of the doughy sweetness filled my mouth. I landed as Sato turned his head, nodding once as if he could sense my silent urgency. Each sensation was like a needle piercing my core. Finding the memory of Sato had pried open a gate, and one by one, reminders of my life leaked through.

Fleur pressed the button and moved back to the armchair, resting her hands on her stomach. "We're getting nowhere."

Sato grinned. "Not true. I hacked into Griffin's office." He turned his computer to face her and pointed to the image, his fingers tracing the line of the bookcase on the far right.

"Dugal has a camera in his office?"

"Activated with his keycard when he exits. You forget, Len had me hack him before. This isn't my first rodeo."

Fleur nodded in approval. "Now we just have to figure out how to get up there. Scaling a glass building isn't in my resume."

"Hellooo?" Viola sang as she pushed open the door. "Fleur? I brought a friend, I hope that's OK?"

Fleur stood. "Vi, now really isn't—" She broke off, her jaw dropping slightly.

Sato looked up, a small smile curling the corner of his mouth.

Viola entered, a paper bag of bagels cradled in her arms.

Beside her stood Opal Barlow.

CHAPTER

FORTY-SIX

FLEUR

F leur's stomach clenched, stymying her movement.

Opal stood, hands in the pockets of her quilted parka, her cheeks flushed from the bitter wind gusting outside the window. Her hair was piled high in a tangle of blonde curls, giving her the illusion of height. Fleur resisted the urge to cower under the weight of her stare.

"Hiya, Opal," Sato said as he hurried to embrace her. "I hear you broke out of the big house."

Fleur cringed, noting Opal's frown as she released him.

"Not my favorite experience." Opal's voice was light, almost teasing as she looked him over. "Do I have you to thank for that?"

Sato grinned. "You can pay me back with those delicious brownies of yours."

"Well"—Viola smiled as she moved into the room, peeling her brown wool coat from her shoulders—"you two look like you're planning something." She nodded to the open laptop, and the crumbled papers littering the coffee table.

Fleur grimaced and gathered them up, gesturing to Viola and Opal to sit. "Did I hear you have bagels?" She couldn't bring herself to look at Opal.

Viola set the bag on the table and pulled out a tub of cream cheese and a plastic knife. "Isn't there something you want to say to Opal, Fleur?"

Gods. The woman had as much tact as a table leg. Fleur turned to Opal, her hands fisting around the crumbled paper.

"Don't." Opal shook her head, her eyes meeting Fleurs. "I won't say I wasn't angry, I was—but I understand why you did it. I asked myself what I would do in your shoes. You didn't know me"—she sniffed—"and Lenora ... it stung. I don't know how you knew where to find the vial ..." She trailed off, shifting her gaze around the room. "It was Lenora, wasn't it?"

Fleur nodded. "I didn't ask her to search your house. I promise." Fleur turned to the butterfly on Sato's shoulder. "She wanted to help. She could tell you were holding back—"

"I know." Opal shuddered. "Well, I don't *know*, but I guessed. You said she had no memory. If she had, you wouldn't have gone to the police. I figured she panicked when she saw my greenhouse."

Lenora fluttered beside her, brightening as her butterfly disappeared. *Tell her I'm sorry. I know what she did for me, how much that must have cost her ...*

"Gods, Opal. We're so sorry," Fleur said, blinking back the tears. "When Lenora told me what she found, I had to tell Javier, Detective Torres—I didn't know ..."

Opal nodded. "I don't blame you. I knew the risks when I agreed to help Lenora." She inhaled, blowing air out of her nose.

"Did you know Lenora's plan?" Fleur wondered, tossing the crumpled paper into the trash and pulling a stack of plates from the cupboard. She paused, turning to Viola. "Wait. How do you know Opal?"

Viola grinned. "You're not the only one with a sixth sense for these things, you know."

"Vi? What did you do?"

Sato chuckled as he helped himself to a blueberry bagel.

"Don't look at me like that, Fleur." Viola frowned. "After you left yesterday, I did some digging of my own. I knew you weren't finished with this—" She paused, holding up her hand when Fleur opened her mouth to protest. "I'm not a fool. I knew you'd wallow for a bit before you realized that sacrificing yourself for Theda won't win her back."

Fleur scoffed. "I wasn't doing that. C'mon, Vi, you know what happened—"

"I do, but I also know you. If you had given up on the case, letting Lenora down—letting yourself down, you'd have to live with that festering inside you. And Fleurie, you're no good at letting things fester."

Fleur frowned, hating that her stepmother was right. "You went to visit Opal?"

"She did." Opal nodded. "Told me everything."

"Everything?" Fleur raised a brow.

"Everything I knew." Viola nodded. "Opal's a part of this, just like him." She turned to Sato. "We haven't met." She held out her hand. "I'm the nosey stepmother."

Sato grinned, shaking her hand. "I'm the ghost's boyfriend."

Fleur rolled her eyes. "Moving on?"

"I was the one who insisted on coming," Opal said, pulling a plain bagel from the bag. "Could I have one of those?" She pointed to the plates still clutched in Fleur's hands.

Flustered, Fleur set the stack on the coffee table and sat on the floor across from the two women. They looked at home on her over-stuffed purple sofa. Warmth curled in the pit of her stomach as she reached for a bagel. Viola and Opal met less than twenty-four hours ago, and they were already friends. How did Vi do it? Fleur shook her head and bit into the cinnamon dough, savoring the delicate spice.

"You asked if I knew Lenora's plan, Fleur," Opal commented as she slathered cream cheese over half of her bagel. "And the answer is no. She asked me to teach her about poisons, and I did against my better judgment. Lenora told me she had a plan, and asked me to create the antidote, taking half for herself. Told me to hold on to the rest in case she needed it again." Opal took a deep breath, blinking back tears.

"I'm sorry, Opal," Fleur said gently.

"I didn't know why she needed it. I should have asked, but maybe a part of me didn't want to know. I knew she was experimenting with belladonna, but I never expected her to use it on herself …"

Sato leaned forward and grasped Opal's hand. "You and me both."

Opal squeezed Sato's hand once before releasing it.

"So, what now?" Viola looked around her. "Did you figure it out?"

Fleur laid out the details, just as she had with Sato, careful to only tell what was important to the case.

"Magick?" Opal's eyes widened. "You're kidding, right?"

"I'm not talking about stage show stuff. True magick is rooted in our cores. Some of us have the gift for it. I was born with the ability to see spirits, a gift shared by my ancestry, but unlike the rest, I am also a seer …"

"You mentioned that before …," Opal murmured.

"And that means I have a few more abilities, namely recognizing a magickal object by its heat."

"It makes sense, in a way …" Opal munched on her bagel. "Dugal invested a lot of money on archeological digs—money the company couldn't afford. As convoluted as the whole thing sounds … it makes sense," she repeated. "Edgar had a head for numbers. Even Rodney had used him to help with some of Khade's bigger projects. Dugal must have realized it was Edgar's genius holding the company together, not Rodney." She paused, her gaze sweeping over them. "I'm not surprised that he was involved in their deaths. Lenora always knew there was something else to it." She shook her head. "I should have listened to her."

"So, is Dugal magickal, like you?" Viola wondered.

Fleur shook her head. "No. That's just about the only thing I know for sure. If he was, I would have felt ... something when Theda and I visited him. But there was nothing but silence and cold. I don't understand how he's able to use it. He's strange, I'll give you that, but there isn't a magickal bone in his body."

Silence descended. Five sets of eyes glued to the corkboard leaning against the wall. Fleur chewed her bagel, her eyes tracing the path of Theda's handwriting on each card. She was missing something. The sensation nagged, pulling her thoughts like taffy.

"You knew my father, didn't you?" Fleur said, turning to Opal. "You recognized him when I showed you the photo. Why didn't you tell me?"

Opal straightened, setting her bagel down, and inhaled. "I only met Arik once."

Viola gasped, her bagel paused midway to her mouth.

"I warned Lenora I wasn't a good liar." Opal huffed and shook her head, then fixed her gaze on Fleur. "I knew who you were the minute I saw you. Arik told us about you during Lenora's last visit. He said you could help but wouldn't—that you were determined to ignore everything about your home. He said your pain cut deep. Lenora believed she could convince you, but she saw you as a last resort. This was her battle, she said."

Lenora brightened beside her. *Would you have helped me?*

The spirit fluttered closer, and Fleur frowned, swallowing back the urge to lie. She turned from Lenora, focusing on Opal once more. "So that's why you said nothing? Because my father told you I was stubborn?"

"Well, no." Opal picked up her bagel. "You were the last person I expected to see, and I didn't know what to do. I made a promise to Lenora ..." She shook her head. "If she had just told me what she was planning, how you fit in ... I-I would have been prepared."

"Well, you're helping now." Viola reached for Opal's hand and squeezed. "That counts for something."

"What do you know about the *Book of Veils?*" Fleur asked.

"Not much. I never saw it or understood Lenora's obsession with it. I humored her. It was good to see her working toward a goal. I didn't realize it was just another part of her parents' mystery. If I had …" Opal shrugged. "I want to believe I would have acted differently, but—"

"You wouldn't," Sato piped up from the armchair. "We both suspected something but did nothing. That's how it was with Len. Left in the dark and loyal to the end."

I should have told her—I should have told both of them. But I was scared, Fleur. You understand that, right? Lenora's voice was strained, and Fleur wondered if she was trying to convince her or herself.

Fleur scooted to the table and picked up the wind spinner. "What about this?"

Opal's eyes narrowed. "I didn't lie about everything."

"The name of the antique shop?"

"It was just a shop, like all the other junk shops. Nothing special about it." Opal paused, her head tilting. "I remember the owner was strange—very intense. He had amber eyes. I remember because they were so bright, I wondered if they were contacts. He seemed to know who Lenora was. Later, I asked her if she knew him. She just shook her head, said he was probably one of Dugal's contacts." Opal blinked. "Dugal dabbled with illegal market antiquities. It wouldn't surprise me if Lenora's hunch was right."

Fleur sighed. It was a significant, albeit vague, lead. There were millions of antique stores in Seattle. Searching for one with an amber-eyed owner was like finding a needle in a haystack. But … if Lenora's hunch was correct …

Fleur pulled up the copy of Lenora's letter they had transferred from the drive onto her computer and scrolled to the end. The letter wasn't the only thing on the drive. Aside from Lenora's research and the scanned pages from the *Book of Veils*, she also included a list of addresses that until now, Fleur had failed to examine. She scrolled until she landed on a name. Just a name, no address, no phone number.

Barker, LTD Antiques.

It was a start.

Opal released a breath. "What about the warehouse? Have you been there? The one Lenora saw Edgar in?"

Fleur waited a beat, letting the change of subject settle. "Not yet."

Viola set her plate on the coffee table and stood. "Well? What are we waiting for?"

"Jeez, Vi, relax. We can't just show up at Griffin's secret warehouse." Fleur arched a brow at her eagerness.

"Why not? No harm in driving by slowly, is there?" Viola frowned as she sat back down.

Opal chuckled. "Can you hack the warehouse's security system?" she asked Sato.

"Maybe?" He shrugged. "If I knew what warehouse to hack."

Lenora pulsed beside her. *The ticket stub. I must have used it to write the address, but the paper tore in the rain.*

Fleur moved to the war board and pulled off the stub. There, in smudged blue ink, *DG1085*. That's what the house was trying to tell her that day. Fleur looked back to her computer, scanning Lenora's list, then up to Sato. "Try 1085 E Marginal Way."

Sato's fingers danced over the keyboard, his brow furrowed in thought.

"Nope," he said, shaking his head. "The warehouse must be on a different network. Damn."

"What do we do?"

Sato glanced up, a grin lifting the corner of his mouth. "Fancy a little recon?"

CHAPTER

FORTY-SEVEN

FLEUR

The gray plaster walls of Dugal's secret warehouse nestled between a boiler supplier and a junkyard. Fleur crinkled her nose as they drove past, noting the perfect anonymity of the location.

Viola turned into one of the random parking lots between build-ings and pulled over, careful to keep them out of view. The weather had kept its dismal downpour, the icy rain pounding against the windshield. Fleur gritted her teeth, begrudgingly thankful for the car's heat warming her toes.

Fleur had lost two battles in less than a minute—the first being her insistence that Viola and Opal wait for them to get back, the second, her ability to drive. Sure, her car stood out, but it was a *classic*, and perfectly drivable, as long as she stayed off the highway. She hated to admit Viola's boring old Nissan was the better choice for their purpose. Fleur frowned as her stepmother turned to face them in the back seat, hating how much she enjoyed the spaciousness.

"OK, Google says it's the building over there." Viola pointed to the smaller of the three nestled beyond the junkyard's tall fence.

Lenora fluttered her wings on Sato's shoulder. Since her memory last night, the Atua spent most of her time in moth form hovering near Sato.

"There's nothing—no sign, no Khade logo ...," Opal murmured from the passenger seat, as she studied the building.

"I doubt this is something Dugal would want to advertise." Fleur smirked. According to Lenora's research, Khade owned the building, but listed it as a storage facility. Fleur chalked it up to Dugal's hubris that he would be so bold as to hide Edgar on company property.

Sato peered into his computer screen, his fingers pounding on the keys. He said he had a plan, a way of getting access to the warehouse's network, but didn't elaborate. Fleur watched his brow furrow in concentration and nudged him. "You ready?"

"Almost ...," he trailed off, his screen flashing with lines of code in the dark car. He scrolled up, scanning his work, before pulling a bright pink thumb drive from the side of his computer. "Do you have the masking tape?"

Fleur fished it out of her bag and handed it to him. "I still don't understand what this is for."

Sato flashed them a broad grin and pulled a Sharpie out of his pocket. "Just wait." He pulled off a small piece of tape and attached it to the front of the drive with the words Bitcoin Wallet scrawled across the top. "Booby trap complete."

"How is that a booby trap?" Viola asked, eyeing the small pink drive.

"You know what Bitcoin is, right?" Sato asked, folding his laptop back into his backpack.

"Digital currency?"

"Yeah, so this is the equivalent of dropping your wallet on the ground." Sato held up the drive. "Dude picks it up, plugs it in—because who wouldn't? Trust me. The guards will be putty in my hands."

"But what if there aren't any guards?"

"Lenora said there were guards," Fleur answered, hoping Dugal had changed nothing since Lenora spied Edgar through the window.

"She's right." Opal nodded to the man in dark overalls rounding the side of the building. "Check out the bulge on his hip."

"Opal, really?" Viola grimaced.

Fleur snorted out a laugh and shook her head. "Get your head out of the gutter, Vi. She means he's armed."

Viola blushed. "I knew that."

"Are you sure this will work?" Fleur asked Sato.

"It has before." Sato shrugged. "Griffin's goons might be loyal, but they lack a certain ... intelligence." He grinned.

Fleur blew out a breath and reached for the door. "You two stay here. Keep an eye out, OK?" She nodded to Viola and Opal.

Sato turned to Fleur. "I'll go around the front and toss this puppy into their path. You head to the crates on the side—that's where Lenora climbed up, right?"

Fleur nodded. "Don't get caught."

"You too."

They pushed open the car doors and moved toward the warehouse.

Fleur pulled her collar up, bracing herself against the rain as she darted toward the crates stacked alongside the building. The sense of déjà vu crept over her as she neared, tightening her stomach into a knot. Lenora was out here, alone, the night before she died. She had planned her death by this point—crafted an elaborate scheme, risked her personal safety and failed.

But she hadn't failed on her own. Fleur could taste the Soulkeeper's interest. The Inbetween needed that Relic, and Lenora was the perfect pawn. Goose bumps trailed over her arms, and she wondered if she'll ever know the extent of their plotting.

This is it. I followed Winston to the door and watched him go inside, then doubled back here. Lenora brightened beside her, her face turned to the window above the stack of crates.

"You remember?" Fleur inched around the building, peering over the corner to be sure no one could see her.

No. But I've read the letter so many times it feels like a memory.

Fleur craned her neck, looking around the roof's edging. There were cameras everywhere. It would be impossible not to be seen ... unless one knew how to cloak themselves.

"Keep a look out, OK?"

It was a simple spell, one every child learns in primary. There was common magick in Evirdahl, magick each tribe shared. Spells rooted in the landscape before they were gifted their individual abilities. She whispered the protection spell, syllables in the ancient tongue blossoming in the back of her throat like an old friend. Words Fleur thought she had forgotten.

The magick warmed her fingertips, spreading like wings in her bloodstream. Her heart pounded, but not in fear. Calm embraced her. Gods. She had forgotten how peaceful magick could be.

Fleur shifted to the side, closer to the crates, and the camera attached above. The spell wouldn't erase her, instead it would blur her, protecting her aura, like an abstract painting made of shadow and cloud.

She pulled herself up onto the crate. The rough splintered wood tore at the side of her hand. Fleur cursed and looked down. A smear of blood on the crate. She wiped it with the sleeve of her jacket, but the same offending sliver caught the seam and pulled.

Wait. Lenora pointed to something beside her. *What's that?*

Dark green threads wound around the wood.

My coat.

"Looks like we're on the right track." Fleur pulled her sleeve loose, ignoring the black threads the wood pulled free and hoisted herself up another crate.

The window was dirty with rain splatter and grime. Fleur peered through the glass, looking for light, movement ... anything but darkness.

A door opposite opened, illuminating the interior. Fleur sucked in a breath and ducked. A man in a dark gray jacket moved inside, flicking on a light at the guard station to the right of the door. She watched him sit in front of the screen, pull something pink out of his coat pocket and plug it into the side of the computer.

Sato's drive.

Fleur shook her head and turned from the guard station, searching the rest of the modest warehouse. A light flared beneath her, and she inched forward, pressing her forehead against the dirty glass.

A workstation—four monitors stacked over a desk. Fast food bags and takeout boxes littered the floor to the left of it, beside a tall bookcase and a bed. Fleur craned her neck, wishing she could open the window and sneak in. Beside the bed was another screen—a television? And a treadmill, a towel hanging from the front of it.

He has to be here.

Fleur shifted feet, inching toward the edge of the crate. She needed a better angle, and twisted her head to peer downward, her eyes darting from screen to screen. The monitor's glow offered meager light, but it was better than nothing. Her gaze swept the workstation until her eyes met a pair of brown ones.

Fleur pulled back, shaking off the surprise before returning to the window.

And Edgar's stare.

Lenora flickered, her light throbbing blue then yellow as she tried to contain herself.

The Edgar Fleur knew from pictures littering Lenora's attic walls was gone. Instead of a boy stood a man, lean with a tangle of over-grown curly brown hair. He wore a pair of dark sweatpants and what looked like leather slippers below an oversized T-shirt, a Seattle Seahawks logo embossed across the front.

Fleur didn't move. She didn't want to break his stare.

Did he see her? Would he sound an alarm? Fleur held her breath. But his gaze was hollow, his face slack. Edgar's hands hung at his sides, as if he forgot they were there.

He doesn't see us. Fleur ... He's in a trance or something.

"Can you get in there?" Fleur whispered without turning. The rain pelted her back, and a shudder threatened to break free. "Len?"

Lenora nodded and flickered once.

A moment later, she was gone.

CHAPTER
FORTY-EIGHT

LENORA

I didn't remember him, but I knew him the moment I saw him. My brother, the reason I forced my death, the missing piece of my puzzle.

His hair was curlier than mine, his jaw squarer, but we shared the same lean build—or we did, weeks ago, when I was alive.

Anger stemmed through me, uncontrolled rage coloring my light red. I wanted to scream, to hurl my voice into the rafters at my family being ripped apart. Fury flickered my light.

Easy, Lenora. You still have a long way to go. Ellory's voice echoed in my head.

She was right. My light dimmed. Anger didn't help anyone. Still brittle from passing through the window, I throbbed as I imagined my heart would on the wings of such a discovery. I needed to be tactful. I could save him, even if I couldn't save myself.

Edgar stood still, a limb of a petrified tree. I slid up beside him, half hope, half wonder. His lips were fuller than mine ... his lashes were longer. His skin was like porcelain, untouched by the sun.

316

I leaned closer, my light mingling with delicate flesh. Goose bumps spread over his exposed forearms. He shivered, and I wanted to cry out. He felt me.

Edgar, I whispered, wishing I could inhale the musk on his skin. *I'll get you out of this. I promise.*

Then I heard it.

Music. The soft strains of melody.

I reeled back. The space was empty except for us. The guard, encased in his booth at the front of the warehouse too far away. I inched toward the rows of monitors, taking in the lines of code on one and the array of images on the other—nature scenes, trees ruffling in a breeze, waterfalls crashing with spray Edgar would never feel. He had an outlet, albeit two-dimensional. At least Dugal gave him that.

My rage sputtered forth like fire and I willed it back. I would free him. I would die as many deaths as needed to do so.

Listen, Lenora. Ellory's voice ebbed, drawing me forward, past the unmade bed and pile of clothing beside it.

It's Dugal, isn't it? Playing the flute?

His reach has grown, but his breath is not his own.

How do I stop him?

You know how. Remember, Lenora. This is why your death is unfinished—why I brought you to Fleur.

Fleur. I glanced up at the window. Her shadow was barely visible. I wasn't alone anymore. Calm radiated through me. I fought this battle once before and failed—but now ...

I turned back to Edgar, my light throbbing with need. I wanted to wrap him in color, to steal him away, to protect him. I lifted my hand, its light brightening the stubble along his jaw. His skin was smooth, unblemished—like the rest of him.

This wasn't my brother. This was only his husk.

I closed my eyes, wishing I could dig out the vivid boy I hardly remembered. I had only snippets of him, but they were enough ... for now.

Can you hear me, Ed? Please? I need to know if you're still there. Edgar? It was a desperate attempt; I knew that. I was dead, and as far as I knew, Edgar wasn't like Fleur ... but I had to try. *Please ...*

Edgar's eye twitched as a shudder raced over him.

I leaned closer, tucking my head under his chin. *I'll get you out of here, Edgar,* I promised, my light flickering with need.

A low growl, like a sob, vibrated the air beside me. I stilled. *Edgar?*

"*Lennn ...,*" he moaned, his face unflinching.

I wanted to cry out. He was still there. Somewhere inside this shell, Edgar heard me.

Oh, Eddie! Shh. My voice shook, my aura pure white. *I'll be back. Be strong.* I pressed my cheek to his, watching as the hairs on his arms rose. My brother could feel me. My light surged with hope.

I rose to the window, sliding through the frenzy of molecules, my light flickering as I pulled myself through.

"Is he OK?" Fleur whispered, her gaze glued to my brother.

He's enchanted. I heard the song.

Fleur cursed. "I really hate this guy."

Fleur ...

"What?"

Edgar could hear me.

Fleur's eyes widened. "That's not possible."

It is. He felt me, and he said my name.

Fleur cursed and closed her eyes.

Do you think ...

She released a shaky breath and shook her head. "His subconscious perceived you. That's crazy. He's somehow in a heightened state of awareness." She glanced back through the window and frowned. "I'd guess his mind fractured. Magick like that ..." She paused. "Your brother is still there, Len, but he might not be the boy you remember."

But ... will he be OK?

"If we do it right. Just using the spinner won't work. Damn. The melody is too embedded, and I don't want Edgar's mind to divide more." She paused and turned to me, her gaze narrowed as if something had just occurred to her.

Do you have a plan?

Fleur nodded. "The beginnings of one. C'mon, let's get back." She shuffled down the crates, a muttering what sounded like a chant.

I have to save him, Fleur. My light bloomed with conviction.

"We will. I promise."

CHAPTER
FORTY-NINE

FLEUR

F leur didn't have a plan—not exactly. But she had an idea.

Edgar's reaction to Lenora changed everything. The wind spinner wouldn't be enough to break him—not if they wanted to keep him from madness. If Lenora's original plan had succeeded, Edgar would be of two minds, manic and scared for the rest of his life. Her mother taught her to be wary of the Relics, that over time if they didn't kill you, they would maim you somehow. And Edgar's situation was a perfect example.

He was stronger than she expected. Most would succumb, losing themselves in the magick, but if Lenora was right and Edgar reacted to her prodding, then he was aware of it. Fleur frowned, staring at the trees and buildings drifting by. And if part of him was aware of it, albeit unable to stop it, Fleur could only guess how that could crack his consciousness.

If anyone in the car noticed her silence, no one commented. Fleur closed her eyes and let the quiet hum of traffic lull her thoughts.

They wouldn't just need the spinner to free him—if they wanted him to return whole, they'd need the flute too.

Fleur sifted through her memories, pulling, and discarding lesson after lesson. Ellory taught her how to counteract the Relics. Each one had its own unique magick, and like all magick, it could be reversed. Fleur should have known it wouldn't be that simple.

She recalled nothing about a counter Relic. The absence of such information was suspicious. Were there more? If so, then why weren't they noted? The Loatheian ruler couldn't have been the only one to employ such methods. To have a failsafe like that ... it was cleverer than Fleur gave them credit for.

She needed more than the pages scanned on Lenora's drive.

She needed the *Book of Veils*. Axel would have put more than words in the grimoire. He would have threaded magick into each page. Magick Fleur needed.

We need both instruments, don't we? Lenora's voice seeped into her thoughts, rousing her.

Fleur nodded but didn't turn her gaze from the window. "I think so."

Think?

"What was that?" Viola chirped from the driver's seat. "You think what?"

They stopped in front of Viola's house. Fleur blinked and straightened, rolling her taut shoulders. "Wait. Why are we here?"

Viola's gaze met hers in the rearview mirror. "It's lunchtime."

"So?"

"Fleur, honey, I have turkey coming out of my ears."

Beside her, Sato grinned and reached for the door handle. "I could eat," he offered, pushing the door open.

Opal nodded as she too opened the door. "I missed Thanksgiving, so ... yeah, I'm in."

Fleur groaned as she pulled herself from the car. Irritated that her musings were cut short, she followed the group into Viola's small bungalow.

If they had both tools, Lenora could plant the spinner in Edgar's subconscious, while Fleur played the reverse melody. Fleur bit her lip, ignoring Viola's chatter as she moved around the kitchen. But would it work? Fleur had tried nothing like this before, and her magick was more than a little rusty. Could she reverse the intention and extract Edgar safely?

They needed to steal the Relics first. Until now Fleur had thought of this as two separate jobs—free Edgar, use his knowledge to get the Relics, maybe even keep him planted in Dugal's employ as a spy until they could assess the situation. But that wouldn't work. Pulling Edgar from the flute's influence now would break him even more than Dugal already had. No. She needed to rethread the tapestry of Edgar's mind before extracting him.

"Earth to Fleur … are you with us?" Viola touched Fleur's arm, shaking her from her reverie.

Fleur blinked, shaking her head. "Yeah. What?"

"I asked if you wanted some of Theda's yams?" Viola moved back to the spread of open Tupperware containers littering the counter.

"Sure." Fleur exhaled, pulling her thoughts into the present, and peeled off her jacket.

Opal and Sato had shed their coats and settled onto the counter stools surrounding the kitchen island. Wine glasses placed in front of them, Opal worked the corkscrew into a fresh bottle.

"What is it with y'all and wine? Don't you have any beer?" Sato lamented as he pulled his laptop from his bag.

"I never liked beer." Viola made a face as she opened the oven door. Three casserole dishes lay in front of her, each as carefully crafted as they were two days ago. Fleur remembered Thanksgiving and cringed. It didn't occur to her at the time that Viola would keep all that food.

"How do you not like beer?" Sato mumbled as he accepted a glass of red wine from Opal.

Viola rolled her eyes at Sato and turned to Fleur. "Now, what are you thinking? I can hear your brain churning from a mile away," she asked as she closed the oven door on the leftovers and set the timer.

Fleur looked from her stepmother to Sato and Opal. Lenora brightened, hovering between them, her eyes as curious as the rest.

She didn't know where to begin. Fleur shook her head and laid out her thoughts carefully, as if unwinding a thread. She paused at the end, her body taut, waiting for the myriad of questions to begin.

"And this book can help extract Edgar safely?" Opal asked.

"I know how to reverse a Relic, but not one embedded so deep." Fleur sighed. "I need the book's magick to guide me."

Sato's wine glass clattered against the counter. "Don't worry." He nodded. "I have a plan."

"Why does that make me more nervous?"

"Rude." Sato lifted his glass and nodded for a refill. "I know a thing or two. Y'all focus on getting the flute from Griffin."

Viola filled Sato's glass and poured herself another, her brow crinkling in thought.

Fleur's gaze swept over them. Silence descended. Even Lenora's light dimmed.

"I think I can help," Opal offered, her fingers toying with the stem of the wineglass.

"Help?" Fleur rolled back her shoulders, allowing the tension to fizzle. "Help how?"

"To begin with, I agree. Your original plan to extract Edgar first was sound." Opal nodded. "Following through with Lenora's plan seemed like the best solution, but now … if you're right about this, I think I can help with getting the flute."

"Second," Opal continued, "Sato is right. Dugal is never without his cane. I never thought much about it, but it makes sense that he'd store the flute in it." Her brow crinkled. "I wonder how many people he's used it on?"

Fleur sniffed and shook her head. The sweet aroma of Theda's yams and the savory warmth of turkey stuffing filled the kitchen. Her stomach clenched as Theda's cry as she pushed back from the table rang in Fleur's ears. No, she ordered herself, stop. She needed focus. "There's no way of knowing."

"What are you think—" Viola broke off as the oven timer chimed. She smiled apologetically and nodded to Opal as she began pulling the food from the oven. "Oh, hold that thought. Fleurie, could you get the plates?"

Fleur grumbled as she moved to the cupboard, grabbed a stack of dinner plates, and set them on the counter. "Buffet style?" she asked Viola, unsure if her stepmother was going to make a production out of lunch.

Viola smiled. "Why not? As long as the food gets eaten." She set the food in a line at the edge of the counter.

"Damn, it looks awesome." Sato grinned as he pulled a plate from the stack and began heaping stuffing on.

Once they were all seated, plates piled high, Fleur turned to Opal. "You said you could help?"

Opal nodded. "Well, we've got two options: wrestle the cane from him or engineer a way for him to lose it."

Fleur smiled. "And how do we do that?"

"I'm sure you guessed I've dabbled with serums and sedatives ..." Opal trailed off, taking a bite of turkey.

"You want to poison him?" Viola's eyes widened.

"Of course not, but maybe we could slip a sleeping draught into his food?"

Sato laughed. "Drug him and take the cane and the other Relic? Then use them to free Edgar? Hell, yeah. I'm in."

"But how do we get the sleeping pill into his food?" Fleur picked at her yams, her appetite fading. Focus, she told herself again. She didn't have time to cry over root vegetables. She leaned back in her chair and met Opal's gaze. "It's not like he'll come to a dinner party."

"The Seattle Art Gala," Viola announced, sitting up in her chair. "Of course, I'd almost forgotten about it."

Fleur bit back a groan. She was not in the mood for another gossip session. "What does that have to do with anything?"

"Khade Securities is a sponsor. The museum holds its annual gala in December ..." She paused. "On the third, if I'm not mistaken. My women's club is hosting this year. Dugal Griffin will be there, no doubt."

Fleur stared at Viola, her jaw dropping. That's it. That's how they'll get in. She didn't know what to say.

"That would work." Opal nodded. "I can craft a sleeping agent. It should be simple enough to slip it into his drink."

"Then we steal the cane." Sato grinned. "I like it."

Fleur's brow crinkled in thought. That would get them in the door, and the flute, but what about the shell Relic? They'll have a slim window once Dugal wakes to find his precious cane gone. He'll put the shell on lockdown. Fleur frowned. "We still need to get past his security to get the other Relic."

"Leave that to me," Sato said, shoveling a forkful of turkey into his mouth.

CHAPTER
FIFTY

LENORA

I listened to them strategize with half an ear. The four of them seemed to feed off each other, building idea upon idea like bricks in our fortress.

Opal to craft, Viola to administer, Sato to hack, and Fleur to steal.

They maneuvered around obstacles—Opal and Viola would be on the floor, chatting Griffin up, planting the drug and extracting the cane. Sato in the security booth, working with Fleur to hack the feed to Dugal's office and Fleur ... I bit back a laugh when Sato mentioned the catering staff. Fleur in a tuxedoed uniform would be worth her grumbling. Fleur would enter with the staff, bypassing security on the first four floors, then make her way to the elevator shaft and the vents beyond.

They planned and drafted.

And I ... I was useless to contribute.

I had only one role. I was the ghost. The lookout. The one to pull Edgar to safety. But what if I missed? What if I couldn't hold him? What if his subconscious was too deep?

Fleur assured me the reverse melody would rethread Edgar's frayed intentions. All I had to do was enter his dreams and plant a memory of the spinner. It would work in tandem to erase Dugal's influence. The key element was breath—wind, whispered demands. Fleur would counteract Dugal's breath with her own, but it was up to me to ensure it reached its destination.

But what if I failed? Like I failed before.

Fleur's gaze flickered to me. If she noticed my silence, she said nothing. I wavered, my light dimming, and she nodded. She understood my need for solace, watching as I vanished.

The Lobby buzzed with the delicate hum of spirits scattered around the tree's trunk. Their auras flickered red with fear. Guardians wove between them, listening, their light deep indigo as they swept between the glimmers.

Amber light throbbed around us, like a candle flame warding off the oncoming night. I paused. Voices tittered with anticipation, mingling with inaudible murmurs as I inched toward the edge of the circular room. The heavy geometric drapes were closed, as always. I shivered at the cool draft wafting from under their thick fabric.

They're closer. Ellory's soft timbre echoed in my mind a moment before she appeared. Like the others, her indigo light stretched over her like a deep chasm.

I throbbed red, glancing up past the dangling lights. *I know which Relic—I'm so close, Ellory ...*

Ellory nodded, her head tilting toward the darkness above. *The flute will only hold them back, it isn't enough, but it is the start we need.* She turned the full weight of her stare onto me. *We must recraft the sheath. I understand the urgency now ...* She frowned. *Hemsut was right.*

My light darkened with memories of my last encounter with the shadow creatures. *But how? And what about the other realms? Are they at war since the sheath isn't there to protect them?*

No, the treaties drawn between realms still stand. The lower nine hold tight to their alliances. It's only Qahil's unruly shadows drawing closer to the core.

What will happen if they reach Evirdahl?

Ellory turned away, her indigo fading as a tinge of red colored her edges. *We must stop that from being a possibility.*

I knew this. Fleur had explained everything, but until this moment, I hadn't understood what that meant. We were getting closer, but will we get them in time?

You must. The creatures reaching the Great Tree endangers us all.

My light flickered with uncertainty.

Trust yourself, Lenora. Your tapestry isn't wrong.

But what if I can't free Edgar? What if Fleur can't get the Relics from Dugal? What if he has a third?

She will. My daughter is capable of many things.

She called Fleur her daughter. If I had breath, it would have caught in my throat at the tenderness of each syllable. Was she free to admit such a thing now? *What of the Soulkeepers?*

I wield more power here than I understood, Lenora. The keepers need me and have not punished my actions, but I must be careful. My gifts will only grant me so much.

What gifts?

Ellory's eyes lifted, and I imagined her smile. *Fleur and I are not that different.* She turned as another Guardian glided past, nodding in acknowledgment. *You must be careful, Lenora. When you descend, do so quickly. Your brother's spirit is ready.*

How do you know?

Ellory tilted her head toward the dark canopy. *The rift in his mind is shrinking as hope winds its way around, but it is still deep. You will free him, and you will bring us the flute. Your death wasn't in vain, Lenora.*

I closed my eyes, allowing her words to sink, their meaning like claws scratching at my spine. My light swelled as my resolve tightened.

Will you help us? I asked, knowing her response, yet hoping otherwise.

But Ellory had gone.

CHAPTER
FIFTY-ONE

FLEUR

S ato's cousin worked for the catering company hired for the gala. If Fleur believed in fate, she would look at this as a positive sign.

But she didn't. Not the way her mother had believed, and certainly not as she was taught to believe. Hemsut be damned. The goddess of time and destiny had overstayed her welcome in Fleur's life. First with her demands, then with her punishments ... Fleur shuddered, goose bumps scattered over her flesh. She glanced up into the thick cloud cover above, knowing Hemsut had just plucked her thread ... a subtle reminder of her place.

"That house—the blue one on the left." Sato pointed out the passenger side window.

"I see it, jeez."

"It didn't look like it."

Fleur grumbled and slowed the Subie, wondering what was chewing at Sato all of a sudden. He didn't have to come with her. In fact, Fleur specifically asked him not to. She could manage this—but

Sato insisted, climbing into her car before she could back up her argument.

"You didn't have to come, you know."

"Ayame is my cousin." He shrugged and Fleur wondered if there was something more to his urgency.

As she angled the Subie into the cramped parking space, Fleur inspected the street where Sato's cousin lived. Quaint was the perfect word for the bevy of colorful homes flanked by cedar fences and well-aged trees. She opened the car door and stepped out onto the curb, listening for the rustle and bark of the bullmastiff —Nova. Didn't Sato say his cousin was taking care of the animal? Fleur moved up the path, her hands fisted in her pocket, Sato trailing behind her.

"Don't worry, Nova is probably in the backyard. Ayame doesn't like the dog around when she's cooking."

"How do you know she's cooking?"

"She's always cooking."

The single-story home was complete with white picket fence and wood shutters over the slate-blue siding. Sato tried the door handle, cursing quietly when it did not open. Then knocked forcefully on the door.

The bark was instantaneous, followed by a sharp command and the thud of paws padding on the hardwood floor.

Fleur took a deep breath.

The door opened, revealing a slight Asian woman in her late twenties. Black hair piled high on her head in a tangled bun, wisps escaped, framing her heart-shaped face and gentle, expectant gaze. She wore an apron over a yellow sweatshirt and jeans. Flour covered her chest and dusted her shoulder.

"Hiya, cuz." Sato ran a hand through his hair and smiled.

"Nope." Ayame frowned and began to shut the door.

"Hey! Wait! I know you're mad—"

"No, Takeo. Mad was two days ago when you left me stranded at the farmers market, because something suddenly came up. Or when you stopped by—unexpectedly, mind you—and handed me Nova's leash with no explanation. Do you know how much that damn dog eats? Huh? Or how much an Uber from Ballard costs?"

If glares were daggers Sato would be cut to shreds.

"I'm looking for Lenora's killer. You know that, cuz. I didn't abandon you. I asked if you were OK, didn't I?" Sato nodded to Nova, pacing impatiently behind Ayame. "And you love dogs! I didn't think you'd mind watching Nova for a bit. It's not like—"

"You should have ASKED, Takeo. I have a family, AND a business to run. It's bad enough that Haru is spending the end of his parental leave watching Yuki alone, so that I can prepare for the gala. Did you even think I might need some help? Huh? Did it ever occur to you to ask?"

Sato looked at his feet and shrugged. Fleur could almost feel the weight of his action on her own shoulders. "I can get a little single-minded sometimes, I know—"

"Not sometimes, Takeo. ALL the time." Ayame exhaled, her expression softening. "I know Lenora's death was hard but, cuz, you're not alone in this. We want to help, but you just ..." She shook her head, her words used up.

Fleur cleared her throat. "Um, hi. I'm Fleur."

Ayame turned to Fleur as if noticing her for the first time, and a flush crept up her cheeks. "The psychic? The one who can see Lenora?"

"Yep. Uh, sorry ... I'm the one taking up Sato's time at the moment." Fleur ducked her head slightly and offered a small smile.

Ayame studied her, her gaze taking in the tangle of Fleur's braided gray hair to the tips of her worn combat boots. Fleur pulled at the sleeve of her leather jacket, wondering if she passed whatever inspection Ayame was giving her. "Can you really see Lenora?"

Fleur nodded, shifting her weight from foot to foot. "Yeah."

"And you figured out who killed her?"

Fleur nodded again, unwilling to admit any more. "And we need your help to make them pay."

"It was Dugal, wasn't it?"

Gods. Ayame didn't beat around the bush. Fleur shrugged. "I can't say yet. Will you help?"

"Please, cuz?" Sato pleaded. "I know I've been shitty, but we're so close. Please? Will you help?"

Ayame narrowed her eyes at the two of them and bit her bottom lip. Behind her Nova whined and scratched at the doorframe, clearing needing attention. Ayame shushed the beast and pointed to the living room, waiting until the dog was settled before turning back to them. "What do you need?"

Fleur turned to Sato, allowing him to take the lead.

"Not much, I promise! Just a uniform. You're catering the gala, yeah? We need to get into the building incognito, and thought Fleur could wear one of your uniforms? Please?"

Ayame raised a dark brow. "Why should I help? Give me one good reason, Takeo, and maybe I have an extra badge and uniform."

Sato took a step forward and grasped Ayame's arm. "Because we're close, cuz—so damn close, this is the last step. And I know I've been the worst, but I'll make it up to you, I promise. I'll watch Yuki every Saturday for a month. But please, Ayame. I need this."

Fleur looked from Sato's pleading face to Ayame's suspicious one, wondering if she should say anything, but thought better of it.

Ayame considered them. "Fine. You can have the uniform and badge."

Sato exhaled and wrapped Ayame in a bear hug. "Thank you. Thank you, cuz. I owe you big time."

"Yeah. You do." Ayame playfully shoved at his shoulder and backed into the house. "Wait here."

She left the door cracked enough for Fleur to see Nova, curled up on an oversized pillow beside a lounge chair. The dog's eyes trained on her, despite her stillness. The beast looked ready to pounce at the slightest word. Fleur met her gaze, daring the dog to move, knowing she could make it to the Subaru in time. Nova growled once, then smiled—if you could call the lopsided tongue roll a smile, content to watch Fleur from the doorway.

Ayame returned with a small canvas bag, the catering company logo stamped across the front, and handed it to Fleur.

"Savory Turnip." Fleur noted the company name as she opened the bag. "What's the badge for?"

"All the staff has one. It supplies access to the lobby and the first three floors."

"Why so many?"

"The gala takes place in the second-floor ballroom and third-floor gallery, but the kitchen is on the first, service elevator in between."

"I owe you. Seriously." Sato smiled as he backed off the small porch.

Ayame pinned him with a final glare. "A month of Saturdays, Takeo! Don't you dare forget!"

THE UNIFORM WAS TOO SMALL.

Fleur stared at her reflection in the mirror and sighed.

She sucked in her stomach and hunched, pulling on the hem of the smock. The fabric was unforgiving and unflattering. It looked more like scrubs than she expected, which would have been fine, if not for the tapered waist. Fleur pulled at the neckline and looked down. Definitely too small. The buttons on the diagonal closure strained against her bosom, no matter how much she tugged.

Gods. She looked ridiculous.

Maybe you could wear it open? Lenora brightened beside her, studying her curvy form in the mirror. *It doesn't look bad, you know.*

"It doesn't look good either."

It's a uniform, not a fashion statement.

"You don't get to comment. You wouldn't understand the big

bosom struggle if it smacked you in the face." Fleur gritted her teeth and eyed Lenora's lean form encased in light.

Don't be rude. Body image is an issue for everyone.

"Oh, yeah? When was the last time you needed a girdle to fit into a smock?"

Lenora rolled her eyes. *It's not that bad.*

"Says you."

"Knock, knock," Viola sang as she rattled the door handle. "Are you decent?"

"Barely." Fleur frowned, glaring at her reflection and Lenora's steady light.

"How does it look?" Viola asked as she pushed the door open, pausing at the entrance. "Well ... that's not bad, is it?"

Fleur glared. "This is a stupid idea."

"No. It's not. It's the perfect idea and you know it. Don't be sour."

Fleur ran her hands down the front of the smock, wincing as the fabric bunched at her waist. "I look absurd."

"It's just to get you in the building, Fleur. You won't be mingling."

She had a point. Not that Fleur was in any mood to indulge it.

"Besides, this might help." Viola held up a brown paper bag and smiled.

"Snacks are hardly the answer, Vi."

Lenora giggled and floated forward. *I don't think it's snacks.*

"Oh, stop." Viola shook her head and emptied the contents of the bag onto the bed. "It's for the vents."

A black jumpsuit, wrapped in a seat belt complete with cinches and carabiner clips, lay before her. "The vents?"

"How else are you going to get into Griffin's office? Sato said the catering pass won't allow the elevator past the third floor."

Fleur blew out a breath and frowned. "How the hell do you think I'm going to fit that under this?" She pointed her image in the mirror.

Think of it as a girdle. Lenora grinned, her light flickering.

"Shut it, Len."

"Oh, Lenora! I didn't know you were back." Viola looked up at the ceiling and smiled. "Hello, dear."

I don't know why you complain so much about Viola. She really is lovely.

Fleur ignored them and studied the black jumpsuit. "So, I'm going to be climbing up an elevator shaft and through the ventilation system, huh? Has it occurred to any of you I don't know how to do that?"

"Sato says the grappling gun will do the trick." Viola nodded at the harness. "This will keep you safe."

"Are you kidding? Vi? Seriously?"

"We're working on a timeline. Opal's sedative will only last an hour at most. There isn't time for you to climb up."

"Why can't I just take the elevator, like any sane human?" Easy in, easy out—and no harness. Between her protection spell and Sato's computer wizardry, she'd stay hidden.

"The upper floors are access pass only. You know that. Stop being difficult."

"I'm realistic, not difficult." Fleur sneered at the jumpsuit.

"Sato has the schematics. He'll walk you through it. You'll be fine."

"Schematics? How the hell did he get those?"

Viola shrugged. "How should I know? Lenora, your partner is very resourceful."

Sato hacked Khade's security system months ago, right? I doubt it was hard to find.

Viola's gaze drifted between Fleur and the jumpsuit. "I could take out the hem of the smock a little. That should work."

"You know how to sew?"

Viola shrugged. "Well, no, but I can figure it out."

Fleur glanced down at the horrible green fabric, fingering the purple turnip emblem in the right corner, then back to Viola. "Why are you helping me with this?"

"Why wouldn't I?" Viola didn't look up.

"Vi? Seriously? This has nothing to do with you."

"Yes, it does." She lifted her eyes. Fleur had never noticed how bright they were before—blue flecked with gold. Viola held her gaze. "It's important to you, so it's important to me."

"Viola—"

"You've kept me out of your life for fifteen years, Fleur. And I've tried, God help me, I've tried so hard to be a part of it. And now? Well, I don't know what changed. I won't question it, but you've cracked the door, and I'd be a fool not to take advantage of that." Tears swam in Viola's eyes. She blinked, taking a step back. "You've spent all this time looking for someone to accept you—all of you, your loves, your magick—all of it. It broke my heart when you and Arik had that falling out, then again with Javier … but things are different now. Look around you, Fleur. We all accept you, want to work beside you, even Theda in her own way. But it's up to you to let us."

Viola rested her hand on Fleur's shoulder and squeezed.

Fleur didn't know what to say. She blinked back tears. Was that true? Had her lack of trust in people been of her own making? She coughed, swallowing back the sob.

"Now," Viola continued, "get out of that smock, and let me see what I can do with it."

CHAPTER
FIFTY-TWO

"We have a problem." Sato slurped up the last of his iced latte. They sat in the coffee shop across from her apartment. A brief escape from Viola and her sewing kit.

"What problem?"

"You've got a tail."

Fleur straightened in her chair and looked around, noting the crush of people around them. "Where?"

"Black sedan parked outside. I noticed it yesterday outside your apartment."

"Shit. So that's why you wanted to take Viola's car to the warehouse," Fleur cursed, remembering the car following her and Theda home from the police station. "Griffin?"

"Probably." Sato narrowed his eyes at her. "Did you say something when you interviewed him?"

"Of course not. But ..." She trailed off, cursing herself for not realizing this sooner. "He knew my name ..." Realization dawned. "Gods.

The book. He knew my name from the book." She shook her head and looked up. "Do you think he knows?"

Sato blew out a breath and leaned back in his chair. "Does it matter?"

"He could use the flute on us, you know."

"Yeah? Then he'd have to stop using it on Edgar. Hmm, not a bad idea."

Fleur's breath caught in her throat. Redirecting the flute would help, no doubt about that, but would it be enough? "He wouldn't. He needs Edgar too much."

"That's a big assumption."

Fleur dropped her head in her hands. "I need that book, Sato."

"Don't worry so much. I'll get it."

"How?"

Sato smiled and tented his fingers under his chin. "Lenora."

"You want Lenora to haunt Griffin?"

"We need her to target the book, haunting is optional."

"That's a big ask. I don't know—"

Oh hell, yeah, I'm in. Lenora materialized at the end of the table, her aura bright.

"Can you do that?" Fleur asked her, glancing from Sato to Lenora.

Sato tapped the side of his head. "It'll work. Trust me."

It shouldn't be a problem. I've got enough anger stored up. I can poltergeist the hell out of him. Lenora seemed almost giddy.

"But how do we lose our unwanted guests?" Fleur nodded toward the black sedan.

Sato's grin widened. "Disguises—and leave the Subaru at home."

Fleur groaned. "You love this, don't you?"

"You have no idea."

～

FLEUR ADJUSTED the edge of her wig and groaned as a bobby pin dug into her scalp. Wig was too generous a term for the bald skullcap hiding her hair. One thing was for sure. Griffin's goons weren't looking for a balding, middle-aged man in a Hawaiian shirt and Crocs.

She shot a murderous glare at Sato.

"Don't look at me like that. You wanted incognito." He smirked, adjusting his baseball cap.

"What Lenora saw in you is beyond me," Fleur joked, pulling at the polyester shirt beneath the boxy denim jacket.

Sato's smile faltered. "Yeah, me too."

Fleur winced and bit her lip. "I didn't mean—"

"Nah, it's cool." Sato cleared his throat. "Lenora could have had anyone, but she picked me. I'll never understand why, but maybe I don't need to, right?"

"Yeah." Fleur turned toward him. "I get that. But Sato, she loved you. I've seen it. She loved you fiercely."

Sato's eyes watered. He blinked and looked down at his computer. "I hate that she's gone. I hate she didn't tell me what she was doing. I hate ..."

"The helplessness?"

"Yeah."

"I know." Fleur swallowed back a sob and rested her hand on his arm.

They sat in silence. Wind swirled and moaned beyond the car door, kicking up leaves and pulling branches into a slow dance.

Across the road sat Dugal Griffin's fortress. The roof jutted through the cluster of cedar trees like a child refusing to move. Windows swept the western wall, reflecting pockets of light peeking through the overcast sky. The house glistened in the setting sun. Cedar shake siding gave the mid-century style a more earthy feel, a stark contrast to the immensely tall metal gate at the end of the winding drive.

Fleur had parked the Nissan at the edge of the property beneath the rain-heavy fronds of a low-hanging cedar. Griffin would have cameras everywhere, but in order for this to work, she needed to be as close to the property as possible without tres-passing.

The car brightened as Lenora appeared, her aura pulsing with excitement.

Fleur cleared her throat. "Are you ready?"

Lenora nodded, her eyes on the bright orange sky. *Are we sure he's home?*

"He's in the library," Sato piped up, oblivious to Lenora's question. His computer screen emitted a light glow as he scrolled through the home's security cameras. "Is she ready?"

Lenora grinned. *Let's do this.*

CHAPTER
FIFTY-THREE

LENORA

I wanted to start small and build to the finale. I wanted Dugal to second-guess every sound, every movement, every shadow.

Energy fizzled, flickering my light red as I moved closer to the broad front door. Rage swirled within me, tangible and dark, elongating my form. I passed through the frenzy of molecules without a thought. The door didn't matter. The walls of Dugal's fortress were nothing to me. My light thickened, oozing into the intricate tile entryway, staining the grout with my wrath.

I reached out, dragging my fingernail over the crisp white wall to my left. The sound was rough and eerie in the silence, echoing in the cavernous angles of his living room.

A light flickered on in the hallway to my left. Again, I scraped my nail over the wall, slowly this time, drawing out the sound.

This was not the wild sense of violation I felt in Poppy's rooms. My rage was controlled. The whirlwind of anger at seeing my last moments taped and tagged in Poppy's room was swift and anguishing. My anger tasted different now. Metallic and raw, sour like putrid milk.

I moved around the room in broad circles, my arms outstretched. Waves of fury rose within me. The world colored red, and I closed my eyes. I wanted to pace myself.

I flung my hand out, knocking over a vase from the side table.

The crash echoed off the high windowed walls.

Footsteps from the hallway.

I grinned and tapped the edge of the glass coffee table, matching the cadence of his footsteps on the polished wood floor.

He paused, but I continued.

"Is someone there?" Dugal's voice was low and grainy, as if unused for too long. He crept into the room, his phone clutched in one hand. He glanced down at the screen, then up around the room.

I rushed toward him, chilling the air as it brushed his skin.

Dugal shivered.

He was shorter than I remembered. Or perhaps it was that I had grown stronger in death? I had only a scant memory of him, but it was enough. His shoulder-length black hair was loose, falling flat against his face. I elbowed one of the framed paintings on the wall beside me. It flopped to the floor, splintering the simple wooden frame.

Dugal turned in a slow circle. His steel blue gaze swept past me, piercing my light with frost. My anger washed over me, a tidal wave of agony. My family ... my life, gone in a flash. Why? I wanted to scream. Why?

My aura flickered and darkened. My phantom heart pounded in my ears. The air grew heavy, lapping at my light.

Dugal tilted his head as if listening, a cruel smile curling the edge of his mouth. "Hello, Lenora," he said calmly.

With that single greeting, my intentions unraveled.

No. No. No. I wailed, my voice crashing against the icy stillness of the room. I tore at the walls, clawing my way to the library.

Book-lined walls circled an antique mahogany desk. I pulled

hardback after hardback from the shelves. I took my time, bottling my fury with each thud. One book fell, then another, again, and again until Dugal entered. I paused. Book in hand, waiting until he drew closer.

With a steady hand, I released it. The book crashed, its spine breaking.

"Is this tantrum really necessary?" His smile was vicious. "Is this the thanks I get for protecting you?"

My light simmered.

"They would have taken you—the courts—after your parents died. They would have abused you, stolen from you, destroyed you. But I stopped them. I protected you."

Lies! I fired book after book at him as if by an invisible bow. *You stole my world.*

The first hit him on the shoulder. He ducked behind the desk. I clutched another book, my wrath intensifying with each word.

"Stop, Lenora. This game has gone on long enough. I don't know what you were thinking—swallowing that poison." He shook his head. "Edgar is gone. They're all gone. The Khade dynasty, as small as it was, has been extinguished. You must move on."

The next book hit his arm, then his torso as he stood.

"I won't cower from you, foolish girl. I bested them—all of them. It was only the first step, don't you see? I'm destined for something greater than your petty, insignificant life."

I hovered above him, my aura sparking like lightning.

Dugal laughed, his pale skin creasing. "And now I have the seer."

I paused, book in hand.

"Delivered by you, I believe."

What did he mean? I flew around the room, tearing pages and scattering trinkets. I shrieked, pulsing the air until the chandelier cracked.

"Temper, temper, Lenora."

My light boiled. My screams shattered the skylight. Shards rained down, piercing Dugal with their arrows.

Blood poured from a gash on his cheek. He cupped his hand against it, his body taut with anger.

"I have a destiny. Fate handed it to me when I was a boy. Power like none imaginable. And that seer—your seer—is going to help me."

I flew around the room, my light pulsing, quaking the air. A storm raged in my wake—I rushed past him, then again, dredging him with my fury, until my gaze settled on the solitary book bound by red yarn. I reached for it, my rage keeping it firm in my hands.

"Admit defeat." His eyes trained on the book, he lifted his hands in mock surrender. "You could never best me."

My light slithered around the volume, highlighting the author's name etched on the side. The surrounding air heated in recognition. Dugal was bluffing. His only connection was her last name. He wanted to scare me.

But it wouldn't work. This time, I held all the cards.

I tightened my grip on the book and held it closer to my chest. Waiting.

Dugal approached, his gaze on the book floating in front of him. "It's all there—but you know that, don't you? The book and its secrets are mine and only *mine*. I'll find them all, and the seer will help me."

I held still, my rage brimming, coloring the book's faded leather red.

His hand reached out, his fingertips a breath away—and I sprinted up, dangling the book overhead, a taunt, a mocking salute to the knowledge I now understood. I tore past him, racing toward the entryway. The book was heavier than I expected, but I held tight, my gaze on the thick wooden door and dark night sky beyond.

"Drop it, Lenora," Dugal shouted behind me.

I didn't look back.

The book clattered onto the tile floor as the buzz of atoms fizzled through me, crowding my essence with the merging clustered of matter. I pulled myself free from the door, bursting into the night, my aura feral with anger.

I drew myself up through the thick canopy of cedars, only glancing down once to see Fleur standing beside the car. She lifted her hand as if to summon me back, but I was too volatile.

Instead, I turned from her and faded into the night.

CHAPTER
FIFTY-FOUR

FLEUR

"You think she's OK?" Sato asked, looking out the window toward the house.

"She's stronger than she looks, you know that."

Sato frowned and looked back at the security footage on his computer. They had watched Dugal scurry around the house, following the damage Lenora left in her wake. They watched Dugal address her, and the shower of books as she rained down on him.

And then she was gone.

Fleur nodded to the screen. Dugal stood, book in hand, in the entryway, a smile crooking the corner of his mouth. Whatever he said to her—it only fed Lenora's rage. "She just needs to cool off. She'll be fine." Fleur prayed she was right.

Sirens cut through the air like a knife.

"We should go," Fleur muttered, getting back in the car and checking the rearview mirror.

"Nah, don't worry. I told Detective Torres we were gonna shake things up a bit."

"What? You told Javier about this?" Fleur balled her fists in her lap and tried not to pounce on the kid beside her.

"Well, yeah, I did." He tapped the side of his head. "All part of the plan."

"Part of the plan? Dammit, Sato. I said no police."

"Relax. I've got it covered."

Fleur cursed. The book was as good as gone now. She frowned and unclenched her fingers, one by one. "Well? What did he say?"

"Nothing, much." Sato looked back at his screen. "You think Lenora's OK? Where did she go?" he asked again.

Fleur shrugged, touching her rubber skullcap, and wiped away a thin layer of sweat. Her fingers itched to pull it off. She doubted Javier had been that accepting of their little plan. Sato was lying. That much was plain, but she didn't press it. "Probably the Lobby. She looked like she needed some time."

"The Lobby?"

"Yeah, kinda like a ghost waiting room, right? It's where she goes when she's not with me."

Sato drew in a breath and exhaled. "I wish she had stayed. What do you think he said to her?"

"Nothing good," Fleur murmured, sinking lower in the seat as a police car flew by. "Can we get out of here, please?"

"Just a minute, OK?"

"What are we waiting for?"

"You'll see."

"What?"

Sato shook his head and grinned. "Patience."

Two more police cars sped past, clustering at Griffin's gate. The gate opened and the flashing blue lights moved deeper into the trees.

"C'mon." Sato adjusted his baseball cap and reached for the door handle. "Let's watch."

Fleur glared at him. "Watch what?"

"Just come on," Sato ordered as he pushed open the car door and slinked off toward Griffin's house.

Fleur made a face and got out of the car, following Sato to the thick visage of ferns lining the front fence. They crept along the outer wall, pausing when another police car pulled into the drive. Fleur frowned. How many police were needed for a haunting? It seemed a little excessive. She glanced up at the now dark sky, her brow furrowing with worry.

"Hey!" Sato whispered, nudging her. "This way."

They crouched in the shadows of a willow tree, the long branches swaying, masking their position.

The final cop car arrived. It didn't surprise Fleur to see Javier. She wondered how long it would be before he arrested her again.

Dugal Griffin stood in the entranceway, his arms crossed over his chest, a scowl darkening his brow above the bandage on his cheek, and the *Book of Veils* clutched in his hands.

Javier and Griffin spoke in muted tones, their heads bent. Dugal clutched the book tighter and shook his head. Javier raised his hands and turned, ordering the officers to search the premises for anything to show who the intruder was.

Fleur turned to Sato, about to ask if he mentioned Lenora to Javier, but a swift shake of his head silenced her. Fine. She'd wait, but if she ended up in jail, Sato was going to get an earful.

Javier waited with Dugal, taking notes and pointing to various parts of the house. The other four officers appeared, each shaking their heads. Fleur smiled in the darkness. At least there was no evidence. Instead, Dugal looked spooked and angry.

Javier pulled Griffin aside, and the two inched closer to their hiding place. He pointed to the book. His tone was calming. Dugal shook his head again, less ardently than before. Fleur strained to hear anything but the low hum of their voices.

"Are you sure the thief was after this?" Javier asked. "Is it valuable?"

"Only to me," Dugal replied.

Fleur snorted, ignoring the poke in her ribs from Sato.

"Can you think of anyone who would want to steal it?"

"Isn't that *your* job, Detective?"

Javier looked up from his notepad. "I'd appreciate any help you'd be willing to give."

"I don't have the faintest idea why this book would interest anyone," Dugal said. "It's just a book of fairy tales, valuable to no one but me."

Javier considered Griffin, his pen tapping the edge of his notebook.

Fleur held her breath. She knew that look. Javier had something up his sleeve.

Javier closed his notebook. "You said the thief dropped it as they made their escape? That makes it evidence." Javier glanced back at the other officers. "Maybe our only evidence."

Griffin cursed. "I want my objections noted, Detective Torres."

"I'll include them in my report, Mr. Griffin." Javier held out his gloved hand.

Fleur watched in stunned silence as Dugal Griffin handed over the *Book of Veils*.

"You'll be hearing from my lawyer, Detective."

Javier smiled. "Of that, I have no doubt."

Sato snorted this time, and Fleur elbowed him.

Griffin turned, his chin raised as he stalked back toward his house.

Javier waved at the other officers, and they moved to their vehicles, then turned to face the willow tree, tapping the spine of the book, before returning to his car.

Of course, he knew they were there. Fleur cursed.

Sato tugged on her sleeve and nodded to the gate. Fleur followed him, her back aching from crouching for so long. They kept to the ferns outside the fence until the last police car passed and the gate slithered closed.

Javier stood beside their car, his own vehicle parked beside it.

"Did the Subie finally die?" he asked, resting his hand on the hood of Viola's Altima.

Fleur gritted her teeth. "Cut the crap, Torres."

Sato grinned and held out his hand. "You were brilliant—perfect."

Javier jerked his head toward the darkened road behind them. "You know you're being followed?"

Sato cursed. "Yeah."

So much for a disguise. Fleur glanced up the road. A glimmer of streetlight caught the edge of a headlight, and she wondered if it was the same black sedan. "We think it's Griffin."

"If it was, I doubt he'd have given me this." Javier didn't look convinced as he pulled the book, bagged and tagged, out of his coat. "Wanna tell me about this?"

"Gods, Javier. You make everything sound so ominous. It's *the* book—you know, the one Lenora stole from Dugal before she died? The one my uncle wrote?"

"Is this about the artifacts Dugal collects? Was Lenora involved somehow?"

"Lenora died because of this book."

Javier narrowed his gaze, waiting for an explanation.

"It's all connected. You know that. You read her letter." Fleur pointed out as she took the book from him. Or he read the revised version of Lenora's letter.

"I've been meaning to ask you about that." Javier shoved his hands in his pockets. "Lenora's claim that she took her own life adds up. The Atropa berries matched the alkaline toxins in her stomach lining. Based on her letter, we've ruled it a suicide. But something's missing—There's more to the letter, isn't there? She claims she died so that she could reach her brother and free him from his imprisonment. My captain chalked that up to mental health issues—" Javier held up a hand as Fleur opened her mouth to protest. "I know that wasn't the case, but seriously, Fleur ... I don't know how else to spin it. The magickal ghost connection isn't gonna fly."

Fleur huffed, hating that he was right.

"The case is closed, thanks to you," Javier continued. "At least on our end, but you're still working on it, aren't you?" He jerked his thumb toward Griffin's gate. "That wasn't you in Griffin's house—that was Lenora, wasn't it?"

Sato cleared his throat but said nothing.

Javier sighed, as if realization finally dawned. "You're looking for Edgar."

"Maybe," Fleur muttered, looking up into the night sky, hoping Javier's inquisition would end before morning.

"If Edgar Khade is still alive, as her letter says, where is he? I've searched every property and found nothing."

Fleur raised a brow.

"Don't give me that look." Javier glared back at her. "The case may be closed, but I know you, Harkyn." He shook his head. "So ... I did a little digging myself."

"You checked all their properties?" Sato asked, folding his arms over his chest. "You sure?"

Javier nodded. "Every asset Griffin owns."

Fleur bit her tongue. He was looking in the wrong direction. Griffin didn't own the warehouse, Khade did. She should tell him, but the last thing she needed was the cops raiding it before they could free Edgar. Who knows what that would do to Edgar's fragile mental state?

"I know you've withheld parts of the letter. Parts that have something to do with you, Fleur—am I right?" He glanced from Fleur to Sato.

Fleur shrugged. "There are a few other elements in play, yes. But you need to let it rest, at least for now. The important thing is that we've solved Lenora's death, right?"

Javier stared at her.

Fleur resisted the urge to squirm.

"Look, we've got a plan, OK?" Sato chimed in. "Nothing too illegal."

"Nothing *too* illegal?" Javier shook his head.

"C'mon, Jav," Fleur pleaded. "We'll tell you everything when we can, OK?"

"I can't keep covering for you." Javier's rich brown eyes met hers. His expression softened.

"I'm not asking you to cover for us," Fleur said, realizing that after all these years, Javier was on her side. She swallowed back the lump in her throat and offered a small smile. "Just give us time."

Javier looked down at his black loafers, invisible on the wet asphalt. "OK. One week—that's it. Then I have to report this."

Fleur nodded. "Thanks, Javier—and for this." She held up the book. "One week will change everything, you'll see."

Javier turned back to his car, then paused. "And Fleur?" he began, looking back at her.

"Yeah?"

"I like what you've done with your hair."

Sato snorted.

Fleur scowled and pulled the cap from her head. "Shut up, Torres."

CHAPTER
FIFTY-FIVE

LENORA

I didn't know what to do with my anger.

It was too raw, too explosive to hold. My light shimmered and sparked like electricity in a Faraday cage, sizzling with energy and anguish, trapped by the metal bars of fear.

At the threshold of Griffin's house, I let it expand, swelling beyond the confines of my light, a rage I had never felt before. In that moment, I was no longer a passive entity, content with the sidelines of my destruction. Was this what I felt walking into the conservatory that afternoon? Was this the conviction that led to my death and failed resurrection?

Instead of fanning the flames, I became the fire.

And for the first time in my limited memory, I was whole.

I coiled into myself—willing my light to calm, barely noticing the amber light throbbing from the canopy. A few of the newer spirits flickered, giving me a wide berth, but the older Atua knew. They nodded, their light bright with understanding. A spirit's first poltergeist was a powerful passage.

I raised my head, meeting the stares and whispers. I didn't want to cower, to indulge in the shame we are taught to feel when our emotions grew too big. I would not apologize.

My light calmed, dimming from blood red to pale beige—the color of pliant flesh, before feathering out in the soft golds of dawn. I pressed my hand to my chest, wishing I could feel the thud of a beat, to know my seams would mend—that I was not the rage I became. I was an instrument, and stronger for it.

I paid little attention to the shadows inching closer to the Great Tree's trunk, darkening its bark, nor the lack of indigo, as the Guardians gathered above—their magick pulsing in amber waves to halt the Shadelings' progress. But I felt a thread of fear that resonated within the pockets of light left below.

I saw only the flickers of memory, spiraling out from my core, unlocked. I closed my eyes, following the prism of life—my life that had eluded me for so long. Dipping my fingers into a barrel of grain, each kernel a secret blossoming with the events of my life. I didn't question how it was possible. The lure of my life was too tempting to ignore.

Images of my parents, my brother, Opal, Sato, friends who were not friends and faces I hardly knew spun around me like puzzle pieces that didn't fit together, and I realized without the emotions, the intimacy of experience, they were reels, no more powerful than before.

It was a tease, a taunt ... a hint of what I could never have again.

Ellory told me it wouldn't work.

The voice crashed through the wall of memory, prying the dream from the reality. I opened my eyes.

This Guardian was tall, broader than the rest, with wide-set eyes and a flat, bulbous nose. Like Ellory, he had no mouth, no expression, but the tilt of his eyes belied his curiosity. His light was darker than most, showing his age. I assumed he was an Elder, one of those closest to the Soulkeepers.

Where is Ellory? I wondered, lifting my head to meet the Elder's gaze.

She is needed elsewhere.

Who are you? What did you do to me? My gaze narrowed, unwilling to let him off the hook.

Ellory said you were stronger than most. She told me of your death—

That wasn't her tale to tell.

I can be very persuasive. The Guardian dipped his head. *I was curious as to what was so special about you. Ellory rarely invests time in the new Atua. But now I understand why.*

Spinning my memories like a film was a cruel trick. Why would you do that?

Most wouldn't know the difference. But you did.

So?

So, you are ready for what lies ahead.

And what's that?

The Relics.

I scowled, unable to house my irritation. I was tired of hearing about the Relics—tired of the constant commentary and impossible demands. I just wanted to be left alone. *What do you want?*

To meet you.

I narrowed my eyes at him.

And to check your progress.

There it was. It wasn't about me. It's never about me. It was about the flute. The damn flute. My light fizzled red, and I fought to contain myself.

You are vulnerable, I understand. An Atua's first haunting is a powerful rite of passage.

What does it matter how I feel? I don't have the flute yet. I'm working on it.

The Guardian nodded. *Yes, we know. Although the situation is dire, the flute would—*

I'm working on it. I repeated harsher than I intended.

The Guardian's eyes met mine, his expression hardened. *Work harder.*

You all gave me—a nobody!—one hell of a task. I know things are dire. I'm not blind. I gestured around me, ignoring the chill lancing the Lobby's spine. *We have a plan. One more day. That's it. Just one more day, OK? Can you hold the Shadelings until then?*

The Guardian's light brightened and dimmed slowly, and I felt the exasperation ebbing around him. *I trusted Ellory when she chose you. So, I will have to trust you, despite my misgivings.*

What do you mean chose me?

She thought it would give Fleur a push in the right direction.

I blinked up at him. *Ellory stole my memories?*

The Guardian laughed. *Of course not, child. Ellory isn't a Soulkeeper. She merely planted Fleur's. Ellory is one of the few with Hemsut's ear. She knew your threads were intertwined.*

I closed my eyes, giving the knowledge a wide berth. Ellory pointed me toward her daughter on purpose. She mentored me only to help Fleur find the flute—the instrument of my family's downfall —the reason for my death and my brother's imprisonment. The urge to burn the thing scorched my aura red.

I wouldn't advise that. There is a greater need than you or me, Lenora. This—he gestured around them—*is sacred ground. If the Shadelings contaminate the magick here, there will be more than a few lives to worry about.*

I want to talk to Ellory. I needed to hear this from her.

You will. She is dealing with our unwanted guests, but she will be back. Tell me your name.

The Guardian shook his head.

If you want the flute, you'll tell me. I stared up at him.

In life, I was called Hamza.

Are you from Evirdahl too?

Hamza's aura brightened. *That, Lenora, is a story for another time.*

So, not Evirdahl? Which realm, then? And how did you die?

The flute, Lenora. Save your brother, then bring it to us. Quickly.

I glanced up into Hamza's wide vacant eyes in surprise. He was too familiar, too insistent. My light flickered as doubt fluttered through my thoughts.

Hamza nodded. *You are right to question me. Talk to Ellory if you must.* He leaned closer. *But bring us the flute.*

CHAPTER
FIFTY-SIX

FLEUR

The book smelled like citrus and clove. Fleur inhaled the delicate fragrance. It blossomed in her heart, spreading through her bloodstream. The tips of her fingers tingled as she turned the page.

A car honked in the distance. The Altima sat in an empty parking lot off Madison Street. Fleur squinted in the half-light of the street-lamp. The urge to open the book was greater than she expected. After dropping Sato off at Ayame's, she pulled over, knowing this rare moment of silence might be her only chance. The binding throbbed beneath her fingers. Fleur chanted the revival spell as she cracked the book's spine.

Its magick flared as its words brightened, swirling into a chrysalis of light. She touched the ink, allowing the magick to seep into her.

Axel preferred quills made of crow. The smaller bird produced a sturdier feather, allowing him to keep his ink thin on the page. Crow feathers held potent magick needed to seal the stories onto parchment. Fleur had only seen his cherished quill once, but it was enough to ingrain his strokes to memory. Her uncle was a born scribe, unlike her father. Where Arik embraced the written word, Axel preferred the writing of it. Two sides of the same coin, her mother once said.

Each quill was enchanted with the words of their ancestors—Fraomadr, the ancient tribe of small magick. The magick hidden in the *Book of Veils* was protection magick able to conceal much from the magickless eye.

The fragile parchment warmed, ruddy and stained with time. Its magick—her legacy—released the tension from her shoulders and stilled the tremor in her hand. It was like returning home.

Harkyns were keepers of history, the scribes, bards, librarians of Evirdahl's words. Recording the tales, spoken lore, and spell etymology for future generations, willed so by the Goddess Gula-Bau herself. Their connection with the spirit world offered them insight few could boast. Fleur stared at the book and its telltale red binding. Gods. How did it get here? Her father's theory about the Dark Purge made sense, but still—how could Axel have been so careless?

The words wrapped around her, spinning stories of the ten realms' origins and the goddess covenant. Ten objects, branded with the trinity seal, but only two realms crafted counter instruments. The fifth, Loatheia, and the ninth, Somm. Fleur knew very little about the ninth realm, only that it existed in a vapor-like mist of sand and wind. Populated by wisp creatures, the Somads, who mined the Vast for silica deposits—heart shards were the highest form of currency in the ten realms.

Fleur had assumed their Relic was a shard, but according to the book, the Somad chieftain enchanted the sand itself, linking it to the Relic from the eighth realm. Fleur blinked at the page. They countered each other. Strange.

The eighth and ninth once held three hands. Untamed travel, stilled by caught sand.

Fleur blew out a breath and turned the page. Focus, she scolded, turning back to the chapter on the fifth realm.

The car pulsed with magick as the book's threads wove around her.

Her index finger tapped the pages as she searched through the lengthy history for the wind Relic's reversal spell. She knew reversal magick by heart, but Fleur needed confirmation. Trusting a discarded, twenty-three-year-old memory was risky.

She paused. There. Finally.

There was a single warning, scribbled in Axel's smooth hand, confirming Fleur's suspicions.

The wind Relic can break its victim's will if supported for extreme lengths. Assess length of time by victim's response to light. The newer the trance, the less the light will bother. If a victim reacts to light, they have fractured. Only the planted memory of the counter and the reversal spell can free the victim. To plant the memory of the counter Relic, an Atua must possess the victim's intellect, drawing down the chaos splintering the mind. Preferable familial relation as the victim must trust the intrusion. The reversal melody should be played in time with the memory, thus cleansing the ill-intent from the mind and mending the frayed threads.

Probability of success: 67%

Fleur scowled at her uncle's grim prediction.

Fleur closed the book and hugged it to her chest. She wasn't ready to let go. She had pushed this part of her aside for so long she'd forgotten the calmness it invoked. And Fleur needed calm right now. She toyed with the red yarn binding and closed her eyes.

Axel used to scare her. He was a great hulk of a man, the opposite of her father's lithe form. He dressed in their family colors of black and gray, a shade to the shadows. His dark gray hair was always too long and his beard too shaggy, but no one could make Arik laugh like Axel. Once—before Ellory's death and Fleur's vision—they were bonded, friends and brothers, through the rebirth of war. Fleur listened with fascination to Axel's tales of the Dark Purge and the dangerous sorceress who tried to destroy them. To her, it was a fairy tale, but to her parents, it was the first breath of terror, and Axel wielded his words like a knife.

Perhaps that was the reason Axel reported her prophecy to the council, ushering in her exile? Did he fear another purge with the death of the queen? Fleur didn't know what caused her uncle to betray them, but his motivations didn't matter. Only his actions.

With a huff, she set the book on the passenger seat. Fleur rubbed her eyes, startled to find her skin damp with tears. She leaned against the headrest, her hands instinctively pulling her tarot cards from her pocket.

Her fingers shuffled, cupping the weight in one hand as she filtered the cards together. The movements reminded her she was safe and whole. Her world might fall apart, but she would survive. That's what Harkyns did. They survived. Fleur thought about her uncle, alone in the empty manse at the cliff's edge. Her family withered and fell, leaf by leaf. With her grandfather's death decades before, Axel became chieftain, a role he had once promised to share with Arik, now a leader to an absent clan.

A card slipped from the deck, fluttering to the floor, and Fleur's hands stilled.

Fate had chosen her card. Fleur reached, holding it face down as she brought it to her lap. With a deep breath, she turned it over.

The Hanged Man stared back at her.

A strangled laugh bubbled up from her throat. Of course, Fleur thought bitterly. A known sacrifice. A change in perspective.

She cursed as she started the car, then again as she backed out of the parking space.

Too many memories for one night.

FIFTY-SEVEN

FLEUR

Viola held up the green smock and grinned. "Piece of cake—here, try it on."

It was a little past midnight when Fleur wove her way back to Viola's bungalow. She was bone-tired and hungry enough to eat a horse. The last thing Fleur wanted was to try on the damn smock. "I guess you figured out the sewing machine, huh?"

Viola shrugged. "Alma helped." She handed Fleur the uniform with a little smile. "Come have some tea."

"Alma helped?" Fleur repeated, her heartbeat quickening.

"Is that a problem?" Viola asked.

"Did you see Theda? Is she OK? Can I call her? No, I shouldn't, right? I should let her call me, right? I'm giving her time. That's what Alma said she needs. How much time, though? A week? Two?" The words tumbled out in a rush, eager to be voiced.

Viola shook her head and put the mug she had just pulled from the cupboard back. Wordlessly, she turned to the small wine rack on the end of the counter and pulled out a bottle of red, twisting the corkscrew into the top.

Fleur eyed the glass of wine Viola set in front of her. "Are you softening me up? Did you speak to Theda? What did she say? Is she still mad? Of course, she is. I would be. Gods, how do I make this up to her? What should I do? Should I go over there? Should I send flowers? A card? A singing telegram? Do those still exist? Do you think they're expensive?"

Viola sipped her wine, eyeing Fleur over the rim.

Fleur resisted the urge to squirm and held the wine to her lips. "Why are you so quiet? Did Theda say something? She's still angry, isn't she?"

"I'm just waiting."

"For what?"

Viola shrugged and took another sip of her wine.

"Gods, Vi! Will you tell me what Theda said?" Fleur didn't bother holding the bite in her tone.

"Nothing."

"Nothing?"

"Well, not really. She was working on some paper, apologized for her behavior at Thanksgiving, and asked who the smock was for. That's it."

"That's it?" Fleur's stomach dropped.

Viola averted her eyes, sweeping the room as she lifted her glass to her mouth. "Is Lenora here? How did the haunting go?"

Fleur glared. "Don't you dare change the subject. Theda didn't ask about me?"

"She asked about Lenora. I guess she saw her suicide in the paper, wanted to know how the ghost was doing with the news." Viola looked down.

Fleur released a shaky breath and stared at her stepmother. Viola was a horrible liar. "And?"

"And, what?"

"Vi. What did she say?" Fleur gritted her teeth.

"Alright! Fine." Viola frowned. "She asked if you were still working on the case."

"What did you tell her?"

"I said yes."

"And?"

"And ... that's it. She said nothing else. I swear."

Fleur didn't know whether to scream or cower. Viola had just confirmed what Theda already knew. Fleur could imagine the hurt swelling in the pit of Theda's stomach, souring her breath as she tried to hold the well of emotion.

"So, she's still mad," Fleur said.

"She didn't look mad," Viola countered.

Fleur laughed bitterly. "Trust me. She is."

"What should I have said?" Viola looked contrite. "I wanted to tell her you quit—I know you did, even if it was just for a day. That means something, but ..."

"No, Vi, you're fine. You told the truth."

"Not the whole truth—"

"It won't matter if I quit, not if I'm working on it now." Fleur shook her head. That was the hard truth of it. She could beg and plead with Theda to forgive her, and maybe she would, but this would happen again. Fleur couldn't keep ignoring who she was. She thought she had gotten past that. She thought Theda understood. Fleur shook her head again, as if the action could dispel reality.

"She'll come around, Fleurie. Theda loves you." Viola reached for her hand.

Maybe she will—Gods, Fleur hoped she did, but would it be enough? If Theda wanted to be with her, she needed to accept her—all of her.

Fleur offered a weak smile and took a sip of wine. Changing the subject, she nodded to her messenger bag sitting on the floor near the sofa. "We got the book."

Viola's eyes widened. "How?"

"Would you believe Javier did it—and Lenora, too?"

"Did the haunting work?" Viola narrowed her eyes and glanced at the bag on the floor. "What was Javier doing there?"

"Sato called him."

Viola laughed. "Smart kid. So, did you find what you were looking for?"

Fleur released a breath and nodded. "I was right. We need both instruments."

"And?" Viola arched a brow.

"And what?"

"You knew that before you opened the book. There must have been more."

More? Fleur bit the inside of her cheek, unwilling to admit it wasn't the book she needed. It was the magick—the reminder. She looked at her stepmother. "I needed confirmation—it's no small thing what we're going to do. I didn't want to rely on my memory."

Viola stared at her for a beat too long, then nodded. "So that's it? Won't Dugal be on his guard now?"

Fleur shrugged. "He's already on guard."

"He knows Opal," Viola muttered. "What if he tries something at the gala?"

"As far as Griffin knows, Opal's been let go. To him, she's a bitter former employee or something. Lenora did an excellent job of keeping everyone in the dark."

Viola shuddered. "I hope you're right."

"Trust me, Vi. It will be fine."

CHAPTER
FIFTY-EIGHT

LENORA

H*ave you heard of someone named Hamza?*

Fleur's eyes widened as she turned to me, her fingers still over the keyboard in front of her. "Where did you hear that name?"

We sat behind the circulation desk at the library. The gala was tonight. Dark circles ringed Fleur's eyes, and I wondered if she slept at all last night. Both Viola and I had urged Fleur to take the day off —she looked like she could use the rest, but Fleur was adamant. Life goes on, she said, and she didn't want to give Lindy any more ammunition, whatever that meant.

I met him—when I was in the Lobby. Ellory told him about me, and he said he wanted to see if she was right. I shrugged, my aura flickering.

"You met Hamza?" Fleur whispered, looking back at her screen. She scrolled to a new worksheet and began imputing numbers, her gaze steady despite the tremor in her hand. "Hamza ...," she muttered, disbelief coating her breath.

Yeah. So? Who is he?

"What did he want?"

What else? The flute, of course. Why? Who is he?

"He was a powerful Aevi Jadu from Saphedvaar—a time mage from the third realm." Fleur spat out the words as if they were poison.

There was more to it. I could feel the unsaid story pulsing all around her. *What else?*

"I only know the legend. He died millennia ago." Fleur focused on the spreadsheet on the screen, leaning in, hiding her face from the rest of the library. "He was in love with another Jadu, a Fire-bearer from a different kindred. Back then, it was forbidden to mate outside your own magick, something about strengthening the tribe's essence—but that kind of thinking is outlawed now." Fleur's brow crinkled. "I guess we can thank Hamza and Orla for that."

What happened? My light brightened with need.

Fleur gave me a sideways glance and snickered. "You really want to know?"

I rolled my eyes. *Cut the theatrics, Fleur.*

"Fine. Forbidden love ... blah, blah, blah. But Orla wasn't having it, so she stole the *Akiseidrbok*, a dark magick grimoire, and cast a spell to sever the ancient tribal ties. But the spell she cast wasn't hers to use, and she couldn't control it. It spun out of control, destroying the sheath—"

Wait. That's how the sheath was destroyed? How strong was this spell?

"Strong, and she cast it incorrectly. I don't know all the details, anyway ... Hamza tried to stop it, but instead of mending the sheath, his magick infected a tribe of humans hiding in the mountain below him, the Fraomadr, and that's where my family sprung from."

Hamza is your ancestor?

"Kinda, we're his legacies, and we're broken into seven factions based on magick. Before the break, we were simple—humans with small magick, but now? We've usurped the power from the ancient tribes and destroyed much of the sacred lands. Typical colonizers." Fleur grimaced.

If Hamza is a Guardian, what happened to Orla?

"Banished to Qahil. I doubt she survived that."

Seems harsh. I glanced at Fleur, noting the crease in her brow.

"She did it to herself. Stolen magick extracts a price. Everyone knows that, and Orla stole a doozy. Exile was better than death—death meant entrance into the Great Tree, and the Soulkeepers would love to have a Jadu with that kind of power."

That must be why Hamza's an Elder Guardian. But ... how do you steal magick?

"The Trinity Goddesses gifted us with a specific set of abilities—all of us, in every realm, new and ancient tribes alike. Using a spell crafted by another's magick is a big no-no. Orla was a Firebearer, the spell she stole was a time spell. When she cast it, the spell extracted blood—the blood of her lineage—her children, and their children, all vulnerable to the call of the *Akiseidrbok*." Fleur's eyes flickered to the stacks, then back to the tables beyond the desk before returning to her screen. "Curses are powerful beings."

Did she have children?

"One—a daughter, with Hamza," Fleur whispered.

What happened to her? My light warmed with curiosity.

"Killed during the Dark Purge."

That's the second time you've mentioned that. What's the Dark Purge?

Fleur glanced behind her, nodded at Lindy seated behind a stack of donated books, then turned back to her screen. "You know the witch trials of the 1600s?"

Yeah. I fluttered closer.

"About a century earlier, Hamza's daughter got a hold of the Evirdahl Relic, a jade stone born of pure creation, able to harness magick without repercussion"—Fleur paused, and I leaned even closer—"and used it to summon an army to attack the Grand Mams of the Disir. She wasn't happy with her mother's banishment, I guess."

The Grand what of the what?

Fleur rolled her eyes. "Queens of the three fairy tribes. Anyway—everyone was scared, and once the Legacy Council got her under control, they purged anything that could be associated with dark magick. Most of it ended up here, in Mundad. Hence the witch trials."

And your father thought that's how the book got here?

"Seems so. It makes sense, kinda."

But—

"That's enough story time. I have to get *some* work done today," Fleur muttered, glaring at the screen. She groaned and rubbed her eyes.

Nervous? I asked, trying to hide my disappointment.

"Maybe." She leaned back in her chair and stretched her arms. "It's a good plan, right?" she whispered, her question belying her doubts.

It *was* a good plan. Sato scanned the vent route from the elevator shaft to Griffin's office, highlighting Fleur's exact path. He would walk her through it from the security room—how he was going to get the security room to himself, I didn't ask, but suspected Opal was concocting a little something for the guards there. Opal and Viola were ready, although I suppose the challenging bit was Fleur's part. Both Opal and Viola had a small vial of Opal's sleeping draught. Back up, Opal said, in case she couldn't doctor his drink. It all seemed so surreal to me—this elaborate scheme.

"Easy in, easy out," Fleur muttered.

You grab the shell, Viola and Opal grab the cane—then we meet at the warehouse. What could go wrong?

Fleur sniffed and shook her head.

I wanted to bite back my words.

We were novices, playing cat and mouse. Everything could go wrong.

CHAPTER
FIFTY-NINE

FLEUR

T he smock was still tight over the harness contraption, but
at least it fit.

Fleur paused at the service entrance to Khade Tower
and took a deep breath. Then another, releasing it slowly.

Her fingers toyed with the lanyard around her neck, the badge
Ayame gave her proudly displayed over the green and purple smock.
It would only get her to the fourth floor. Once she was inside, she
was to take the service elevator to the fourth floor, then pull the
emergency and climb onto the elevator roof. She had an array of
industrial strength carabiners attached to her harness—thanks to
Alma's skill with a sewing machine and a grapnel gun in her
backpack.

Until yesterday, Fleur didn't know grapnel guns were real. But
there was no denying the weight of the mechanism and the rope
tucked into her bag. All she had to do was shoot the hook up twenty-
one floors, attach the end to her harness, and push the button that

would haul her up, then enter the ventilation shaft above the elevator door. Griffin's office was on the other end.

Gods. Fleur swallowed a groan and willed her feet forward. Please, let this work.

A murmur of voices grew closer, and she turned to see a trio of green smocks heading toward her. Blend in, she told herself, falling in step behind them, mimicking their actions as they pressed their badges onto the screen at the door and nodded to the guard posted there.

Fleur fumbled slightly with her badge—her fingers suddenly too big for the slender plastic card. She smiled weakly at the guard, praying he didn't notice.

"You've got a long night ahead of you," he said, his eyes crinkling. "Don't spill any drinks on the guests."

Fleur cringed. "Don't jinx me." She laughed, sliding past him and into the wide hallway leading toward the kitchens.

She trailed behind a cluster of waitstaff, biding her time until they turned the corner to the kitchens before she tapped her earpiece. "Are you there?"

"Nice going with the guard. You play flustered well," Sato's voice flowed into her ear.

"Are you in position?" Fleur asked, resisting the urge to touch the Bluetooth in her ear. She studied the pen marks on her palm. The elevator should be around the next corner.

"Yup. No problems."

Fleur didn't ask how Sato managed the takeover of the control room. If this went badly, plausible deniability might be her savior—still, she was sure one of Opal's sleeping tonics was involved.

Valerian root, lavender, ashwagandha, chamomile, melatonin, and benzodiazepine—but not too much. They wanted him sleeping, not dead, Opal said, but Fleur wasn't so sure she meant it.

"Remember, don't enter the vents until Vi and Opal have Griffin with them. We can't take any chances," Sato reminded.

Fleur wanted to laugh. This whole thing was one giant chance. "Do you have eyes on Vi?"

"Yeah, they just entered. Viola is chatting up some frowning old lady—"

"Probably Louisa Whethermore," Fleur muttered, rounding the corner and eyeing the elevator ahead.

"Not a fan?"

"Not really." Fleur pressed her badge to the elevator call button, glancing over her shoulder. The corridor was empty. Perfect.

Fleur! Dugal just walked in. Lenora's voice bloomed in Fleur's head just as the elevator doors slid open.

"Griffin's here," Fleur murmured, entering the elevator.

"Right on time."

Fleur knew Lenora wasn't happy monitoring the gala. The spirit wanted to join her in the elevator shaft, but Fleur had insisted. Lenora could give her a more exact view of Griffin than Sato could from the cameras—and Fleur hated to admit she was worried about Vi and Opal. Having Lenora at the gala, an element of unseen protection, offered Fleur a sense of peace she needed to complete her task.

The doors slid shut. Fleur released a ragged breath and pushed the button for the fourth floor. The elevator hummed as it climbed. Fleur watched the numbers illuminate on the screen above the door.

The elevator stopped.

Fleur looked from the screen to the door, her heart pounding. It wasn't supposed to stop at the third floor. She pressed the number four, her thumb playing a staccato rhythm on the plastic button.

The doors opened, and Fleur cursed.

Two servers in the same green and purple smocks grinned at her as they entered and pressed the ground floor.

Fleur offered them a weak smile, her gaze sweeping the crush of people scattered through the lobby until it landed on one.

Theda. Standing at the edge of a group, swath in a flowing dark blue dress, one shoulder bare. She held a wineglass in her hand and tilted her head—her gaze on Fleur.

Blood drained from Fleur's face. How could she have forgotten Theda would be here, lobbying funding for her newest project?

Theda turned fully, frowning as her eyes swept Fleur's uniform. She broke from the group and moved forward.

Fleur swallowed back the urge to race from the elevator, to pull Theda into her arms and away from the vile magick lacing the building. Fist clenched, she shook her head and turned away, watching in her periphery as Theda paused midway to the elevator, her shoulders hunching.

The doors slid closed.

Fleur's lip quivered. She looked up, centering on the glowing numbers of descent. She would not cry. Not now. Not yet. Focus, Fleur scolded herself, ignoring the other two servers flanking her in the small elevator.

The doors slid open, and Fleur gestured for them to exit. Thankfully, they were too engrossed in their conversation to notice the doors close behind them.

"One more time," Fleur muttered as she pressed the button. Her shoulders slumped against the metal walls. Please don't open, she chanted as the third floor slid past.

"What the hell, Fleur? You're supposed to be in the shaft by now," Sato's voice crackled in her ear.

"Minor setback, but I'm on my way."

"You better hurry. Vi is already chatting with Griffin."

CHAPTER
SIXTY

LENORA

Viola was a social wizard. If she wanted to talk to someone, there was nothing, and no one, that could stop her. And she did it so gracefully, including everyone around her in her warmth and candor. It was a remarkable sight.

I hovered beside her, watching as she plucked two glasses of wine from the nearby server's tray and handed one to Opal, all the while continuing her conversation on sheer versus cotton drapes with the woman standing beside her.

Opal hated crowds. That fact feathered over me as I watched her anxiously scan the sea of faces. You wouldn't know it to look at her. The ease with which she nodded along with the conversation, laughing quietly, made her look at home. Only the nearness to Viola and the faint tremor in her hand belied her efforts.

"You've done wonders with that room, Louisa," Viola was saying, resting her hand over the older woman's arm.

"It is lovely, isn't it? The room needed a facelift. But finding a good designer ..." Louisa closed her eyes and exhaled. "Don't get me started."

Opal took a sip of her wine, a smile curling the corners of her mouth.

"Now, Louisa," Viola began, her eyes suddenly flickering to someone behind her friend's shoulder. "Chin up, my dear. I see our host." Viola nodded as she spoke. "Can you imagine—losing his ward one week and burglarized the next?"

"Oh, yes. I read about his misfortune in the *Times*." Louisa shook her head. "Come, Viola, let's see how he's doing."

Viola turned to Opal. "Opal, dear, would you get our host a glass of wine? His hands are empty."

"Oh, Viola, you do think of everything." Louisa nodded in approval as she pulled Viola forward.

I didn't move, awed as I was by Viola's performance. Not only had she set the scene, but she had enlisted a credible ally in her quest. Fleur would be proud.

Opal moved to the bar. I followed closely, my gaze sweeping the room. A sense of foreboding settled over me. I drifted over the crowd until a flash of blue beside Viola's green lace caught my attention. I inched closer, curiosity getting the better of me. A woman in a flowing blue dress wrapped her arm around Viola, her face turned slightly toward me.

Theda.

Did Fleur know she was going to be here? Why didn't she tell them? I glance back at Opal, still at the bar, then back to Theda, chatting with Viola.

She didn't look angry or sad—just calm.

Viola squeezed Theda's shoulder and leaned closer. I watched Theda's head bow, a frown tilting her mouth. What was she telling her? Viola wouldn't break confidence, would she? Frustration fizzled around me as I looked back to Opal.

Opal inched toward a nearby table, her back to the crowd, and set the glass of wine down. The sleeping draught was in powder form, encased in a hollowed-out ring on her finger. Easier to get past security, she claimed as she showed us the mechanism.

A man sidled up to the bar, bumping Opal the same moment she opened the ring. Powder spilled onto the table. I watched in horror as he turned to apologize. There was no way to mask her purpose now. I hurried forward.

With the slam of my fist against the bar top, I knocked over his glass. Amber liquid sloshed against his sleeve, eliciting a curse, and deterring his actions. My light flickered. It was a close call—too close. Opal glanced around her before scraping the remains of the powder into the glass and swirling the dark red wine.

I wanted to ask if it would still work. I didn't know how much was needed, or if any had escaped onto the floor.

"Everything's fine," I heard Opal mutter. Sato must have seen the event from his perch in the booth. "Just a minor hiccup."

I followed her into the crowd, noting that Theda had vanished, and created an invisible barrier between Opal and the flailing arms and elbows.

"Such a shame," Louisa was saying as we approached. "Your ward was so young to die like that." She and Viola had successfully cornered Dugal Griffin and were peppering him with questions. "And then a burglary so soon after." She shook her head. "Do you think they're connected?"

Dugal cleared his throat and looked around the room, his expression pained. Like everyone else, he was clad in black-tie attire. His unremarkable tuxedo blended into the scenery of like-minded patrons until only his cane was distinguishable.

He gripped it tightly. More decoration than useful. Dugal Griffin was able-bodied, but old-fashioned, if not ridiculous. A gentleman always wields a cane, he said once, looking me squarely in the face. I laughed at him then. The humor was refreshing until I realized he was earnest.

I smiled. This ought to be good.

"Naturally, I didn't know the girl was dealing with such things," he said finally, resigning himself to the conversation. Louisa Whethermore was a pillar of society, and a very generous contributor. He'd have to put up with her if he wanted her donation.

I snickered. At least that's what he wanted everyone to think. It was a fine cover—I had to admit—for the theft he had Edgar commit. Inflate prices and skim funds off the top. It was double-entry bookkeeping and not very original. Then present his ill-gotten gains as donations to his archeological society. I didn't know if Louisa ever contributed, but the appearance of it was worth its weight in gold.

Dugal's gaze fell on Opal. The air grew warm and sour. Of course, he knew her—she worked for him for almost ten years, and in that decade, Dugal spoke to her once. "Hello, Barlow," he said smoothly.

"Griffin." Opal nodded at him. "How are you holding up?"

"I should ask you the same."

"I miss her every damn day." Opal's voice was commanding, but sincere.

My aura burned, and I clutched my hands together over my chest, wishing for the thud and swell within.

"As do I."

Liar.

Viola turned. "Do you know each other?" She looked between Opal and Dugal.

"I worked for him years ago at Khade House," Opal remarked.

"Of course! I almost forgot." Viola smiled sadly. "Such tragedy." She took the glass from Opal's hand. "Should we toast to Lenora's light, extinguished too soon?" Viola thrust the glass into Dugal's hand before he could protest, a sympathetic smile pasted across her face.

The woman wasn't just a wizard; she was amazing.

Dugal clasped the glass, raising it in unison with Opal and Louisa. "To Lenora," he muttered, swallowing back the glass of wine.

Glee rose within me, bubbling my light yellow. He drank the whole damn thing.

Dugal rarely drank, but on occasions like this he wouldn't refuse. He had a persona to keep—the image of an elegant recluse to foster. He would drink the wine, but only if forced.

"Thank you, dear ladies. Your compassion has been a balm." He nodded his head to them, empty glass held loosely between his fingers, and turned slightly.

He was trying to escape. I flickered, moving to the other side of him, as if I could somehow bar his way. If Opal was right, we now had twenty minutes before the draught worked.

We couldn't let Dugal out of our sight.

"If you please, Mr. Griffin. I've recently learned of a dig in Turkey that uncovered an unusual monolith ..." Viola latched on to his attention and pulled him back. "Was that your foundation?"

It worked. Dugal turned back, his gaze fixed on Viola as if her voice had hypnotized something in him. "Not mine, no. But I have been following it. There were three stones, not one. Quite fascinating, too. They are etched with glyphs of some unknown origin."

I shook my head. Viola nodded along to Dugal's observations, mimicking his enthusiasm, and doing her best to keep Louisa engaged.

Fleur? I said, willing my voice forward. *The package has been delivered.*

CHAPTER
SIXTY-ONE

L enora's voice echoed in Fleur's head just as she yanked open the elevator hatch and hoisted herself awkwardly through.

"What? You don't need to use code, Len. No one can hear you."

It's fun. Don't be a stick in the mud.

Fleur frowned as she peeled off the green smock and tugged on the hitch on her belt. Straps, like seat belts, hugged her upper body and thighs. The harness was uncomfortable, but it was better than that damn smock. She tossed the offending garment into the elevator and leaned back, staring at the cool metal interior of the lift shaft.

Gods. She really hoped this worked.

Did you know Theda was going to be here?

"No."

She spoke with Viola. You don't think she'll do anything, do you?

"Define anything."

I don't know ... tell Javier?

379

"Maybe?" Theda was an unknown, but only if she suspected anything. Fleur's brow furrowed. Problem was she was sure Theda did. "I can't worry about that now. She wouldn't put us in danger, that I know for sure."

But what if she tells Javier? Lenora insisted, her voice sounding more frantic.

"Then I'll probably go to jail again."

But—

"I'm kinda in the middle of something, Len. Don't worry so much. Theda won't do anything."

Right. Sorry.

Fleur huffed. She squinted up the shaft and pulled the grappling gun out of her backpack. She braced her feet apart, imagining them glued to the cool metal roof, and tightened her grip on the gun.

"What are you waiting for?" Sato's voice buzzed in her ear.

"Just shut up. Who made you our leader, anyway?"

He laughed. "Shoot the damn thing already."

Fleur craned her neck and lifted the gun. It was awkward. The bulk of it rested on her forearm. Her muscles strained and quivered. She took a deep breath, then another, and peered through the scope at the beam above.

Gods. Please let this work.

She pulled the trigger and almost dropped the gun, unprepared for the recoil. The rope unraveled rapidly, and she tightened her grip. Fleur looked up. Did she hit it? The rope dangled in front of her, and she tugged on it before attaching the end to a trio of carabiner clips.

"Nice shot." She could almost hear the smirk in Sato's voice. "Now, get the hell up there."

Fleur grumbled as she finished attaching the rope, praying it would hold her weight. She squeezed her eyes shut. A thousand curses blossomed on her tongue.

Just push the button and the hook will pull you up, she told herself. You can do this. Don't think. Just. Push. The. Button. Fleur held her breath, gripped the rope tightly with one hand, and pressed the button at her waist.

She flew upward, stale air slapping at her cheeks, threatening to pull her black beanie from her head. The beam grew closer and closer until it practically slammed into her. The rope jerked to a stop, leaving her dangling just below it.

Fleur grunted and released a ragged breath.

She never wanted to do that again.

"The vent is right in front of you," Sato announced. "You'll need a flathead screwdriver."

Fleur gritted her teeth. "I know what screwdriver to use," she muttered as she opened the tool kit attached to her sleeve.

The vent opened easily. Fleur slid in, unlatching the rope from her waist once she was inside. It was a tight fit. She scrambled to right herself, the sound of metal scratching metal echoed in the shaft behind her.

"OK. Two turns ..." Sato paused. Fleur imagined him squinting at the blueprints on the screen in front of him. "The first at fifty feet, the second after another twenty, then you're home free."

Great. Fleur crawled further into the vent, her hips rubbing against the metal lining.

The further she went, the darker it grew. With a tap of the button on her shoulder, a small flashlight flared, brightening the space in front of her. Where did Viola get this jumpsuit? Fleur crinkled her nose, wondering what else her stepmother was hiding from her.

She didn't know how long she crawled, but by the time she made the first turn, her joints screamed at her. She paused, rubbing her knee with her palm, trying to stimulate circulation. There must have been an easier way. Couldn't she just have walked through the office, like a lost intern or something?

Fleur righted herself and continued onward. Second turn, then straight on until ... "How will I know I'm at the right vent?" They all looked the same to her.

"I'll tell you."

"Could you give me a hint?"

"If you hit the end, you've gone too far."

"Gee, thanks."

Sato was getting on her last nerve.

"How's Viola doing down there?" She needed to think of something other than the pain in her knees.

"Concentrate, Fleur," Sato muttered. "You're almost there."

"Fine," she huffed, stretching out on her belly as the tunnel narrowed.

"Just a couple more feet ..."

She passed another grate, then another, noting that the air had grown cooler. "Where am I?"

Silence.

Fleur paused and angled her flashlight straight ahead. Only two more grates before she reached the end. One of these must be Dugal's office. She inched closer to the slats and peered down. She was over the hallway—the white paneled one she and Theda had followed the pantsuit lady down a week ago. Had it only been a week? Fleur repressed a shiver as the memory of silence washed over her.

She looked up. It should be the next grate.

"Sato?"

"Next one. You're doing good."

"Where were you?"

"Talking to Viola. Package activated."

Fleur released a breath and scurried to the next grate. "Alright, then ... showtime."

CHAPTER
SIXTY-TWO

LENORA

D ugal paused mid-sentence and frowned.

The pill was working.

He looked at Viola and offered a weak smile. "Would you excuse me?" He didn't wait for an answer before he turned, swaying slightly, his hand grasping the edge of the bar table beside him.

Viola nodded to Opal. "Follow him," she whispered, her eyes on the back of Dugal's jacket as he vanished into a sea of evening attire.

It all happened much faster than I expected. Opal and I followed him to the men's room. Opal glanced at her watch, then back to the door—guarding it. After a few minutes, she knocked lightly on the door, cracking it open.

"Excuse me?"

A snore bubbled up from the last stall.

Opal smiled and touched her earpiece. "Activated," she whispered, alerting the others.

She pushed through the door and locked it behind her before rushing to the stall.

Dugal Griffin lay sprawled on his stomach over the toilet seat.

Opal pressed two fingers to his neck and nodded—my light flickered. He was still alive. Relief and disappointment warred within me, pulsing my light orange. To say I didn't want him dead was a lie, but I wouldn't want it done by Opal's hand. No, Dugal's death was mine.

His cane lay at his side, one arm thrown over it. Opal pulled it free and stood, twisting off the top etched with the goddess symbol. She peeked inside, then delicately extracted a small wooden stick.

"Is this it?" Opal whispered as she recapped the cane and lay it back at Dugal's side. She turned the stick over in her hands. "Len? Are you here? Is this it?"

I knew from the *Book of Veils* that it was a plain wooden flute—twig-like, with no embellishments. I hovered beside her, studying the tiny holes along its side. There, just above the slivered opening at the top, carved into the petrified bark, the crescent moon symbol.

I tapped the side of the stall, wishing I could answer her.

"One for yes, two for no," Opal muttered, looking up from the stick.

I tapped again—just once.

We had the flute.

Opal sighed and slid it into the small purse hanging from her wrist. She looked down at Dugal, her eyes hardening, and drew back her pointed black heel. She kicked him squarely in the stomach. "Rot in hell."

I wished I could hug her.

SIXTY-THREE

FLEUR

M oonlight feathered over Griffin's desk, streaking over the marble floor like an arrow from Eros's bow. Fleur pushed open the grate and crawled out, her knees protesting as they hit the hard marble floor. They creaked as she stood, and Fleur winced slightly as she hobbled over to the bookcase displaying the conch shell.

The office felt different at night—louder, more alive. The din of street noise seeped through the wall of windows, giving the room's chill some much-needed warmth. Fleur released a breath and rolled her shoulders. In and out. She didn't have time to mess around.

The shell's warmth twisted around her, digging into her flesh, and pulling her in. Fleur leaned closer to its glass case, her fingers seeking the latches on either side. It was a curious Relic, born of a now deserted realm. The Svinkraken had sought sanctuary in Evir-dahl during the invasion more than a millennium ago. She knew them as the warriors of the north and had only met one of the squid-like warriors—once, at the Jaser high court. She could hardly believe she remembered it. How old was she? Four? Fleur shook her head.

She pulled the glass away, setting it carefully on the floor. Svinnka was lost to the realms long before the sheath was destroyed. But she wondered ... what if reuniting the Relics could manage the destruction of that world? What if there was still magick in the oceans, magick the heat from the volcanos deep below couldn't destroy? Magick that could heal?

Fleur knew only one person capable of answering her questions, and she had a bone to pick with him. Once this was over, she was going to give Axel a hefty piece of her mind.

But for now, she needed to grab the shell and head to the warehouse.

The conch was thicker and heavier than it looked. Fleur closed her finger over it, careful not to pierce her skin with its sharp edges. Each Relic had a catalyst, a missing ingredient needed to spark its magick. For the flute, it was breath. For the shell—blood. Blood Relics were rare. Fleur frowned as she wrapped the delicate conch in the scarf she took from Viola's closet and slid it into her trouser pocket—the conch shard was one of two Relics activated by blood. The other ... ice crystal arrowhead from the fourth realm.

A shiver trailed down her spine. The room groaned as silence descended once again. Fleur stilled, her heart pounding in her ears, and turned slowly, careful not to disturb the rolling quiet, her eyes searching the room for shadows.

One by one, the shades thickened, pulling from the room's corners like ink splattered on paper. Fleur held her breath, touching the key around her neck. It throbbed against her palm, warm with a spark of her mother's magick, as the dark bodies crept closer. What was happening? She was no Atua, no fresh essence for them to feed. Fleur may not remember everything, but she knew she was more of an appetizer to the Shadelings, not the main course. Their wispy fingers left trails of ice over her flesh. Smoke curled around her, tugging at her limbs. Grima would sap her despair, their smoke seeping through her jumpsuit, a dangerous caress—the lull of sorrow bit into her, and tears sprang into her eyes.

The protection chant tumbled onto her tongue but froze before she could breathe her magick into it. Fleur gasped as icy fingers clasped the delicate skin of her throat.

Focus. She blinked, backing slowing into the center of the room. The image of her father's frail body—void of life—bloomed in her mind, her stomach cramped with remorse. She had been too stubborn, too angry to see him until she was too late. Fleur never understood him, never tried. His inability to understand his daughter consumed her. But was she so different? Fleur swallowed back the tears clogging at her throat, coughing—her shoulders hunching slightly.

Arik was trying to protect her, and she did everything in her power to defy him. Agony tugged at her heart. He was dying, and she couldn't be bothered to visit. She thought she had time. She thought things would mellow out. She was wrong.

Focus. An unfamiliar voice echoed in her mind.

Not Lenora. Deeper.

"Sato?" she whispered but heard only a faint crackle in her Bluetooth.

Don't let the despair take hold, Fleur.

Fleur's eyes blinked open, crusty with sleep. Had she slept? Darkness swirled around her, a sandstorm of smoke. She stood frozen in the center of Griffin's office, a sliver of moonlight illuminating his desk.

Moonlight. Of course.

With heavy legs, Fleur stumbled toward the desk. The air thickened, her lungs strained.

One more step. The light is upon you! Take my hand. The voice sounded frantic.

Something gripped her fingers, pulling her forward. The shadows clung like cobwebs burning to embers as the light fell over her.

KRISTA FAZENDIN

Fleur groaned and rubbed her eyes. Awkwardly, she stumbled into Griffin's chair and dropped her head into her hands. Her chest heaved—with each breath, she pushed the sorrow back, shutting it away in the cage at the pit of her stomach.

"You're OK." That voice, steady ... and real.

Her breath hitched in her throat as she looked up.

A man in a tuxedo, his black hair streaked with silver, stood beside her. He glanced around the room, his arms crossed over his chest. Fleur studied his clean-shaven jaw, noting the absence of wrinkles and laugh lines.

"Who are you?"

He turned to her. His eyes were bright amber. "A friend."

Fleur frowned and stood, needing to distance herself from the stranger. "Most of my friends have names."

The man smiled. It was an amiable smile, one Fleur suspected he used to charm, but it held no warmth. He tilted his head—as if considering her—and blinked, his lids moving vertically across his eyes.

Shit. Shit. Shit. Fleur backed away, her hand raised, palm splayed in front of her.

He was Entomali—one of the keepers of the Great Tree. She would know the insect creatures anywhere.

"Am I dead?"

The creature laughed. "No."

"But you're a Soulkeeper."

"That is true."

Fleur narrowed her eyes at him and waited.

"I am not here to harm you, Fleur." He didn't move.

"How do you know who I am?"

"It's my business to know those who can help me."

Fleur released a strangled laugh. "Help you?"

The creature nodded. "We can help each other."

"I doubt that."

"You'll see."

"I don't enjoy cryptic conversations, mister. So, either tell me what you want, or I'm leaving." Fleur's patience unraveled a little with each word. She inched away from the desk.

He sighed, his shoulders relaxing as he folded his arms loosely across his chest. He looked bored, resigned ... disappointed. Fleur lifted her chin and met his amber gaze.

"You're a fighter," he said cautiously.

"Only if I have something to fight for."

"You'll do nicely."

"Do what?"

The creature leaned forward. "Not yet, seer—but soon."

"Fine." Fleur rolled her eyes, fighting the tremor racing up her spine. She turned toward the vent. "Then, if you don't mind, I've got places to be."

"Come find me when you're finished with your little intrigue." He handed her a business card, a smile flickering in the corners of his mouth.

Lazlo Barker Antiques. LLC. The antique dealer who sold Lenora the wind spinner. Fleur frowned. An Entomali living in the second realm was unheard of. She narrowed her gaze at him as she pocketed the card. "What do you know of my intrigue?"

"Enough." Lazlo grinned. "Haven't you wondered whose breath powers Griffin's flute?"

Fleur opened her mouth, but her words drained down her throat. Soulkeepers allowed the dead to choose but bargained with the living. Fleur swallowed back a curse. If Griffin was using the Entomali's breath, what had he traded in return? No Entomali would give his breath for free. Fleur sucked in a breath as she recalled Lazlo's words. "*Not yet, seer—but soon.*" A chill slid over her skin, and she knew, somehow, she was part of the Soulkeepers' bargain. But how? And why? Questions frenzied, words twisted and swelled with need. Fleur opened her mouth, then closed it, unsure if she was ready for the answer.

"It's you in the black sedan, isn't it? You've been following me since we met with Griffin."

Lazlo blinked, tilting his head knowingly. "You fascinate me."

"What do you want from me?"

Lazlo merely smiled and nodded toward the open vent. "There'll be time enough later. I'm eager to see how you fare tonight, Fleur."

Fleur narrowed her gaze at him. "Why?" she asked, tempting fate.

The Entomali shrugged. "Watch out for Griffin. He knows more than you think, and he's twice as devious."

With a frown, she turned back to the vent. Fleur's fingers curled around the card in her pocket. "How——," she began, swinging back around.

But the Soulkeeper was gone.

CHAPTER
SIXTY-FOUR

FLEUR

It shouldn't have worked, but somehow Sato's half-baked plan to lure the guards away from the warehouse did.

Fleur was against Viola and Opal being involved, but Sato insisted. Fleur argued that the security team would see through the ridiculous argument or—worse—they'd ignore it completely. Who cares if two middle-aged women had a screaming fit on the sidewalk right next to your secret warehouse? Surely, Griffin's guards were smarter than that.

For the first time in her life, Fleur was glad to be wrong.

It took less than ten minutes for the guards to intervene in Viola and Opal's staged disagreement. The three guards wandered over, trying to keep the peace until Viola lured them into the fight. One innocent question, one vicious accusation, and they were hooked. Fleur wasn't even sure what they were fighting about—something to do with a stolen casserole dish that escalated into something far more sinister, no doubt. Whatever it was, it gave Sato time to loop the camera feeds.

While she and Lenora slipped through the unguarded doorway.

Edgar sat on the edge of his bed, his eyes trained on the floor. He looked bewitched, mystified by the hard concrete slab. If Fleur wasn't holding the flute, she would wonder if he wasn't being controlled at that very moment.

The trick with the magick was to hold your subject enthralled. Over time, the melody waned, needing to be recharged. After ten years of recharging, Edgar's mind would depend on the song—that's why they needed the spinner. Like a bottlebrush—the mandala's magick should scrub the tight edges and corners of Edgar's mind, washing him clean with the reverse melody.

Fleur had never done this before. Aside from a brief, half-remembered conversation with her mother when she was a kid and the few lines in the *Book of Veils*, Fleur was totally guessing.

Gods. Please let this work.

How do I do this? Lenora's voice wavered, betraying her worry.

"Remember Madam Olga?"

I have to possess him?

"Same principle, except you're not possessing his body, just his mind. Do you remember how you did it?"

Kind of ... I just focused on her, imagined her limbs were my limbs, and stepped inside of her. It was like moving into a dark room with only a sliver of window. Muscle memory helped me with her limbs, but they were heavier than I expected.

"Well, she wasn't exactly a small woman. Anyway, focus on Edgar, OK? His memories of you together—happy memories. Pull yourself into them just like you did with Olga."

What if I can't? I only have snippets of memories—the exercise Ellory taught me is helping, but I'm still not strong enough to remember entire events.

At Ellory's name, Fleur looked up. Her conversation with the Soulkeeper burned in her mind. Focus, she scolded herself. There would be time enough to investigate the creature later.

"Then we regroup and try again." Fleur paused and looked down at the flute in her hand. "I can still reverse the hold and free him without the mandala, but his mind might fracture. Even if we succeed, he might not be the brother you remember, not after all this time."

Lenora nodded, and Fleur swore she saw her gulp. *OK. I can do this.*

Fleur turned to Edgar, still seated, still staring, completely ignorant of their presence. She took a step closer, the melody staining against her memory. She hoped she remembered the cadence recorded in her uncle's book. Edgar flinched and rubbed the back of his neck as if he could feel their stares. Fleur took another step and lifted the flute to her lips.

Gods. Please ... let this work.

～

LENORA

The first memory I had was of summer. Edgar lay next to me in the grass, our heads close together, our skin bathed in sunlight, eyes on the clouds.

Edgar found the cloud game tedious, but I loved it.

"Look! A mandala!" I pointed to a cumulus cloud curling around the wind spinner's curves. My finger traced the outline of the goddess symbol on the air, and I gripped Edgar's hand tightly in mine.

Edgar frowned and squinted. "You mean those cumulus clouds there?"

"Use your imagination! Look!" I pointed to another, wispier cloud. "That one looks like the spray of water when a wave hits a big rock."

"Cirrostratus. It'll rain later."

I turned, propping myself up on my elbow. "What's with you today? You're not even trying to humor me." The grass was warm, tickling the delicate flesh of my arm.

Edgar sighed one of his deeply dramatic sighs and stretched his arms over his head. "I'm just not in the mood to pretend."

Earlier, our father had called Edgar into his home office. It was a rare thing—to be summoned. Rodney liked to keep his work and home life separate—the office was just for show, he'd say. My actual work stays downtown. I stared at my brother, wondering what had changed in the brief time between now and breakfast. "What did Dad want?"

Edgar pressed his lips together, his gaze still on the summer sky. "He showed me some documents, figures from their annual shareholder summit, and asked me to interpret them."

"Why?"

"Because someone is skimming profits. He asked me to review the quarterly reports for anomalies."

I bit my tongue. Edgar had a gift for numbers. One that added a sparkle of pride to our father's eye. He was the golden child. Having graduated from high school a month before his twelfth birthday, he already had an acceptance into MIT—while I struggled to configure a matrix. It would be a lie to say it didn't bother me, but I tried not to think of it as second best. Eddie and I were different. My skills lay in the arts and languages, while his ... his endeared him to our stoic father.

"And?" I asked, realizing that Edgar wouldn't elaborate.

He shrugged again. "The thing is ... I hate it, Len. Everything I see is like a scope of rationalizations and algorithms—at school, in chess club—none of the kids know how to talk to me, and I don't know how to communicate either. I'm a freak. I don't want to do it. I don't want to be the gifted kid anymore."

"But Ed—"

"No, not you too, Len. Do you know what those gifted programs are like? Everyone wants something from you. They praise every little thing you do and pull you aside as if you're a trophy—their trophy. I hate it."

"But your friends—" I didn't want to admit that he was right. I knew how frustrated he felt. This wasn't the first time he'd mentioned it. But I let my optimism get the upper hand, even though I knew it wasn't what he needed.

"You mean those posers who lap it all up? They're not my friends. They want to be seen with me, the boy wonder. They're the worst. They're told how special they are their whole lives, and they believe it. They're elitist assholes, Len."

I looked back to the house, praying Opal didn't hear his language. "Why didn't you say anything? Talk to Mum if Dad won't understand. She'll get it."

"Will she? Sometimes I think she hates me."

"Jeez, Ed." I sat up, dusting bits of grass from my arms. "She does not. She just doesn't know how to relate to you."

"I'm just a kid. A dumb kid who doesn't know what to do with himself. It's not hard. She could try a little."

The clouds darkened suddenly. Drops of rain fell on my bare arms. Freezing rain. I looked up. We needed to get inside. A shiver raced up my spine, and I turned, ready to race Edgar to the house, but he vanished, leaving only the imprint of his aura on the air.

The earth slanted, and I tumbled, my hands clawing at the dirt. The clouds elongated, pulling apart, their wispy fingers swirling around me, tugging at my shirt, my hair. I fell through them, and they latched on to me. Sticky like sap, they coated my skin. I tried to stand. Sap dripped around me, blurring my vision.

This was Edgar's mind. I turned frantically, searching for an exit from the cavern I had tumbled into. Warm amber light poured from above, and I shielded my eyes as I looked up.

Not a light. A window—a door.

An oubliette.

My brother had trapped me.

~

FLEUR

The melody wasn't hard. After a few false starts, Fleur got the hang of it. The flute felt delicate in her hands. Her fingers pressed against the rough holes. It was a lifeline devouring her breath.

Edgar barely moved.

But she pressed forward, inhaling deeply with every note, inching closer to him until she sat beside him on the narrow cot.

Lenora had vanished, leaving only a thin trail of light—a halo around her brother. Was it the residue of her aura? Fleur wasn't sure.

Dimly, she heard a scream—high-pitched and ragged.

Fleur didn't falter. She would not stop playing until Lenora returned.

Another scream—the sound came from Edgar.

And this time, he swayed.

Lenora

"EDGAR!" I shouted again, heaving the scream from my stomach.

Silence. The air grew thick and sweet, filling my throat until I gagged.

I slugged through the sap, feeling my way around the circular interior. There had to be a way up. Why would he trap me? I was trying to help him. Maybe there's a hidden lever? My fingers tripped over the slick crags, scrapping my knuckles against the instances of dried sap covering the walls. The pain—sharp and deep—pulsed through me.

I took a deep breath, startled by the wheeze of air curling through me.

My face. My body—tangible. I touched my cheek, swallowing back the urge to cry. Pliable skin—warm flesh.

I was whole again.

Music. The flute's low soulful moan wound around me. It ebbed, dipping from crescendo to staccato in a fluid motion. It wasn't an unpleasant tune. I hummed a few bars, recognizing the melody.

It was the lullaby Ellory taught Fleur.

"Edgar!" I shouted again, lifting my face to the light. "Please ..."

"Shh!" The air rumbled. "Stop shouting, Len."

He knew me. I wanted to cry out—my body trembled, and I struggled to keep still. "Edgar?" I whispered. "Are you there?"

"Of course I am. It's my mind."

Air vibrated around me, hardening the sea of sap until the oubliette gleamed amber.

I didn't know what I was expecting, but the skeletal man with shaggy hair and sunken eyes who appeared before me was hardly it. Edgar looked like a shadow of the man seated in the warehouse. He was the painting to Griffin's Dorian Gray.

"Hello, Len." His cheek dimpled. "What brings you here?"

I threw myself at him. To touch his face, to feel his breath against my skin. My little brother—grown, alive. My resolve hardened as I wrapped him in my arms. "I'm here to get you out."

Edgar shook his head. "It's impossible. If he finds you—"

"Who? Griffin? We have the flute, Ed. Dugal is out cold. We're going to get you free."

"We?"

"Me and Fleur. She's ... well ..."

Edgar took a step back, his eyes brown pools. "How are you here, Lenora?"

"I found a way, Ed. It's Dugal. He's behind all of it. Mum and Dad's death, your imprisonment, the embezzlement—everything. He's holding you captive with a magickal flute."

"I know, Lenora. I've known about Dugal since the day of the crash. What I don't know is how you're here. In my head." He squinted at me. "Is this another trap? Another lie?" He shook his head. "It won't work this time, Griffin." His voice rose.

"I'm not a lie, Edgar." I spoke quietly, unsure of how to tell him the truth. "I found a way to undo what he did to you ... only I made a few miscalculations."

Edgar groaned. "You found his book, didn't you?"

"You know about the book?"

"Of course. Years ago, when I was just a kid, trapped in a hospital bed. Griffin had me memorize it—said we were going to collect all the Relics and renew this realm. He said that the time for magick was now. I thought he was full of shit, or crazy, or both, until he pulled out the flute."

"You knew everything." I could hardly believe it. "And you didn't escape?"

"Are you kidding? I've tried a million times. But I'm trapped. The me in the world is just a husk—a giant computer that bows to Griffin's will."

Fleur was right. I grasped his hand. "We found a way to unite you and pull you free of the spell's influence." I paused, tilting my head toward the melody. "Listen ..."

Edgar clapped his hands over his ears. "No. Lenora. Don't—don't!"

"Shh! Ed! It's OK—listen. The tune is different."

"No. It's a trick." He shook his head, covering his head with his arms.

"Look at me, Edgar! Please ... I've missed you. I love you—I'm not a trick. This is the truth. My truth. I was told you were dead, that you were all dead. But I didn't give up. No, Eddie! I never gave up on you," I cried, wrapping my arms around my brother.

"How are you here, Lenora?" Edgar stared at me through tear-stained eyes. "Tell me the truth."

"I died, Edgar," I whispered, tears clogging my throat. "It was the only way."

Edgar screamed, a wail of tears streaming down his face. He backed away from me, his head shaking. "No. No. No."

I reached out, my fingers tugging at his ragged clothes, trying to pull him back to me.

"Why would you do that? How can I go on now, Len? Why should I?" He wept into his hands. His body wracked with sobs.

I knelt at his feet. "Please, Eddie ... I need you to listen to the flute. I did this to save you ... I wasn't supposed to die, I promise. But I misjudged my abilities ..." I offered a weak laugh. "You know me, Ed —always go big." I sniffed. "I messed up, but I found a way. Fleur, she's ... my friend. She knew how to free you. She's playing the flute. Please, Eddie, just listen."

"The music is evil, Len. It did this to me," Edgar muttered, allowing me to pull him closer.

"It was, but I fixed it. Remember the mandala cloud?"

Edgar scoffed, his shoulders relaxing. "You and your dumb cloud games."

It worked. He remembered the game, if not the spinner. I released a breath and hugged him closer. "I need you to trust me. Can you do that?"

He nodded his head against my shoulder.

"Listen to the music, Edgar."

CHAPTER
SIXTY-FIVE

FLEUR

Edgar tilted his head toward the flute, tears blossoming in his eyes.

Fleur took a deep breath and continued the melody. She shifted her gaze to his clenched fists. C'mon, Lenora, focus on the melody. It was working—slowly.

As she played, her mind drifted, touching on the forgotten things in her youth, the freedom of childhood, the innocence of life before exile, before doubt. Fleur added each delicate strand of her own threads to the song, weaving the freedoms she had taken for granted into each note. Edgar deserved to know the taste of strawberry air on her lips and the feathered touch of sunlight on her skin. She couldn't do much more than blow her intentions into the thinly veiled melody—the lullaby her mother taught her, and the laughter she had forced herself to forget.

Tears trailed down her cheeks as she recalled the soft call of her mother and the rumble of her father's chuckle. She drew back from the bitter cage she placed around the frail memories, allowing them breath, allowing them to bloom.

Edgar's fingers unfurled, his hand grasped his knees, his once limp body tensed and shifted beside her.

Fleur turned slightly, renewing the song. Edgar blinked. Once. Twice. His face coloring, his aura quickening in the gloomy warehouse.

"Fleur!" Viola's shout pierced the rafters.

She couldn't stop. Not now. Not yet. Fleur stood, the flute still at her chapped lips, her breath filling the slender cavern.

"Fleur! Get out of there!" Sato shouted from the window behind her.

Still, she played. They had come so far, sacrificed too much for her to stop now.

"Yes, Ms. Harkyn. Please join us," Dugal's voice echoed in the space between notes.

Fleur stood at the entrance to Edgar's cove. Watching the scene move toward her as if it was a grainy reel of film. Somehow, the melody still played despite her gasp.

Dugal held Viola's arm. A gun pointed at her side.

Fleur's heart dropped, crashing into the pit of her stomach. Anger swirled with fear, welling until her breath faltered. Gods. No. Her body tensed, and she pulled the flute from her lips.

Behind her, Sato dropped from the window. He landed with a crunch on the desk below, but Fleur didn't turn. Her eyes were on Viola.

"I must hand it to you, Ms. Harkyn. Your plan almost worked," Dugal sneered as he moved closer, dragging Viola beside him. "That sleeping brew was potent, but the delivery was poorly done." He jerked his head toward the door behind him. "Opal still has much to learn."

"If you harm her—" Viola struggled against him, her face red with anger.

Griffin laughed. "My guards will keep her safe."

Viola huffed and tried to crush his toe under her heel. Griffin sidestepped her and pushed the gun further into her side. "None of that, Mrs. Harkyn."

Fleur gripped the flute, praying that Lenora had enough time to make it out, and took a step forward. She needed to bide her time. Spooking Griffin would only hurt Viola. She lifted the flute. "I'm guessing you came for this?"

"That, and you."

"Me? What the hell does that mean?"

Viola whimpered softly as Dugal dug the muzzle of the gun into her side. "Don't be a fool. You're a seer, just like your mother. I didn't realize your importance at first, but after Barker's request, I did my own research."

Fleur's eyes widened. She was right. The Soulkeepers bargained for a seer. But why? The Entomali didn't need to forecast the future or speak to the dead. Hell, they owned the dead. Realization dawned like an arrow to her heart. Lazlo wanted a seer to find the Relics. She cursed—and Griffin wanted to beat him to it. "So, you want your own seer to do your dirty work for you?"

"Finding the Relics would be easier, yes." He shrugged as if he hadn't just admitted to what she had already guessed.

"Why do you want them? You can't use them." Even as she asked, Fleur realized the answer. She was the damn prize.

"No. But you can."

"I won't."

Dugal cocked the gun. "I think you will."

Sirens. In the distance. Fleur paused. This wasn't part of the plan. Everyone stilled as the sound grew closer. Realization slapped at her.

Shit. Javier.

"You kill her—or any of us—and the police will be here in seconds. There's no way out, Griffin," Fleur shouted, playing on the whine of sirens getting louder.

"I call your bluff," Dugal growled. "You've just spent the night stealing from me—why would you call the police? You'd only implicate yourselves."

A car door slammed.

"Don't be so sure, Griffin. Let her go."

"Police!" Javier's voice boomed over them like a cannon, followed by the rush of feet. "Drop the gun, Griffin."

Fleur grinned. "Hiya, Javier."

"This isn't your fight, Detective. I'm only here to collect what's mine," Dugal growled, tugging on Viola's arm as he moved.

Fleur's gaze held steady as Griffin dragged Viola in a wide arc. He inched closer to Edgar, now fully conscious. Anger flushed Edgar's pale skin, twisting his mouth, and hardening his jaw—a feral creature released after a decade of imprisonment. Lenora glistened beside him, her aura pale white, her eyes trained on Viola.

Griffin prowled, his gaze darting from face to face, eyes wild with desperation. He hadn't counted on this. For the first time, the odds were against him.

The window was slim, but it was one Fleur had to take. She jerked her head from Sato to Griffin, praying he would have her back. Sato's eyes met her from the desk, and he nodded.

"Let the hostage go, Griffin. This isn't looking good for you," Javier shouted from behind them.

Griffin's brow furrowed. It was all the hesitation Fleur needed. With a grunt, she flung the flute at Sato and launched herself at Griffin—heaving into him with all her might. Javier shouted. Viola screamed as Fleur shoved her away, grasping the gun with both hands. Griffin was unprepared. He stumbled backward under the weight of her. His arm cracked beneath him, and he shrieked in pain. Viola scurried behind her.

Fleur leveled the gun at him. "You were saying?"

Gods, it felt good to have the upper hand.

"Fleur. Set the gun down," Javier shouted, his own firearm trained on her.

"In a minute," she replied, her gaze fixed on Griffin.

403

Griffin groaned, holding his injured arm close. "Do you have any idea what we can create together?" he grunted, scooting awkwardly to his knees. "This realm is ripe for the picking. You know it—I know it. Its magick isn't gone, just dormant. It is waiting for the call of strength."

"And you think that's you?"

"Why not?" Griffin lifted himself, groaning as he did so, and cradled his arm close to his chest.

"You're artless, Griffin. You don't stand a chance against true magick."

Griffin threw his head back and laughed.

"That man is totally insane," Viola muttered behind her. "Don't hurt him, Fleur. He needs help."

"Fleur. I said, put the gun down," Javier shouted again.

Fleur ignored him, her gun still aimed at Griffin. "Where did you find the book? Huh? Griffin?"

"It found me," he sneered. "It was waiting for me."

Fleur shook her head. "It would *never* have chosen you."

Griffin ignored her, his gaze sweeping the room. "Stupid people. This is my destiny. I have powerful connections."

"Barker?" Fleur scoffed.

Dugal paused. "You've met him? Of course. He's been looking for you for a long time."

"What is he? A competitor? An accomplice? Do you both plan to rule this realm together? Fat chance, Griffin. Without me, you've got nothing."

Griffin shook his head. "Such ego." He stepped forward.

Fleur aimed the gun at his leg. "I said, don't move."

"Fleur!" Javier warned, exasperation coating his tone.

"Do you really think I'd be fool enough to load the gun?" Dugal laughed again, wincing with pain as he shifted his arm. He crept closer, undeterred by the weapon. "Tell me, Harkyn. Have you spoken with Lenora? I suspect she's involved in this operation. Did she ask you to free her brother? Did she cry on your shoulder, weaving her fairy tale about how I murdered her family?"

Fleur tracked him with the gun. Loaded or not, she wouldn't let him go. She'd throw it at him if she had to. "What do you care?"

Griffin paused, inches away, his gaze on someone behind her. Edgar.

Fleur didn't dare turn. "I know the truth, Griffin. You're not the hero of this story and you know it."

"No," he said, taking a step closer. "But neither are you." His gaze met Fleur's, and she saw anger and malice swirling in his steel-blue eyes.

A flash of movement flared in the corner of her eye, and Fleur turned—time elongated and slowed, trapping them in an instant of shock. A low gurgle bubbled up from Griffin's throat, his face reddened as he sucked at the air, his skin graying. Eyes wide, his good hand grasped his chest, his neck—he stumbled, his body rickety and tense. He wheezed fast and faster, spittle foaming, flying from his blue lips. Fleur jumped back as Griffin fell to the floor, flailing, tears streaming down his face.

A bloody gash on the side of his neck.

Fleur spun around, dropping the gun, a curse spilling from her lips.

Edgar held the conch shell; a drop of Griffin's blood stained the jagged white edge.

Damn. It must have fallen from her pocket when she attacked Griffin.

Griffin rasped, blood oozing from his mouth, his face tight and pale. He writhed as if he could somehow save himself. A moment later, he stilled, his fisted hands slumped against the cold concrete.

Javier rushed forward, his firearm lowered, and pressed two fingers to Griffin's neck. He shook his head and glanced up, first to Fleur, Sato, and Viola before finally landing on Edgar. "He's dead. Want to tell me what's going on?"

"He drowned." Fleur shrugged. "It happens."

"No, Harkyn. It doesn't happen like this."

"Nobody needs to know that." Fleur shuddered, turning away from Dugal's body.

Edgar stood beside the cot. Flushed, he glared at the body and straightened his spine. Sweet Gula—did it work? Did the melody really work?

"Edgar?" Fleur asked gently. "Are you OK?"

He nodded, his eyes watering. "He deserved that."

"Yes, he did." She nodded to the shell in his hands. "How'd you know to use that?"

"It's all in the book." Edgar held up the shell, examining it. "I expected it to be bigger."

"It was once." She held out her hand. "Can I have it? It's safe with me."

Edgar lowered the shell into her hand and watched as she pocketed it. "You're Fleur?" he asked, studying her, his hands clasped in front of him.

"Yup. Heard about me, have you?"

"Lenora said you were her friend."

"I *am* her friend," Fleur said gently. "She's right here."

Lenora fixed her eyes on her brother. *He's going to need time, Fleur —you were right. But he's free.* Her light pulsed softly.

"She said she was dead." Edgar frowned, looking around him.

Fleur nodded. "But she's not gone, Edgar. I promise you that."

"So Dugal was right. You're the seer."

"Among other things." Fleur shrugged.

Behind her, Viola let loose a ragged shriek and fanned herself with both hands. "Fleur! Oh my God, Fleur ... is he? What the? Oh God!" She shook her head. Her teeth chattered even as she grinned and leaned against the wall behind her. "I *never* want to do that again."

Fleur laughed and rushed up to her stepmother, wrapping her arms around her. She didn't expect the rush of emotion the moment she saw that gun. She didn't expect the swift clutch of her heart at the thought of losing Viola, too. "You OK, Vi? Did he hurt you?"

Viola smiled through her tears. She squeezed Fleur. "I'm fine. Don't worry about me."

Sato hopped down from the desk and handed her the flute. "Nice throw, by the way."

"Thanks." Fleur pocketed the flute, nodding to Sato. "Nice catch."

Sato grinned and turned to Lenora's brother. His dark eyes sizing him up. "You look like Len."

Edgar shook his head. "No, Lenora always looked more like our father."

Sato shrugged and inclined his head. "Anyway, I'm Sato, Lenora's … friend."

Lenora flickered, swaying closer to her brother.

Edgar frowned, his body tense as he looked around the room. "I don't know what to do."

Sato chuckled softly. "No worries, Ed. I don't either."

"How about one of you tell me how Dugal Griffin drowned on the concrete floor of his own warehouse?" Javier interrupted.

Sato slapped him on the back good-naturedly. "Magick."

"Shit, Sato. You're not kidding, are you?"

"Nope. Good luck, Torres." Sato laughed. "C'mon, let's leave them to it." He turned to Edgar and jerked his head to the door.

"Not so fast. I have some questions for Mr. Khade." Javier stepped in front of them.

"Can they wait until he's had a breath of fresh air?" Sato challenged.

"Fresh air can wait, Sato." Javier shook his head and pulled out his notepad. "I'll be with you in a minute."

"As you wish, Detective," Sato replied with a mock salute, ignoring Javier's scowl.

Lenora turned to Fleur, her glow warm and cautious. *Fleur—*

"OK, what the hell is going on?" Javier turned to Fleur. Oblivious of Lenora, he spoke over her, his brows furrowed in thought. His gaze danced between them. "Fleur? Vi?"

"Calm down, Jav." Fleur grimaced. "It's no big deal. Drop him in the Sound and file it under drowning—self-inflicted. Sato can draft up a fancy suicide note for you."

"How are you so calm? A man is dead." Javier shook his head at her.

"He wasn't a good man." Should she be upset? Death was death—the Soulkeepers will deal with him. Lazlo Barker's face swam behind her eyes, then faded. *Barker will make him pay*—she didn't know how, but she was sure of that.

Fleur turned to Lenora, noting eagerness coloring her light yellow. She held up the flute. "You need this, right?"

Lenora brightened and drifted forward. *But how* ... she tried to grasp it, but her fingers slid through the tiny wooden flute.

"Damn," Fleur muttered, her mind wandering once again through her mother's lessons. Gods. She really should have paid better attention all those years ago.

Javier bristled at Fleur and Lenora's exchange, his face flushed with confusion. "Do you have any idea how many laws you've broken tonight, and how many you're asking me to break?" His tone was grim.

"Oh, yeah? Where's the cavalry?" Fleur gave him a pointed look, knowing Javier had broken protocol the moment he entered the warehouse alone.

Javier pulled off his glasses and rubbed his eyes. "Fair," he groaned.

"Now, gimme a minute ..." Fleur looked from Javier to Lenora and exhaled. "I need to figure this out."

"Figure what out?"

"How to give this to Lenora, OK? Now ... shh." Fleur waved the flute in front of him.

"What?" Javier shook his head. "That's evidence. You can't just—"

"Javier, I know this looks crazy—," Viola interrupted, her voice steady despite her still trembling hands.

"Vi—this is chaos. What the hell are *you* even doing here? I expected Fleur, not both of you." He shook his head again.

Viola took a shaky breath. "Someone had to make sure Fleur didn't get killed."

As Viola argued with Javier, Fleur tugged and twirled at memories she had ignored for far too long until one, the slightest glimmer of a spell, pulled free, enveloping her in warmth. "Got it."

Lenora brightened. *What do I need to do?*

"Nothing. Just … wait …," Fleur muttered, closing her eyes and allowing the magick to wash over her.

It began in her fingertips, the laughter, the giddiness of youth, of fresh strawberry-scented air and musk from the Barbard trees that lined the south gardens. In late winter, when the hellebores peeked through the frosty earth, spilling their muted elegance onto the once decaying leaves—the tang of milky dandelion tea still on her lips, Fleur cast her first spell. She needed that memory. She needed the warmth and nourishment, the abundance of youth … Fleur needed to remember how to be whole again.

It was as simple as that. Her skin sizzled lightly, heating her cheeks, her chest, her arms … warmth … magickal warmth. How long had it been since she allowed it in? The spell wouldn't work with a half-hearted existence. Fleur paused as the truth—her *real* truth sunk in, and the chant she once knew by heart tumbled from her lips. The Atua spell was a common incantation in her youth. It offered physical form, albeit momentary.

"Fleur?" Lenora voice was quiet.

The whole warehouse was quiet.

Fleur opened her eyes. Both Javier and Viola, mouths agape, stared, their eyes glazed in wonder. Fleur's gaze feathered over them, landing on Sato, and Edgar, their eyes wide, then the woman gaping behind them.

Theda stood frozen, her hand covering her mouth, but her gaze wasn't on Fleur.

It was on Lenora.

"Fleur?" Lenora's voice was thick and raw. She cleared her throat, the sound echoing off the warehouse rafters, falling on six pairs of startled ears.

Sweet Hemsut. It worked.

Lenora stood beside her, raw and tangible flesh wrapped her in amber light. She looked around her, tears welled in her eyes and splashed her cheeks. Fleur took a step back, pride straightening her spine and held up the flute.

Lenora grasped it, gasping softly as her fingers slid over the cool wood. She gripped it to her chest, her eyes wide in wonder.

"You have one minute, Len, before you change back," Fleur whispered to her friend.

CHAPTER
SIXTY-SIX

LENORA

I couldn't stop crying. I didn't know what to do ... how to act. My gaze flew around the room. They could see me. Everyone. Edgar ... Sato.

"Lenora?" Edgar moved first, and before I knew it, I was wrapped in his arms. My brother wept into my hair as I did on the rough fabric of his T-shirt ... rough fabric. Dear God. I reveled in the sensation, rubbing my arms over his back as if I could absorb him into me.

I pulled away first, cupping his pale, damp face in my hands, memorizing the constellations of freckles scattered over his nose. "Listen to me, Eddie. I never forgot you, and I never will." He sobbed and tried to pull me closer, but I wasn't finished. "You're not alone, you hear me? You're not alone anymore. You're brave and amazing, and Opal and Fleur, and ... Sato ..." His name stuck in my throat as my heart—my real heart swelled. "Everyone here freed you, and they are here to help you and me. OK?"

Edgar nodded. "You want me to trust them."

"I trusted them with your life, and they trusted me. Edgar, I have less than a minute, but ... I love you, little brother. I'll never leave you."

"Love you back, Len." His words were thick with sobs as he let me go. Viola wrapped her arm around him, his tall frame bending to curl into her embrace.

"We'll take good care of him." Viola smiled at me. "You're family, Lenora."

Warmth enveloped me, and I nodded my gratitude.

"Len?" Sato's face was red and damp, his voice hoarse.

I didn't speak. It only took a shared glance for us to come together, arms wrapped tight around each other as if we could stay like that forever. I inhaled the bittersweet aroma of black coffee and peanut butter toast—his favorite and pressed my lips to his. Fire warmed my stomach as he pressed me closer, deepening the kiss before quickly pulling away.

"Len. I have to say this. OK? I love you. There. I didn't say it enough before ... and"—he wiped his eyes and took a breath—"and I should have. I should have said it every day. I should have made you tell me what you were doing. I know you were protecting me but, Len, you should have told me ..."

"I didn't know how." I spoke honestly, my heart pounding for the first time ... and the last. "Sato, love ... would you have believed me?" I shook my head, wiping my tears with my fingertips, and sniffed.

"Maybe? Hell, I don't know. But you should have given me a chance." Pain washed over Sato's face, and I realized how callous my actions were.

"You're right." I pulled him toward me again. "But it didn't mean I didn't love you."

He sighed and held me close. "I know, Len ... I know," he muttered into my hair.

I sighed loud and true, my heart singing, my cheek pressed against his. I shifted to feel his stubble, to memorize the feel of him, but it was that moment my body slipped ... my form collapsed and faded.

And Sato's arms were empty once again.

CHAPTER
SIXTY-SEVEN

FLEUR

Lenora shimmered gold as the spell wore off.

Fleur wiped her face with the sleeve of her coat and looked from Viola, still holding Edgar, to Sato, his face flushed as he crossed his arms over his heart, trying to keep Lenora's warmth tucked away.

"You OK?" she asked the spirit.

Lenora flickered and dimmed, a small smile curled over her face. *Thank you for that, Fleur.* She looked down at the flute in her hands. *I should go ...*

Fleur nodded, suddenly unsure of herself. Was this goodbye? The case was solved ... Lenora had the flute ... Fleur cleared her throat and turned from the group, keeping her gaze on the Atua. "So ... yeah. I hope you get it there in time," she said quietly, nodding at the flute.

I'll never forget you, Fleur.

Gods. She was gonna cry. Fleur sniffed and crossed her arms. "So, this is it?"

I think so.

Fleur nodded curtly and straightened her shoulders. "We'll watch out for Edgar. I promise."

I know you will. Lenora inched toward her, her fingers uncurling as if to reach out, then paused. *I trust you, Fleur.*

Fleur opened her mouth, but only a strangled sob escaped. What was wrong with her? Why, when she needed them most, did words fail her? Fleur fixed her gaze on Lenora and nodded, tears dampening her cheeks.

An instant later, Lenora was gone.

Fleur's face warmed, and she released another strangled sigh, half laugh, half sob. Why was she crying? Isn't this what she wanted? To get back to her life? She helped the spirit, and that's it. It was over. Lenora could continue to the Glorious Feast, and she ... well, Fleur wasn't sure what she was going to do. But an annoying part of her knew she would miss the damn spirit.

Someone touched her shoulder, pulling Fleur from her reverie, and she wiped her eyes, surprised to see Theda standing beside her.

"You OK?"

Fleur cleared her throat. "Yeah ... yeah. I'm good."

"Is she gone?"

Fleur nodded and cleared her throat again, trying to swallow back the tears clogging her throat. Focus, she told herself, staring at Theda—flesh and blood Theda. "What are you doing here?"

"I saw Opal in the parking lot. Watched her use some fancy moves to take down Dugal's guard. Who knew she could do that? Kickboxing, maybe? Anyway, I raced over to help, but—" She broke off as her gaze fell on Dugal's body. Inhaling sharply, she looked at Fleur, questions furrowing her brow, and she pulled Fleur into her arms. "Oh, Fleur ..."

Fleur inhaled, burying her nose in the crook of Theda's shoulder and allowed a shudder to wash over her. Theda's arms were steady and safe, her heartbeat thudded against Fleur's chest as she pressed her closer, unwilling to let go. "She's gone ...," Fleur whispered.

Someone cleared their throat. Probably Javier. Fleur frowned as Theda pulled away and looked at Dugal's body.

"If you two are finished?" Javier released a ragged breath, cursing softly. "Ghosts, a cursed piece of shell, an enchanted flute—how am I going to explain this? Magick? Spirits? I need *something* to work with here."

Theda stepped closer to the body. "Looks like he drowned. How is that possible?"

"C'mon, Theda." Viola averted her gaze as she moved around the body. "Let me fill you in."

Fleur watched her stepmother lead Theda and Edgar out of the warehouse, trying desperately to ignore the ache seeping through her veins. She wanted to tell Theda the whole damn thing was finally over. But it wasn't. Fleur didn't move, listening with half an ear as Javier began his tirade of questions. The case may be solved, Lenora might be gone, but *this* was far from over.

CHAPTER
SIXTY-EIGHT

LENORA

E llory was waiting for me.
I knew she would be, but the fear flickering her aura yellow and the tremor in her voice surprised me.

Thank Hemsut, you're back. Do you have it?

I held out the flute. It looked too small for such importance, too fragile to save a world.

Ellory snatched it from me, her light stilling. *Come.*

She turned, drifting upward, past the almost barren branches and the darkened bark. Below us a bevy of souls gathered, their light flashing red with fear, a few indigo spirits fluttered around, trying to calm, but failing.

Have they reached the Lobby?

Not yet, but they are close ... too close. Ellory spoke in concise tones as if trying to contain her anxiety. *We've held them off, presented a united front, but still, the darkness pushes forward. It is like—*she paused, turning to me—*they have no fear. Their hunger consumes them. I've never seen the like.*

Ellory continued, drifting past branches as the canopy grew closer. I tried to calm myself, willing my already frazzled light to strengthen. I was ready for this—whatever this was. I had only just left my family and now I floated closer to a war, a war I didn't fully understand.

She spoke as we moved, her voice less staccato, as if she sensed my worry and sadness. *They are of a hive mind, the Grima. We didn't understand this at first, but Hamza and Oliver have managed to single out the Alpha.*

Wait ... Hamza and Oliver? Is Oliver a Guardian now?

No. But he is powerful enough. As are you.

Me? What? No way. I stilled, forcing Ellory to turn. *What do you mean me?*

You have magick within you, Lenora. You always have. That is why Axel's book sang to you. That is why you understood his text and the stories preserved there—

Dugal read it too.

Dugal only saw words, not truth. That is why he enlisted the help of a rogue Entomali. Lazlo fed him the lies necessary to get Dugal to do his bidding, and in return, he offered his magickal breath for the flute. But you, Lenora ... your magick has been there the whole time. That is why we tasked you with this mission. Your plan to save your brother was solid, fueled by your passions and unflinching will. It would have succeeded had the Soulkeepers not intervened—

My light throbbed silver, my phantom heart stopped. *The Soulkeepers intervened?*

I knew of your connection to our world and Fleur ... when I planted her memories. I knew you were strong enough to undo the Soulkeepers' spell. Ellory smiled. *And you were.*

My light flickered rapidly as rage funneled through me, rage and ... understanding. I moved from Ellory, her presence like a burn too recently singed. Understanding? If Ellory hadn't planted Fleur's memories ... Gods. I would be lost. I wanted to thank her, but the words stuck in my throat. Bitterness swept over me, darkening my light. *They did this to me ... and now ... now you expect me to help them?*

No. Ellory's gaze drifted to the flashing light above us. *No. Lenora, now I expect you to help me, and Fleur, and all the other souls who, like you, didn't get a say in their afterlife. This isn't about the Soulkeepers. It never was. Their arbitrary and hurtful spells have done more damage than good, but without them, we wouldn't exist. They are our keepers, literally. If their world dies, then we all die—and that, Lenora, would break the thread every realm has with its soul. Do you understand that? That thread is what keeps the ten realms alive. Without a soul, every creature would turn to dust ...*

So, I just have to accept it? I just have to move forward and accept that the Soulkeepers killed me?

You are not the first spirit they have meddled with, nor will you be the last. Lenora ... Ellory turned fully toward me, her eyes meeting mine. *I will not deny you your rage. I only ask that you use it as fuel and turn it to the darkness above.*

My light simmered. I stared at her, my ghostly limbs trembling with rage, with desperation and righteousness. My life was stolen. The words chanted over and over—syllable by syllable until my light beamed red.

Ellory darted forward, her light brightening with every broken and diseased branch we passed. I followed, my focus on the splintered rays of light flung into the abyss ahead. Maybe she was right? Maybe I was meant for more than a life on Mundad. Maybe Ellory had saved me when she gave me Fleur's memories ... but none of that mattered. Not at this moment.

We broke free of the canopy on the crest of a light wave, my aura throbbing with fury. My light thick and incandescent, blinding the wisps of Grima lashing out. The Shadelings squealed as they retracted, slithering back like a wounded snake.

Hamza, Oliver, and a few Guardians I didn't recognize stood at the front lines, glowing like a laser beam, warding off the Alpha's minions. The Shadelings were crafty. They sought the creases and cracks within each tide of light. It was unreal, almost too fantastic to believe. Magick, warm and bright, blazed like a spotlight. Was I capable of the same brilliance? Was Ellory right? My anger dimmed as doubt flooded over me.

Fight it, Lenora! Ellory's voice punched through my doubts. I turned to her, watching as she, too, blazed and shimmered, magick beaming from her. *Take my hand!*

I reached, surprised when I felt her fingers lace through mine. Fury flooded me, brightening my light, my aura matching time with the others.

The flute! Oliver screamed.

Ellory pulled the flute free and pressed it to her lips. Breath? Did she have the breath to play it? But how?

The spell—the same one Fleur had used on me in the warehouse. Dear God ... was I whole? Was I whole and still glowing? I dragged my gaze from Ellory to my legs—I had legs! Braced apart, light rippling from me. Wonder mingled with my fury as I allowed the depth of my emotion free. With a burst of light, I focused my energy on the darkest Shadeling behind the rest—the Alpha.

The notes were muted and low. I could barely hear her through the roar in my ears. Ellory raised her head, her light twice as bright and pulsing to the lullaby. She directed the song to the Alpha, her body swaying with the melody, her aura filtering through a rainbow of color, each one projecting the notes forward.

The darkness screamed. The sound seeped into my core. Agony, like nothing I'd ever felt before, tore at me. A carousel of memories slapped at me, anger and hatred plucked at my threads. I shuddered, my light fading ...

FOCUS, LENORA! Hamza's cry pierced my despair. *Don't let them in!*

I straightened my shoulders and lifted my chin. Pulling the images of my family close to my heart. I wouldn't focus on them ... no. No, I only needed one. Dugal. Wrath pooled in my core, blocking out the shrieks and moans of the Shadelings surrounding us.

That's it! Oliver shouted. *You can do it, lass!*

The Alpha throbbed, pulling Shadelings back. They swirled around it—a whirlwind of madness and shadow. The screeching amplified, thickening the air with the sour stench of decay, but still, Ellory played.

My shoulders ached, but I didn't lower my arms. I embraced the pain. I wondered if I'd ever feel it again. I wanted to tuck the sensation away.

One by one, the Shadelings dissolved, their bodies blotting like a stain on the brightness of the sky. Our light pierced the pockets of blue that once again began to appear. Slowly like a sweater unraveling, the Grima faded, their Alpha the last to vanish.

And still, Ellory played.

We didn't move. Even after the last shadow had faded, we stood, braced, in position, our auras golden in the dawn, our bodies swaying to Ellory's song.

The last note fluttered on the wind and faded. Ellory pulled the flute from her lips and blinked as if seeing the world for the first time.

In a rush, our bodies deserted us, and we were once again essence. I stumbled, unprepared to let my mass go, my eyes meeting Hamza's as he sunk back into his indigo shell.

You did well, Lenora. Oliver stood in front of me, his light a prism of relief. *I knew you would. Didn't I tell you? Eh? Hamza?*

You tell me many things. I rarely listen. Hamza grumbled as he floated closer to Ellory. *May I?* He held out his hand.

Ellory nodded and released the flute. *Thank you for the honor of playing it.*

I turned to Oliver. *Honor?*

Aye. Hamza was tasked with using the flute, but he believed Ellory would wield it better.

I watched Hamza tuck the flute into his folds of light and drift back toward the trunk. I wanted to say something, but I didn't know what or even if it would be welcome. The other Guardians faded, their indigo light pulsing in our direction in thanks as they returned to the Lobby until only Oliver, Ellory, and I remained.

The sky was blue and cloudless. I could see nothing but the reaching limbs of millions of trees, each one broader and greener than the next. Color was returning to the Inbetween. *How many Great Trees are there?*

Only one, Ellory said. *We all spring from the same root.*

The All-being. Oliver grinned. *How does it feel? To know yourself again?*

How did it feel? Sad, joyful, tepid ... I didn't know what to do now. *I'm not sure.*

Ellory smiled. *Give it time. The Inbetween isn't finished with you yet.*

What do you mean?

Oliver's light dimmed and flickered. *The Grima won't stop. That much we know to be true. We gleaned the Alpha's intentions, albeit only a whisper of them when it was stunned by the flute. We—the whole of the ten realms—won't be safe until the sheath is reconstructed.*

Ellory leaned closer, her voice tender. *There are more Relics to find, Lenora. You and Fleur have only just begun your journey.*

EPILOGUE

The metal was damp and cold beneath her hands. Light glimmered on the dark water below, trailing its fingers through the waves of Elliot Bay. A ferry horn sounded, alerting the passengers to its approach. Fleur sucked in a breath and leaned on the rail, basking in the warmth of the rare winter sun.

The hum of voices ebbed and flowed with tourists and vendors; the soft strain of a lone violin echoed off Pike Market's splintered beams. It was a typical Saturday afternoon. Not even December's chill could dampen Fleur's spirits.

"No. I said I needed a *male* therapist. I really don't know how I could speak any clearer."

Poppy's voice punched through the market's din like a bucket of icy water. Fleur cringed. Dammit. She turned slightly and caught a glimpse of a bright pink puffer coat. Had Poppy seen her? Gods. She hoped not.

Pulling her beanie down further, Fleur hunched over the rail, willing the woman to continue on her way.

Whatever the response was, Poppy was clearly not having it. "No, you listen. Do you know who I am? I can't just have *any* therapist, and certainly not that horrible woman" She paused. "Let me speak to your supervisor." Poppy's voice faded as she moved further down the sidewalk.

Fleur released a pent-up breath and allowed the tension to swirl out of her. The last thing she needed was a confrontation with Lenora's stalker. Fleur knew Poppy had a long road ahead, and she was pleased the woman was seeking help, but that didn't mean everything she did could be easily forgiven.

Her mother's lullaby played softly in the back of Fleur's mind, a constant hum since Lenora left. A month ago, it would have driven her mad, but now? She was wrong to allow it to grow quiet. Running away didn't move her forward. Her mother died, defying the goddess to protect her. Her father had honored Ellory's wish and spent his time in this realm doing his best to temper her, all the while healing himself, and what did she do? She defied them all. She ran away.

Fleur lifted her face to the setting sun. Slipping her hand into the pocket of her jacket, she toyed with the corners of Lazlo Barker's business card. She knew enough not to trust him, but she had so many questions—about the Lobby, the Great Tree—Dugal Griffin. If she was going to continue her mother's quest and find the other Relics, Fleur had a feeling she was going to need Barker's help.

"Watch you don't get a sunburn from all those rays," Theda remarked behind her.

Fleur closed her eyes and let her voice wash over her. She turned slowly, fighting the urge to throw her arms around her. "You came."

Theda smiled softly and moved to lean against the rail beside her. "How are you, Fleur?"

"A mess, as usual. You?"

Theda was quiet. Her gaze skimmed over Fleur's face before she turned to face the bay. "I miss you."

"I miss you too." Longing scratched at Fleur's throat.

Theda laughed, her breath puffing in front of her. "We're a fine pair."

"Theda, I'm sorry—"

"No," Theda interrupted, shaking her head. "I was wrong to ask you to stop. I see that now." She closed her eyes and took a breath. "I was jealous and spiteful—neither are good looks on me."

"I was so wrapped up in everything, I didn't even think of how it was affecting you." Fleur sniffed, blinking back tears. "But the thing is ... Theda, this is who I am—the ghosts, the weird requests, the getting arrested, the visions. This is me. I can't make it go away even if I tried, and you know what? I don't think I want to. It's time I made peace with all the unusual parts of me." Fleur took a deep breath, knowing this next part was the hardest. "I'm not going to stop, Theda. My mother left me with a mission, one I've half-assed until now, and I'm going to do it right. My life is chaos, and that's not going to change—but it's not a whole life without you in it."

Theda exhaled and leaned forward until their foreheads touched. "I know."

Fleur closed her eyes, waiting for the rejection, waiting for the kiss goodbye.

"I didn't understand what all that meant before, and I still don't, but the truth is, I would rather be with you than without. I didn't just miss you this last week—I missed *us*, our world, our chaos. I can't promise I won't get frustrated or angry with you and your insane spirit world, but I'm going to try."

Fleur opened her eyes and pulled away, her gaze fixed on Theda's warm brown one. "So ... you're in?"

Theda nodded.

"Really in? Even if Javier arrests me again, or Viola is held at gunpoint, or I have to—"

"Yes. To all those things. I'm in." Theda laughed and kissed her.

Her heart pounding, Fleur wrapped her arms around Theda and pressed her tight, deepening the kiss. She was warmth and sunlight to Fleur's shadow, and she'd be damned if she'd lose her again.

~

Javier was smarter than Fleur expected—she had to give him credit. He cleaned up the Griffin mess with care. He even took her advice, she snickered, skimming the front page of *The Seattle Times*.

Dugal Griffin was found late Saturday night. His body washed up on Alki Beach in West Seattle. Apparent cause of death was drowning. Benzos were found in his system. Fleur shook her head and read on, noting that the police were calling it an accidental death or overdose.

Neither they nor the warehouse were mentioned.

Fleur sighed and took a sip of her coffee. She pulled Lazlo's business card from her pocket, her fingers tracing the gold-foiled letters embossed across the front. What did he say? They could help each other. An Entomali never gave anything freely—there was always a trade. Griffin suggested that her family was part of his trade with Barker. That explained why he acted so weirdly to her name all those weeks ago.

Not that any of that mattered now.

Griffin was dead, she had the shell Relic secured in her cabinet, Lenora and Ellory had the flute, and Edgar was free.

All was right in the world.

Fleur traced the business card with her fingertips, hissing when the cardstock's sharp edge sliced into her skin.

Damn. She sucked on her finger, swallowing back the metallic taste of blood.

A bad omen.

Something was brewing.

COMING SOON

If you enjoyed Moths and Moonlight, be sure to check out Fleur and Lenora's next adventure!
The Soulkeeper's Bargain
A Fleur Harkyn Mystery
by Krista Fazendin

Fleur slipped past the streetlamp, skirting the low fence bordering the expansive Victorian house. Making sure her grey hair was hidden, Fleur pulled her black beanie over her ears and glanced at the street behind her.

Empty. Perfect.

She pulled herself over, flinching as the fence rails scratched her wool leggings and landed with a squish on the still damp moss. The rain may have let up hours ago, but Fleur would have to be careful not to leave a mark.

If her stepmother's flippant remarks about the Whethermores' malfunctioning alarm system were right, this should be a simple grab and go job. Thankfully, Viola loved gossip, and Louisa Whethermore's ugly gray pendant with its horribly faded etching was just the intel Fleur needed—assuming it was what she thought it was. Viola wasn't known for her accuracy.

Fleur hustled up the garden path, keeping to the shadows. Her step was light, careful never to leave much of an impression on the soft soil. She crept past the hedges and onto the obscured porch, inching closer to the keypad on the door.

A chill tripped down her spine, lancing her with fear. Fleur stilled, sinking into the porch's gloom.

Her gaze darted over the bare winter branches and rows of juniper until a shimmer, like water rippling in sunlight, caught her eye. Her heart sped up and for a moment the urge to call out, to greet Lenora, bubbled in her throat.

But it wasn't Lenora. A month had passed since Fleur had helped her free her brother from captivity. A whole month without a word, without a single peep from the Inbetween. Not that Fleur really expected one. The case was closed. Lenora had the flute—although it would have been nice to know if the flute had worked safeguarding the Great Tree. Fleur took a breath and focused on the glimmer, irritated that she'd thought it could be anything other than a nameless spirit.

Fleur held her breath as it wove, expanding and contracting in the chill. It lingered, its light faded, erasing all sound until only a vast opaque shadow hovered over the garden.

Damn. Not a spirit.

She pressed into the dark gray siding, her hand creeping upward to the slender key at her neck. To most, it was unremarkable — small, rusty and round, a faded goddess symbol etched on the bow, its teeth dull with age, but to Fleur the ancient key was a talisman, given to her by her mother. It was all Fleur had left of the woman who gave her life.

The metal warmed against her soft leather glove, warning her.

The darkness swelled, closer this time. Fleur gripped the key, a breathless chant on her lips. She eyed the halo of dusk stretching from the creature's core. Grima, or Shadelings as her father called them, were getting bolder. They fanned out in recent weeks, breaching the delicate balance of this realm in droves. Fleur had only encountered them a handful of times in her twenty-nine years, but now they were everywhere. They hunted in packs, seeping from darkened corners on unexpected prey. To see one alone was rare. It paused, smoke webbing over the garden.

She willed the Shadeling to continue, adopting the stillness of a tree, her mind bright with fear.

Frigid air brushed her cheek.

Smoke filled the garden, dusting the dormant shrubbery with darkness. A spirit fluttered in the center, its body heaving as if it still held breath. A new soul, freshly harvested from its body, an Atua, in the ancient tongue, reaction gilded its light, coloring its aura gray with confusion and fear, the perfect prey for Shadelings. Grima feasted on emotions of both creatures and spirits. The more potent—like the Atua—the better the taste, and the dammed creatures' hunger seemed insatiable. The spirit flickered and faded, its energy too new to fight off its attacker. The chill dissolved, leaving the cold, damp winter air void of magick.

The Shadeling vanished.

Fleur released the key and rolled her shoulders, moving away from the wall. She turned to the keypad lock and tugged off the plastic cover. Pulling two wires loose, she threaded them together, and waited until the pulsing red light turned green, then keyed in a series of zeros, praying the You-tube video she had watched earlier was accurate.

The door opened with a dull click.

The safe should be upstairs, if Viola's gossip was correct. Fleur closed the door softly, ignoring the tinge of guilt in the pit of her stomach, and eyed the security box on the inside wall. The red light pulsed — a silent trigger. Fleur moaned. Viola said it was malfunctioning, not broken, she reminded herself as she hurried over the Persian rug and up the curved staircase. Her boots tapped on the polished hardwood. She didn't look back; she didn't glance around. In and out. She wasn't there to window shop.

She was there for the jasper stone relic. Her stepmother would have something to say if she ever discovered Fleur's new hobby, especially as it involved the president of Viola's Women's Club, but she didn't want to think about that. This wasn't about Louisa, or Viola, or even her... this was about the stone relic upstairs. The one Louisa claimed came from a royal lineage and flaunted endlessly; the stone Viola hated enough to gossip about—the stone, composed of fossilized algae and three billion years old, was ancient biolumines- cence, growth magick, forged in the darkness of the tenth realm. The jasper was all that was left of the life that once inhabited Qahil and served as a beacon for Grima—but that was long ago, before its magick faded...or so Fleur hoped. After spying the Shadeling outside, she was having her doubts.

Fleur hastened down the upstairs hall, peeking into each room. The safe was behind a framed Chagall lithograph. Fleur frowned and moved to the end of the hall, wishing she had thought to ask which room it was in.

Dark drapes cloaked the turret room at the front of the house. Pulling a penlight from her pocket, Fleur cased the room from the desk to bookcases. There. Above the narrow brick fireplace hung the Chagall, encased in a gilded frame.

The lithograph was stunning. Roughly 9x12, it largely pictured a woman's face, long drooping nose and wide blue eyes. A smirk crooked her mouth, as if she knew the secret hidden behind her. Fleur slid her hands over the frame, feeling for wires tied to the alarm system.

Upper left corner thinly concealed. Fleur tilted the frame from the wall, careful not to disturb the wiring, and examined the safe. Fairly typical, albeit ancient, large Sentry safe with a key lock.

Fleur pulled her leather lock pick case from her jacket pocket, extracting a small tension wrench and curved diamond pick. Sweat beaded over her brow. She could do this. She'd practiced on every lock she could find, but this...this was her first safe-cracking. Using the mantle for leverage, Fleur rested the edge of the frame against her shoulder and worked quickly, biting her lip as the lock clicked.

The safe's heavy door swung open, revealing a mess of files and loose documents. Fleur's hands shook as she searched the stacks of paper and family mementos until a velvet box knocked against her thumb. It pulsed warm to the touch. A sign of the magick within. Fleur flipped open the case and examined the oval jasper pendant nestled inside. There, barely visible, unless you knew to look, the Goddess symbol etched into the back—crescent, eye, sun, balancing light and dark.

It was a relic — one of ten, their magick once harnessed within the powerful Sheath that protected the ten worlds. Time and human hands almost destroyed all evidence of the shimmering algae that once laced the stone like filigree.

Stuffing the box in her pocket, Fleur closed the safe. Her hand slipped ever so slightly, tugging the edge as she rehung the picture over its bulk.

And triggered the alarm.

Fleur raced down the hall, her feet tripping over themselves. She flew down the stairs, leaping for the door before cracking it open and peeking outside.

Stillness.

She closed the door behind her and moved swiftly through the garden to the fence. Her heart pounding in time with her frantic breath. With a groan, she hoisted herself over the wrought iron and onto the darkened sidewalk, willing her legs to move at a normal pace. No suspicious movements. She stuffed her hands in her jacket pockets.

As she rounded the corner, her ancient white Subaru 360 flared to life. White paint faded and chipped around the wheel well of the tiny car, specks of rust darkened the chrome edges of its condensed form. It growled and puttered, a cloud of exhaust leaking from its rear. Fleur cringed and glanced around, praying the noise would go unnoticed. She jogged over, yanked open the passenger's door, and slid onto the cracked red leather seat.

"Did you get it?" Theda turned, moonlight illuminating the curve of her cheek. She wore the same dark clothing, her tight curls piled high and wrapped in a black scarf. She waited; anticipation flushed her brown skin.

Fleur patted her pocket and leaned closer, pressing her lips to Theda's. Her skin was soft and warm, a balm to Fleur's frenzied nerves. Theda kissed her back, caressing the delicate flesh behind Fleur's ear as she broke away. She smelled like jasmine and citrus, like the darkest part of the night, like hope. "Yup."

"Can I see it?"

Fleur pulled the velvet case out of her pocket and opened it. The stone gleamed in the dim moonlight.

"I expected something... more." Theda studied it.

"That's the trick. Most Chieftains enchanted whatever they had on hand. This used to be a plain old rock. This world cut it and made it into a pendant."

"Where is this one from?"

"Tenth realm, Qahil." Fleur tilted the pendant. There were few records of the magickal items, aside from her uncle's ledger, but most of it was folk lore. Legend passed down as a lullaby — a series of couplets her mother taught her. Fleur hummed the melody softly, offering Theda a small smile. *The tenth, now bleak, once flourished with life...* She squinted at the stone's striations. Goosebumps scattered over her arms as she closed her fingers over it. Barely any heat, Fleur released a breath. "It's inactive."

Theda nodded and shifted the car into gear. "So, it could just be another random piece of junk?"

"No, look." Fleur turned the pendant over and pointed at the faded symbol. "It's a relic." She looked up at Theda, pride widening her smile.

"My little thief."

The newness of her current situation hovered over Fleur's shoulders like a weighted blanket. She wasn't a thief. Not really. She was simply completing the quest given...finally. Her mother had made that clear when she sent Lenora's spirit to help, hadn't she? Ellory Harkyn wanted Fleur to resume her quest, the one given to her by Hemsut, the goddess of fate herself and was then passed down to Fleur after her mother's death. A death Hemsut has caused, Fleur's stomach twisted at the thought, for years Fleur had resisted the lure of magick, of her world, this quest. Her anger at the goddess of fate had only been part of the reason.

But the magick beckoned, softly at first, a whisper in the dark, a reminder of who she was, and Fleur ignored it for as long as she could. It had been too long, too much bad blood, and after helping Lenora, well, it was time. Time to grow up. Time to stop running. The certainty she fought against for so long was strangely comforting.

It was time to finish what her mother started by finding all ten relics and using them to rebuild the Amaranthine Sheath that once protected the realms.

Still, she shrugged. "Not a thief, a collector. Besides, they don't belong here. This realm is sapping them dry."

"And that's bad."

"Don't make fun. It *is* bad. The balance depends on these little pieces of junk. Without them, we won't be able to restore the sheath..." Fleur crossed her arms over her chest and watched as they chugged away from the Whethermores' Victorian. A flash of blue light illuminated the pavement. The Seattle PD had arrived. Fleur blew out a breath as they turned the corner.

"I was only kidding. I know the stories."

"They're not *just* stories, Theda." Fleur slipped the pendant in her coat pocket, her gaze on the side mirror, tracking the blue lights. "You know that."

Theda reached for Fleur's hand and squeezed. "I do. Sorry. Sometimes all this," she pointed to the box in Fleur's pocket, "is just kinda unbelievable."

Fleur turned to her. "But you believe it, anyway."

Theda lifted Fleur's hand and pressed a kiss to her knuckles. "You're very convincing."

"I think you mean charming."

"Hell, no." Theda snorted out a laugh, the Subie speeding up the hill towards home.